STOLEN

A. R. KEOGH

Stolen

Copyright © 2023 by Arianna Kehoe

All rights reserved.

Editor: Genie Rayner, Magic Lamp Editing

No part of this book may be reproduced in any form or by any electronic or mechanical means, including information storage and retrieval systems, without written permission from the author, except for the use of brief quotations in a book review.

Author contact: author.a.r.keogh@gmail.com

Cover Design by Getcovers

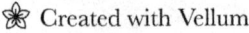 Created with Vellum

For my Gangi, Mom & Steph
Thank you for being with me every step of the way.

CONTENT WARNING

This book is for mature audiences. Reader discretion is advised. This book contains depictions of emotional abuse, assault and trauma. Sexual violence is strongly inferred.

CONTENTS

Chapter 1	1
Chapter 2	14
Chapter 3	32
Chapter 4	50
Chapter 5	70
Chapter 6	87
Chapter 7	98
Chapter 8	105
Chapter 9	116
Chapter 10	125
Chapter 11	134
Chapter 12	150
Chapter 13	154
Chapter 14	174
Chapter 15	186
Chapter 16	200
Chapter 17	212
Chapter 18	217
Chapter 19	232
Chapter 20	241
Chapter 21	247
Chapter 22	260
Chapter 23	267
Chapter 24	277
Chapter 25	285
Chapter 26	299
Chapter 27	308
Chapter 28	318
Chapter 29	327
Chapter 30	337
Acknowledgments	349

CHAPTER ONE

Elle

"Why are you sneaking around our territory?" I snarl at the rogue we've just caught who's been stealing from our pack, vandalizing property, and killing our livestock. Looking down on him, he looks like he's been on the run without a pack for quite some time. The smell alone is enough to make me vomit, almost like rotting flesh. Even though everything in me says to back off, I step closer. I can't show any weakness, not now, with all the warriors of my pack watching, including my father.

The wolf doesn't answer. He just stares down at the forest floor, refusing to fully submit. I kick him in the chest, the momentum sends him sprawling on the ground. Grabbing him by his throat I make him meet my glare. "*Why are you here?* To steal and terrorize my pack?!" I shake him and bring my face closer to his. This was a mistake – I forgot about his hands. His fingernails rake across my face, digging into my skin. Shit, it burns. I momentarily loosen my grip on his throat and the rogue takes his chance and lunges. He pushes me back, but I easily overpower him and send him back onto his knees in front of me. *Thank you, Alpha blood!*

I can hear the warriors murmuring behind me. They were probably waiting for me to slip up even the slightest bit. Now I have to prove to them that I can handle this. I square my shoulders and step closer once again. Placing both of my hands on either side of the rogue's face I make him meet my eyes. "I'm sorry for your life and what it has become. I'm sorry for what I have to do to you to keep my pack safe. May you find peace once you are not on this earth." I brace myself and twist hard, feeling the rogue's neck snap. He falls from my grip limp to the ground.

My stomach knots. I just took a life. I feel dizzy. Even though it was for the safety of my pack, it still doesn't sit right. Footsteps approach behind me and I take a breath to calm my nerves. I turn and face my father. "He wouldn't answer my questions. I had to make a choice, and I didn't think sending him away would've worked out in our favor," I say as I steadily meet his gaze. "It was for the safety of the pack."

My father grabs my shoulder and squeezes it in comfort. He doesn't offer any words or order the rest of the warriors to do something with the body. No, that's my job now. Or it will be when my dad officially steps down as alpha and I take his place. This was a trial of sorts, to see how I, a she-wolf, could handle a rogue problem. I think I did pretty damn good, except for the part where I let myself get distracted. I know I won't hear the end of that for a few days. They'll all be questioning if I have what it takes to be an alpha.

"Sam! Noah! Bring me the shovels and then head back to the town. We can meet at the packhouse once I return."

"Uh, don't you want help taking care of the body, Elle?" Sam asks.

"No, I want you to go tell everyone that the rogue situation has been dealt with." Really, I just want to be alone for a while, and even though I'm exhausted from the skirmish with the rogue, I could really use the workout digging his grave will give me. "It's fine, Sam, go home." My voice is on the edge of being a direct order. Sam and Noah both look at me then at each other and shrug. Both head over to the other men to tell them what the plan is. Sam keeps looking over at me with concern on his face, not really wanting to leave me alone right now. But that's what I need, to be alone.

I watch as they all gather and leave my sight. I give it a few minutes longer before I look down at the body I have to bury. The body of a man whose life I took. *Oh fuck!* I lean against a tree as I puke my guts out. I'm like that for a few minutes because every time I think of the task at hand I start vomiting all over again. "Get yourself together, Elle. You're gonna have to do this more than just this once." Yeah, a pep talk to myself, that's what I need.

A deep chuckle comes from behind me. Fuck, I wasn't alone after all. "I got sick my first few times as well," my dad says as he hands me a handkerchief for my face. He leans against a tree and looks at me. My dad, Roman, is the alpha of our pack. He's in his forties but you wouldn't know it looking at him. Werewolves' aging slows down once we hit peak age, females twenty-one, males being twenty-three. Not sure why there's a difference between male and female, that females mature faster. I think it has to do with mating and breeding. My dad looks like he's in his early to mid-thirties, though. He's got a strong build, and standing at well over six feet tall he's pretty intimidating. Though you kinda have to be when you're alpha.

He leans down and grabs the shovels and hands one to me. "It's when you stop getting sick, that's when it should bother you."

I give him a smile and start digging. We're already at the edge of our territory so we thankfully don't have to lug the rogue's body through the woods. As we both dig in silence, the crunch of our shovels hitting the dirt the only sound around us, I let my mind wander to how I, a she-wolf, am the one who will be alpha for our pack.

Twenty years ago, I was born to my parents, Alpha Roman and Luna Jillian. I don't remember my mother— she died in a rogue attack about two years after I was born. My parents never had any other children so it's just me. Usually, it's the first-born male who takes the role of Alpha. My father never found another mate after my mother died, so he never did get the chance to have a son. I think he was too heartbroken to venture out and meet someone new. He held it together, though, for the pack and for me. He was my only parent after all.

When I was eleven, I went through my first shift, that's when my dad asked me if I wanted to train to be the Alpha. The prospect of being the first female alpha felt right to me. I wanted to prove to my dad that I could do it. I stayed by his side most of the time, listening in on pack meetings, watching how he handled situations within the pack. Even now, nine years later, I still devote my life to this training. I have to prove, not only to my dad and the pack but to myself, that I can do this.

We get the hole dug, about six feet, and we climb out and roll the body into it. Ugh– we still have to put the dirt back in the hole. Maybe I should have kept the others around. This would have gone a lot faster. Though I'm not sure if I would want them to see me toss my cookies. It was a lose-lose situation. About half an hour later, all that was left of the scene that unfolded two hours ago was a mound of disturbed dirt. I really hope that's the last of the rogues for a while. I don't want to do that again anytime soon.

Walking beside my dad on the path back towards town he lightly shoves me. "Hey!" I yell, turning around to see a playful look on his face.

"Let's run back!" he says as he tiptoes around me.

I groan. "Dad, I'm really mentally and physically exhausted. I just want to get home, shower, and meet up with Sam and crash hopefully before dawn."

"*Pfft*, chicken," he teases.

"I'm NOT a chicken."

Dad laughs. "Why are your hackles up? Huh? Afraid you will lose against an old dog like me?"

I shake my head and laugh because my dad is anything but old. He can still out lap a lot of the younger wolves here. He won't start slowing or aging until he officially steps down and stops shifting all the time. But if he wants to race, we can race. "All right, *old man*, let's run!"

* * *

I GO into my room in the packhouse at three AM, heading straight to the shower to wash all the grime I have accumulated from the night's events. Stepping into the hot shower I grab my washcloth and scrub hard. The feeling of taking someone's life is still all over me. Even though realistically I know I can't scrub the feeling off, I wash until my skin is red and tender. Toweling off my body and wrapping my hair in a towel to dry, I find an oversized t-shirt to wear to bed.

My body is ready for sleep, but my mind keeps racing. When my dad and I returned from the forest, Sam, Noah, and a few pack members were still waiting inside the kitchen of the packhouse. Apparently, Sam explaining the night's events wasn't enough for some of the pack and they waited to hear from my father and me about it. Mainly my father. They need assurance that my decisions on how to handle these high stress situations have his approval.

Most of the pack is on board with me becoming alpha, but there are those few closed-minded ones who have their doubts about a female leading a pack. They would rather see me mated to another future alpha and be his luna, or have Sam become alpha. Sam is my chosen beta. He'd make a good alpha, but it's not in his blood like it is mine. Many of them had hoped that Sam and I were true mates, but when we turned 18 it wasn't there. But then that would give the Elders the excuse to let Sam be the alpha, and I his luna. Sucks for them because it didn't happen. And they will be stuck with me as their alpha whether they like it or not.

* * *

THE SUN IS SHINING through my window and the brightness wakes me up. I look at my clock and see it's already ten AM. Shit, I'm running late. I rush and throw on some jeans and a t-shirt, grabbing my Chucks along the way as I slam the door behind me and run downstairs.

My dad and his beta, Jon, are already there. So are Sam and Connie, an older she-wolf who took on the upkeep of the packhouse after my mother died. By the looks of things, I've definitely missed breakfast because the kitchen looks freshly cleaned, besides the few coffee cups in the hands of the men sitting around the table.

"Good morning, Eleanor," Connie says as I make my way over to the coffee pot and pour myself a cup. I don't know why she insists on calling me by my full name after all this time. I've told her a million times that I prefer Elle, but she says my mother named me Eleanor so someone should call me that. She is a sweet lady, who lost her mate in the same attack that killed my mother. Both of her children are mated now, her son mated to a she-wolf in our pack, while her daughter is mated to a wolf in another pack across the country.

"Can I make you anything for breakfast?"

"Oh no. Don't bother with it, you just cleaned up, I'll make some toast and I'll be good."

"The future alpha of our pack can't just have 'some toast and be good'," Connie scoffs. "I'll make you some eggs and bacon to go with your toast, and *then* you'll be good."

Shaking my head, I walk over to the table and sit down to go over patrol runs and supply runs into the city. My father, Jon, and Sam are already deep into the conversation by the time I join them.

"Think we should cut down on patrols since the rogue has been taken care of. I don't see the reason to keep our warriors out there day in and day out, running them ragged, on top of their regular training." Jon takes a drink from his coffee and looks around the table.

"I see what you are saying, Jon, but I think we should keep the patrols heavy for the time being," my dad replies, keeping his face nuetral. "It keeps the rest of the pack feeling safe after feeling so vulnerable, and what if there are more than the one that was ... taken care of last night?"

"But we're wasting valuable time for them to be training as well! What if another alpha comes through here and decides he wants our land? Our resources? It's a definite possibility, especially with an alpha change coming soon. That's when packs are at their weakest, during the transition period between alphas."

I glare at Jon– everyone knows that a pack is only as strong as their alpha. The pack looks to the alpha for guidance. Weak alphas equal a weak pack. Is Jon finally voicing his true opinion of me? Does he think I'm weak? Maybe he does think this so Sam, his son, can become Alpha and not I.

He sees my glare and holds his hands up. "I don't think you're weak, Elle. Quite the opposite actually." He rests his hands around his mug. "But there is truth to what I said. Anytime *any* pack goes through a leadership change is when they are most at risk for attack. It's not in offense to you or how I think you will lead us."

I snort. "Or maybe you just think Sam would be a better alpha than I, and you hope to get under my skin and get me to step down. Well, that's not going to happen, Jon. It's my birthright to become alpha. And I am going to see it through, and I am *NOT* going to be a weak alpha."

"I never said you were."

"But you insinuated it!"

"No, I didn't! I just laid out some facts."

"But you just said—"

"ENOUGH!"

We all turn and look at the head of the table, my father now standing over us radiating frustration. He sits back down once he has our attention. "Now we are here to discuss how to handle the patrols and the trip into the city. Not to get into an argument of who thinks Elle is capable of being alpha or not."

I open my mouth to retort but he holds his hand up to silence me and continues. "Do you have an idea on the patrol situation?" my father asks.

Reflecting back on what was said before the outburst, I can see both of their perspectives on the patrols. My father would want to keep them going longer, which I understand because he still hasn't gotten over my mother's death fully, and every time there's a rogue in the area he goes a little overboard with the patrols. But Jon has a good point, too. A lot of packs know my dad is stepping down soon, and as much as I hate to admit it, he is right. We will be most vulnerable at that time during the transition months. It takes time for a pack to fully accept and trust their new alpha, so warrior training is a must. There has got to be a middle ground here.

"Perhaps we will continue with the heavy patrols for a few more weeks." I hold up my hand to stop Jon as he's about to protest. "I agree we need to get our warriors back into training. But also we need the whole pack to feel safe and secure. I am sure they feel somewhat vulnerable and violated since the last rogue. Starting tonight we could have three shifts for patrols, twenty wolves per shift. The following week go down to fifteen wolves per shift, and keep going like that until we're back to our normal patrol schedule. As long as there's no threat it shouldn't take more than three weeks, or a month tops, to get back to normal."

After a few moments of silence that feel like an eternity, Sam speaks for the first time since I arrived in the kitchen. "Well, damn, that could work. I'm all for it." He grins at me from across the table and I flash one back. Sam shows no hard feelings about my comments about me thinking his father wanted him to be alpha. He's always had my back and given me full support.

I look at the end of the table toward my father for his reaction and receive a nod of approval.

Well, shit, maybe I can do this.

* * *

SITTING on a rock on the beach I try to relax, my body still tense from the stress from this morning's meeting, and lack of sleep. Even though I got the approval from my father on the plans for the coming weeks, I feel it's not enough. I need the approval from ninety percent of the pack, having that kind of support would put some of my thoughts at ease. I feel as though Jon is right in some way—our pack *will* be at its weakest point in over thirty years.

Sure, the majority of the pack supports my becoming alpha— probably about seventy-five percent of the pack is in my corner. They know how long I've been training for this. But it's the other twenty-five percent who will give me trouble. Some already have. A group of guys who joined our pack a few years ago love to throw down challenges, physical fights to prove who is the strongest. Obviously, since I'm still actively the next in line to take over I have always won, but the fact they initiate the challenges to begin with states what they think of me being the next leader of the pack.

A challenge is when a wolf decides the alpha isn't fit to lead the pack anymore, and so they fight until there's only one standing. Years ago there was a unanimous decision among the packs that challenges to the death should be forbidden. So now it's basically until one wolf surrenders or doesn't have the strength to join the fight again.

There's one guy who has challenged me more than once—Rafe, a twenty-two-year old wolf who thinks he should be the next alpha. He's a little crazy, I think. He has radical ideas that would take the pack back in time over 100 years.

Come to think of it, Rafe is my biggest annoyance right now. He's challenged me five times in the past two years. His followers, Raul and Glenn, have only challenged me once each, and never again after I kicked their asses. But Rafe hasn't given up.

The wind slightly changes direction and I catch a scent that wasn't there earlier. "You shouldn't sneak up on people, you might get hurt," I say, turning to look at Sam, who is walking on the beach toward where I am sitting. To someone who doesn't know Sam well, he can be very intimidating, standing at six foot five inches, with muscles that humans have to take steroids to get, and a hard face that says "I won't put up with your bullshit." But I've known him all my life, he's my best friend, my confidant. That's why I chose him to be my beta. We've always had each other's backs, and he's not afraid to disagree with me if he thinks I'm going in the wrong direction with issues in the pack.

Sam sits next to me. "Now you and I both know no one can sneak up on you unless you let them." He winks and gives me a playful shove.

"Hey!" I yell, smacking him on the shoulder.

"What are you thinking about? I could hear the gears in your brain going from down the beach."

"Oh, you know ... that maybe I'm not cut out for this alpha thing."

"Ha! What are you going to do? Step down, look for a mate, and help breed the next generation?" He picks up a stick and starts aimlessly drawing lines and circles in the sand. "That's not you and you know it, everyone knows it. You're meant for something more than that."

I find some rocks and start placing them in front of Sam to add to his sand art. I don't say anything back. Sam gives a frustrated sigh and throws the stick. "You know, if you don't ever get out of your head and believe in yourself, no one is going to believe in you. It's gotta start with you, though. The meeting this morning? Yeah, it got a little tense, but that's gonna happen. Not everyone is going to be one hundred percent on board with everything, it's not possible. But what I saw was you listening to both points and finding a compromise. That's what alphas do, they find middle ground when listening to others."

Damn, he's right. If I'm gonna do this, which I am, I have to stop doubting myself and making second guesses. The pack can feel my indecision and that alone will make them antsy and question my abilities.

Standing up, I brush the sand off my jeans. "I guess I should head back. My dad probably wants to go over some things before the day is gone. I also have to make rounds around the pack members and see how they're doing. Did you drive or run here?" I ask Sam.

"I ran, needed to get a run in and let my wolf out."

"Want a ride back?" I nod toward my Jeep in the pull-off.

"Yeah, that would be great."

Our ride back is quiet except for the radio. Both of us are lost in our own thoughts. That's why I love spending time with Sam— he doesn't have to fill the silence with endless rambles. Sometimes I find myself wondering what it would have been like if we had been mates. It would have been an easy transition, especially with the bond. It would make going from friends to lovers easier and not awkward.

We tried when we were sixteen to take our friendship to the next level. Hormonal teenagers of the opposite gender who spent all their time together, it was bound to happen. I smile at the memory. We were on the same beach we had just left, and Sam had grabbed my hand and pulled me in for the most awkward kiss in history. We tried, but we kept knocking noses and foreheads together and ended up just laughing. A little laugh escapes my mouth. Sam turns and looks at me with a perplexed look on his face.

"You okay over there? Or are you officially losing it?"

"I was just remembering when you tried to kiss me."

"When *I* tried to kiss *YOU*? Ha! It was mutual and I was rather good. It was you who ruined it."

"Like hell it was me! You're the sloppy kisser!"

"I am not! I'll have you know that Suzie said I was the best kiss she's ever had!"

"Well, seeing how she has only kissed you and Noah, that's a no brainer!" I'm now laughing so hard I have to try and stop so I can see the road. I love this banter– sometimes it feels like we're still teenagers the way we pick on each other. And not like we're about to run a whole pack in a few months.

Turning the Jeep into the driveway I see my dad sitting on the porch with Jon. I can't read the looks on their faces, but as I approach the house I can feel the tension in the air.

"Dad? Jon? What's going on?"

My dad steps forward with a grave look on his face. "We're going to have a visit from another alpha."

CHAPTER TWO

Elle

The tension in the pack is thick. It's smothering. Alphas don't typically visit other packs. They send lower-ranking pack members to bring word to each other. And hello, even werewolves have cell phones and email, which is the way alphas prefer to communicate.

The reason alphas don't typically visit other packs - and if they do it's not for very long periods of time - is because the need to be the dominant wolf is too strong between them. There are never two alphas in a pack – it would be a bloodbath.

Alphas only visit when they're invited, when building an alliance against another pack, when they're looking for their mate, and then when they want to take a pack over and expand their territory.

The way my dad and Jon are acting I'm thinking it's

one of the latter two. If this was an ally, they wouldn't be making sure there are warriors at every post on the territory, though I'm told it's just for precaution. No, this is an alpha my dad sees as a potential threat and wants to be prepared for anything.

* * *

WALKING along the paths to each post on the northern and eastern borders to make sure the warriors have the supplies they need and making notes of who needs what, I'm intercepted by Jon and Sam. They were doing the same along the south and west.

"Sam and I have the rest of this covered. Your father needs you back at the packhouse now."

"But we can get it done much faster with the three of us."

Jon gives me a stern look. "Maybe I wasn't clear enough. Your alpha orders you to stop what you're doing and head back to the packhouse immediately." He sighs, his expression softening. "Look, you know he never sends direct orders to you. What he needs to tell you is important. Sam and I have this covered. Give me your list of which station needs what and head on home." He holds out his hand for my notebook and I begrudgingly turn it over to him.

"All right. Do you have any idea what he needs to talk to me about?" I ask, even though I already know what his answer is going to be.

Jon shakes his head. "No, I don't. And even if I did I couldn't tell you because *he* wants to talk to you." He makes a "go along" motion with his hand.

As I'm about to step into the trees to shift into my wolf, Jon calls out to me once more. "Oh, and Elle?" I turn around with, I'm sure, a look of annoyance on my face. "Just know, he needs to put the best interest of the pack first, and that means you, too. So whatever it is he needs to talk to you about, just agree and don't give him too much of a hassle." And with that he turns back to the north and takes off running to catch up with his son, leaving me alone on the road once again.

Once I'm in the forest I take off my shirt, pants and shoes. I put them all in the bag I carry before shifting into my wolf. She's quite a sight if I do say so myself. My fur is all white, and I'm large for a female. Almost the size of a male wolf. It's not common for females to get so big. No, we're not *Twilight* werewolf big, that would be cool though. When I stand next to Sam while he's human my head reaches his elbow.

I take a moment to take in my surroundings with my heightened senses. Squirrels fight over acorns, the stream flows few miles away. The scent of corn from the fields and the smoke from the village come through on the wind. Making sure I grab my bag, I take off at a sprint and wind through the trees. It should only take me ten minutes to get to the edge of the woods. I love running, it's in our nature to run. Whether we're hunting, playing, traveling, or even running for our lives, wolves need to run.

As I come closer to the edge of the forest I slow down to a walk. I don't want to startle anyone thinking I'm running from something or with bad news. Right now the pack is on edge and it's best not to make it worse.

I shift back into human form, redressing behind a tree before walking out onto the road. Hearing footsteps coming near me I turn to face who's approaching.

"Hey, Elle!" A small figure comes out from a fort made out of logs and tarps and greets me.

"Hey, Josh. Whatcha doing?" I smile at him as he runs down the path to me.

"Just building my fort closer to the house. I have a way cooler one in the woods, but Mom told me yesterday she wants me closer to home for now." He rolls his eyes like he thinks his mother is being overprotective. "You should come see it sometime! Do you think Sam would come, too?"

I laugh. "Of course we will. We gotta make sure it's sturdy and safe for you guys to play in, don't we?" I give him a high five and then kneel down so I'm eye level with him.

"Listen, Josh, I know it might seem like your mom is being overprotective and nagging about you being safe, but she is right. You shouldn't be out in the woods right now, especially without an adult. It's just for a week or so." Looking into his big innocent eyes I try to convey the importance of what I'm saying. "Do you think you could do me a favor and listen to your mom and stay out of the woods for now?"

He shrugs. "Yeah, sure, I can do that." He starts shifting his weight back and forth on his feet, eager to get back to his fort.

"All right, kid, pound it." I offer my fist up for a fist bump, which he gladly returns.

"See ya, Elle!" he yells over his shoulder as he runs back to his yard. I stay and watch to make sure he goes back to his fort before heading in the direction of the packhouse.

Smiling to myself as I walk up the road, I think of all the kids who follow Sam and me around. The boys idolize Sam and hope to be big and strong like him someday, while the girls follow him because they all have crushes on him. He hates it, absolutely loathes when we go into the village, because they swarm and it makes him uncomfortable. And I think it's hilarious, which he says is no help to him.

I enter the house and see Connie busy in the kitchen. "Hi, Connie, what's for dinner? It smells so good."

"Good evening, Eleanor. I'm making one of your favorites! Beef stroganoff," she responds, not even looking up from cutting up mushrooms. "You're late, your father expected you here ten minutes ago. So when you go in there and he's in a mood, you know why."

Stepping into the hallway heading towards his office I groan. *Ugh what could be so important that ten minutes makes a difference?* Once I get to the office door I decide to knock and not barge in. Maybe that will ease some of his anger.

"Come in," I hear from the other side before I can even knock. *Well, it's the thought that counts, right?* I open the door and sit in the chair across from him.

"You're late. Didn't Jon tell you to leave there and come straight to me?" The tone of his voice tells me this isn't a time for jokes or sarcasm.

"I ran into Josh— you know, Joyce's and Ron's pup?" I look at his face to see if he's even interested in my reason for being late. He doesn't stop me so I continue. "He was complaining that his mother wouldn't let him go into the woods right now. I didn't give him full details, but I told him that his mother was right and for the time being he shouldn't be there without an adult. Isn't that what I'm supposed to do? Make sure orders are followed by everyone?"

My dad runs a hand down his face. "Yes, that is what you are supposed to do. Especially with young ones who don't fully understand. Sometimes it's easier for them to follow the rules when a higher-ranking wolf talks to them."

He smiles at me and I can feel the tension in the room dissipate.

I relax and sag into my chair. "So what's so important that you take me away from doing my rounds?" I ask.

The tension and stress return to my dad's face. I brace myself for whatever it is he has to say. We're not normally like this. Usually the conversation flows freely between us, but whatever he has to tell me now, he doesn't want to.

My dad lets out a big sigh. "For the time being, for a couple of weeks, we need to take a break from your training."

"What? Why?"

"With this alpha stopping by for who knows what reason, we can't let him know that we're starting to transition leadership. Not only that, but that the new pack alpha is a she-wolf. It will show that we will have a weak point, and I can't endanger the pack. We have lived here peacefully and quietly- besides a few rogues here and there- for almost two decades."

"I can't believe this!" I snap. "You doubt me! Why go through all these motions? Years of training just to rip the rug out from under me?" I should have known, eventually my father would think I'm too weak to lead. That a woman shouldn't be in this role. Next thing he'll be saying is that I should find a mate and start having pups!

"Now, Elle, that's not what I said. It's only for a couple of weeks and then we can go right back to your training."

"Bullshit. A couple of weeks will turn into months, which will turn into a year!"

"Stop and listen to me! An alpha has to do what's best for their pack. You should know this by now. And right now, having an unknown alpha coming in, we need to play things safe."

I stand and place my hand on his desk and lean over him. "If it were Sam in my place, or if you had a son, you wouldn't be doing this," I snarl. "It's all because I'm a woman and not a man."

My dad shoots up from his seat and gets right in my face. "I am not explaining myself again! You are to stop training until further notice and that's an ORDER." The amount of authority in his voice makes me shrink back and retreat into my seat. I forgot how scary he could be. But he doesn't stop there. "And if you keep acting like a spoiled brat you won't be alpha. I'll stop all the training. You'll be banned from warrior training as well."

I sit there looking at the floor. I'm speechless. He has me completely submissive now, something he has never done to me before. It's unnerving, being born a dominant wolf and being forced into submission. I hate it.

"Also, you believe everyone thinks you're too weak? Maybe take these next few weeks you have off and think about that. Because if, deep down, you think you're too weak to be alpha then you really shouldn't be. Now I have some things to take care of before dinner. Close the door on your way out."

"Yes, *Alpha.*" I sneer the last word heading for the door. I slam it behind me. Rounding the corner to go up the stairs to my room crash into Jon. He looks at me, a look of concern– or is it pity?– on his face.

He places a hand on my shoulder and gives me a reassuring squeeze. "It will be okay. In a few weeks everything will be back to normal."

"What do you care?" I scoff and wrench out of his hold. "You'll probably get what you want, your son as alpha." I push around him so I can get by, but he grabs me by the wrist. "HEY!"

"Elle, I have always been in your corner. I have always thought you would be a good alpha. I'm sorry if you think my disagreeing with you and giving you a hard time has made you think otherwise." I must look confused because he goes on. "I'm doing what a beta does— we're supposed to give you all options, so you see things from more than just one angle. I know Sam does that for you all the time, and I'm sure it's more acceptable coming from him. I am your fathers Sam"

Again his hand squeezes my shoulder and he goes down the hall into my father's office.

Maybe Dad's right. Maybe I should do some self-reflection in the next few weeks. Because apparently I'm reading everyone wrong.

* * *

IN THE KITCHEN WITH CONNIE, I help her finish the dishes since I'm no longer allowed in my father's meetings. Connie is busy setting the table and I see her put my plate in my usual spot, to the left of my father.

"Actually, Connie, I think I'll take my dinner upstairs tonight." I don't feel like sitting downstairs with everyone pretending everything is okay. Especially after what happened between my father and me a few minutes ago. His words still sting like a slap across my face.

Connie puts her hands on her hips and glares at me. She hates dishes going upstairs. "I promise to bring the plate down and wash it myself." I send her a pleading look with my eyes. *Please bend your rule this once, for me?*

"Oh, all right, Eleanor! But if I find that dish isn't brought down by morning," she emphasizes, pointing her finger at me like I'm a child to be scolded, "I'll have some words with you."

"Thank you." Smiling at her scowl, I quickly get my plate filled with the best beef stroganoff ever and run up to my room before anyone else can enter the kitchen.

I enter my room and shut the door, setting my plate down on my desk. I grab my remote and put on an old show for background noise. I'm not used to eating alone. There are usually at least eight people eating at the packhouse for dinner. Mostly from pack meetings and people stopping in to see my dad. It's not uncommon for others to join us for dinner unannounced. Connie seems to have a sixth sense for this because there's never not enough or too much, no matter how many people show up.

Taking a bite of my dinner I didn't realize how famished I was. I must've skipped lunch today while doing my runs to the posts. I wonder if they got what they needed. I'm sure they did. Sam and Jon wouldn't leave them without, but still I don't like seeing things go unfinished on my part. Tomorrow I'll go make sure everything is okay.

Fuck, that's probably considered an alpha duty and I'm banned from those for now. Well, what am I supposed to do with myself? Ask Connie to teach me how to knit? Shaking my head I continue eating.

But seriously, what am I supposed to do now? I've been training since I was eleven! I don't know anything else.

I'm sure *Alpha Roman* will have an idea, but I don't even want to talk to him right now. I feel like he betrayed me, like he doesn't have faith in me at all.

At that last thought I push my plate away, no longer hungry. I suppose I could take a shower before going to bed.

*　*　*

WHEN I HEAD down to breakfast the next morning there's no one around. *Odd, I'm not that late. Am I?* I place my empty bowl from last night in the sink. Even Connie isn't here. I listen closely and I can hear her in the laundry room. I can also hear voices coming from my father's office.

Yep, some orange juice and toast, then. Grabbing the bread I pop it in the toaster, and while waiting for my toast I pour a glass of juice. Just as I finish putting butter on my toast, I hear my father and some others coming down the hall. I toss my cup in the sink, snatch my food, and run out the door before I can be stopped.

I drive over to the training grounds, taking the route through town. Our "downtown" is one street full of shops, a barber, hair and nail salon, a small diner, and the school. We don't have much here to do. If we want to go out shopping we have to go into the human world, which isn't a big deal. We leave them alone, they leave us alone. They think we're some weird version of the Amish, I think.

We have about 300 wolves in our pack, making it decent sized in numbers. Our actual owned property is about 200 acres, but our territory is much bigger than that. We're on the edge of the National Forest so that gives us the breadth to run, hunt and fish.

When I arrive at the training grounds I'm met by David, one of the leading commanders of our warriors, which also means he's the man in charge of training. "Hey, David, I'm going to go change and I'll be out on the field." I stop and turn back to him. "If I'm allowed to be here that is."

David cocks his head, looking perplexed. "Why

wouldn't you be allowed here? No one's said anything to me."

"Oh, no reason. Forget I said anything." I rush into the locker room to change into my sweats, and to get away from awkwardly trying to explain that I was temporarily demoted. At least Dad didn't take this away, too. I kinda thought after last night I would be learning to knit.

Out on the field everyone is gathered towards the middle. This is odd – usually they're all in smaller groups. I walk over to find out what's going on.

"Yo, Elle! Over here!" I look and see Noah making his way through the crowd and I meet him halfway. "What's up? I haven't seen much of you since the rogue deal."

I'm very aware that Noah's words were heard by the majority of the others because the hum of voices died down and they're all looking at us.

"Yeah, it was a crazy night. Just been busy trying to figure out how to handle patrols now that that problem was taken care of. I've been beat, honestly." I shuffle on my feet. Normally I'm not this uncomfortable in front of people, but now I'm wondering if they all know that my dad decided to stop my training for the time being.

"Well, what happened? Noah told us some stuff but we want to hear it from you," a voice yells out.

A chorus of "Yeahs!" comes from around me.

I notice David and Karla, the other trainer who focuses mainly on self- defense, walking over to us. "Later, guys. We can have a fire on the beach and I'll tell you everything."

"Sweet."

"Awesome"

"I'll bring drinks!"

I have no clue who said what because the chatter was back among the group.

"All right, everyone listen up! If you're here for self-defense, then go with Karla. The rest of you follow me," David barks.

* * *

I LAND on my back hard. *Ow.* We are doing one-on-one drills right now, and I'm paired with Rafe, one of the guys who "challenges" me all the time.

He raises his foot to come down on my stomach but I grab his leg and twist, sending him sprawling on his stomach. Taking my chance, I stand back up and get into stance, preparing to take his next move. In training we're supposed to do *some* moves but not intentionally hurt one another, so when his fist comes at me so fast that it definitely would have broken my nose, I know we're not running simple drills.

However, I cannot let my anger get the best of me. It makes you sloppy, and sloppy fighting means you can lose.

Everyone is watching now. I have to be careful how I handle this. David will report my behavior back to my father, and I don't need any more issues there.

Lowering my stance just enough, I take a chance. "Rafe, this isn't the time or place for this. We're supposed to be learning and working on our strategies."

He doesn't listen, he never does. Instead he starts circling me. I in turn also start going in circles so I never have my back to him.

"Fuck the strategy, fuck this training program. It's a bunch of bullshit. You know it, I know it, and everyone here knows it." He gestures to the crowd that seems to have gotten bigger. I notice Sam now— someone must've gone to get him. He steps forward and I see my father behind him,

I shake my head, hopefully conveying to both of them to stay out of this. It's between Rafe and me.

Looking back at Rafe I lower my arms. I hear some gasps come from the crowd. "Listen, Rafe, if you're not happy the way things are here, the road out is that way." I point towards the road that heads off the property to the south. "Challenging me all the time and getting your ass handed to you every time isn't the answer. Pack your shit and leave if you hate it here so much."

He stalks closer to me, until he's looming over me, his foul breath making me hold my own. I still keep my arms down, though. I'm ready for an attack but I don't want him to know it.

"This pack needs a new leader. This pack is weak, you're weak, and so is your father. Bunch of pathetic weak losers who don't want to fight! We're wolves! We're meant to fight, draw blood, and kill." Spit is flying from his mouth, hitting me in the face.

I stand my ground. "No, Rafe, you need to stop, stop before you say or do something that gets you killed. You don't like how things are done here?" I point at my father. "There's your alpha. I suggest talking to him once you've calmed down. I'm done here."

I turn my back on him. Some would say it's a mistake, but it was my calculated move and it works. I hear him right before he grabs my arm. "You're not done here! Not until I say we're done." His teeth bared, he's practically growling, not talking. He yanks my arm and throws me to the ground. I kick him in the balls and scramble back to my feet.

Fuck this. I ram into his chest with my shoulder. He pulls me down with him and gets me with an elbow to my ribs. Shit, I think he cracked them. Fighting through the pain I grab Rafe by the shirt and punch him in the face and one more in the gut, *asshole*. He pushes back and I go in with another punch. We take turns beating each other into the ground, neither one of us giving up. It feels like this has gone on forever.

Blood spewing out of Rafe's nose and down his cheek from a cut. "Are we done now?" I ask, wiping blood and dirt from my mouth.

He doesn't answer. Instead he lunges out and grabs my hair and once again I'm on the ground. I've been up and down so many times now I'm starting to get dizzy. He kicks me in the gut before straddling me and I have to force myself to not vomit . He wraps his hands around my throat he starts to press. *Holy shit, this is a true challenge. He wants to kill me.* I reach up with my hand and press my thumb into his eye. I feel blood or something ooze onto my hand.

"AAGHHH!" Rafe screams in agony. I feel his weight suddenly gone– someone must have intervened and pulled him off of me. The next thing I know Sam, Jon, and Karla are surrounding me.

"Are you okay?"

"Someone call the nurse and send her to the packhouse!"

"He tried to kill me, didn't he?" I ask whoever will answer me. I close my eyes. My head is pounding– that's to be expected after getting punched a few dozen times. I reach up to rub my throat, stopping when the pain shooting in my ribs becomes unbearable.

"Don't move, Elle." Sam lightly takes my hands and holds them down. "We'll get a stretcher and get you back to your house and the nurse can see you."

"*Pfft*, I'll be fine, we heal fast. I don't need the nurse, just a nap," I argue.

"You'll need some pain medicine to help you sleep. I'm sure you're in a lot of pain."

"Sam, Jon, help me get her on the stretcher and into the truck, would you?" I feel more hands on me as they try to gingerly roll me on the stretcher Karla set down.

Wait, where is Rafe? "Rafe?" I ask aloud. I can't even hear him yelling anymore.

I'm hoisted up and slid into the back of a pickup truck. I hear two people get in and the tailgate slam before the engine revs and we're bouncing down the road. Couldn't they drive slowly? All the jostling is making me hurt more.

"Your father and David are taking care of him," Jon says gruffly.

"Why aren't you with him?"

"Because he needs to be in two places at once and that isn't possible. So I'll stay with you until he can be here."

That figures. When your father is the alpha, family comes second. He has to deal with Rafe first before he can tend to me. It sucks but I get it. Rafe needs to be dealt with by an alpha, he's gotta be put in place by an alpha. Yeah, betas have a lot of say, but when wolves get out of control and they try to kill another pack member, that's something the alpha has to handle directly.

The truck lurches to a stop. "Jesus, don't you know how to drive?!" I yell. The sudden stop made my whole body shift and pain shoots through me.

"Oh, quit your whining." I open my eyes and see Sam grinning down at me. "We're gonna put you on the couch in the living room. Kinda figure you don't want to be hauled up the stairs."

"I can stand. Let me get down and I can go over there myself."

Jon and Sam look at each other and shrug. They both

know how stubborn I can be. I swing my legs off the stretcher and gingerly put my feet down. Everything hurts. Thank god, werewolves heal fast. After I sleep for a few hours I should be golden.

Sitting down on the couch I let out a pained groan. Fuck, this *hurts!* The nurse, Rose, comes into the living room. She looks me over and then promptly turns to the guys. "All right, all the men out! I have to remove her clothes so I can examine her." She fishes through her bag and removes scissors that are meant for cutting through clothes, like what paramedics have.

Jon leaves immediately, probably heading out to the porch to call my dad. Sam, however, comes over to me and kneels so he's not standing over me.

Touching the only part of me that isn't too hurt he takes my hand in his. "I have to go into the city today. I'm part of the group that's going to get supplies, so I probably won't be here when you wake up. I'll be back in a few days."

Knowing it's probably killing him to leave me when I'm all busted up, I reach up and ruffle his hair to ease his stress. "Good luck, have fun, and bring me back something nice."

Sam chuckles. "I'll bring you back some M&Ms. If they have a ten-pound bag, that's what you'll get." He still doesn't get up, he doesn't want to leave me. I can see Nurse Rose losing her patience, standing behind him with her hands on her hips.

"I'll be fine, Sam. We better let Rose do her job and patch me up." He lets go of my hand and heads out of the house.

Rose walks over to me. "Now I hope you're not too fond of your shirt and pants," she says as she begins cutting through the fabric.

"Well, since they're just sweats for training, I think I can let them go."

She examines me thoroughly, noting where she touches and I cringe in pain. Once she's done, she helps me into a long button-up shirt.

"The healing process has already begun. Do you think you can make it up the stairs and into your bed before I give you the pain medicine?" Rose looks at me over her reading glasses.

I nod. "Yeah, I can manage that." My head isn't pounding so hard anymore, and my ribs are just burning and no longer a fire.

Jon is waiting in the hallway and with Rose's help they assist me up the stairs. By the time we get to my room I am out of breath and shaking. Regardless, I head to the mirror and not my bed. Rose *tsks* in disapproval at me.

I'm a mess. My face is all cut up, though the cuts look like they're a week old and not from a few minutes ago. There's bruising around my neck from where Rafe tried to strangle me. I don't bother looking at the rest of my body, knowing it looks bad based on how much pain I'm in from just going up the stairs. And don't even get me started on my hair. My dark brown hair, pulled back into a braid for training, looks like a bird decided to make a nest in it. I'm not covered in blood or eye ooze, Rose must have cleaned me up while examining me.

Disgusted, I turn away from my reflection and head to my bed. Once I'm settled in, Rose comes over with a bottle of water and some pills.

"Take these— one is for the pain and the other is to help you sleep and stay asleep so you can heal faster."

I take the water and the pills and swallow them down. "Thanks."

Jon waves. "Have a good sleep. I hope to see you out and about tomorrow." And with that he's out the door. Rose is still in my room, packing up her bag.

"If you wake up in pain, call me and I'll be over with some more meds. Though I'm sure a young healthy wolf like yourself won't need any more." She gives me a tight smile and walks out of my room, shutting the door behind her.

I settle in my bed and get as comfortable as I can. The meds must be kicking in, I'm starting to feel sleepy. I hear voices in the hall but I'm too tired to try and listen. Sleep is taking over and everything goes dark.

CHAPTER THREE

Elle

I'm running through the forest, weaving through the trees and jumping over fallen logs. My hair whips behind me. I feel every pebble under my feet, every branch tickles my skin as I run past them.

I'm completely exposed, barefoot and naked, running on an unbeaten path.

Running because something or someone is chasing me.

But I'm not scared. No, I feel free. I feel safe.

Hearing the trickle of a stream nearby I change my course and run toward it. When I get to the flowing water, I walk up the bank into a small clearing and I sit and wait.

Closing my eyes, I listen. I hear whoever's been chasing me coming closer. The soft sound of leaves touching fur, his paws padding on the forest floor making the softest crunch from disturbed plants and fallen needles.

I take a deep breath, smelling his scent in front of me. His breath on my face.

Tilting my head up I open my eyes. He's standing over me. I should feel threatened with this big black wolf looming over me, my throat exposed to him because I'm looking up into his amber eyes.

He growls softly and nuzzles into my neck. I reach and grab onto his fur. We stay like this for a minute before he backs away.

"Wait! Don't go." I stand to stop him. "Please," I whisper.

The wolf cocks his head and then he lunges at me. He has me pinned to the ground, but now instead of a wolf he's a man.

He kisses my neck. "Be careful what you wish for, mate."

I startle awake. *Well, THAT was a weird dream.* Must have been because of the pain meds. I mentally shake it off. I look at my clock— it's one in the afternoon. Stretching, I say aloud, "There's no way I only slept for a couple of hours and feel like this."

A chuckle comes from the corner. "More like twenty-five hours." I look and see my dad sitting at my desk. "How are you feeling?" he asks. How long has he been here? He looks exhausted, dark circles under his eyes, his clothes all rumpled like he'd been sitting in them all night in that chair.

Flexing my arms and shaking off the sleep I smile at him. "I feel great. I don't feel like I got my ass handed to me." I pause and ask, "How's Rafe?"

Dad's face goes grim. Running his hand through his hair, something he does when he's uncomfortable or when something is bothering him, he says, "He's been taken care of."

"He's dead?" I ask and Dad nods. I'm not quite sure how I feel about this. Rafe was an asshole, definitely, and he was trying to kill me, but they stopped him. He didn't kill me, so why did he have to die? I look at my father. "Was it you?"

Instead of answering me he gets out of the chair and comes to sit on my bed. We sit in silence for a while, my dad just looking at the floor and me waiting for his answer.

Finally breaking his gaze from the floor, he faces me. "Yes, I did. His intentions were clear. At least toward the end it was."

Holy shit, I don't think my dad has ever executed a pack member. Exile? Sure. Probation? Yes. But he's never killed one of our own.

"What do you mean 'at least towards the end'"?

"Elle, I knew you'd have a few scuffles here and there when you turned eighteen. Every wolf goes through it, it's how we establish dominance within the pack. Even more so when you're the soon-to-be alpha. People try to challenge you, mostly to see if you're strong enough to lead them. Others, though, they challenge for the position itself." He stops and rubs his temple before continuing. "After David and I pulled Rafe off of you, we took him into the woods and he was uncontrollable. Kept trying to go back to you and finish the job he had started. He had this crazed look in his eyes- or eye, I should say."

I dip my head down. Holy shit, I took out his eye?

"Hey." My dad puts his arm around my shoulders and squeezes. "You did what you had to to survive. It's nothing to be ashamed of." He pulls away and looks me in the eye. "Do you want me to continue? Or do you want to leave it where we are now?"

Taking a deep breath to get my bearings, I square my shoulders and face him. "Continue, please."

"So Rafe's going absolutely crazy, still trying to break past our hold on him. Thankfully, Noah showed up and with some reinforcements. They also brought the silver cuffs with them. We bound his arms behind his back and his ankles as well. I told him that he attempted to kill you and therefore broke one of our laws. I told him that since he was unable to kill you he had the option of exile." Dad smiles but it doesn't reach his eyes.

I'm not sure if I should say something or just keep my mouth shut. Before I can even find the words I want to say he continues. "He told me, and the whole forest actually, that I was a pussy and the weakest alpha he had ever met." I gasp, but Dad ignores me and goes on. "Rafe said if I didn't have the balls to kill him right then and there that when he came back he'd make me watch him kill you. Then he'd kill whoever didn't submit to him as their alpha. He kept saying it over and over, and after watching what happened between the two of you, it set me off. I slit his throat and watched the light leave his eye."

Holy fuck ... I'm truly speechless now.

Dad shakes his head. "I don't think he would have lasted long on his own. I think he lost his mind so much he wouldn't know to eat or drink. I had to kill him. He made it clear that he would hurt the pack, and more importantly, he'd come back and hurt you again. I couldn't risk it, Elle, I just couldn't." His eyes meet mine, pleading for me to understand. "I didn't want to kill him, I *had* to."

"Seems like the shitty part of the job, doing things you don't want to."

His chuckle is dry. "Elle, one thing to remember, an alpha sometimes has to do things they don't want to, especially when it keeps the pack safe." He looks at his watch. "I gotta go, I'm supposed to meet Jon and go over some things." He's almost out the door when his head pops back in. "Oh, you might wanna fix your hair and clean up a bit before coming downstairs." I catch his wink as he shuts the door.

Gah! My hair! I jump out of bed and run to the bathroom mirror. The rat's nest that was there yesterday has gotten worse from my whole day of sleeping. Grabbing my brush, I try to work out the tangles before giving up and turning on the shower. It will be easier to untangle when there's conditioner in my hair.

Once I'm out of the shower I towel dry my hair and head to my full-length mirror. Oh good, the bruises are gone and the cuts have all healed. Full body inspection checks out, I look good as new. Heading over to my dresser I pick out my favorite oversized t-shirt, a very well-worn *Metallica* concert tee, and some jeans. Quickly throwing my hair in a messy bun, I take one more look in the mirror and leave my room.

Bounding down the stairs, I smell grilled cheese and tomato soup coming from the kitchen.

Mmm, comfort food.

Rounding the corner into the kitchen I take a seat at the table. Connie is busy at the stove, but she turns and gives me a smile. "I'm glad you're feeling better, Eleanor. The kitchen was quiet for a day without you coming in to taste test everything."

"Gotta make sure it's safe to eat, it's a safety precaution." I shoot her a grin.

"Oh, you know no one has ever gotten sick from my cooking!" she scolds me, but I see the smile on her face as she turns back to the stove.

The front door opens, I hear two sets of footsteps, and my dad and Jon come into the kitchen.

"Hey, Elle, how are you feeling?" Jon sits down across from me, while my dad takes his normal seat next to mine.

"I'm feeling pretty good."

"That's good to hear. I already called Sam and told him you were awake." He pours some lemonade that Connie had put on the table. "They should be back in two days. I know I'll feel better when they're back."

"Oh good, I hope he brings me some M&Ms like he promised."

"He's bringing something back all right," he says wryly.

What's with the smirk? Dad chuckles but tries to hide it by taking a drink.

Now I'm really confused. "Uhh, okay. What's going on?"

Jon shakes his head. "I promised my son I'd let him tell you."

"Whatever." Clearly, I'm not going to get anything out of these two clowns. It doesn't matter anyway, because Connie brings over the food and I'm starving. I take a bite as soon as I dunk my grilled cheese into the soup. *Mmmmm, this is amazing.* "Thanks, Connie. It's delicious, as usual." Dad and Jon both nod in agreement, their mouths too full to talk.

"You're welcome, Eleanor," she grins at me. The dryer buzzer goes off and she disappears from the kitchen to take care of the laundry. Man, what would we do without her?

Deciding to test my luck I look at my father and ask, "So what's going on with the visiting Alpha? When's he supposed to be here?" Dad stops chewing, clearly not expecting the conversation to go this way. Since this is a topic I have already been privy to I think it's safe to ask. Looking back and forth between Dad and Jon, I begin to think I have overstepped the boundaries of my new "rules."

Dad finishes chewing, pushes his plate away and rests his arms on the table. "Well," he says and shoots a glance at

Jon. "We're not really sure. He won't give us any definite details. All we know is that he'll be here at some point this week or the next."

"Which is why we asked the team that went into the city to wrap it up and be back in two days. We need Sam and the others back ASAP," Jon adds.

"I'm confused. Do we know this man is a threat? Is that why you're on red alert? Do we know *anything* about him?" I ask.

"No, we don't know for sure that he is a threat. And we're not on red alert, we're just taking precautions that are probably unnecessary." He shoots me a glare that says I'm overstepping my new boundaries. I hate not being in the know. It's beyond frustrating– all I've done is ask questions and get answers. He has know it's hard for me to not ask questions, even if it is for only a few weeks.

"I'm sorry, Dad. This is hard for me, I'm not used to not knowing what's going on. We've gone from talking about everything to me being a regular pack member. If I've crossed a line let me know and I'll back off."

I get out of the chair and take our plates to the sink. Might as well get used to this for a while. Besides, Connie doesn't have to come back to a sink full of dishes, especially since I have nothing better to do.

Dad sighs, I hear both chairs scrape against the wood floor. Jon excuses himself, leaving my dad and me alone. I continue washing the dishes, not pushing for any more explanation than I have already received. We don't speak. The only sound filling the silence is the water running from the tap and dishes clanking around.

"I'll dry them and put them away," Dad says, taking the dish towel from its home on a handle. Once the dishes are done and put away, I go to clean the surfaces.

Dad is still lingering. Why doesn't he just go? Doesn't he have a million more important things to do besides stand here?

"His name is Drake, and his territory is north of us in Canada."

I turn around and look at him, kind of shocked he offered more information to me.

Giving him a small smile, I nod once. "Thanks."

There's sadness in his eyes. "You know, this isn't easy for me either, Elle." And with that he walks out of the kitchen and I'm left alone.

* * *

IT'S BEEN two long days of doing basically nothing. I went back to the training grounds this morning, where I was paired with Noah today. He kept trying to go easy on me, until I laid him out three times. I'm now sitting on the porch with my dad, Noah, Jon, and his mate Rhea. Jons and Rhea's younger children are playing in the yard. They're twin girls and eleven years younger than Sam. Allison pushes Cait to the ground.

Cait squeals. "Hey! I'm telling Mom. MOM—"

"I'm right here, Cait, no need to yell." Rhea doesn't even pick her head up from the blanket she's knitting for a couple who's about to have their first pup. "Allison, don't push your sister."

"Why do you always have to cry to Mom?"

"Why do you always have to push me around?"

"I was born first, meaning *I'm* the boss, because I'm older and more mature than you."

Cait scoffs, "You were born *two whole* minutes before I was, you're not that much older or mature than me." She crosses her arms, turns away from her sister and sits on the ground. "And I don't want to play with you anymore!"

"Fine!" Allison yells back and she sits facing the opposite direction.

"Kids," Jon says to no one in particular. "They're a handful." He takes a sip of his beer and Rhea reaches out and smacks him on the knee.

"Life would be boring without them and you know it," she says, giving him a pointed look.

"Yes, it would, and I wouldn't trade them for anything." He looks at his daughters with so much love in his eyes. I wonder if they know how much he adores them?

I yawn for what feels like the hundredth time this afternoon. The strange wolf keeps visiting my dreams and it's putting a damper on my sleep. I don't even fully remember the first one. Hearing about Rafe kind of put that on the back burner.

"Why are you so tired, Elle?" Noah lightly nudges my head with his hand.

Smacking his hand away, I take a deep breath. "Just been having weird dreams. They wake me up. There's a wolf who I don't know that I keep seeing." I shrug and turn around to face everyone else.

Noah's chortling with laughter. "That's it? You're seeing a wolf when you're sleeping and you're waking up, losing sleep like it's nightmares? That doesn't seem scary."

I smack him again. Who invited him anyway?

"Hey! I'm only picking."

"But why is he there? Who could it be? And what does he want with me?" Dream or no dream it makes me unsettled. I turn to look at my dad, Jon and Rhea, who all seem to be looking at each other with odd expressions.

"What?" I ask

My dad shifts in his chair. "Well, it could mean that your mate is nearby, or that your paths will cross soon." He takes a deep breath before continuing. "Could be a threat, though, too. The wolf inside us, even though it's just an extension of ourselves, can be more in tune with others."

"Have any of you had this type of dream before?"

"A few months before I met your mother." He closes his eyes and smiles. Probably reminiscing on memories I don't want to hear about. I look at Jon and Rhea.

"What about you guys? Any strange wolf dreams?"

They both shake their heads. "No, I haven't." Jon says.

"The only ones I hear about it happening to are alphas and lunas. Either sensing each other or it's a warning of a threat." She stops knitting and comes to sit by me on the stairs. "What's he look like? What's the feeling you get from him?"

"Uh ..." I'm not very comfortable with all the questions. I start twirling my hair around my fingers. I take a deep breath and let it out. "He's big, has, um dark fur. Black maybe. He doesn't seem threatening." I shake my head and stand suddenly. "What are we talking about? It's just a dream, it doesn't mean anything."

I step off the porch and pace. *But if it doesn't mean anything then why has he been in my dreams since the day Rafe almost killed me?* I don't get it. I just want this alpha to get here so we can get this damn visit over with and I can go back to my normal life.

Noah comes over to me. "Hey, I didn't mean to laugh at you. I didn't think it was serious stuff."

"It's fine, man. And it's *not* serious."

It's just a dream. I have no desire to find a mate, not yet anyway. It would throw everything off, it would change my entire life. I don't want to be linked to someone like that, mind, body, soul, and heart. I've seen what can happen when you find your true mate and then lose them. You lose a part of yourself. No, I'd rather wait until after I turn twenty-one and I can choose my own mate. I can still get the bond, the blood bond, it's just not as intense.

It's strange how it works. But again, I think it comes down to breeding and making sure our population is added to.

The exhaust from a truck breaks me from my thoughts.

"Sam's home! Sam's home! Sam's home!" Allison and Cait chant, running to the edge of the yard, jumping up and down with excitement.

"Mom! Dad! You see his truck?! It's him!" Cait yells.

We all laugh. Well, there's one stressor gone. Now that Sam's home we can relax a little. All of us head to stand with the girls while he parks his truck.

"Hi, everyone— ugh!" Allison and Cait both tackle him as soon as he's out of the truck, sending them into a tangle of limbs on the grass.

"What did you bring us, Sam?"

"Did you bring any candy?"

"Was it fun in the city?"

"You were gone forever."

Sam laughs and pulls them in for a hug. "I missed you monsters, too. Were you good for Mom?"

"Yes!" they say in unison, grinning up at him.

Rhea and Jon each grab a girl and free Sam from their grip. "All right girls, that's enough. Let your brother breathe," Jon says, holding Allison in one arm. He offers Sam the other to help him up. They do that awkward one-arm man hug. "Good to see you home, son."

"Thanks, Dad. It's good to be home." He's very cheerful, more so than usual. Hmmm, what's with him?

Sam hugs his mother and gives her a kiss on the cheek. "Hi, Mom. You can stop worrying now, I'm home."

Rhea shakes her head. "Foolish boy, when will you learn that a mother never stops worrying about her children? No matter how old they are or how strong they get." She pulls him in for another quick hug before releasing him.

"Noah," Sam nods in his direction. Noah waves back.

My father steps forward and offers his hand. Sam takes it. "I'll give you the inventory report soon, Roman," he says.

"Don't worry about that right now. Get settled in tonight and we'll meet in the morning." Dad grins at him. "Glad you're home, Sam." Dad slaps his shoulder then heads over to talk with Rhea and Jon.

Sam comes over to me. "Hey there." He looks me up and down. "You sure look a lot better than the last time I saw you." He flashes me a grin and I smile back.

"And you don't look any worse than the last time I saw you," I reply. "Which is good because you were pretty ugly before."

He bursts into laughter. "Man, I'm glad you're still you. After that last fight with Rafe, I wasn't sure if your brain got all scrambled."

Something's off about Sam. He seems fine, but he's treating me differently. Usually we hug when one of us is gone for a period of time, but he's kept a few feet between us. What's changed? I hear the sound of something in the truck. I try to look but the windows are tinted so dark I can only make out movement. Who's Sam got with him? And why haven't they left the truck yet?

Sam notices me stare at his truck and turns to look, then quickly turns back to face me.

"So, uhh, who's in your truck, Sam?"

He rubs the back of his neck, not quite meeting my eyes. It seems like he's struggling to find the words he wants to say.

"Elle, I have to tell you something. But I- I don't know how to. You see, I, um, I brought someone back with me."

Why is he so nervous? This isn't like Sam, fumbling for words and fidgeting. "Okay, who is it?" I look to Sam, who still won't meet my gaze, and then to everyone else. They're all standing around awkwardly, too, minus the girls, who are rummaging through a bag they found.

Getting fed up with Sam not being able to give me a straight answer I push past him and head to the passenger side of the truck.

"Elle ..." Sam starts but it's too late. I have already whipped open the door and come face to face with a woman. She's got long dirty blonde hair, big blue eyes, and a slender face to hold it all together. She also smells of flowers. The mystery woman looks shocked and nervous to see that I ripped open the door to her safe haven.

I'm staring at her, wondering why Sam brought this she-wolf back with him. Sam steps in between me and the open truck door. When she sees him her eyes fill with adoration and love. Seriously, what is going on here?

Sam looks at her. "Hey, you okay?" She nods and smiles shyly. He turns back and faces me. "Meghan, this is Elle, Alpha Roman' daughter." She gives me a small wave, which I return. I'm not a complete bitch. Sam takes a deep breath. "Elle, this is Meghan. My mate."

I stare at them both, my mouth drops.
What. The. Fuck.

* * *

I FIND solace in the kitchen with Connie. Everyone else stayed outside on the porch, enjoying the summer evening and getting to know Meghan. Sam's got a mate. Wow. I wasn't expecting this. I mean, now I understand what Jon meant the other day when he said "He's bringing something back."

After fumbling out the lamest greeting and then giving some lame excuse about peeling potatoes, I ran into the house. God, I probably seem like a jealous bitch right now. But come to think of it, I probably am a little jealous. Not in the "she took my man" type of jealousy– no, Sam and I tried that years ago and it didn't work out. We're friends, best friends. A duo, and sometimes Noah, too. I'm also not jealous that he found his mate and I haven't. Nope, I'm still camped out on "no mate island." But then why *am* I jealous? Because Sam didn't call me himself and tell me. Like why wouldn't he? Why did he wait until he showed up with her and completely shock me? He should have called me, or even texted me. "Hey Elle, you'll never guess what! I found my mate. We'll see ya in a few days, she's coming back with me." Our friendship is already changing and I'm not ready to let him go.

Okay, that's selfish of me. I'm happy for him, of course I am. But how is this going to change us? I throw the potato I was peeling in the bowl and grab another. I'm enjoying this. It's giving my hands something to do while I think things through. I take a deep breath. I'm just going to have to talk to Sam. Yeah, that's it. I should probably try and get to know Meghan, too.

"You keep peeling more potatoes and we're going to have to invite half the pack to dinner." Connie pulls me out of my head and I look at the potatoes I have peeled.

"Shit, sorry, Connie." I pick up the bowl of potatoes and take them to the sink to rinse.

Connie takes out the cutting board and starts cubing up the potatoes and adds them to a large pot. We work together in silence. I can tell Connie wants to say something.

Sighing, I set the knife in the sink. "Just say whatever you want to say, Connie."

"Don't you take that tone with me, Eleanor," she says, standing there with her hand on her hip, the other one pointing a finger at me. "When I'm ready to tell you what I'm thinking I will, and not a minute sooner." She turns back to the stove and fusses over it.

Rolling my eyes I go back to the sink and start the dishes. *Whatever.*

"And don't roll your eyes at me either, Eleanor!" Connie chides. *How does she do that?* I have my back turned to her and she's not even looking at me! Bewildered, I whip around to look at her. She laughs. "Darling, I have two pups, all grown up. I have been through this two times, and I have been in this house with you for eighteen years. I probably know you better than you know yourself."

She goes back to stirring one of the pots on the stove, and I continue to stare at her.

"For instance, I know that you're feeling overwhelmed, and like you have lost your best friend." She gives me a small smile. "I know it feels that way and it will be a while before you and Sam are used to your new normal, but you need to keep an open mind here. A way to keep your and Sam's relationship close would be to befriend his new mate. Now I have only talked to her for a few minutes, but she seems like a nice young woman. You should give her a chance."

"Okay," I say, not really knowing what else to say.

Connie huffs. "No, it's not just 'okay.' That young lady out there is out of her element and probably feeling very vulnerable now. The only thing she has right now that feels safe is Sam. When you leave your home, and everyone you know, to go be with your mate in a new pack, it's very overwhelming. I should know." She closes her eyes, the memories of her leaving her home to come here with her mate probably flooding all back to the front of her mind.

"I didn't think I was acting *that* horribly," I amend, dipping my head down to look at the floor. Connie's hand grabs my chin and makes me meet her gaze.

"You're not, dear– at least it's not how everyone else is probably seeing it. They know it's a shock to you, even Sam understands you may need some time to adjust." She brushes some hair that had fallen into my face behind my ear. "But to Meghan, she already feels like an outsider, like an intruder. She's out there thinking she has made an enemy of the alpha's daughter, the highest-ranking female in the pack, and I'm sure that's a scary thought for her to have."

I shake my head. "But wouldn't Sam just tell her that's foolish thinking?"

"If she mentioned it to him, yes. But she will probably keep her mouth shut. Knowing how close you and Sam are she knows it could cause a rift between you two. Even if it was temporary and minor."

I cock my head to the side, even more confused now. Wouldn't she rather Sam *not* have any sort of relationship with me? No matter how platonic it is.

Connie must sense my confusion because she pats my arm and says, "You don't understand the true mate bond. She knows you're not a threat in a way to take Sam away from her. But she wouldn't do anything to jeopardize your relationship because it would hurt Sam so much. And that's the last thing she wants to do."

One of the pots on the stove starts to boil over and Connie rushes over to tend to it, ending our conversation.

* * *

AFTER EVERYONE HAS LEFT to go home after dinner I head to my dad's office, knocking on the door before entering.

"Hey, Dad," I greet him before walking over to the small library of books he has.

"Hey, Elle, what brings you in here?" he says, looking up from the pile of paperwork he was reading. An alpha's work is never done. Well, until you retire.

"Nothing really, just wanted to run something by you." He looks at me, waiting for me to go on. "Meghan seems nice, quiet but nice," I add.

"Mhm, she does."

I fiddle with a metal spinning thing he has on a shelf. "I was thinking maybe I could go over tomorrow and show her the main parts of the pack land. Sam's gonna be busy with you and Jon, Rhea has the twins to tend to. I figured that since I have some free time available, I could use this as a chance to get to know her." I glance over at him, waiting for an answer. When he doesn't give one I add, "That is if it's okay with you?"

Dad leans back in his chair. "I think that's a great idea, Elle." He smiles at me— he looks pleased with this idea. He's probably sick of me moping around the house when there isn't training and bugging Connie all the time.

"Okay! Cool, I'll show her some of the paths if she wants to go for a run or explore a little bit." I'm excited,

I've never had a good chance to make any girl friends my age. Most females shy away from me because I'm such a dominant wolf, but her being the next beta's mate brings her up in ranks sort of. Plus I know Connie is right, befriending Meghan will make her transition into the pack much easier for all of us.

Dad stands up and walks over to me. "Now wait, Elle, you can only go on the paths that have been marked as safe. We brought our perimeter in for the time being. We don't want anyone running into trouble until this Alpha Drake has come and gone." He sighs. "I know you're used to having free roam, but could you please stay in the perimeter? You can show her all the sights and paths you want as soon as we know it's safe."

He looks at me, giving me a silent plea not to argue with him on this.

Deciding it's better not to argue again, I nod in agreement. He's just trying to make sure everyone is safe, and I get that. I don't need to add anymore stress than he already has.

Giving him a hug I say, "Thank you."

He squeezes back. "Your mother would be proud."

CHAPTER FOUR

Elle

With the windows rolled down and the music playing, I steer my Jeep down the road to Sam's house. It's a nice summer day, so I'm hoping Meghan wants to walk around today.

When I left the packhouse I only saw Sam from a distance. We waved to each other but I didn't go and greet him. I'll let my dad fill him in on what my plans are. I drive past Josh's house and see him playing outside in his yard with some other boys. I honk my horn and wave at them, they run down the road a ways, chasing my Jeep.

I laugh, remembering when Sam, Noah and I would do that to my father, or any of the warriors.

Pulling up next to Sam's small ranch house I put the Jeep in park and turn off the engine. As I'm stepping out I see the curtains moving. Well, hopefully she answers the door. I jog up the steps on the small porch and the door opens before I can knock.

Meghan gives me a shy smile. "Good morning, Elle." She steps to the side and I step in. "Would you like some coffee? I just made a fresh pot."

"Coffee sounds great, thank you." I follow her into the kitchen. Even though I know my way around this house, I want her to feel somewhat in control of her new life.

Meghan brings two mugs over and puts the cream and sugar on the table. She takes a sip from her mug and sighs. "So what brings you over here? Sam didn't send you, did he?" She sounds a little annoyed.

Deciding to answer the second question first I shake my head. "No, I hardly saw him this morning. Didn't even get a chance to talk to him. I came over to see if you wanted to get a tour of the land. Sam's busy and I have some free time today." I shrug and take a sip of coffee. Mmm, it's strong. "I also thought it would be good if you and I got to know each other. I'm not good at the girlfriend thing, but since you and Sam are a package deal now, I'd like to get to know you."

Meghan ponders this for a moment and then smiles broadly. "Call me Meg."

* * *

As we walk around town, I point out what there is to do in our little village.

"And that's the school where the younger kids go. Once they get into high school, and if they have their shifting under control, they can go to the high school in town. We have a bus that shuttles them into town." I sit down on a bench. "And that's about it."

Meg sits next to me, looking up and down the street. "I'm glad it's on the smaller side and not a town mixed with humans. That's what my pack was like. We all lived on the outskirts, but our downtown was shared with the humans."

"Wow, it must be hard keeping the secret when you live so close to them."

"You have no idea," she laughs. "I'll miss it, though, my friends and parents."

"Well, what did your parents say when you told them you found your mate?" Even though it's hoped for and normal, I'm sure it's still a shock when it does happen.

Meg snorts. "Are you kidding? As soon as they found out he's the future beta and talked to your father, they packed up my clothes and brought them halfway." She closes her eyes— I think she's fighting back tears. "With my family it all comes down to status and 'the image'." I must be making a face because she waves her hands. "No, no, it's not what you think. They love us kids, and we love them. They're great parents, really they are. It's just that they had always hoped that I would mate with someone in a higher rank."

"Well, what rank are you from? If you don't mind my asking."

"Not the bottom, not the top, in the middle, I guess." She shrugs. "We never wanted for anything. Dad is actually the pack lawyer, but he also has a practice in town and works with the humans. So moneywise we were about the same. It just came down to where we fell in the pack."

I nod. "Some of our pack works in the town next to us. Construction and stuff like that." I didn't really know what else to say, I couldn't imagine if I found my mate and my dad just shipped me off like that. Seems crazy to me.

"What's your family like?"

"Oh, um ... well, my dad is the Alpha, but you already know that. My mom died in a rogue attack when I was two so I don't really remember her." I take a deep breath. It's strange to feel sad and miss someone you didn't really know. "So, it's been Dad and me, and Connie. Her mate died in the same attack as my mother. Her pups had both grown and moved out of her house, so my dad asked her to come live in the packhouse with us."

Meg looks at me with sympathy. "I'm sorry about your mom, that's gotta be tough. Like who do you have to talk to about girl stuff?" Picking up a stick she begins breaking it into tiny pieces. "I mean, I really couldn't imagine going to my dad about periods and boys." She cringes at the thought.

I laugh. "Well, Connie and Rhea helped a lot with that stuff." And they did. Connie was there when I had to call her from the school because I started my period. Rhea took me bra shopping, and both women were there to hear about my crushes and first kiss. "My dad and I were close, though. *Some things* I could talk to him about. I talked about boys with him, though I'm sure he wished I didn't, but that's what happens when you spend all the time you can together." I don't elaborate on my training to become alpha– I'm not sure if Sam has told her or if I'm even allowed to talk about it right now.

"You're really close, huh?"

"Yeah, we are." I feel a smile on my face. "He's taught me everything I know." Standing up and stretching, I ask, "Are you ready to go?"

A crestfallen look comes over Meg's face. "Oh yeah, that's fine."

"I don't have to take you home. We can do something else."

"Like what?"

"Do you wanna go for a run?"

Her face lights up in excitement. "Hell yeah!"

We get into the Jeep and I drive us in the direction of one of the trail heads. On a tree is a green ribbon, which means this one has the all-clear to use. I point out the ribbon to Meg and explain that we should see these every fifty feet or so on the trail. Also the trail will have the heaviest smell of wolves from all the patrols.

Meg nods. "Sam mentioned something about things being strict because an alpha is coming. Thanks for explaining the ribbon, though."

Nodding my head I start down the trail. "Come on, we can leave our clothes here and come back for them later." I motion toward a tree that has a waterproof can at its base.

"Cool." Meg goes behind a tree to shift and I go to do the same, but first I send a quick text to my dad.

> Still with Meg.
>
> We're going for a run.
>
> I saw the ribbons so I know what trails are safe

DAD
> Be safe
>
> Use the mind link if there's any trouble

"Right, use the mind link. It's a useful tool werewolves in the same pack can use to communicate with each other. It has to be directed, though. We can't hear each other's thoughts. It's basically like talking but it can be done over a long distance"I sent my dad a text saying what we're doing, he'll probably tell Sam."

"Okay!" Meg calls out.

Closing my eyes I shift into my wolf and trot out onto the trail. A light brown wolf, Meg, sees me and flattens out on the ground.

Ah shit, my size probably freaked her out. I lower myself onto the forest floor to make myself smaller.

"*Meg, it's just me. I probably should have warned you that my wolf is rather large.*"

"*Holy shit, you're beautiful! And, I'm sorry to say this but you're HUGE. And it's not just your size that's intimidating, you put out an aura of dominance.*"

Stretching my limbs, I snort. Sam must not have told her anything about me. I'm not sure if that's good or bad, though. I shake out my fur.

"*Yeah, it's why I don't have any friends who aren't male. It's hard to play and run when you always beat them.*"

Meg barks, "*What? I'm offended! I know we just met like, literally yesterday, but I thought we were now best friends forever.*" She hangs her head and covers her face with her paw, making an overplayed motion of despair. "*I thought we were kindred spirits!*"

She flops down as if my comment was unbearable for her to hear and she's completely devastated. I laugh, "*Oh my god. I cannot wait for you to pull these theatrics on Sam. Let's go, my 'bosom friend'.*"

We set off at a nice trot. "*We can run back,*" I tell her. "*I

A. R. KEOGH

just want you to get familiar with this trail since it's one of the only ones we can use for now,"

"*Okay!*" Meg looks at our surroundings and stops to sniff as well, familiarizing herself with the path and getting a whiff of some of the other wolves.

I wait patiently, not wanting her to feel rushed. I'm listening to the stream babble in the distance and the leaves rustling in the breeze. My mind wanders to the wolf who keeps visiting my dreams. I know I don't know him. I have never met a wolf or man who makes me feel so safe. All I remember is he follows me in the woods, sometimes I'm in wolf form, sometimes I'm human. He stalks me, which shouldn't be comforting at all. But for some reason it feels okay.

If Rhea and my father are right and he *is* my mate, do I want to meet him? No, I don't. I'm supposed to be alpha. But why does he keep showing up in my damned dreams? Is he even aware of it? So many questions and I have no answers, it's unsettling.

"*Hey, earth to Elle!*" Meg breaks through my train of thought, making me look up.

"*Sorry, I must have started daydreaming while I waited for you to explore,*" I explain, completely embarrassed to be caught off guard.

"*No kidding, I've been trying to get your attention for like five minutes. I even pretended to be hurt and nothing.*" She starts dancing around me in circles. "*So, spill the beans. Is it a guy?*"

Without answering I start heading up the trail. "*We gonna keep going or what?*"

"*Ooh, avoidance,*" Meg snickers. "*So it IS a guy. Is he dreamy? Handsome? Sexy? Is he strong? I. NEED. DETAILS!*"

"*Stop badgering me, I don't know. I've never seen his human face.*" Meg cocks her head, obviously confused. "*I've only seen *him in my dreams, he's got black fur, and he's big, really big."* Meg yips, lowers her front half and wags her tail. *"Not like that— sheesh, Meg, get your mind out of the gutter."*

Standing up, Meg heads back in the direction we came from. *"Let's head back. I can explore later. We have to talk about this."*

"Um, okay ..." I don't understand the big deal about it. It's just a dream.

Once we get back to the tree that has our stuff, we shift and get dressed. Meg turns and looks at me expectantly. "Well? Where are we going? Sam's house or the packhouse?"

Shaking my head, I start back to the Jeep. "It's not that big a deal," I say, trying to get her to calm down. I can feel the excitement and curiosity rolling off her in waves. I really don't think it is, it's just a dream. Nothing more, nothing less. How would my subconscious know what my mate looks like? Or smells like for that matter. No, this is just my imagination going wild.

"You didn't answer my question, Elle," Meg huffs. "Come *on*, I want all the details!"

Sighing in defeat, I turn the Jeep in the direction of the beach. "Fine, I know a place we can go."

Meg claps her hands, excited she's getting her way. "Yay!" she squeals.

"I'm surprised you don't want to get back to Sam, honestly." Glancing at her from the corner of my eye, I see her face drop a little. "I mean, isn't the mate bond super strong when it's new?"

Sighing, she looks out the window and starts wringing her hands. "Yeah, it is that strong. You've been a good distraction, though. I'm not sure how to explain it. It's intense, that's for sure. I don't think I'm in love with him yet, but it's like I've known him forever and that it hasn't just been for a couple of days. Even though we still have so much to learn about each other."

"Hey, if there's anything you want to know about Sam, I'm your person- or wolf. Especially on the extremely embarrassing stuff." I shoot her a wink and she laughs.

"I'll keep that in mind."

Turning into the pull-off I cut the engine and we both jump out of the Jeep. The ocean air feels cool on my face. I love this place. Dad says my mom used to bring me here all the time when I was little. But I don't remember that, though maybe my loving this place is from those distant memories.

Meg and I walk along the beach. "This is so pretty! We don't have many beaches where I'm from, just stinky marinas polluted with chemicals from boats." She wrinkles her nose in disgust. "But this is so clean and fresh, I can see myself coming here a lot." She bends down and picks up a smooth stone, rolling it around in her hands before throwing it into the cresting waves.

We come to the spot where rocks and a few logs are sitting in a half-circle with a fire pit in the center. It's the place where we have our fires and small parties. We sit in silence listening to the waves crash on the beach and the seagulls cry overhead. It really is peaceful here, probably my favorite place to be other than the forest.

"So what do you want to know?" I ask hesitantly.

"Sheesh, Elle. You make it seem like I'm strapping you down and waterboarding you for answers." She chuckles. "Which I may do if you don't start talking," Meg jokes.

Laughing and shaking my head, I decide to put her out of her misery even if it is all just joking. I wanted to befriend her, right? And friends talk about this stuff all the time, I suppose. "There really isn't much to say, Meg. I have these dreams where a large black wolf stalks me through the forest."

"Yeah, but wouldn't that be threatening?" she asks. "You don't seem upset or shaken up by this at all." Her face is full of curiosity that is probably from all the questions running in her head.

"That's what's weird, though. You *would* think it would be intimidating and threatening, but it's not. I don't wake up in fear or stress. I feel safe near him, like he's watching out for me, protecting me."

"Do you know when these all started?" Meg asks. She's now picking the bark off a stick she had found on the ground next to us.

Grabbing a handful of sand, I begin letting it fall through my fingers, watching it drift back to the ground. "I think it was last week, after my fight with Rafe."

Meg nods. "Sam told me a little about that. An experience like that could definitely trigger weird dreams, especially where a presence feels safe and comforting rather than threatening." She pauses for a minute, looking to the sky as if it has what she wants to say next written in the clouds. "It could just be your subconscious looking for a way to feel safe after that, but …" She stops talking, leaving me with an unfinished sentence.

"But what?" I prod, but she shakes her head.

"Forget it, it's stupid and probably just old wives' tales."

"No, seriously, I need your input."

"Well, it could be your mate." She looks at me sheepishly. I blink in surprise. Oh, come on, her, too? I snort in disgust.

"Whoa, hey! Elle," She holds up her hands in surrender.

"It's just an old legend. Nothing says that it is true, it's just something I've heard before," Meg amends.

"I don't want to find my mate, not yet anyway." I stare out at the waves, watching them crash against the rocks on the cliffs, the ocean spraying water. Meg inhales sharply.

"But why? Every wolf I know, especially girls, dream about finding theirs."

Not meeting her gaze, I look at the ground. "Because it would ruin everything." She cocks her head, obviously confused. To most wolves, finding their mate is the answer to everything, not the problem. Taking a deep breath, I decide to answer her question in full. Damn, these new rules, she's Sam's mate, and I want to be friends with her. She needs to know everything if I'm going to explain it right to her.

"I'm supposed to be the next alpha." I hear her gasp but keep going. "Right now I can't train, Dad doesn't want this Alpha Drake to know that we are in transition. Something about it showing the pack could potentially go through a weak period while I get my bearings in the new role."

I close my eyes and rub my temples. I miss the training and all the chaos that comes with it. I feel like I'm at a standstill and I don't like it.

"Is that why that guy attacked you? I had asked Sam why he did it, but he wouldn't go any farther than to say 'This asshole almost killed my friend. But he's been taken care of, so he isn't a problem anymore.'"

Laughing at Meg's imitation of Sam, I nod. "Yeah, he was constantly challenging me. We had fought a few times before and I had always sent him home with his tail between his legs."

"But wow! A female alpha! That's so cool!" She pauses

and thinks for a moment. "Is that why you don't want to find your mate?"

I nod. "And because I'm from a long line of alphas I would most likely be mated to an alpha. Or maybe even a beta." Standing up I start to pace. "I don't want to be a luna, stuck at home with pups, cooking and doing laundry. I like being part of the decision-making, getting my hands dirty. Actually doing things that matter."

"I see your point. But maybe, if you did find your mate, you could change that. I think it's more of a habit now, that lunas stay home. All I'm saying is, if you do meet him, it might not be so bad."

"Yeah, maybe," I say. But I'm thinking that there is no way an alpha would let his luna lead operations of a pack on an equal basis. A lot of them are set in their ways. It's only just in the past few years that females have been able to become warriors and enforcers in their packs. Some packs still don't allow them to be warriors.

Meg jumps up, snapping me out of my thoughts. "Sam!" She barrels towards him, his arms extend as he welcomes her into his arms. They melt into an embrace and I turn my head, not wanting to intrude on their moment.

Sam and Meg come back toward me. "And we went for a run– well, more like Elle let me sniff around the woods so I know where to go. And now we're here." She beams up at him, and Sam looks like he's heard the most interesting story and not just about our wanderings today.

Sam smiles at me and I grin back. Meg is still going on about the day and she doesn't notice Sam mouth "Thank you" over her head. "Oh, and that brings me to this." She playfully smacks him on the chest. "Why didn't you tell me Elle is going to be your alpha? Hmm? You kinda left that detail out." She crosses her arms and glares at him.

His eyes narrow as he turns to face me. "I didn't think Alpha Roman wanted anyone to know right now."

"It's my life," I snap. "I can tell Meg if I want. Besides, I think she's trustworthy. She's your mate after all."

"When it comes to the safety of the pack it's not just your life. It's all of us, Elle."

I look at Meg, who looks shocked by our exchange. "You see? *This* is why I don't want to find my mate!" I point at Sam. "Always withholding information because they think they know better. Because they're men," I growl out. I'm not sure where this hostility towards Sam is coming from, maybe it's because he didn't call me when he knew I was awake after the attack. Or maybe it's because he didn't call me himself and tell me he'd found his mate. Whatever the reason is, my anger is coming out now.

Meg takes a step back, holding her hands up, looking between both of us. "Listen, I'm not getting involved in this power struggle. But I do know you guys are best friends, so figure it out and leave me out of it!" She turns and starts to walk in the direction of town.

"Where are you going?" Sam calls after her.

"Home!" she yells back. Sam's face falls. Meg must see this because she shakes her head. "Let me clarify. I'm going to your place, our place, whatever you want to call it. That's where I'm going. You two obviously need to talk." And with that she heads up the path and disappears from our sight.

Sam and I stand there, not talking and not looking at each other. It's tense. We've never been in this situation. First time for everything, I guess.

Finally getting sick of just standing there stewing, I groan. "Look, Sam, I know my training is on hiatus, but I really didn't think it would be an issue if Meg knew the truth."

Sam takes a deep breath and rubs the back of his neck. "It had nothing to do with keeping things from Meg because she's a woman." He meets my gaze. "It was what your father told me after I told him I found her. I couldn't not follow what he said. And he wouldn't tell me his reasoning either." Sam comes closer to me, his eyes pleading. "Now, can you *please* tell me why you're mad? Obviously it's not because of Meg, though I was worried about it being that. It's been you and me forever, and I know what people thought about us. But then I realized no, it's been years. We tried it once and it was awkward as hell." He takes a deep breath and blows it out. "So please, Elle, why are you mad?"

"I'm not jealous or mad that you found her," I say, looking at my feet. "I'm mad that you hid it from me. I'm mad that you didn't call me after your father said I was awake." I look at him and his face softens.

"Elle, I'm sorry. We had to cut the trip short, then the whole Meg thing." He picks up a rock and throws it down the beach. "I didn't think about it, honestly. I just wanted to get home." He smiles at me and bumps into my shoulder. "You still mad?"

"You know I can't stay mad at you." And I can't, it's impossible for me to stay mad at him. We've never had a fight last longer than a day. I smile at him.

"Good, because if you were, I was going to withhold some important information from you."

I roll my eyes. "You're unbelievable. And such a child! I feel sorry for Meg, she's gotta put up with you." I grin at him so he knows I'm joking.

"Well, that's the thing about being mates. We can't stay mad at each other for long."

"What is it you have to tell me?"

Sam's face goes serious. "That Alpha Drake should be here the day after tomorrow." He clears his throat. "Could you do me a favor, Elle?"

He looks so anxious right now, so I nod.

"Can you keep Meg close to you? I trust you with her."

"Of course I will," I say.

Sam relaxes. "Thank you." He holds out his arms and I walk into them. "Thank you, and not just for that. Thank you for taking your time to get to know her and make her feel welcome." He pulls back and looks at me. "She was nervous you wouldn't like her. But I knew it would all work out somehow— you're my best friend."

I pull away. "Of course, Sam. If she's in your life, she's in mine. And I really do like her."

"That's good to hear. You two will be friends in no time."

"Oh, Sam, don't you get it?" He cocks his head. "You've been demoted. I have a new best friend now." His face drops and I laugh at his dumbstruck expression.

* * *

KNOCKING on the door to my dad's study, I wait for him to answer.

"Come in," I hear from the other side. I open the door and see that he's not alone. I pause in the doorway.

"Hey, Elle." He approaches me and kisses my head. "What brings you here?"

His company is Karla, a she-wolf around my dad's age. She's one of our top-ranking warriors. "Um, I can come back later if I'm interrupting something." This is awkward—I know my dad and Karla have a personal relationship— but he thinks I'm clueless.

"You're fine, Karla is about to leave." He winks at me and heads back to his chair.

Karla gets up from her seat. "Have a good evening, Roman." She stops in front of me. "Elle, good to see you, too. When should we expect you in the field again?"

I'm caught off guard. "Oh, ah, probably tomorrow. Unless Dad needs me elsewhere." I look over her shoulder at him, but he's busy writing an email or something and doesn't even notice.

Karla smiles. "Sounds good. Some of the guys are getting too cocky. I'm going to need you to put them on their asses a few times to remind them of their place." She winks at me and I smile back. She's always been pretty cool, a badass that's for sure. I'm actually surprised she hasn't been promoted again. I make a mental note to ask Dad and David once my privileges are back.

The door clicks shut and it's just my dad and me. He's still typing away on the computer so I pull out my phone and wait. There's a message from an unknown number.

> UNKNOWN
>
> Got your number from Sam :)
>
> I had fun today!
>
> Text me whenever.
>
> Especially if you have more alpha wolf dreams ;-)

THE WINKING FACE makes me laugh. My dad stops what he's doing and looks at me, puzzled. I hold up my phone. "Meg," I say before typing out my response.

> Ok, I will ;-)

LOOKING up from my phone I see my dad still looking at me. "What?" I ask.

He shakes his head and smiles. "So, I take it your day with Meg went well?"

"Yeah, she's really cool. I think we're friends already." And I'm not just saying that. I really like her. I can definitely see us getting closer.

"Well, that's good to hear. When I told Sam where you were going this morning he got all nervous," he chuckles. "I had to assure him you weren't going to play any tricks on her or anything."

I'm offended. "Why would he think I would do that?"

Dad bursts out laughing. "He didn't think you were going to be malicious. He thought you would be like how you are with him and Noah. You know, kinda rough."

"Oh, I see. I could see why he would think that, though. I've never had a girlfriend before. It's definitely different. She asks questions Sam and Noah would never ask." I giggle. "It made me uncomfortable at first, but afterwards I realized I've been missing out on a lot. It sucks when almost all the females here stay away from me, besides Connie and Rhea."

Dad nods, leaning back in his chair looking pensive. He groans, "Maybe that's where I missed something when it came to raising you." Sadness comes over his face. "I was too wrapped up in my grief to notice that missing a mother could really affect your upbringing."

"What the hell?" I look at him, completely bewildered. "I don't think there's anything wrong with how I was raised. Yes, it sometimes sucked not having a mom, but you made it work." Taking a deep breath I try to reign in my emotions. "Even if I did have my mother around it probably wouldn't have changed how I am much. I probably still would have been a dominant wolf. You can't tell me that just because there's not another kid in your bloodline that's the reason I am so dominant. I was *born* this way. Sure, she would've been easier to talk to about boys, periods, and all that, but you let me talk to you about those things. Maybe not in the same way as a mother, but you never told me that you didn't want to hear it, or that you were too busy. You did what you could with what you had."

I finish my rant and look up at him. He looks amused, there's a small smile on his face.

"You're so much like your mother. You have her spirit, you know." I'm confused– everyone always points out the differences we have. "You don't have your traits just from me. Your mother was strong, and stubborn, too." He laughs. "Did you know she was the one who told me we should train our women in more than self-defense?"

I shake my head. "No, I didn't know that."

"Yeah, she did. She told me that when I complained one night that our biggest weakness was our numbers of trained warriors. She said, and I quote, '*Roman, we have the numbers to build and train more. There are she-wolves who would love to learn but aren't given the chance. Utilize them, they may surprise you.*'" Dad snorts, "Of course it was an argument we had over and over again."

"So what changed your mind?" I ask him.

His face softens. "You were born, and I knew I would want you to be able to not only protect yourself, but I also knew that, like your mother, you would want to protect those around you. That day I told Jon to spread the word that all women could train to be warriors if they wanted to." His expression amused, he added, "Our army doubled, and I had to admit to your mother that she was right."

Why is he choosing now to tell me this? He's had eighteen years to tell me, but he chose today? "I wish I could remember her," I say. "Last night you said she would be proud of me. What did you mean by that? Was it because I chose to help Meg, because that's what a luna would do? What my mom would have done?" I ask, not sure how talking about my day with Meg brought us here.

Dad walks over to his liquor cabinet and pours two tumblers of scotch, holding one out to me before sitting back down. I take a sip, feeling the heat from the liquid scorch down my throat and settle in my belly. We sit there in silence. Deciding to not pressure Dad for an answer I continue to drink until my glass is empty. I stand up to leave, figuring I'm not getting an answer tonight, and Dad breaks the silence.

"No, that's not why." He glances at me as he takes the last swig from his tumbler and sets the empty glass on his desk. "I realized I don't say it enough to you. She would be, and I'm not just saying that to say it. But last night, when you told me what you hoped to do today, it made me proud of you in a way I haven't felt before." A smile comes across his face. "You hate that you have to wait now. You feel like I put you on the sidelines for the time being, and in a sense it's true. You could have continued to mope around the house and feel sorry for yourself, with even more reason because you also felt like you lost your best friend."

He pauses, closing his eyes like he'll find the words he wants to say. "Instead, you took control, you decided what the best thing would be, not only for you but for Meg as well." Sighing, he gets out of his chair and leans on the desk in front of me. "That's why your mother would have been proud, because you took control."

I wonder if my mother would have been proud of what I have done for over half my life. All the training, the late-night hours, everything that comes with being an alpha. Or would she have preferred that I focus on finding my mate? It's hard to know because she's not here to give me guidance.

I look up at my father. "Would she have been proud? Would she have backed me up on my decision to be the next alpha?"

Dad leaves his chair, he places his hand on my shoulder and squeezes. "She would have been your number one supporter, Elle." And with that he walks out of his office, leaving me with a million thoughts swirling in my head.

CHAPTER FIVE

Elle

I'm standing in a clearing in the forest— it's become my 'go to' place now. The moonlight is shining through the opening in the trees, illuminating my skin. It's a full moon, making everything brighter. The energy around me sends goosebumps down my neck. Where is he? Looking around I don't see him. Sadness comes over me- he's usually here. Why isn't he here?

Closing my eyes, I surrender myself to my other senses. I can smell the pine sap oozing from trees, the fresh scent of water and moss coming from the stream. I hear the rustling of leaves in the soft breeze, the water in the stream flowing over the rocks. And then I hear the leaves on the ground crunch behind me. He's close. Still keeping my eyes closed I wait for him to get closer. I feel his hot breath on my back, and my body settles.

"I thought you weren't going to come tonight," I say and turn to face him.

"Am I ever going to see your face? I don't think it's fair that you have seen mine and I haven't seen yours."

He huffs and steps forward, nuzzling into my neck. I reach out and touch his fur. We stay like that for a while.

Clouds cover the moon, darkness blankets the clearing. The large wolf steps back, his hackles rise and he starts growling. Looking at something behind me, he steps between me and the threat I cannot see.

"What is it?" I ask, even though I know he can't actually answer me. He continues growling, snarling aggressively at whatever it is he sees. I can feel his tension. Whoever this is, they aren't friends.

A large gray wolf, almost the size of my new companion, steps out of the trees. He's snarling, making his threat clear. I notice his eyes keep moving to me. He advances, trying to get closer. The black wolf moves, blocking the intruder from getting close to me. He's protecting me. He looks back at me and snaps at me, his eyes pleading for me to understand. He pushes me back with his massive shoulder, still growling at the advancing wolf.

"You want me to run?" I ask. He snaps at me again, making me jump back. Then he's barreling towards the gray wolf. *No!*

I know he wanted me to run but I can't leave him. I shift into my wolf and start toward where the other two are circling each other. The gray wolf notices me and charges at me, my black wolf lunges at him and shoves him to the ground.

"RUN!" he yells in my head.

I bolt straight up out of bed, adrenaline pumping through me like I just ran for my life.

Holy fuck, what was that? I look at my clock— four in the morning. I get out of bed and head into the bathroom. It's not worth trying to fall back asleep when I'll just be getting up in a few hours.

Turning on the shower and letting it warm up, I brush my hair from the tangles that accrued through the night.

Noticing the steam come from the shower I undress and step in, letting the water run down my body.

There are a million questions running through my head. The main one being, who is this black wolf? I grab the shampoo, squeeze some into my palm, and begin lathering my hair. My dream self obviously feels comfortable with him, even safe with him.

If I were to buy into the whole 'your mate can visit you in your dreams' hoopla, I'd say that's why. But I don't buy into it. It's just ridiculous, how can your unconscious know what your mate looks like? It can't, it's impossible. So scratch that idea. Dipping my head under the stream of water I rinse my hair. Once it's suds-free I put conditioner in to set and do its magic of making my hair silky smooth.

I start shaving my legs, more questions battering my mind. And now a gray wolf shows up, obviously a threat in my dream. I have no idea what that could be about. I wonder if it's supposed to be Rafe? No, Rafe was red, not gray. And he's also dead, so he's not a present threat. Maybe it's a warning of a threat close by, and the black wolf is just a figment of my imagination. I finish rinsing off and step out of the shower, snatching my towel.

Who the fuck am I kidding? They're dreams for god's sake. That's all they are. Nothing more. Nothing less. That settled, I grab some clothes for the day. I throw my towel on the chair and pull my shirt over my head.

Pushing my foot through one leg hole and then the other I pull up my jeans. I'm not going to waste any more time on this. It's nothing, absolutely nothing.

I sit on my bed, my face in my hands. But if it's nothing, why can't I shake this feeling that something horrible is going to happen soon?

* * *

It's only four thirty when I get to the kitchen. Connie isn't even up yet. Starting a pot of coffee, listening to it brew, drumming my fingers on the counter, I feel uneasy. Like today is a day I shouldn't let my guard down.

Hearing footsteps down the hall I tense up, until I notice the familiar pattern. My dad is up. I let out a long breath and let my body relax.

"You're up early," he says, grabbing a mug, leaning against the counter next to me.

"Couldn't sleep." Looking over at him I notice his shoulders are tense and his face set hard. Maybe it's not just me and my crazy dreams making me uneasy.

"Me either. Tossing and turning for the past hour it seems." He smiles at me but it doesn't reach his eyes.

The coffee pot settles down, I pour us both cups, and we sit at the table drinking in silence. Should I tell him about my dreams? Or would it cause him more stress? It seems silly to unload them on him— he's got enough on his plate.

Dad chuckles, bringing my attention to him. "What?" I ask, wondering what could be so funny before the sun is even up.

"You." Setting his mug down he turns his body to face me. "I can hear the gears turning in your head. I'm surprised smoke isn't coming out of your ears." I roll my eyes— how can he tell I'm having an inner battle in my head? "So? Are you going to tell me?"

"It's stupid, nothing to worry about," I sigh. I keep my gaze on the coffee in my cup, not meeting his prying stare.

"Nothing is stupid when it comes to you. And I always

worry about you." He pats my arm. "But you don't have to tell me anything you don't want to."

Groaning, I give in. "I had another dream, that's all."

"That can't be all it is if it's making you lose sleep and you keep thinking about it more than a few minutes after waking up."

Folding my arms on the table I hide my face in them. "Seriously, Dad, it's nothing," I mumble to the table.

"Was it the black wolf again?"

I shoot up in my chair and glare at him. "How did you know?" I demand.

"I'm your father, I know everything." He winks at me, making me smile. "So what happened in your dream?"

"I thought you knew everything." He doesn't answer, choosing silence as a way to get me to talk. And it works. "Yeah, the black wolf was there, but this time it wasn't just him." I peek over at him and he raises his eyebrows to tell me to keep going. "There was a gray wolf there, too, and the black wolf didn't like that. He kept putting himself between me and the gray one, both were snarling. I shifted, and the black one told me to run. Then I woke up."

I shrug, trying to show nonchalance, like the dream didn't bother me too much.

Dad looks at me for a long time. He doesn't speak, but he studies my face. "Sounds to me like the gray wolf is a threat to you, and the black one is trying to protect you." He drains his coffee in a long swig and sets the mug down on the table with a light thud. "The mind is a powerful thing, Elle. It might not be a premonition, but it's warning you about something." He stands up and fills his mug with more coffee. "You'd do best to listen to it. Keep your guard up."

"But why? They're only dreams, Dad, my unconscious

going crazy with the imagination." I refuse to put any stock in my dreams. They mean nothing.

He puts a hand on my shoulder. I look up at him, his face hard with stress again. "Like I said, the mind is a powerful thing. Come get me when breakfast is ready, please. I have some work to catch up on." And with that he walks down the hall to his office, leaving me alone with my thoughts in the dark kitchen.

* * *

MEG and I are sitting on her back porch, enjoying some lemonade, fresh- squeezed, made by Meg. Yep, she's definitely a keeper. Anyone who can make fresh-squeezed lemonade taste this good can't be let go.

Meg looks even cheerier than usual, all smiles and jokes. She's the exact opposite of Sam, which is probably why they're mates— two halves of the same coin.

"What's up with you? You get laid more than two times last night?" I waggle my eyebrows at her, making her giggle.

Meg throws a balled-up napkin at me. "Well, someone around here has to!" she laughs.

"Yeah, I've noticed a big change with Sam. His scowl isn't as scowly anymore," I tease. "And you're over here making fresh-squeezed lemonade, making him amazing dinners, the list goes on. Obviously something good is happening in that bedroom."

Meg snorts. "Like you would know," she laughs, clearing our plates from our small lunch.

"What's that supposed to mean?"

She blinks at me. "Well, you're a virgin, aren't you?"

I sputter my drink. "What? No, I'm not."

"Really?" she asked, bemused by this clarification.

"Why do you look so shocked?"

Her face flushes. "Well, um, don't take this the wrong way, but ..." Meg clears her throat. It's obvious she's now uncomfortable.

"Just spit it out, Meg," I snap, feeling annoyed now.

"It's your scent, honestly. You, you smell so ... I don't know how to say it. I guess 'pure' is a good word to describe it."

I stare at her, my eyes wide. "What the hell? Pure?"

"It's not a bad thing, you just smell like a fresh mountain morning. Like a river that hasn't been polluted yet." She glances at me sideways. "And I know it's not your shampoo because that smells like citrus. You just smell good, Elle." Meg looks away, still blushing.

I sit back in my chair. I have never associated someone's scent with being a virgin or not. I guess it could make sense, in a way. "You smell like flowers." I say laughing, hoping to ease her discomfort.

Meg lets out a long breath and smiles tentatively. "Yeah, Sam told me." Her face was reddening again. "So um, who was it? Or has there been more than one conquest?"

Leaning forward I put my hand on hers. "It wasn't Sam, if that's what you're asking."

The relief on her face is obvious. "Well, that makes me feel a little better, honestly."

"Please tell me Sam told you about our fumbling kiss when we were sixteen?" I pray out loud. She nods, but I can tell she's not over her insecurity.

"I just wasn't sure if there was ever a night where, after a good run and the adrenaline is pumping, something more happened. Not that I could hold it against either one of you if it did." She grabs her cup and starts pushing on the ice in it with her straw.

God, why did this have to get so awkward? "Look," I say, standing up and walking around so I'm standing right in front of her. "Sam and I are close, we did *try* to have a relationship. I'm not even sure if it was because we were attracted to each other or if it was because everyone thought we were." I sit on the small ottoman so I'm eye level with her. "We found out very quickly that we're just friends. It actually made things easier," I muse.

"What do you mean by 'easier'?"

"Well, you see, if Sam and I did work out in the relationship department, I would've had to find a new beta. Also, everyone in the pack would then expect *him* to be the next alpha and not me, essentially ruining everything I worked for." I shrug, trying to show her it's not a big deal. "Plus, I think he really needed you."

Meg nods and looks out at the sky, thinking about something. After a while she turns to me, a devilish look in her eyes. "So, who were these conquests?" Leaning her arms on her legs she looks me right in the eyes. "I want *details.*"

Glad we're out of the rocky part of the conversation, I chuckle. "We have these allies, I guess the closest you could call another pack 'friends'. Well, the alpha and his son were visiting us, to go over pack business and strengthen our alliance. The alpha's name was Matthew, and his son was Jared." Pausing, I think back to remember why they came. "I think they were here to introduce Jared and me as the next alphas of our respective packs. Anyway, Jared thought it was funny that a *girl* would be the next alpha, we got into a scuffle, in which we both decided it was a draw. Next thing I know we're out for a run in the woods so our fathers could get some business done, and he kisses me." I laugh. "We fumbled around on the forest floor for a while before actually doing the deed. He was more experienced than I was."

Meg looks absorbed with my story. "Well, was there anymore? Guys— I mean."

"No, Jared and I hooked up a few more times when we visited each other's packs." I smirk, "Jared and his father are stuck in the past and think women belong in the house raising pups and cooking. While the men do all the fun stuff. I think Jared found his mate, and from what I hear she's a firecracker." The thought of Jared's mate being the exact opposite of what he expected amuses me.

"Wow," Meg says. "That was absolutely boring. You're a terrible storyteller, Elle." She feigns boredom, dramatically throwing herself back into her chair.

Laughing and shaking my head at her antics I say, "What did you want me to say? That we fucked like crazy? Actually, that's the truth, we did fuck each other like crazed hormonal teens." Stopping to take a drink before continuing, "but it was always a power struggle – who could end up on top, literally."

Throwing her head back and laughing, Meg's shirt moves around her neck, revealing something I didn't see before. It's a mark.

I pull on her collar so I can see it better. She stills, watching my face, waiting for my reaction. "Holy fuck, you're blood bonded now." It's not a question, it's a statement. Anyone could see the mark on her neck and know what it means. "Holy shit! Why didn't you say anything? How do you feel?".

Pulling away from my grasp, Meg blows air from her lips. "I didn't think of it, honestly."

"Didn't think of it?" I exclaim. "This is huge! Something you're supposed to tell your best friend."

"To answer your other question, I feel fine. Great, actually." She looks down, avoiding my stare that probably feels like lasers into her skin. "I can *feel* him, like he's here with me. We can feel when the other feels anxious or scared."

Her phone goes off. Stopping to check it she smiles. "Sam felt me getting nervous and wanted to know if everything was okay." She shows me her phone.

"That's absolutely insane," I laugh. Meg's face falls, and she pulls her phone back and types out a response. Ah shit, she thinks I'm picking on her. "Hey, I wasn't picking on you. The only people I know who have mates don't share this stuff with others. It's mind-blowing to me, how in tune you are to each other."

Nodding, Meg grabs the plates to take inside. "Wanna go for a run?" she asks, turning to look at me, a grin on her face. I have been forgiven.

* * *

Running isn't the release I thought it would be, not today. I keep looking behind me, feeling like we're being followed. I have a feeling in the pit of my stomach something bad is going to happen. My fur stands on end, I have to keep forcing myself to relax, there's no invisible entity out there. I need to chill.

Meg comes trotting over to me, her sandy fur wet from splashing in the small stream. *"Hey, everything okay? You don't seem to be having fun."*

"I thought this would help," I say. Sitting back on my haunches I cock my ears in different directions, trying to hear everything I can. Just squirrels and birds.

Meg lies down, her eyes shifting up to me. *"Thought it would help what?"*

"*Don't you feel it?*" I ask, now pacing in a circle around her. "*Don't you feel the tension in the air? It's so quiet.*"

"*The only thing I'm feeling is dizzy. Could you please stop circling me, Elle?*"

"*Oh, sorry.*" Sitting back down, I try to release the tension in my muscles.

"*Maybe you need some sleep,*" Meg says. "*Don't take this the wrong way, Elle, but you look like shit. Have you been sleeping?*"

Flashing my teeth to show my annoyance, I follow her lead and lie down on the forest floor. "*Jeez, Meg, you could've been nicer about it.*"

"*Nope,*" she puts emphasis on the "p" making a popping sound. "*Best friends don't tiptoe around each other to spare feelings.*" She lets out a sigh. "*You never answered my question, though. Are you getting much sleep?*"

"*No,*" I yawn, helping to prove that I haven't been sleeping.

Resting her muzzle on her paws she peeks at me. "*We could nap here,*" she suggests. "*We'll hear if anything happens. Sam knows we went for a run.*"

Naps. I don't normally nap. They seem like a waste of time to me— there's always something to be doing. I yawn again and that's enough to convince me that just this once a nap won't hurt anything. Settling down next to Meg, the sounds of the forest soothe my thoughts and I fall asleep.

"*Elle! Meg! Where are you?*" Noah's voice wakes me up, the urgency making me jump to my feet.

"*Noah? What's wrong?*" I see Meg is already awake and standing, looking as confused as I feel.

"*Is Meg with you?*"

"*I'm right here, Noah. What's going on?*" Meg replies.

"*Good, you're together.*" The relief evident in Noah's voice.

"Listen, both of you, you need to get back to Sam's now. Connie will meet you there."

"Wait, Noah!" I yell, hoping I catch his attention before he shifts and reports back to my father and Sam.

"What? I gotta go, Elle. Your dad is waiting to hear back from me that you're okay," he snaps.

I growl at him, also making Meg shrink down low to the ground. *"Listen, shithead, I still outrank you and I can kick your ass into next week!"* I snarl. *"Now tell me what the fuck is going on."* The last demand comes out an order.

"He's here, Elle. Alpha Drake is here." I can hear him whine, *"Now please go to Sam's and stay there until you're told otherwise."*

Dread fills me to my core, I feel my heart drop into my stomach. Looking at Meg and not saying a word I take off in the direction of Sam's house. I can hear Meg behind me, doing her best to keep up. I slow down so I don't lose her.

"C'mon, let's get to your house!" I yell to her.

"But what about our clothes?"

"Forget them for now, we can grab them later. We'll get dressed at your house." Hopefully Connie's sixth sense has kicked in and she brings me some of my own. I won't fit in Meg's clothes. We focus on running, not talking to each other as we navigate the forest. Sam's house comes into view and we pick up our speed. We stop in the back yard and look around, the back door opens, we growl.

"Oh, stop growling at me, you two, and get in the house!" Connie yells, throwing two blankets to us. We shift and put the blankets around us, covering our bodies, and run into the house.

Connie throws a bag at me. "Here, change into these. I thought of it just before I left the house."

I smile at her in thanks. "What would we do without you, Connie?" She shoos me to get changed and I head into

Sam's bathroom, examining the contents of the bag Connie packed.

A baggy long-sleeved flannel shirt, a tank, a pair of jeans, and a set of underwear. Throwing the clothes on I head into the main room. I'm almost down the hallway when I realize I don't have shoes.

"Uh, Connie?" I'm about to ask her about footwear when a pair of Chucks and socks are shoved into my chest.

"Yes, yes, I figured you would've been out on the trails and not have time to grab your shoes." She smiles at me.

I smile back– the woman thinks of everything. Sitting on the couch I shove my feet into the socks and shoes, making sure the laces are tight in case I have to run.

Looking over at Connie I can see she's nervous. "Connie?" She turns to look at me with worry in her eyes. "Where's my dad? Is he okay?" I glance at Meg. She's curled up in a ball on the other end of the couch. "What about Sam?" I ask on her behalf.

Connie starts fretting around the kitchen, needing something to do, never sitting still. I glance over at Meg, hoping Connie's actions aren't upsetting her. She gives me a small smile and a half shrug, saying she understands.

"Oh, they're just fine, Eleanor," Connie huffs. "Your father just wanted to know where you are right now, that's all."

Nodding, I understand. It's easier to concentrate on what's in front of you if you don't have to worry about the whereabouts of the people you care about. This must be why I have been so anxious all day, because *he* was coming today. It all makes sense now. Even with my stomach in knots, it makes me feel a little better knowing that by tomorrow morning things will subside.

We settle in the living room. Meg flips through Netflix aimlessly, Connie had brought some knitting with her, and I kept checking my phone for notifications. It's useless— no one is going to text me right now. My dad will send either Sam, Noah, or Jon in person to let us know the coast is clear.

Meg groans and lobs the remote to me, unable to decide on anything. "This is pointless. I can't find anything because I can't concentrate! You pick something, anything, I don't care."

Grabbing the remote from where it landed on the floor next to me, I scan the options, opting for a sitcom I used to watch when I was younger. The TV fills the room with noise, making the waiting slightly more bearable. We get comfortable and continue to wait.

After about three episodes of the show, Connie asks if she can make us something to eat. We say "No thank you," too nervous to eat. Well, at least I am. I'll eat when I can see my dad again, and I'm sure Meg feels the same way when it comes to Sam. Connie must understand because she doesn't seem bothered by our refusal and goes back to her knitting. It's not until after another two episodes go by that we get an update from the packhouse.

Breaking into our small sanctuary, Jon bursts through the door with Noah behind him. His eyes scan the room, making sure everyone is where they're supposed to be. Jon's eyes land on me. "Elle, your father wants me to take you back to the house."

"What about Connie and Meg?" I ask, standing and stretching out from sitting for so long.

"They're coming, too."

We hustle out the door and climb into Jon's truck. "What's going on? Is the alpha gone?"

"No, he's still here," Jon growls. He's on edge— something hasn't gone well with this meeting.

"He's brought an army with him," Noah adds. Jon shoots him a glare.

Ignoring Jon's disapproving growl, I ask more questions. "An army? Like more than the usual crew that goes with an alpha into another's territory?" Usually my dad only takes eight other wolves with him, not enough to pose a threat, but enough to feel comfortable in unknown territory.

"He's brought enough that our warriors are either evenly numbered or slightly outnumbered." Jon hits the dashboard in anger. "Fuck, this is a mess!"

Meg speaks up for the first time since Jon burst into her house. "Do you know what he wants?" Her voice is small. She's scared. I wrap my arm around her shoulder to comfort her.

Noah turns to look at us. "No, we don't. At least when Roman sent us to get you Drake hadn't shown his hand." He runs his fingers through his hair. "But that could have changed since we left." He turns around to face the front, a snarl on his lips. I turn to look at what caused this reaction and see men I don't know standing beside big trucks and SUVs.

Reaching out I smack Noah on the head. "Are you fucking nuts?" I growl out. "Do you want to give them a reason to think you're challenging them?" Jon shakes his head, muttering something about "stupid pup." And it was stupid for Noah to do that— it looks like this guy is looking for any reason to fight. As much as we may want to growl and show how much we dislike this, we can't.

As soon as the truck comes to a stop in the driveway, Meg's out of the truck and into Sam's arms. I can see him murmuring in her ear, probably reassuring her that everything is okay. My dad strides purposefully down the porch steps. When he reaches me he pulls me into a tight hug.

"Dad, I'm okay." I pull back to look at his face. The stress that was there this morning has increased tenfold. "What's going on, Dad? Where is Drake?"

"He went back to talk to his men." He looks at Connie. "Thank you for going to sit with Meg and Elle."

He turns to where Meg and Sam are standing and she gives him a small smile. "Thank you for sending us the company, Alpha." Sam gives her a reassuring squeeze.

"Dad," I say, getting his attention again. "What's going on?"

"Listen to me very carefully, Elle." He grabs both my shoulders, forcing me to look at him and give him my full attention. He takes a deep breath and lets it out. "He's looking for a mate. All unmated females are to meet him and he's going to see if there's one he likes." Dad closes his eyes– this isn't something he wants to do. He looks at me, his eyes pleading for me to understand. "I can't tell him 'no,' Elle. He has too many men with him. He did this on purpose, he knows it puts us in a spot where we can't refuse."

I'm completely appalled. "So we're going to offer up our packmates like cattle?" I snap.

"You act like I have a choice! And I don't!" Dad yells, making me flinch. "Hopefully he doesn't see anyone he likes, and then he leaves and we won't have to see him again."

"I'm sorry, Dad, it just seems completely barbaric." I hug him, trying to convey that I'm sorry and that I'll listen to whatever he says to do. "Wait, you said "choose." If he's looking for his mate wouldn't it be simple? If his mate is here, wouldn't the bond tell him?"

Dad pinches the bridge of his nose. "No, Elle. He's in his thirties or forties, so he's past the point of finding his true mate." Shit, this makes it worse, because now he can choose any woman over the age of twenty-one.

"So, every she-wolf over twenty-one has to do this?"

"No, he wants to see all unmated females eighteen and older." He grimaces as he says it. Dad doesn't like this but what can he do? The safety of the whole pack is at stake.

I wonder why he looks so sad and worried, not just stressed. Slowly it dawns on me. "You said eighteen and older?" I ask.

Closing his eyes, he nods.

I finally got it, all the worry I saw in his eyes a minute ago. I'm twenty, I'm unmated, I have to stand in line, too.

"Well, fuck."

CHAPTER SIX

Elle

*W*aiting on the front lawn of the packhouse, I watch as the young women and their families come and greet my father. The women look confused, their parents terrified. This may be the last time they see their daughters. The thought is unsettling. My father approaches each family, explaining the predicament our pack is in and offering his sympathies. I stood by him for a while, but the sadness was too much. I had to walk away.

Now I stand alone. Meg had come over to talk to me, but I don't feel like talking at the moment. She is now standing with Sam and Jon. Rhea is in the packhouse with the twins, not letting them see the quiet chaos that is happening.

The other young women, ages ranging from eighteen to

twenty-five, come over and stand by me. All of them are looking at me for answers I cannot give them.

"Elle." Rachel, a girl I went to school with, steps closer to me. I look at her, seeing the fear in her eyes. "What's going on? Why is this happening?"

Shrugging, I meet all of their questioning looks one at a time. "I don't know. I wish I did," I sigh. "All I know is that if my dad refused, we'd be in the middle of a fight." Closing my eyes I remember what my father had told me. "Hopefully he doesn't see anyone he likes the looks of and moves on." I open my eyes and see them all nodding.

Another voice comes from the crowd that has formed around me. "We can do this. Who knows? Maybe he won't be that bad if he's looking for a mate." They all murmur in agreement, but I can't help but wonder that if this alpha needs to have all the unmated she-wolves lined up to pick from he must be an asshole.

Dad walks over to us. "All right, form a line." His voice is grave– he doesn't want to be doing this. He looks at me. "Stay in line, keep your eyes down, and for god's sake, Eleanor, keep your mouth shut."

I blink in surprise. "What?"

Grabbing my chin he forces me to look at him. "You're going to see him inspect your packmates, it's going to piss you off. He's going to want to look all of you over." Closing his eyes, he takes a deep breath, regaining control of his emotions. "Just don't do anything to draw attention to yourself." He lets go of my face and walks over to Jon, who is standing where I assume this Alpha Drake will be showing himself.

Even with all the people here, it's silent, like they're all holding their breath. Everyone's heads turn when the sound of tires on gravel breaks the silence. A large black SUV pulls up beside where my father and Jon stand. The door opens and a tall, muscular man steps out.

Huh, I wasn't expecting this guy to be good looking at all, considering he has to force packs to allow him to check out their women for a potential mate. I was expecting someone *much* uglier. Drake walks over towards my father—well, strut would be a better description. He's arrogant that's for sure. He has dirty blond hair, and his eyes seem light, they must be blue. Drake looks down the line of women.

"Is this all you have, Roman?" He laughs. "Kind of a sorry bunch, aren't they?" He's trying to provoke a reaction from my dad, but it doesn't work.

With a face showing no emotion, my dad steps forward. "Let's get this over with, Drake." Drake nods and begins walking down the line, stopping to look longer at some.

He reaches out to one girl and strokes her hair, another he touches her face and skims his hand down her throat. She whimpers, shrinking down trying to make herself look smaller. He grabs her hair and pulls her back up. "What's the matter, sweetheart?" he sneers. "You've never been touched by a man before?" I want to snarl, I want to push him off of her. I feel my lip start to curl.

My dad steps forward, forcing his way in between Drake and the girl.

"You're not here to antagonize and harass my pack, Drake."

Drake's face remains in a sneer for a moment as he stares at the girl. Then he looks at my father, a smile forming on his lips. "You're right." He lets the girl go and she steps back in line, holding onto herself because she's shaking so hard. "I apologize, Roman," he says, though there's no remorse in his face or voice.

Dad walks back to where he was before he intervened. Drake continues down the line, keeping his hands to himself for the most part. This asshole needs to hurry up and get the fuck out of here.

Drake stops two girls down from me. "You!" He points at her. She's petite and has red hair. "Step forward." She complies, stepping out of the line, keeping her eyes down. Drake circles her, looking her up and down. "What's your name?"

"N-Na-Naomi," she stammers out. It's barely more than a whisper.

Drake laughs. "Can you speak? It doesn't matter, for what I have in mind you won't be able to talk." She cringes away from him and low growls come from the crowd. We all know what he was insinuating. It makes my skin crawl. *He* makes my skin crawl. I can feel the anger brewing inside of me, wanting to lash out.

Placing his hand on his chin he stops circling her. "You know, I can't really see what you look like, with that hoodie on and all." He reaches out and in a fluid movement he unzips her hoodie. She's wearing only a tank top underneath, leaving not much to the imagination. She's exposed.

Naomi crosses her arms trying to cover herself, pulling on her sweatshirt. "Stop, please!" She's crying. He just laughs at her.

I see red. No, this asshole isn't getting away with this. I see my dad shout something, but I can't hear it. Blood pounding in my ears, I step out of the line. "ENOUGH!" I yell. Drake turns to look at me and my dad stops midstride. I walk toward Drake and Naomi. Getting right in Drake's face I say it again. *"Enough."*

He shoves Naomi away from him. "Get out of here!" he

sneers. She stumbles past the line of women and runs to her family, sobbing and holding on to them.

Drake turns back to me, his blue eyes cold as ice, piercing into mine, trying to make me look away. "Well, well, what do we have here? "He glances me up and down. "A bitch who doesn't know her place in front of an alpha?"

"I know my place. It's making sure assholes like you don't harass my packmates." I refuse to back down, not to this bully.

He backhands me, sending me stumbling. I spit out blood. When I look up I see my dad start to charge Drake. Fuck, this isn't good. He tackles Drake, both falling to the ground. Two of Drake's men grab my dad and hold him back. Looking around I see more of his men holding everyone at gunpoint, keeping them from helping my dad, their alpha.

Holy fuck, they came armed? What is this?

Drake gets up from the ground. Looking to make sure his attacker is held, he walks over to me. Grabbing my hair, he yanks my head back and tilts my face to his. "What's your name, sweetheart?"

"Eleanor." I wince in pain. Drake sees this and he pulls tighter. As I cry out in pain, his smile widens. He's enjoying this.

Taking his other hand he runs his thumb over my mouth. "Tell me, Eleanor, why would your alpha risk attacking me for you? It could have started something that would have ended bloody, and he knows that." He glances at my father who is struggling against the two men holding him back.

"I'm his daughter," I spit out.

He lets go of my hair and I feel relief immediately. I

look at my father. He's stopped struggling now that Drake has let me go.

Drake glances at him, then brings his icy stare back to me. "Interesting. Roman, why didn't you tell me you had such an ..." He pauses, his eyes roving over my body. " ... exquisite daughter?" My dad growls, Drake steps closer to me, so we're almost touching. He pushes my hair back behind my shoulder. "You are beautiful, Eleanor, but I must say, it's hard to tell what you really look like with that shirt on. It covers too much." He yanks on my shirt, which sends the buttons popping in all directions. All that's covering me is my bra. "That's a little better," he says, his hand touching my breast.

"Don't fucking touch me!" I snarl, wrenching out of his trouch and punching him in the face. His stance falters and he steps back. Emotions flit on his face, shock, rage, and then something I can't read. Amusement maybe?

Leaning toward me, Drake grabs me by the back of the neck and throws me to the ground. Holding me there he bends down. "Do you give up? Do you submit, sweetheart?" he asks me, his breath right on my cheek.

Struggling against him I turn my head and spit in his face. "Never."

Wiping my saliva with his sleeve, a grin splits his lips, the grin of a predator who just caught his prey and is about to enjoy the meal. Grabbing a fistful of my hair again he shoves my face into the dirt. Drake gets in my face again. "I'm going to enjoy it, you know."

Breathing heavily, I turn to look at him. "Enjoy what?"

He chuckles. "Beating the fight out of you," he whispers. I still, his words sending chills down my spine. *No, he can't choose me.* He stands, hauling me up with him. "Well,

Roman, I've made my decision." Drake stands in front of my dad.

"NO!" Dad headbutts Drake, knowing what Drake was going to say. The men who were holding my dad restrain him again. Drake wipes the blood from his face, his nose broken, and then punches my dad in the stomach.

Sam and Jon are both trying to get through the men holding them back, growling profanities. But it's hard for them to do anything when there're guns pointed at them and they know their mates are at stake.

"You're going to tell me 'no,' Roman? It doesn't matter what you tell me— I will have everyone in this pack slaughtered in front of your eyes, and then I'll kill you slowly, after you watch every one of your pack members die, friends, loved ones, women, children." He grins and punches my dad in his stomach, making him double over. "And then I'll still take her, mate her, fuck her, and beat her. Until everything that makes her your daughter isn't there anymore."

He raises his fist to assault my father again. I can't take it anymore— I know he's not bluffing, he'll kill everyone here and still take me. He has calculated every move he has made. He knows there's no way our pack could win this fight, he made sure he outnumbered us.

I don't want to do this.

"Stop!" I wrap my hand around his arm before he can give my dad another blow. "Please stop!" Drake looks at me. "I'll go with you, I'll be your mate, just please stop, and don't hurt anyone else."

He stares at me, bewildered. He wasn't expecting me to do this, he was expecting a fight. He looks around. "If this is a trick, I'll—"

"It's not a trick," I cut him off. "I will go with you, but I have some conditions."

He cocks an eyebrow. "What are your conditions?" Crossing his arms over his chest as he glares at me.

I don't let him intimidate me, staring him in the eyes as I approach him. "You don't hurt anyone in this pack again." He sighs, as if this is the most boring conversation he's had. "I want your word, Alpha Drake, that you will leave this pack alone, no hurting anyone, and no killing anyone."

We stare at each other for a long time. Finally Drake inclines his head. "You have my word, sweetheart. If you come with me, I won't attack your precious little pack." We shake hands and he pulls me into his chest. "You're mine now," he whispers in my ear, sending chills down my spine. *What have I done?*

Drake throws me to the ground in front of my dad, who is now unrestrained. I glance around to see Drake's men moving back to their vehicles. "You have fifteen minutes to say goodbye, then you're getting in that car even if I have to drag you." He walks away to talk to one of his men.

"Dad," I cry as he pulls me into his arms. The reality of everything is hitting me now.

"What have you done, Elle?" he chokes out. Pulling back, he holds my face in his hands. "You didn't have to do that."

"He was going to kill you, Dad, and everyone else, too." Tasting the salt from my tears on my tongue, I add, "He would have taken me anyway. This was the only way to save the pack."

He wipes my tears with his thumb. I lean my face into his palm. Taking a deep breath I look into his eyes. "An alpha sometimes has to do things they don't want to, especially when it keeps the pack safe," I quote what he told me a few days ago in regards to killing Rafe. "I did what I had to do."

He pulls me in for another hug, holding me like he did when I was a child. Looking over his shoulder I see Meg crying, holding onto Sam like he's the only thing holding her up. We've become so close in just a few short days. I'm going to miss her.

I let go of my dad and walk over to them. She lets go of Sam and throws herself at me. "You're such a fool, Elle!" she sobs, "such a fucking fool! What were you thinking?!"

"I'll miss you, too, Meg." I clear my throat, cries starting to catch in it. "Take care of Sam, and visit with Connie. She'll get lonely without me bugging her every day." She chuckles a little, and nods, not able to form words.

Sam looks at us. I pry away from Meg and hug him. My first best friend, my confidant, the man who was supposed to stand by my side as my beta. "I'll miss you Sam," I say.

"Oh, Elle." He hugs me tight. I realize it's the last Sam Hug I'll ever have. The thought breaks my wall and the tears flood out.

"Take care of my dad will you?" I ask. "Make sure he's okay after this." Sam just nods. "Thanks," I say and I run back to my dad. I don't know how much time I have left. Not much, maybe a few minutes.

Jon gives me a quick hug. "Stay strong, kid."

"Thanks, Jon. I'll try." He leaves us to go stand with Meg and Sam.

"I told you to keep quiet, Elle," Dad huffs.

"I couldn't let him do that to her, humiliate her like that. I had to do something."

"I know you did, Elle."

Hugging him again because I know I'm never going to see him again, I let myself go and let the tears come through. "Sam's your next alpha now. He'll be a good one, Dad. I know it." I pull back and look at him and he nods. "Okay, good." Glad I got a say in one more pack matter.

I turn to look for Drake– he's still talking to one of his men. I have a few more minutes. "Listen to me, Elle." Dad says, pulling my attention back to him. "He's going to want to break you. Don't let him."

"I won't, Dad. I'll fight."

Dad shakes his head, "No, Elle, that's what he wants. He wants you to fight."

"You want me to submit?" What the fuck?

"I want you to survive." He kisses the top of my head. "I love you, Elle."

Behind me now, Drake grabs my arm. "Time's up," he says and pulls me toward his car.

"Wait!" I break free from his grasp and hug my father one last time. "I love you, too." Letting go, I walk back to Drake, he takes my arm again and pushes me into the back seat, sliding in behind me.

The engine roars to life and we head down the road. I watch out the window as my childhood home passes by.

* * *

Hours passed, along with the scenery flying by my window. Drake hasn't said anything to me, and I refuse to initiate conversation with him.

The tears stopped long ago, my face no longer puffy from crying. Hopefully my father is resting, letting Sam and Jon take care of things. I wonder how long the pain of leaving them will be so raw. Weeks? Months? Years? Maybe it will never go away, maybe this pain will always be in my heart for the rest of my life.

"We're getting close." Drake's words pull me back into the car, away from my home hours away.

"How close?"

"About an hour," he says, tossing a piece of fabric at me. I examine it, it's a hood. "Put that on. I don't want you seeing how we get to my territory." He smirks. "Can't have you running away, now can I?"

I throw it back at him. "I'm not putting that fucking thing on," I snarl.

He chuckles. Lunging out he grabs my arm, twisting it with one hand. With the other he smashes my head into the window and holds me there. "Part of our bargain was that you would come with me quietly." He loosens his grip and I shove him off. *Asshole.*

Rubbing my arm where he's twisted it, I shake my head. "I never once said anything about coming quietly." I sneer, flashing my teeth at him. "And I don't plan on being quiet for a long time, so you might as well get used to it."

He laughs, a sound with no humor in it. "I'm going to break you, Eleanor." He picks up a bag from the floor and rummages through it, pulling out rope. I notice there are shiny threads woven in. *Silver.* He sees my eyes widen and his smile returns. "Now be a good bitch and put the hood on or I'll have to restrain you."

He holds the hood out for me, knowing he's already won my compliance.

I take the hood, his grin widening. *Asshole.* Putting the hood on, my world goes dark. I have no idea what to expect now that I can't see. Leaning against the window I close my eyes, plotting how I can survive this new life of mine.

CHAPTER SEVEN

Cedric

I'm lying on the dirt in the forest. Sore and unsure why I am here.

Looking around I see a clearing, it's next to a stream. Where is she? Where's the woman who's been there every time I visit this place?

It all comes back, hitting me like a freight train. Her, me, we've been here alone every time, but last time someone else was here, too.

A threat. Him. "No!" Jumping to my feet I bolt over to where I last saw her. I was trying to keep him away from her, he's dangerous. He'll hurt her. He will take her away from me.

Sniffing the air and ground I try to find her scent, but it's like she hasn't been here in a while.

Panic starts to set in. Keeping my nose to the forest floor I keep smelling. But I never find her.

I go back to the clearing, our clearing. I'll wait for her here, this is where she will find me when she comes back.

Sitting in the moonlight I howl at the moon, sadness in every note.

What the fuck? Sitting up in bed I try to figure out why I woke up. Swinging my legs off the bed, I bend down to pick up my shirt. I feel the bed move and a hand touches my back.

"Baby, what are you doing? It's too early to be up, come back to bed," Jasmine says, looking up at me still half asleep.

Pulling my shirt over my head, I grab my pants and pull them on. "I can't sleep, go back to bed."

She pouts, her red hair looking like fire on the pillow. Sitting up on her elbow she looks at me, her face suggestive. "We don't have to sleep," she says, reaching for my hand.

I pull away and give her a quick kiss. "Sorry, but I should be going anyway. Meeting Cory early this morning." Shutting the door behind me, I walk down the hall of the small one-story house, making my way to the front door.

It's still dark outside. Checking my watch I see it's only three-thirty in the morning. What the fuck. These damn dreams— sometimes I wish oracles were real. I'd ask where this chick is and why she is in my dreams. *But she wasn't there this time*, that is the biggest question now. Where did she go? And why did I wake up feeling her loss? I don't know her, don't even know her damn name.

Shaking my head, I tell myself I won't waste my time thinking about her or my stupid dreams. At the door to the packhouse, my house, I let myself in and head upstairs to my room.

Ripping off my clothes I throw them in the hamper, turn on the shower and step in, washing last night's activities off my body. Thinking about last night I smile. Jasmine is certainly good at making me forget the stress that comes with being an alpha. She sucks the stress right out of me, literally.

The water cascades down my back as I think back to Jasmine on her knees in front of me, her red lips wrapped around my cock. Feeling myself get hard I wrap my hand around my favorite part of my body and begin to jerk off. I imagine holding onto a mane of red hair, then the hair isn't red. It's dark brown, and instead of looking down, she's looking up. Brown eyes, burning up at me with a fire in them.

What the fuck?! I stop stroking and turn off the shower. *Now she's taking over my fantasies?* Drying off, I wrap the towel around my waist. Looking in the mirror I decide to shave and trim my beard— it's getting a little long. Leaning on the counter I feel my still-hard dick twitch in protest. *Sorry, dude, no getting off this morning.* Fucking annoying.

I'm still annoyed with the events in the shower when I go into the kitchen, wearing a scowl on my face. Cory and Reg are already at the table drinking coffee and eating breakfast.

"Good morning, sunshine," Cory says, picking up on my sour mood.

Reg smacks him on the shoulder. "Stop antagonizing him!" she scolds. "Coffee's fresh, Ced," she says. She rolls her eyes and looks pointedly at Cory.

I've known Cory and Reg my entire life. Cory is my cousin. Reg— Regina, though if you call her by her full name, may god have mercy on your soul— she's been our friend since we were younger.

Cory and Reg turned out to be mates, which was a fun day for all involved in that fiasco. I smile to myself remembering the day. Cory and I had gone off, trying to make alliances with other packs. We left Reg at home in charge of things. We were gone for two months, during which they had not seen each other during their eighteenth birthdays.

When Cory and I returned, Reg was there to greet us, and when she saw Cory and he saw her they stopped in their tracks.

"It's you?!" Reg screams and stamps her foot. *"Of course it's you! Why wouldn't it be? It's bad enough I have to put up with your bullshit every day, but now you're my mate and I have to go home with you? Now I don't get a break?"*

Cory had had his own reservations as well.

"You think I want to be mated to you?" he snapped at her. *"You're such a controlling nightmare, always correcting me. Do you think I'm enjoying this?"*

Of course they got over it. We've all been close for years, but they bickered all the time. It was irritating. After a few weeks of fighting the bond, they gave up and their bond is stronger than ever. They still argue over everything and tease each other, but now they do it with fondness in their eyes.

And here I am, twenty-two and I still haven't found my mate.

Jasmine makes up for the loneliness I feel, but it doesn't fill the void completely. I know she hopes that after I turn twenty-three I'll choose her. I shake the thought from my head. Grabbing my coffee I take a sip, waiting for my bagel to toast. It pops out of the toaster and I spread peanut butter on it, I take a bite and go sit at the table.

"Heard you come in early this morning," Cory smirks. "Where were you last night?"

"Who are you? My mother?" I snap. He knows damn well where I was.

Laughing, Cory throws a piece of toast at me. "Oh, lighten up, asshole." I take some of my bagel and hurl it at his face. I hit my mark, peanut butter smearing his cheek. "What the fuck?" Cory exclaims.

"That was for calling me an 'asshole,' asshole."

Reg rolls her eyes. "You two are *supposed* to be the leaders of this pack, building it back up, yet here you both are, acting like ten-year-old boys," she scolds.

"We're just having some fun, babe." Cory gazes at her. The guy is seriously pussy-whipped.

Taking the last bite of my bagel I look over to Cory. "Any word from Abel?" I ask, wiping the crumbs from my face.

The humor drains from his face. "Some, but not much that could help us. I don't think so, at least." He glances at Reg, who is now cleaning the dishes from their breakfast.

"Some news is better than none," I say. Leaning back on my chair, I take a sip of coffee, looking at Cory, waiting for him to continue.

He leans his arms on the table. "Apparently Drake's out scouring packs, looking for a mate."

My eyebrows rise. Wow, that's a new low. "Is he meeting any resistance?"

Cory shakes his head. "No. Most packs don't like to allow it, some alphas don't care and have no problem. Like it's still the fucking medieval times and offering up their daughters is normal." Grimacing, he grabs his mug, taking it to the sink. "It's crazy, man."

"Ha!" Reg throws the dishtowel on the counter. "It's fucking disgusting and wrong." She stands in front of us, hands on her hips, glaring at us.

"What do you want us to do about it?" I ask her, completely perplexed. "We have seventy-five wolves in our pack, Reg. Not like we can just storm into his territory and stop him."

"I know how many we have in our pack! He's the reason why there are so few of us!" She lets her arms fall from her hips, sadness replacing her anger. "He's the reason we're barely surviving. I'd hate to hear of him destroying another pack like he did ours."

Cory wraps his arms around her, giving her comfort.

Resting my head on my clasped hands I can't help but feel her sadness. It's all our sadness. Drake came onto our territory and wiped out everyone over the age of twelve. The memories come flooding back.

I'm asleep in my bed, my mom comes into my room and wakes me up.

"Cedric, honey, you have to wake up!" There's an urgency in her voice, something's wrong.

Wiping the sleep from my eyes I look at my mother. "What's going on, Mom?" I yawn.

Mom grabs my hand. "Come on, Cedric, we don't have a lot of time." She rushes me out the door and down the stairs. Cory and Reg are here, along with other kids from the pack. We're all huddled in the living room, Mom showing more kids where to stand, handing babies and toddlers to us older kids.

Once the door stops opening and parents stop bringing their children inside, Mom takes us down to the basement. She moves a shelf out of the way—there's a door in the wall. Wow! So cool!

"All right, kids, inside." She starts helping them into the tunnel when there's a loud bang from outside and lots of shouting. Mom looks out the small window that's just above the ground outside. "Hurry! Get in, get in!"

The shouting gets louder. "Mom, what's going on?" My heart is pumping so hard it feels like it's going to burst out of my chest. I'm scared.

She grabs my shoulder. "Listen to me, Cedric. Do you remember the man who was here yesterday?" I nod. Another alpha came for a meeting with my dad, he called me 'Champ.' I remember my dad being mad after he left. "He's back and he's not happy with your father. Now, you have to stay here and protect the little ones." She hugs me. "Can you do that for me?" I nod into her shoulder. She's sniffling.

"Mom, are you crying?"

Clearing her throat she holds me at arms' length, her eyes warm but full of sadness. "Here." She hands me a bag. Looking inside I see food and water in it. I look up at her, confused. "Lock the door behind you. I'm going to push the shelf back into place. Stay here until someone comes and gets you. Whatever you do, don't open this door."

She kisses me. "I love you. Now go!" Mom pushes me into the tunnel, shutting the door behind her. I realize I didn't say it back. But it's too late, she'd already pushed the shelf back in place.

I don't remember how long we were down there. A few hours? Maybe closer to a day. I remember there being lights and games down there to play and some toys. Blankets and pillows, too, but why?

When no one came and it had felt like forever went by, Cory and I decided to open the door. The others stayed inside. We ventured up into the house. No one was there.

Stepping outside we saw what had happened the night before. Cory and I walked around, both of us taking turns puking. There were bodies everywhere.

We called out names, but no one answered. We had to go back and tell everyone their parents were dead, that we were the only ones left of our pack.

I was twelve years old and both of my parents were murdered. I was twelve and I had to tell everyone their parents were dead, that we were all that was left. I was twelve years old when I became alpha.

CHAPTER EIGHT

Elle

The car comes to a stop but I can't see where we are because of this damned hood. As if Drake can read my mind he moves closer to me. I freeze when I feel his hand close to my neck. He pulls the fabric off my face.

I take a deep breath of fresh air. Having the hood on for what seemed like two hours felt suffocating. Drake's breath is on my neck. "Welcome home," he says, though nothing about his tone is welcoming.

My hand reaches for the door handle, but before I can tug it to open the door his fingers clench my arm, twisting me towards him.

His face was right in mine. "You don't open the door until I say you do, understand?"

Giving him a murderous glare, I rip my arm from his grasp. "Don't fucking touch me."

Smirking, he gets out on his side, comes around to my door and yanks it open. Pulling me out of the car he holds me close, the proximity making me nauseous. "You'll do best if you don't talk back to me, especially in front of my men." Drake looks down at me. "Now be a good mate and give me a kiss."

"Fuck you," I spit, trying to remove myself from his grip.

A perverse smile spreads across his face, his eyes light up in excitement. He grabs my face, his fingers pressing into my flesh hard enough to leave bruises. He forces his mouth on mine.

I wait for my moment. He pulls away and says, "There, that wasn't so hard, wa—" His words are cut off by my fist hitting him in the jaw. He lets go of my arm, I run. I make it a few feet before I'm tackled to the dirt.

"Fucking bitch!" Pulling me up by my hair he slams my face back into the dirt. "You disrespected me in front of my men. I can't have that, sweetheart." He pulls the hair that has fallen in my face into his hand. "You're going to learn to obey me and show me respect."

I growl at him.

He chortles. "I'm going to love breaking you in— so much fire in you, Eleanor. I hope it takes a long time."

Sick bastard.

"Now, come along nicely." He pulls me up onto my feet. "There, now let's go inside the house."

Looking up I finally see the house we pulled up to. If you want to call it a house, it's more like a manor. The exterior is all stone. It's a beautiful sight, but it lacks the warm feeling of a home. My new prison is beautiful, but still a prison.

Next to the house are a half a dozen men who are all staring at me. I glare back. I'll punch them, too, if they touch me. They all have smug looks on their faces, like they know what's going to happen to me and they're more than okay with it.

One man catches my attention. Drake is busy talking to one of the other men. I assume it's his beta. Even though Drake has a firm grip on my arm I allow myself to study the man who caught my eye.

He stands tall, his dark hair peppered with gray. Unlike the other men, whose eyes are unreadable or have a sinister look to them, this man's eyes are soft, kind even. Our eyes meet, he studies me just as I study him. Maybe there will be a somewhat friendly face around here.

"Kane!" Drake barks. The man's, Kane's, face changes, going hard and inscrutable.

"Alpha." He glances at me. "I see your trip was successful."

Drake laughs, tugging me close again. "Yeah, it was. Though she's got a bit of an attitude problem, as you saw a few minutes ago."

Kane nods, his lips twisting into a sneer as he looks at me. "Nothing that can't be beaten out of her, sir." Well, I was way off on my first impression. He's an asshole just like the rest of them.

Drake looks down at me. "Oh, I'm sorry," he says, though he looks anything but sorry. He's enjoying this, being in control. "Eleanor, these are my men. I'll only point out two because they're the only ones who have permission to beat you if you get out of line."

Lovely. How sweet of him to at least tell me their names.

Pointing at the large man he was talking to before Kane, Drake continues. "This is Maxx, my beta." I look him over. Standing around six-four, he's tall, with big beefy arms. He has beady black eyes that are too small for his face, a wide nose, and lips so thin they're nearly non-existent. I narrow my eyes at him. "Maxx, this is Eleanor."

"Luna," he says, inclining his head. I grimace. I don't want to be their Luna. I don't want to be here at all.

"And this is Kane, the enforcer." I glance at him and look away. I already know what he looks like. "Like I said, they have full permission to put you in your place if you forget it," he taunts.

"Kane, take her inside and show her to my room." He looks down at me smiling– there's a dark look in his eyes that makes my skin crawl. "I have things to take care of before I welcome her properly."

My stomach knots, bile rises to my throat and I swallow it down. There's no way I'm going to puke in front of these men. I won't show weakness.

Scowling at Kane, who has now grabbed my arm, I snarl, "Don't fucking touch me!" How many times am I going to say that? "I can walk on my own just fine." Squaring my shoulders, I walk up the stone steps with Kane right behind me. Taking a deep breath I open the door to my prison.

Behind the door there's a massive entryway, archways leading to different rooms and hallways, and a staircase with black iron railings that leads to the upstairs.

For a moment I forget the situation I'm in. "Wow," I whistle. This place is huge yet it's sparsely decorated. No plants, no pictures on the walls. There's only furniture, nothing to make it warm and cozy like a home. *What did you expect, Elle?* I chide myself. *Knitted afghans and hot chocolate? Connie to come bustling around the corner asking if I want anything to drink?* I shake my head, the thought of Connie making my heart ache with pain.

Tears threaten to escape my eyes– I'm never going to see them again. The thought brings a chill to my bones and I wrap my arms around myself.

Movement to the side of me snaps me out of my thoughts. Kane is now standing next to me, looking at me. That soft look is in his eyes again.

"What do you want?" I snap. "Don't you have some poor pack members to punish?" I notice the whips he carries on his right side. *Why does he have two?*

He must have seen me looking at them and touches one. "This one has silver sewn in." Kane looks at my face, gauging my reaction.

Silver, the only thing that can scar us werewolves. It weakens us, especially when it gets into the bloodstream. I'm appalled.

"Come on, I'll give you a short tour." Kane walks into one of the rooms, not waiting for me. Deciding to follow, for fear of being on the receiving end of either of those whips, I enter the kitchen.

It's cold, everything black, white, and stainless steel. There's nothing about this that's beautiful, I used to look at design magazines and imagine remodeling ours just like this one. Now I know why Connie refused. This isn't a place where family meals are made, where laughter bounces off the walls. It's cold and sterile.

"Do you want anything to eat?" Kane asks, breaking the silence.

"No." I wrap my arms around myself, trying to find warmth.

Shrugging, Kane walks past me. "Let's keep moving, then."

I follow him, not listening or looking at the other rooms he shows me. When we start climbing the stairs I begin to shake. I know what's upstairs. Bedrooms. I stop at the top of the landing. Kane, who is now halfway down the hall, turns and sees that I haven't moved.

"Let's go," he says coldly.

But I can't move, I know what's going to happen once I step into that room. Fear locks me in place. I glance down the stairs. Maybe I can make it. Maybe I can run.

Kane hasn't moved. He stares at me, watching every move I make. "Don't even think about it." His hands twitch to one of the whips, and looking in his eyes, I know he wouldn't hesitate to use it to stop me. Growling, I step down a step. Fuck it, I'm trying.

"I don't want to hurt you, Elle," he says firmly, taking his hand away from the whip. What he says makes me stop.

"What did you say?" I stare at him. *Who are you?*

"I said I don't want to hurt you."

"No, you called me Elle, not Eleanor." Drake never called me Elle. When he introduced us he said 'Eleanor'.

Shock comes on his face, and as quickly as it was there it vanishes. "Elle is a shorter version of Eleanor. Now let's go, I have more important things to do than chase you around."

He strides down the hall, stopping in front of a door in the middle of the hall.

Begrudgingly I follow. I don't believe his reason for knowing what I prefer to be called. I have no reason to not believe it. I don't know anyone named Kane, let alone this sadistic prick who walks around with two whips.

We stand there— he's waiting for me to open the door

and go in. Closing my eyes I turn the knob and, pushing the door open, I peer inside. The room is huge. Dark hardwood floors, a fireplace on the far wall with a TV hanging on the wall above it, a black leather couch sitting directly across from the fireplace. In the far corner I see a desk and chair. It's so clean it doesn't look like it has been used.

Feeling curious I step in a little more. Around the other side of the room, hidden by the open door, I see the bathroom. From where I'm standing I can see that it too is over the top with luxury. Damn, it must have cost a fortune to remodel this place.

My eyes continue to wander, exploring the room from the doorway. I finally look at the bed. A lump forms in my throat. *I have to sleep in that bed with him.* Shivering at the thought, something on the posts catches my eye. Something metal is attached to each of the four posts.

Gathering up all the courage I can muster, I walk closer to the bed to inspect the foreign addition to the wood. Picking up the links in my hands, a gasp escapes from me. "There's chains. He has chains on his bed," I say to no one in particular.

Hearing a sigh I turn to look at Kane and our eyes meet. "For what it's worth, I'm sorry this is happening to you."

Rage burns through me like a wildfire. "I don't want your fucking pity!" I snarl, getting right in his face. "If you feel sorry for me, help me get out! Your pity is worthless to me."

"There's nothing I can do to help you. I suggest you take what kindness you get here, because it's not given out often," he says, his face deadpan. "Don't go begging for help to escape because you won't find it. Just be a good girl and submit to him."

Like a fire hitting a propane tank my rage explodes and I punch him in the jaw, sending him into the wall behind him. He's stunned momentarily, rubbing his head. I see my moment and I take it.

I kick him in the sternum and bolt down the hallway. Reaching the stairs, I hear him cursing. Without looking back I run down them. "Stop fucking running! It's only going to be worse when I catch you." Hearing him tear down the stairs after me I reach the door I came though minutes ago. Yanking on it, nothing happens. It's locked.

Kane tackles me to the ground. Using one hand he holds my wrists behind my back, the other hand yanks my hair, pulling me to my feet. "You shouldn't have done that, bitch!" he growls, pulling on my hair. He brings me closer to him so my back is against his chest. "I told you not to take the kindness offered to you lightly." He moves us up the stairs, still restraining me by my arms and hair. "I give you advice on how to survive him, and how do you repay me?" He gives my head another sharp tug, tilting my head back at a painful angle.

"Agh!" I yell. "Your advice sucks, I'm not going to submit," I say, clenching my teeth, trying not to give him the satisfaction of a scream.

We reach the bedroom door and he violently shoves me in so I land on my hands and knees. I grab onto the bed, pulling myself up. "Then I hope you enjoy the pain, *Eleanor*, because that's going to be all you feel if you keep this attitude up." He slams the door. Hearing the latch click in place I know I'm locked inside.

* * *

DARKNESS FALLS OUTSIDE THE WINDOWS. I've been trapped in this room for hours. Kane came back once about an hour ago, asking if I wanted some food. I told him to fuck off.

Within the first hour of being locked in this room I contemplated my escape. I thought about the windows, but they didn't open. I looked around for something to smash one open, but then how would I get down? And they would hear the glass breaking as well and come get me before I could get far enough away.

I thought about destroying Drake's belongings. Smashing his TV, ripping the mattress on the bed, breaking the frame and posts into nothing but splinters. I found a pair of scissors and thought about stabbing them into his leather couch and tearing it until the foam spilled out.

I thought about a lot of ways I could destroy this room, but it wouldn't change anything. The outcome would be the same. I'd still be stuck here.

So I just sat down on the couch, waiting for him to show up, in the dark and silence.

Hours later I'm still sitting on the couch, holding the scissors in my hand. Hearing the door click, I know it's him. Drake walks in, shutting the door behind him, locking it again.

My heart rate quickens, my breath becomes shallow. Clenching the sharp scissors in my hand I wait. He comes into my sight, glances at me, then goes over to the fireplace and starts a fire.

He breaks the silence first. "Heard you and Kane had some fun." Drake continues to stare into the flames. I don't answer. He turns his icy stare on me. "He went easy on you, but pull a stunt like that again and he has the full authority to beat you until you're black and blue." Drake saunters over to where I'm sitting. Looking down he spots the scissors in my hand. "And what are you planning to do with those?" he asks, a sly grin on his face. He's amused.

Staring into his eyes I tell the truth. "I was thinking of all the ways I could stab you."

His grin widens. Kneeling in front of me he unbuttons his shirt, exposing the flesh covering his heart. "Go on, I won't give you another chance, Eleanor." The glint in his eyes tells me he wants me to try. I hold the scissors up and Drake's eyes brighten. Waiting for me to make my move so he can hurt me.

This is pointless. He wants me to try and kill him. I turn the scissors over so I'm holding the blades. Taking the handle he grabs them from my hand and sets them down. "Good girl," he says, getting up off his knees.

Drake sits on the bed. I gulp. Shit, the bile rises back into my throat.

"Come," he orders. *I'm not a fucking dog.* Well, I guess I am, but that's beside the point. I don't move, he growls, aggravated with my dismissal. "Come here before I drag you over by your fucking hair and chain you to this bed."

He means it, I know he does. Reluctantly I walk over and stand in front of him, waiting for his next order.

"Strip."

"Excuse me?"

"Are you deaf? I said strip. I want to see you, all of you."

I don't move, I'm not putting on a show for this asshole.

"Fine," he chuckles, "we can do this my way." He yanks on my shirt, popping the remaining buttons and tearing through the knot I made to cover myself. The shirt and buttons fall to the floor. Reaching behind me he unclasps my bra. I feel exposed to his stare as he takes in the sight of my body.

His hand covers my throat, squeezing until it's hard to breathe. "Try anything stupid and I'll fuck you in the ass so hard you won't be able to sit for a week."

Yeah, I definitely don't like the sound of that. This is bad enough.

Content with my silence, he releases my throat. I want to rub it, but I don't want to give him the satisfaction of knowing he caused me pain.

"Now your jeans." I notice he's undressing himself, too. Closing my eyes, I unbutton them and pull them down my legs, kicking them away from my feet.

"Mmm" he purrs, his body pressed up against my back. "Turn around and get on your knees."

The fire comes back. *No, I'm not doing this.* I turn around and slap him across the face, my hand stinging from the contact. "Fuck. You." I spit the words out slowly through gritted teeth.

Drake looks at me, enraged. He takes me by the throat, and picking me up he easily throws me on the bed. Straddling me he flips me on to my stomach. "You're going to regret doing that, sweetheart," he hisses into my ear. I feel his tongue on my neck, sliding it down to my collarbone and back up. "After tonight you'll be bound to me."

I try bucking him off, twisting and turning but it's no use, he's stronger than me. Feeling his teeth on my neck I close my eyes. When his elongated canines puncture my skin I scream.

CHAPTER NINE

Elle

The sun is peeking over the horizon, making the sky a mixture of pink and blue.

I haven't slept, my face is covered in dried tears. My body hurts all over, the spot on my neck where he bit me is tender. But most of all, my heart is shattered. The things he did to me last night, I wouldn't wish them on my worst enemy.

Drake sighs, the bed moves. He's awake. I lie there waiting for another assault but it doesn't come. The bed jostles when he gets up. Hearing the bathroom door shut, I release the breath I was holding in my lungs. When the shower turns on, I relax a little more, knowing there's some distance between us.

What have I gotten myself into? I can't beat him, he's too strong, too evil. This isn't one of the punks from my pack trying to challenge me. No, he's something different. I thought evil only belonged in storybooks, but now I know it's real. I've seen it, felt it, and now I'm trapped in it.

If I had just kept my mouth shut I wouldn't be here. But Naomi would be, not me. Guilt lances through me at the thought. No, I had to say something. It's better I'm here than her. I'm a fighter, Naomi isn't. She couldn't survive this.

I gave myself up so my pack could survive, putting their well-being before my own. I did the right thing.

I close my eyes, taking a long deep breath to center myself. *No, I'm not going to lie here and feel sorry for myself. I'm going to endure whatever it is he does to me and, in the meantime, I'm going to find my escape. I'm getting out of here.*

The water shuts off, a few minutes later the door opens. Closing my eyes I listen as Drake's footsteps come closer to me. They stop right beside me.

"I know you're awake, sweetheart. Sit up," he orders.

Keeping the sheet around me I do as I'm told. Hating that I'm obliging him, but I have to get my strength back, and getting knocked around isn't going to help my recovery.

He tugs the sheet off, seeing all of me, his face smug as he looks me over. His hand comes near my face and I flinch. He pinches my chin between his fingers and turns my face. His fingers trail lightly over where he left his mark on my neck. "Now everyone will know you're mine."

Anger courses through me. Standing, I walk towards the bathroom. "I'll never be yours."

"You are mine, mind, body, and soul. I can do with you as I please and there's nothing you can do about it."

The anger turns to rage, boiling in my blood. I turn to face him. "You can take me from my family, you can take me from my home. You can break my body as much as you like." I stride over to him, my chin high, refusing to back down from his empty ice blue eyes. "But you'll never break my soul. I'll wait for my moment, no matter how long it takes." I'm now right in his face, fueling my hatred and rage into my glare. "And I'll fucking kill you."

His grin is malicious as he tucks a strand of hair behind my ear. "I look forward to your efforts, sweetheart."

* * *

I'M LYING on the couch, waking up from a nap. I couldn't sleep on that bed, but I needed rest. Stretching out I feel the pain and soreness from the bruises on my body.

After I gave Drake my declaration that I will kill him someday, I went into the shower and scrubbed my body. I scrubbed until it was too painful, my skin aggravated and red with anger at my assault. And even then I still don't feel clean.

When I saw my body in the mirror I was horrified. Seeing more bruising than pink skin made the pain more prevalent.

Looking out the window I see the forest. I wonder if that will become my safe haven here. Or will he turn that into a nightmare, too?

My stomach rumbles. I haven't eaten in twenty-four hours. Sighing, I get up— I'm going to have to eat. No one has knocked on the door, so they're not bringing me food.

Fuck it. I try the door and am shocked to find it unlocked. Hmm, I'm allowed out of the room it seems.

With tentative steps I walk to the stairs. No one comes out yelling, no fists are flying telling me to go back to the room. I slowly walk down the stairs, listening for any threat that may come my way.

Reaching the bottom, I encounter no one. *Okay, I'm alone.* Turning into the kitchen I head straight for the fridge. Finding the inner makings of a sandwich I take them out and look for bread, opening different cabinets until I find it.

My attention is on building the sandwich when there's a thump, someone setting something on the table. I freeze. "Well, well, well, look who's finally come out of hiding." Whipping around, my body screaming in protest at the sudden movement, I see Kane lounging in a chair at the table.

"What the fuck are you doing here?" I turn back to my task, putting everything back where I found it before grabbing my plate and sitting at the table.

Kane has a stupid grin on his face. "Babysitting you. Making sure you don't try to make another run for it." He places his hand on the whip on his side.

Peering at him from over my sandwich I ask, "So what did you do wrong to be saddled with babysitting?" Taking a bite I roll my eyes. Not having eaten in over a day, this sandwich is the most delicious sandwich ever made on the planet.

"I didn't do anything. My job is to enforce the laws and rules of the pack, and punish those who cause any trouble." He nods at me. "You're the only trouble we're worried about."

"Well, gee, sorry I don't enjoy getting the shit beaten out of me," I snap.

"I told you how to avoid it, not my fault you didn't listen."

"I can't believe you can idly stand by as your alpha beats me. You're just as sick and twisted as he is."

Kane stands and walks around the table. Leaning down so we're eye level he says, "Oh, Elle, I won't just idly sit by." He smirks, "If you give me or anyone else any trouble, I'll gladly beat the fuck out of you myself."

He leaves the room, letting me sit in silence. I slowly pick at my sandwich. His words should have put a damper on my appetite, but I find myself still able to eat.

Once I finish eating, I clean my plate, unsure if there's someone else here who does them. Drake doesn't seem like the type to do his own cooking or dishes, though. Maybe Kane told me yesterday, but I don't remember much of the tour and whatever he said.

I find a greenhouse on the back side of the house. Taking in my surroundings I see different herbs probably used in the kitchen. Hearing humming on the other side of a shelf I go to see who it is.

An older man is there, picking off various leaves from different plants. My toe hits a garden trowel, sending it skidding across the stone floor. "Oh! Shit, I'm sorry," I say to the man.

He looks at me, a half-smile on his face.

"Oh, Luna Eleanor. It's nice to have a face to put to the name," he says pleasantly.

"Just Elle, please. And what's your name?"

"I'm Gerald, I'm the chef." He looks at me pointedly. "Do you need me to make you something? I know you sent your food back down last night."

My face reddens. "Sorry, I didn't mean to offend you. It's just that …" He raises his hand, cutting me off.

"Luna, there's no need to explain. I know how hard it is to move into a new pack, let alone becoming Luna."

"Please, call me Elle. No need to bother with the whole 'Luna' thing."

Gerald shakes his head. "But, my dear, that would be disrespectful. Both to you and our alpha who chose you." He grabs his basket with the herbs he just trimmed. "If you need anything to eat, I'll be in the kitchen." He disappears from my view. Well, at least there's one seemingly nice person here.

There's a door on the other wall leading out to a patio. I could use some fresh air, I hate being stuck inside. Weaving through the tables and shelves full of plants I make my way to the door. Grabbing the knob, I start to turn it when a voice comes from behind me.

"What do you think you're doing?"

"Ugh!" I exclaim, "I just want to go outside." I turn to see Kane standing in the doorway. "Is that breaking the rules?"

"Without an escort and permission, yes, it is."

"You're really annoying, you know that?" I say.

"Funny, I was going to say the same thing about you," he retorts.

Fuming, I jerk open the door and step outside. I stomp out into the middle of the patio and sit down on the stone. I know I'm acting like a petulant child, but I need to test something out.

Kane pinches between his eyes. "Jesus Christ, will you get back in the damn house?"

"No, it's a beautiful day outside." I wave my arm in the air, showing him the sky, to prove my point.

He storms over to me. "Let's go. Now."

Using my hand to shield the sun from my eyes, I look up at him. "Fuck off, Kane. I'm not hurting anything or anyone."

Uttering curses aimed at me, Kane takes me by the arm

and hauls me up. "Can't you do as you're told? For fuck's sake."

"Why do I need permission to go outside?" I ask. "I didn't even leave the yard."

"Because the alpha doesn't need you running off or causing a scene." Kane stops once we're back in the house and lets go of my arm. "You need to get something through that thick skull you obviously have." I open my mouth to retort but he holds his hand up to silence me. "You don't get a say in what you want to do, *Luna*. You want to go for a walk? You gotta ask. You want to go into the town and shop? You gotta ask. You want to take a piss? You gotta ask. Just like—"

Slapping him across the face I cut off his rant. Seeing the anger in his eyes I know I fucked up.

He grabs my arm once again and drags me up the stairs. "I try to tell you how to survive here, give you advice, and all you do is throw it back in my face," he growls. We reach the door to Drake's bedroom. Kane throws me in and locks the door behind him.

Well, that was interesting. I learned something today—Kane is easy to piss off. But after all his threats of having no issue with beating me to a pulp, I realize I have provoked him twice now and he has yet to follow through with his threats.

Once yesterday, when I punched him in the face and then kicked him in the chest, he only restrained me when he caught up to me. He wasn't nice about it, but he never hit me.

And then today, even with my temper tantrum and slapping him across the face, he just hauled me back up here.

For a man who says he has no problem beating me or

putting me in my place for the smallest infraction, he hasn't actually hit me.

* * *

Scrolling through movies and shows trying to find something to watch, I hear footsteps outside the door. The lock clicks– they don't open the door but I hear something clatter as it's set down. Whoever is out there doesn't come in and their footsteps retreat down the hallway.

I wait a few minutes to see if they return. Nothing. Curiosity getting the best of me, I leave my spot on the couch and open the door to see a tray with dinner on it sitting in front of the door.

Must have been Gerald, I think. Grabbing the tray I head over to the desk and take a seat. Examining its contents, tonight's menu consists of chicken parmigiana and a soup of some sort. It smells delicious. I dig in, not wanting to offend Gerald a second night in a row.

The taste compared to the smell is incomparable. *This has to be homemade sauce.* I devour my meal, even taking my bread and wiping the rest of the soup out of the bowl. Making a mental note to thank Gerald in the morning, I neatly stack the dishes on the tray and set it back out in the hallway.

Another hour goes by before the door opens and Drake struts into the room. *Asshole.*

"Did you miss me, sweetheart?" he asks, smirking at me.

"About as much as I'd miss syphilis."

He chuckles. "Oh, that mouth of yours." He muses, "I know what would make it stop running."

Ugh, I shiver. "You put your dick anywhere near my mouth I'll bite it off."

Grabbing my face his blue eyes meet mine. "I'd love to see you try, and when you do, I'll enjoy beating you, I'll enjoy taking you, fucking you until you scream in pain, begging me to stop." He pulls something out of his back pocket. Handcuffs. "Let's see how long it takes to make you scream for mercy tonight."

CHAPTER TEN

Cedric

Sitting in the living room, I stare at the fireplace, watching the remaining embers flicker, trying to stay alight. Cory and Reg went to bed hours ago, leaving me alone with my bottle of scotch and my thoughts.

Every night it's the same. I plot the death of the man who killed my family, who destroyed our lives.

Aggravated I sigh– we're nowhere near ready to take him on. Slowly we have added to our pack, taking in rogues who aren't too far gone, making allies with other packs. But it's hard to convince other alphas to join our fight against a much more powerful pack.

I can't blame them. Drake has the numbers to ruin any pack. They're also ruthless, not caring if they kill women and children. We learned that the hard way. Not every child made it to the packhouse that night, my older sister among them.

She was only seventeen. When I found her there was blood everywhere. Her face, chest and arms, even on her legs. It wasn't until I got older that I realized what must have happened to her.

Rage burns in my chest. Letting out a growl I throw my glass into the fireplace, the glass smashing against the brick and sending shards all over the place. When one nicks my cheek, the sting of air hitting the small cut twinges.

"You keep throwing glasses, we won't have any more."

Whipping my head around I see Bryce enter the room. Grabbing a glass, he holds it out for me to pour him some scotch.

He sits on the other end of the couch.

"You gotta stop just sitting in here and chewing on ideas. We gotta make a move soon," Bryce says, sipping on the scotch, staring into the fire. Bryce helps with the dirty work, the stuff Cory and Reg have a hard time with.

When your enemy is evil and powerful, you have to do evil things to get information. We have tortured to get information, and then killed them. Cory understands to some extent– he's not happy about it, but he gets it. Reg, hates it. She keeps things going smooth in our everyday life of the pack and even helps with training everyone how to fight. Fighting and killing when your life's on the line, she can handle that. It's the torture and execution she has a hard time with.

And that's why I have Bryce. You have to be somewhat sick and twisted to understand the mind of someone sick and twisted.

Rubbing my eyes I sigh, "We're not ready, man. I wish we were."

"Wishing is for pussies, Cedric. Men do what they have to do. Stop wishing and start doing."

"It's not that simple. How can we accomplish anything besides getting ourselves killed?" I shake my head. "We don't have the numbers."

"We have allies, use them."

He really doesn't get it. "I can't ask another alpha to sacrifice his pack for our cause."

Bryce snorts. "Why not? They know how bad he is. So they lose a few people, so what? As long as he dies, who gives a fuck?"

Bewildered, I stand and pace the room. "'So what?' It's not 'so what.' Those are lives we'd be responsible for. We would probably lose our whole pack, leaving another generation of teenagers and kids to pick up the pieces." Taking the bottle of scotch, I drink straight from the bottle, not bothering to get another glass. The burn warms my throat down to my stomach.

And it's true. That's what would happen, the kids left behind would have to pick up the mess we would leave them. The youngest two in our pack are nine, who were only infants when their parents died.

None of the ones who are mated have had pups, all afraid of history repeating itself. They don't want to leave their children orphaned like they were.

Bryce raises his hands in surrender. "Okay, man, okay." Resting his chin on his fist his eyes meet mine. "So what are we waiting for now? More information from Able?"

"Yeah," I say, sitting down on the couch, exhaustion heavy on my eyes.

Draining his glass Bryce sets it on the table. "Well, when word gets back let me know. We gotta get this going." He leaves the room. I'm alone with my thoughts again.

Closing my eyes, I try to make the thoughts go away. I need a moment where I'm not the alpha of this pack. My thoughts drift to the brunette from my dreams. I haven't seen her in a few weeks, instead it's just me in the forest, sometimes waiting for her to show up at our spot by the stream. The other times I'm searching the forest for her.

Who is she? And why do I get the feeling she's important?

The sound of the front door opening and closing tears me from my thoughts. I can tell by the click of heels on the floor who my visitor is.

"Cedric," Jasmine purrs. I open my eyes and see her kneeling in between my knees. Her hands running up and down my thighs, she looks at me with desire in her eyes. Reaching for my belt she starts to unbuckle it.

Any thoughts of the woman in my dreams are pushed aside. Why bother with dreams when I have someone right here to take my stress away?

She gets my belt undone and unbuttons my jeans. Stopping there, she stands. She yanks off her top and I see her tits, pushed up in her bra, almost spilling out of the cups. Unbuttoning her pants, Jasmine shimmies them down to her ankles and kicks them away. The sight of her black thong has my cock twitching in approval.

Jasmine kneels between my legs again, grabbing the waist of my pants. She gazes up at me. "A little help?"

I smile, lifting up off the couch so she can remove my pants. My dick pops out, lying on my stomach. Grabbing it she begins to gently stroke me, then, bringing it to her mouth, she takes me. Throwing my head back I let her, my hand in her hair, guiding her. *Oh fuck.* She sucks hard, bringing my cock to the back of her throat. I feel her gag and she pulls off, taking a breath. Holding me at the base, she swirls her tongue around the head of my dick. She takes me deep again, her hand cupping my balls, rolling them in her palm.

"Enough," I say, releasing her hair. She lets my dick pop out of her mouth, slick with her saliva. Licking her lips as she climbs on top of me, she guides me into her wet pussy and begins riding me. She's trying to go slow, but I don't want slow and steady. I need fast and rough. Grabbing her hips I keep her in place, pounding her hard. Jasmine's tits are bouncing in my face as she takes me stroke by stroke.

Jasmine throws her head back and moans, "oh god." I can feel her juices coating my dick, lubricating it. She's close. I keep my rhythm, sweat beading on my forehead. She screams, coming around my cock. I slow as I feel my release.

Panting, she leans in and kisses me. "Feel better? I know I do."

"Yeah," I smile at her, "I do." Pulling her in, I give her a kiss. She breaks away, bending down to pick up her clothes, and I smack her ass.

"Hey!" she yelps, playfully swatting my arm. I hold out my hoodie to her.

"Here, put this on. No point in getting dressed just to get undressed when we climb in bed." Jasmine looks at me through her long lashes. "I'll be up in a minute."

She pulls the hoodie on. It's huge on her, covering the important things, leaving her legs exposed. Pulling my pants on, I watch her walk out of the room and up the stairs. Once she disappears around the corner I head into the kitchen. I get a glass from the cabinet and fill it with water. I take a long drink, thirsty from the workout I got a few minutes ago. Draining the glass, I rinse it in the sink and put it in the drying rack.

Tired, I head up the stairs, dragging my feet. When I reach the top of the landing I'm greeted by Reg, her blonde hair pulled up in a messy bun, strands of hair falling out from lying on a pillow. With her arms crossed she glares at me.

"Late night visitor?" Her eyebrow rises.

Pushing past her I head to my room. "I don't have time for this." I don't want to hear her opinion on who occupies my bed. It's none of her business.

"Then make time, Cedric."

I rub my face and groan. Guess I'm not going to bed yet. "Just say whatever you have to say." Leaning against the wall I look at her, waiting for the tirade I know is coming.

Her nostrils flare. "Don't push me, Cedric. You know how I feel about your relationship with Jasmine."

I roll my eyes at her. "Yeah, you nag me about it constantly."

"I wouldn't call it nagging. Look, Cedric." She places her hand on my arm. "All Jasmine is trying to do is fuck her way into your bed permanently. And it's working," I open my mouth to protest but she holds up her hand, stopping me. "It is working when people ask if she's going to be your Luna and you don't flat out deny it anymore. If you loved her, it would be different. If she loved you, it would be different. But you don't. She looks at you and she doesn't see the man behind the alpha title. Jasmine only sees the title that comes with being your mate."

"Are you done?" I ask, annoyed that I'm having this conversation at two in the morning rather than sleeping.

Reg shrugs. "Until you give me your dumb excuse as to why you still let her in your bed." She smirks. "Then I'm sure I'll have more to say."

"I'm sure you will," I huff. "What's your problem with

her? She's strong, doesn't take any bullshit, and she's tenacious. I haven't found my mate yet, and I probably won't at this point. My time is up for that and I'll be able to choose my own, not fate or whatever makes it work. What's wrong with choosing her? Because we don't love each other? News flash, Reg, not everyone gets love, not everyone gets a happy ending."

"The problem is you're thinking with your dick," she snaps.

"Who I fuck is none of your business, Reg," I snarl, getting pissed that I'm having the same conversation with her over and over again.

"It is when there's a possibility the person you're fucking may become the Luna of our pack!" she shouts.

The door down the hall opens and Cory steps out, rubbing sleep from his eyes. "What are you two shouting for?"

Reg wheels around on Cory. "We're talking about how this one," she points at me, "needs to make a wise decision when it comes to choosing his Luna. And that letting Jasmine sink her claws into him is clouding his judgment."

"She's not clouding my judgment," I snap back.

"She clearly is if she's in your bed every night!" Reg shakes her head. "Look, Ced, I just want you to *really* think about this. Your choice of mate affects the whole pack, not just you." She gives me one more glance and heads into her room. Cory doesn't follow right away, staying in the hallway looking at me.

"What? Do you have something to say, too?" I'm over this, I want to go to bed.

He rubs his head. "Dude, I don't care who you fuck. But she's right, you need to be sure the woman you choose is the right choice to help you lead the pack." He turns down the hall. "And for the record, I don't think it's the one occupying your bed tonight," Cory says over his shoulder.

The door shuts and I lean against the wall, groaning as I slide down to the floor. *What the fuck am I going to do?* I sit there, on the floor in the dark, not wanting to go in my room and face Jasmine. There's no way she didn't hear all of that.

Letting out a sigh I get off the floor. There's no avoiding this. I turn the knob and enter my room. Jasmine is in the bathroom, washing the makeup off her face. Rummaging through my dresser I find a pair of basketball shorts and throw them on.

Sitting on the edge of the bed I bow my head looking at the floor. Staring at the knots in the wood, I try to make sense of the argument Reg and I just had.

The water shuts off. After a few moments the bed dips. Jasmine comes up behind me, rubbing my arms and nuzzles my neck. "What's wrong, baby?"

"Don't pretend you didn't hear all of that," I mumble, still staring at the floor, refusing to look at her.

Jasmine laughs. "Yeah, I heard it. But I don't pay any mind to it." She begins rubbing my back, kneading into my tense muscles. "You know Regina has been jealous of me since we were younger, and Cory will go along with whatever she says because he's her mate."

I relax into her massage. She's right, she and Reg have always bumped heads. "Do you remember when they found out they were each other's mates?" Jasmine asks, now working her hands down my lower back.

"Mmm," is the only response I give her.

"I think the reason she was so mad at first is because it wasn't you."

"That can't be it, she loves Cory." I turn to look at her, which ultimately ends my massage.

Jasmine flips her long hair over her shoulder. "Yeah, now. But have you ever wondered why she was always with you two? She and Cory didn't get along then at all, they were always fighting. She put up with him because it kept her close to you." Her finger taps my nose.

Shaking my head, I don't quite believe it. Sure, they fought and argued a lot when we were younger- hell, they argue all the time now- but Reg never once said or even hinted that she liked me more than as a friend.

Jasmine lies down next to me, propping herself up on her elbow. "Trust me, Cedric, I know when a girl is jealous."

"Yeah, but even if she did like me more than as a friend back then, that doesn't explain her issue now."

She scoffs. "That's easy to explain. No, she doesn't like you that way *now*. But the *idea* of someone else having you, what she couldn't have, *that's* what pisses her off." Jasmine sighs. "Also the fact that you might find someone would change everything. You would no longer be a trio, there would be someone else in the mix. Another female." She leans over and kisses me. "Goodnight, baby. Try not to fret over the petty stuff. She'll accept me someday."

Jasmine shuts off the light and darkness blankets the room.

Punching my pillow, I get comfortable. Closing my eyes I try to shut my brain off. As sleep pulls me under, the last image I see is the white wolf that haunts my dreams.

CHAPTER ELEVEN

Elle

Twenty days. I have been here for twenty days. A few weeks that feels like ten years. Looking in the mirror I can see how much I have changed. Dark circles shadow my eyes from lack of sleep. Bruises cover my body, new ones replacing the old ones before they can heal.

That's what happens when you're beaten and raped on a daily basis. The only place I haven't had a bruise is my face. Probably because he doesn't want the people in his pack to know he's a sadistic asshole.

Everything hurts, my ribs, my back, my arms and legs. Everything is constantly sore. The pain isn't enough to stop me from fighting, though. No, I'll never stop fighting him.

I try so hard not to cry, but the tears win every time. I can't help it. I fight to keep from crying and screaming because I know Drake gets off on it. But they always escape.

Someone knocks at the door. Answering it I see Kane standing in the doorway. "What do you want?" I demand, crossing my arms over my chest.

His eyebrow cocks. "Well, good morning to you, too." He stays outside the room, never entering fully.

"Do you want to come in?"

"No," he says abruptly.

"Okay. Well, as much fun as it is standing here in the doorway, I have some much needed plotting to do." Slamming the door in his face I start towards the couch. He knocks again. What the fuck? I go back and whip the door open. "What?" I snap.

"I was going to ask you if you want to go into the town, since you've been in this house for a week." Shrugging, he turns down the hallway. "But seeing as you have some major planning to do, I'll leave you to it."

I can leave the house? "Wait!" He stops and looks at me. Shoving his hands in his pockets, he nods. I take that as my cue that he'll wait for me. Running to the closet I grab my vest and race out into the hallway, almost bumping into Kane in my haste.

He smirks. "Ready to go?" Nodding eagerly, I bounce on the balls of my feet, waiting for him to go first. He leads me down the stairs and out the front door, heading toward a black pickup truck.

I stop walking, my excitement dissipates.

Kane notices I'm not following him anymore. "What?" he snaps, turning to glare at me.

"Can't we walk?" I've been sitting all week, I need to stretch my legs.

"No, we're driving. Don't worry," he adds, "we'll do

plenty of walking in town." That's good enough for me and I walk towards the truck, tugging on the handle. Kane pushes the door shut. What the fuck?

"First, some ground rules."

Groaning, I lean against the truck. What a buzzkill. "Let me guess," I say, holding up a hand and ticking off on my fingers, "if I run, you'll beat the shit out of me. If I try and get anyone to help me escape, you'll beat the shit out of me. If I give you too much attitude, you'll beat the shit out of me, drag me back here by the hair, throw me back in that room and lock the door."

Kane smiles. "Yep, that sums it up pretty good." He opens the door and I climb in. "You're catching on." He winks at me. *Fucking weirdo.* Kane gets into the driver's seat and starts the truck.

Turning onto a paved road and passing large fields, I watch the scenery, wondering what this pack is like. Are they happy? Content? Are they sad because they know their alpha is a sadistic psychopath? Or do they turn a blind eye to it? Do children run around the streets playing without fear? Or do they stay close to their parents? Will they give me a chance to get to know them or will they automatically assume I'm like their alpha?

"What's the pack like?" My voice breaks the silence in the cab.

Kane looks at me from the corner of his eye. "We get by." We're in a residential area now, passing about two dozen large two-story and split-level houses with, to human standards, large yards.

"Looks like you more than get by."

"The pack itself is very … well off, I guess you could say." He waves his hand out the window. "These families are all the ones who are most beneficial to the pack.

Lawyers, doctors, the higher-ranking members of the pack."

"So people like you and Maxx live in these homes?"

Kane nods. "The pack is split into three neighborhoods basically. This one is for the rich and those most loyal to Drake. The second one, they have smaller homes. They all help run the stores and schools." He turns the truck down another road, showing me the neighborhood he just told me about. These houses aren't as big as the other ones, but they're still nice.

"And what about the third?" I ask.

Kane sighs. "That's where I spend most of my time. Or I did until you showed up." He gives me a pointed look.

I glare at him. "Oh, like it's my fault I'm here? And your job description changed from 'high and mighty enforcer' to 'babysitter.'"

"From what I understand it is. Did you or did you not offer yourself to Drake so he would leave your pack alone?"

"He was going to destroy my home, kill my family. What else was I supposed to do?"

"You made a choice. Regardless of the circumstance, you chose to come here." We pull into a parking lot, and, looking around, I notice we're on a street lined with shops and businesses. Kane gets out of the truck and walks around to open my door. Our eyes meet. "So yes, Elle, it is your fault."

* * *

WE SPENT the late morning stopping into the shops, getting things like meat, eggs, and other various items.

Many people stopped us, but when Kane introduced me as their Luna their smiles disappeared. Some people just got serious and became more formal. Others, I could see the pity in their eyes.

So they must know how he is. It's not only behind closed doors or within the presence of his men that he shows his true colors.

We set our bags in the bed of the truck. "So who's been doing your job? Since you have been stuck with me?" I ask Kane.

"Maxx." He lets out a puff of air, looking at the sky. "I should go there and see how that's going. He's more strict than I am, I guess you could say." He looks at me. "He's easier to provoke, and hands out harsh punishments for minor infractions"

"Can I see it?" Kane shoots me a confused look. "Not the punishments. I want to see the area that causes the pack trouble."

He glares at me and I hold up my hands to him. "I'm not going to try anything, Kane," I say, trying to placate him. "I haven't done anything at all today, have I?"

"You've been annoying," he growls under his breath. "But I don't think that's something you can help," he grumbles. He stares at me, and I stare back. This is something I need to see. I'm not going to back down from this.

"Please? I just want to check it out. I don't even have to get out of the truck if you don't want." Maybe showing compliance will help me get my way.

Kane mumbles something to himself, shaking his head as he slams the tailgate shut and walks to the driver's side. "Get in the fucking truck." Grinning to myself because I know I got my way, I hop into the passenger side.

"Thank you," I say softly. I want him to know that I do appreciate this. Plus it keeps me out of the house for a little while longer. Who knows when I'll be able to come back out.

"If you try anything, and I mean *anything*—"

"I won't," I say, making an X over my chest. "I promise I won't."

"Don't interrupt me, I'm already regretting this." I don't say a word, not wanting him to change his mind. Satisfied with my silence, Kane growls, "If you try anything, I will make your life a living hell. Even more than it is now," he adds, knowing my life is hell.

I nod. "Okay, I get it. I'll listen."

He seems to believe me. The truck roars to life and we take off down the road.

* * *

WE DRIVE for about ten minutes before we stop, pulling to the side of the road.

Kane jumps out of the truck, keeping his door open. "Slide over and hop out this side. Don't want you falling in the ditch."

I hop out of the truck and look at my surroundings. My jaw drops. "This is part of the pack?" I ask. The houses are barely houses. Small buildings with sagging roofs, missing shingles. The place is falling apart. It looks like a bad part of town you don't want to go walking in.

Some of the houses have little gardens out front, trying to spruce them up and bring something pretty to the sad scene. But it doesn't change the fact that these people live in horrible conditions. The roofs probably leak and the windows most likely let in drafts of cold air.

I'm bewildered. I look at Kane, who has no emotion on

his face. Like he doesn't care that some of his people live like this. The fact that he sees this as normal infuriates me.

"How? Why?" I don't understand this. At home, people either bought, built, or inherited their houses. You could tell who had more money, but it wasn't based on their place in the pack. Some houses looked shabby and unkempt, but that was based off of that family's want of doing the upkeep. No one lives like this.

Kane never answers my question. Instead he walks down the road farther into the sad neighborhood. Not wanting to make him angry, I jog to catch up, slowing to a walk when I reach his side.

A squeal steals my attention from the houses. There are a couple of pups playing in the road, wrestling and chasing after one another. At least the kids seem happy. Looking around I spot who I think their parents may be. They look tired. Like they don't get enough sleep and the stress of their lives keeps them up at night.

The kids see us, their eyes zero in on Kane. With fear in their eyes, they run to their mothers, hiding from the man who probably is the cause of their nightmares.

"So what do these people do for work?" I ask.

"Grunt work, mostly. They tend to the livestock and fields. Harvesting them and taking the goods to the shops in town."

"Sounds like long hours and hard work." I stop walking. He stops, too, and looks at me. "And I'm guessing they don't get paid much."

"You would be correct," he says, his eyes void of any emotion. I can't read him. Does he not care? Or is he just good at hiding his feelings about it? "It's the way things are, Elle. You might as well get used to it. Not every pack is like your father's."

Ignoring his jab, I start walking again. "How many?"

"How many what?"

"How many wolves live here? Approximately."

"Around six or seven hundred, more than half of them being trained for combat."

Holy shit, that's more than double my pack at home. "And how many live here?" I wave my arm around to the dilapidated houses.

"I'm not sure. Roughly three hundred."

No wonder my dad didn't fight back. Drake wasn't kidding, it would have been a slaughter. Now I truly feel like I did the right thing, at least for my pack. It's better that I alone suffer, knowing they're safe, than being responsible for all their deaths and still be here with him. Yes, even though this sucks for me, at least they're alive.

"Have you seen enough for today? Gerald will be upset if we don't get this food to him in time to prepare dinner."

I look around one more time, wishing I had time to talk to some of those who live here. But I don't want to push my luck. "Let's go," I nod to Kane, leading the way back to the truck.

I'll come back here— maybe there's a way I can help them. In the truck Kane makes a wide u-turn, steering us in the direction of the manor.

* * *

BACK AT THE house I decide I'm tired of sitting in that room all the time, taking my meals there, and lying on the couch all day. Helping Kane with the groceries, against his protests, I put them on the countertop.

"What can I help you with, Gerald?" I ask the older man who is busy dicing onions.

Without stopping he looks at me. "Finally sick of being cooped up all day?" he smiles.

"Yeah," I grin back. "If I keep lying around I'm gonna get fat." I poke at my stomach to emphasize my point.

Gerald barks a laugh. "That would be a compliment to me, Luna."

"Yeah, I guess it would be." Looking at what he has out on the counter for ingredients I ask, "So what's on the menu tonight?"

"Shrimp scampi. Are you afraid of raw shrimp?" he asks, his eyes alight with humor.

"I'm not afraid of anything."

"Now that doesn't surprise me," Gerald says with a smile. Handing me a bowl of shrimp with the tails and legs still on. "You can peel them, then."

Set with my task, I stand at the counter and begin peeling the shrimp. We work in comfortable silence together, with only the sounds of pans sizzling and Gerald's knife hitting the cutting board.

Gerald breaks the silence. "I know this may be a foolish question but I can't help but ask; how are you feeling here, overall?"

I blink at him. It is a foolish question. His boss is a sociopath who enjoys inflicting pain on me. I fucking hate it here. I don't say it out loud, though, fearing it may get Gerald in trouble, and I don't want that. He's the only truly nice person here.

"Well, the food's amazing." I give him a tentative smile, hoping he understands I won't go any farther on the subject.

Gerald nods, his face softens, his eyes full with sympathy and understanding. "Where do you live, Gerald?" I ask, changing the subject and out of genuine curiosity.

"Down the far hall." He waves the knife in the general direction.

I freeze. I didn't realize other people lived here. *He's heard my screams.* Looking down at my hands I realize the shrimp are all peeled. "Where would you like these?" I ask, holding up the bowl.

Gerald gestures to the counter by the sink. "Right there would be fine, Luna."

"I'm going to go check out the study, see if there're any books that I may like." Walking faster than a normal person would, I head for the door, wanting to get away from Gerald. Knowing he has heard my screams of pain, it's too much for me. I can't look at his sympathetic stare.

"For what it's worth, Luna," Gerald calls, making me stop mid stride. I don't turn to face him, too embarrassed to look him in the eye. "Life is what we make of it. If you don't like how things are going, do something to change it."

Saying nothing, I leave the room, unable to stay in there with him any longer. I want to be alone.

* * *

I'M NOT ALONE for long. Sitting in a large wingchair in the study, I'm reading a book I found, trying to immerse myself in the world the author has illustrated, looking for any escape from my reality. Footsteps on the hardwood floor take my attention away from the story, a shadow casts over me. I don't have to look up to know it's Drake.

Choosing to ignore him, I try focusing on the text in my lap. He grabs the ottoman and sits across from me, taking the book from my hand and throwing it across the room.

"Hey! I was reading that, asshole," I snarl, moving to

get the book from where it fell. Drake grabs my arm and pushes me back in the chair.

"When I'm in the room your attention should be on me, unless I say otherwise."

"Wow, you really are an arrogant son of a bitch," I retort. That earns me a backhand, my cheek stinging from the impact.

"That's a warning, sweetheart." He points his finger at me. "Next time it will be my fist."

Glaring at him I say nothing. I'm sure I'll get more later anyway.

"That's better." He drags a finger down my cheek, trailing it down to the mark he left on me. It makes my skin crawl. "There, that's not so hard, is it?"

My lip curls up. I allow my canines to extend just a little and I growl at him.

He chuckles. "Well, I can see I haven't beaten obedience into you yet." He stands and heads towards the door. "You'll be dining at the table with me tonight."

"And if I don't want to?" I challenge, standing up, crossing my arms in front of my chest.

"I'll drag you in there and chain you to the floor by your neck, like the bitch you are."

How charming.

Drake comes back to me. "Between you and me, I hope you don't show up and I get to do just that." He kisses me and then leaves.

I wait a few minutes before I leave the study, not wanting to give him a reason to chain me to the floor by his feet.

Kane and Maxx, Drake's beta, are in the hallway talking. While I'm still unsure of Kane, I know Maxx is just as sadistic as Drake. I try to avoid him – it probably wouldn't take much more than a sigh to set him off.

Kane spots me, his eyes meet mine. Maxx notices Kane's stare and follows it. His eyes land on me. "What are you doing out of your room?" He leers at me with his beady eyes.

"Last I checked I wasn't required to stay there."

"A bitch's place is in two rooms in the house," he sneers, "the kitchen making food, and in the bedroom spreading her legs."

Fuck this. I charge down the hall, closing the distance between us. As I raise my fist to punch him, someone stops my arm mid-swing. Looking at who stopped my assault I see Kane holding my arm as he pushes it down.

Maxx is furious. "You were going to hit me, weren't you, you little bitch?" he roars.

He grabs my neck and throws me into the wall. I fall to the floor, my head pounding where it hit the wall. Looking up I see Maxx getting ready to kick me. Closing my eyes I brace myself for the impact. It never comes.

"Stop!" Kane's standing in between us.

"Get out of my way, Kane." Maxx shoots me a glare. "She needs to learn respect. She tried to punch me – I'm the beta, no one disrespects me."

"But she didn't and you still threw her into the wall. I'm sure that's a good enough lesson." Kane looks down at me. "Isn't it, Elle?"

I stand and lean against the wall. "Yeah, lesson learned." *Not.*

Maxx grunts and leaves, heading down to Drake's office.

"Asshole," I mutter under my breath. Kane chuckles.

"What's so funny?"

"You are. You're not very good at making friends here."

"Well, that's because everyone here is psychotic." I let out a sigh. "Besides Gerald, that is."

He snorts. "Come on, let's go in the dining room before you get yourself into more trouble."

"Good idea," I agree.

Following Kane, we enter the dining room. The table is set for four.

"Uh, where do I sit?"

Kane pulls out the chair to the left of the head of the table. *The same spot I sat in at home.* I shake the thought from my head, sitting down in the chair. "Okay, who's next to me?"

"I am." He sits next to me. We wait in silence.

Drake and Maxx enter the room a few minutes later. Drake spots me, surprise on his face. *Yeah, you're not chaining me up like a dog, bastard.*

He sits next to me. "Well, maybe Kane is right. Maybe you are learning." He takes a sip of the wine Gerald just brought out for us.

Maxx snorts. "Didn't seem like she had learned anything when she tried to punch me. Pure disrespect."

"I didn't hit you. Kane stopped me, but you still threw me into the wall."

"You shouldn't have stopped me, Kane, you should have let me beat some respect into her."

"Maybe you should have some respect beaten into you!" I snarl. "You don't know how to talk to a lady– maybe if you learned you would get laid." Tilting my head I grin. "Though with that ugly mug of yours I would also recommend a hood." I stab at my salad. "No one could look at that face and come." I fork the salad into my mouth, watching Maxx's face contort with anger.

Kane bursts out laughing. Drake ignores us all, sitting there quietly eating and drinking his wine.

"You fucking bitch!"

"Shut up!" Drake yells. Maxx immediately sits back in his chair. Kane stops laughing but hides his smirk by taking a drink of wine.

Drake looks at me. "You, stop antagonizing my beta. And you," he rounds on Maxx, "the only one here who can talk to her like that is me. She is your Luna, therefore you will show her some respect."

"Alpha, I—" Maxx starts but Drake cuts him off.

"Unless she is running away, or defying my laws, you have no reason to attack her."

Hmmm, odd. Before he told me Maxx had full authority to beat the crap out of me. What's changed?

Gerald brings out the shrimp scampi I helped him with. No one talks, we're too busy eating our food. The sound of cutlery on the plates makes the only noise.

After fifteen minutes Drake sets his plate aside and looks at me. "So, Eleanor, Kane tells me he took you to see the main part of the pack territory."

I shoot a look at Kane— was I not supposed to leave the house? "Yeah, he did." Placing my fork on the plate, I push it away and take a sip of my wine.

"What did you think?"

Choosing my words carefully I take another sip of wine. "Most of it seemed nice and fine. The shops were nice."

"Most of it?" Drake seems bothered, like my saying it wasn't all wonderful is an insult to him. *It should be.*

"Well, there's that one part of the living area, the people are living in really horrible conditions." I swallow, my mouth goes dry. They're all looking at me. "It's not right," I say, looking Drake directly in the eye.

Maxx is the one to answer. "They're the slobs, the troublemakers, trying to cause trouble by defying our alpha. When that happens, they're sent there to live." He looks smug, like that's the best answer he's ever given.

I let that sit, thinking about it before answering. "So it's like a work camp? Do they get paid?"

"They get rations," Drake says.

"Why does Kane or Maxx or whoever have to be there?"

"Don't you listen?" Maxx snaps. "They cause trouble, they need punishment."

I stare at him, appalled and shake my head. "That's so wrong."

Kane clears his throat, bringing all of our attention to him. "Maybe the Luna should make an appearance there. She can talk to the people. As a woman she won't be as intimidating as we are."

Opening my mouth, I close it suddenly. Kane's foot presses onto my mine, and he shoots me a look telling me to keep my mouth shut. He carries on as if I hadn't tried to interrupt him. "She can get information from them, and maybe find a solution to the problem."

Drakes leans back in his chair, drinking from his wine glass. He doesn't speak. He eyes me and I want to shrink in my chair. *Did I say something to piss him off?* I'll find out later either way.

Maxx stands, pacing the room. "I don't like it," he says. "I don't trust her." He looks at Kane. "To be honest I don't trust you either."

Kane shrugs, unaffected by Maxx's declaration.

Drake looks at me, his cold eyes sending chills down my spine. "Leave us," he says quietly.

Taking my cue to leave, I hurry out of the room, taking the stairs two at a time.

Even though I've been outside all day I decide to not take a shower. I'm going to want one later anyway.

Grabbing the throw blanket that I have claimed as mine, I sit on the couch and wait for Drake to come upstairs.

I only have to wait fifteen minutes, then I hear the door open.

"You'll be meeting Kane downstairs at 8 AM."

"What?"

"You'll be going with him so you can talk to the people of the pack. Figure out why they defy me, and report back to me." He unbuckles his belt, laying it on the back of a chair.

"What happens to them when I report what they say back to you?"

Drake glares at me. "That's not any of your business." He walks over to the liquor cabinet and takes out a bottle of gin. After he pours himself a glass, he sits next to me on the couch. "You're to get the information and tell me what's going on. That's it. How I choose to deal with them is my decision." He grabs my chin. "Do you understand?"

I nod. I could always change their words. How would he know? He won't be there.

Drake drinks from his glass. "If you fuck me over in any way, I'll chain you to that bed and you won't leave this room for six months. Do I make myself clear?"

Meeting his stare I nod. "Crystal."

CHAPTER TWELVE

Cedric

I'm in my office, reading an email from Alpha Jared, asking me to call him. I don't have any time to think about what that could be about when my office door slams open and Cory and Bryce come charging in.

"Ced, we just got word from Able," Cory says. Any annoyance I had at them dissipates.

"Drake has a mate," Bryce says.

My eyebrows rise. "Wow, poor girl." Feeling a pang of sympathy for whoever it is, I think she's probably wishing she was dead right now.

Cory and Bryce sit in the chairs in front of my desk. "This is big news, Cedric," Bryce says. "We could use her."

"Use her how?" I ask.

"Find a way to get to her, take her away, and torture her

for information." Bryce's eyes are wide with excitement. "Or we could send pictures of her to him, after we mess her up a bit, or a lot." He grins that grin that makes me wonder if he's a sociopath. Bryce is pretty twisted.

"Holy fuck, dude, are you nuts?" Cory looks at Bryce like he grew an extra head.

"Who's to say it would work? He probably doesn't give a shit about her." This isn't the first time Drake's had a woman for a long period of time. They all end up the same, dead. Who's to say the same won't happen to this one?

Bryce shakes his head. "No, he marked her, Ced. She's different." He chuckles, "Able says she's a spitfire, constantly fighting back."

He's marked her? This changes things. If he marked her, that means he wants her around forever, she's special to him. He's never marked any of the others. They were expendable. She's his weakness. There's no way Drake loves her, but he must be possessive, keeping her hidden like a prize jewel.

"How could we get to her?"

Cory scoffs. "Dude, you can't be serious. Trying to get her would be a suicide mission. And torture her?" He shoots a glare at Bryce. "Are you serious? She's probably been through hell and back already with him. You want to kidnap her and do some more?"

Bryce shrugs, nonchalant like this is everyday conversation. "Every-thing's fair in love and war, Cory. And this is war."

Standing up I look out the window, though there's nothing to see. No pups playing in the yard, no older couples taking an afternoon stroll to stretch their legs. Drake stole that from us. Now it's our turn to steal from him.

"How do we get to her?" I ask Bryce. Cory groans, throwing his hands up. I ignore him. "Well?"

Bryce grins, like he's just won the lottery. "We'll need a diversion."

* * *

AFTER A FEW HOURS of deliberating and arguing, we have a plan. Cory storms out of my office, in agreement with the plan but still pissed. He doesn't like the idea of torturing Drake's mate. I told him when we get there, we'd discuss it more. He's mad that I'm even considering it at all.

Bryce leaves my office next, much happier than Cory. He loves chaos and lives for it, I think. There really is something not quite right with him. But he's always been loyal to me.

Remembering my email, I take out my phone, and call Alpha Jared.

"Alpha Cedric," his deep voice greets me.

"Alpha Jared." I wouldn't go so far as to say Jared and I are friends, but he's a good alliance to have. He has a pack around the same size as Drake's, making him a damn powerful alpha. The only difference is he's not a psychopath who slaughters other packs. No, that's just Drake. "You emailed me telling me to call you," I say into the receiver, twirling a pen in my hand.

He laughs. "Yeah, like two hours ago. Something come up?"

"Yeah, you could say that." I won't divulge my knowledge and plans to another alpha. He may use it against me.

"Still trying to find a way to get to Drake, huh?"

"What did you want to talk about, Jared?" I snap, getting annoyed with his prying.

I hear him clear his throat. "Yeah. You may want to check into a pack to the northwest of you. There's some no-man's-land in between your borders."

Rolling my eyes I toss the pen. "And why would I want to do that?"

"You have a common enemy— Drake fucked with them." He sighs. "I don't know, I just thought it could be something worth checking out for you. Join forces or something."

"Thanks, I'll look into it."

"No problem," he says. Hanging up the phone I look over my notes, trying to see if there's anything wrong with the plans we have set.

Bryce is right. We may lose a few men, but for the cause it's worth it. Everyone will agree, I won't have a problem getting volunteers for this.

We'll go in six weeks. Under the darkness of the new moon we'll hide better.

In a few weeks Drake's mate will be my prisoner.

CHAPTER THIRTEEN

Elle

*F*or the first time since I've been in Drake's captivity I find myself in the forest. I'm a wolf this time, my white fur illuminated by the moonlight.

Hearing breathing behind me, I know I'm not alone. His presence is dominant, intimidating. I know it's the gray wolf without even having to turn around. I'm on edge, my hackles raised, my lips curling up, showing my sharp teeth.

The black wolf never brought this response out of me. He was the feeling of safety and comfort.

The gray wolf steps in front of me and tries to push me back, snapping at me, making me retreat.

He's herding me. Pushing me back from the clearing, trying to keep me from finding the black wolf.

Snapping back I try to push forward. He snarls at me, grabbing the nape of my neck, pulling me away from the clearing.

I try getting loose from his grip, but he bites harder, making me yelp in pain.

Soon I can't see the clearing, the moon obscured by the trees making the forest dark. The gray wolf keeps dragging me farther into the darkness.

A howl piercing through the night makes me stop. The black wolf. The sound full of sadness, his song continues, fading away the farther I'm pulled into the woods.

I wake up and, looking at the window, I see it's still dark outside. The sun just peeking its way over the mountains, creating the thin line of light that will soon illuminate the valley. I haven't had a dream since I've been here. They have all been nightmares.

Drake sighs in his sleep and rolls over, settling back into what looks like a peaceful slumber. *Asshole.* I hate him. Anyone who can sleep so soundly after tormenting someone needs to burn in the deepest depths of hell. Leaning over to look at the clock on his night stand I hope my movements don't wake him. Four in the morning. I snort softly. Figures— I have four hours until I'm supposed to meet Kane.

What the hell am I going to do for four hours? I could shower, hopefully that won't wake Drake up. Scooting to the edge of the bed I quietly roll off, tip-toeing around the bed. Halfway to the bathroom my arm is snatched into a vice-like grip.

"What are you doing?"

So much for not waking him up, I think to myself. I step back, looking at him, moving so that my arm isn't twisted in an uncomfortable angle. "I woke up, thought I'd take a shower." I glare down at him. "Or am I supposed to ask for permission?"

"The only time you don't have to ask for permission is

when you service my cock." A wry smile widens on his face. His eyes full of lust, looking at my breasts, he reaches out and pinches my nipple showing under my shirt, squeezing and twisting it to the point of pain. "You have the perfect body," he drawls. "It will be a shame to ruin it with pregnancy."

I feel the blood drain from my face. I've been so caught up in trying to survive living with this sadistic asshole I never thought about having to carry his pups. The idea is unsettling, making my stomach churn.

His hand moves down to my hips, he pulls me closer to him. Lifting my shirt up he licks my navel. Pulling away I slap him across the face. "You have me at night, asshole." I snap. "Let me have my mornings in peace."

Drake snarls, and throws me on the bed. Pushing himself between my legs, he uses one hand to restrain both my wrists, holding them above my head. The other hand wraps around my throat, his grip tightens. He's done this before, choking me until I pass out so he can assault me without a fight. "You keep forgetting, sweetheart, I fucking own you," he growls in my face, his hips pushing his erection against my core. "I can touch, fuck, and beat you whenever I want."

"You don't own me, no one owns me," I hiss. He releases my throat, raising his fist. "Wait! You really think that's a good idea?" I ask him. Surprised, he stops, holding his fist, ready to punch me.

"You clearly aren't learning your place. Maybe a black eye will help you remember."

I nod. "Yeah, fine, whatever. But do you really think it's a good idea to send me out to talk to the members of the pack with a shiner?" I'm going out on a limb here, assuming he still lets me go out today. Also assuming he cares what his people think of him. "You wouldn't want them to think you beat on me, right? An alpha beating his luna." I pause, shaking my head. "That doesn't send a good message to them."

Drake lets go of my arms. Stepping back he looks at me and he chuckles, shaking his head. "Maybe Kane is right. You *are* smart." Leaning down he presses his mouth to mine. Pulling away, his eyes meet mine, the sadist shining through. "You'll get it tonight, sweetheart. More than usual to make up for this morning." He walks into the closet to get ready for the day. Taking my chance I bolt into the bathroom, shutting the door behind me.

I might have gotten away with slapping him for now, but I'll definitely pay for it later.

* * *

It's six-thirty when I enter the kitchen. "Good morning, Luna," Gerald greets me. "Would you like a croissant?" He holds up a basket of warm pastries.

My mouth waters. "Mmm, yes, please," I say, taking one from the basket. Turning to sit at the table to wait for my coffee— I've learned not to get it myself because Gerald gets offended— I see Kane sitting there already.

"You're early," I say, taking my seat, reaching for the butter. Pulling apart my croissant, I spread butter on it, which melts into the nooks and crannies.

Kane looks up from his coffee. "I could say the same to you," he winks.

"Yeah, but I'm stuck here," I say, my words muffled by the food in my mouth. "You have your own house, or do you not stock it with food and coffee?"

Kane just chuckles, continuing to sip his coffee. As I

tear off another bite of my breakfast and pop it in my mouth, a thought comes to mind.

"Hey, I have an idea," I say, looking at Kane.

He snorts. "This oughta be good."

Ignoring his remark I carry on. "Could we go for a run? I haven't shifted since I've been here and I'm itching for a good run." Kane gives me a pointed look, not happy with my idea.

"We don't have to run," I plead. "We could just walk. Or hell, even just stand there." I'm desperate, begging for this. "Please? I promise I won't try anything."

He doesn't answer. Running his fingers through his hair he grunts. "Fine," he snaps. A smile spreads across my face. Yes! Kane points at me. "If you try anything stupid, like running, I'll tell the alpha that you can spend some time with Maxx."

The smile falls from my face. It's bad enough having Kane around all the time. Maxx would be worse. Kane hasn't hit me, not once, just restrained me. Maxx would beat the hell out of me for breathing too loud.

"Trust me, with that warning, I'll do anything to not get that punishment."

"Let's go, then." Kane stands up, finishing his coffee and setting it down as he looks at me, waiting.

I pop the last bit of food in my mouth, taking almost no time to chew, and I drain the last gulp of coffee. "Thanks, Gerald!" I call over my shoulder, all but running to the door.

"Have fun, luna!" I hear him call out.

Waiting at the door I'm bouncing on the balls of my feet. Kane gives me a look, annoyed with my excitement. I can't help it, I used to shift every day and run.

Kane shakes his head, grumbling something about

babysitting not being part of his job description. Opening the door, he waits for me to exit the house. Once we're outside I wait for him to show me which way to go, not wanting to ruin the highlight of my morning.

He sets off in a jog, heading towards a tree line. I follow him closely.

"We can shift here," Kane says as we step into the cover of the trees.

"Okay." I take off my shirt, not self-conscious of being naked. Most wolves see each other naked sometimes— especially when we first shift it's hard to control. Lots of ruined clothing and naked bodies. It's only Drake who makes me feel vulnerable.

With my back to Kane, I hear him growl. Turning my head I see him looking at me. He's not looking at me with want or desire— the look he has on his face is anger. *What's that about?* I look down, seeing all the bruises.

Snapping my head up I glare at him. "If you don't like it, don't fucking look," I snap. "What did you expect anyway?"

"It's different seeing it," he growls.

"Oh yeah? Well, try living it." Yanking my pants off I shift, keeping my back to him so he can undress.

"Let's get this over with." Kane's words come through my head. I guess the mind link works.

Kane's wolf is about the same size as mine, neither one of us looking down on the other. His fur is dark brown, like chocolate.

We set off at a steady run, not sprinting but faster than a trot. We run for a while, not talking to each other. He's letting me be alone. We run through the woods for a few miles, then Kane stops when we come up on a large rock. I trot back to him quickly, not wanting him to think I'm running away.

"*Let's stop here,*" he says, sitting on his haunches. I don't sit, I continue to romp and play, sniffing around the surrounding area, knowing I go too far when Kane growls.

Walking up to Kane, I lie down. "*I have a question.*"

"*Of course you do,*" he huffs.

I try to gauge the expression in his eyes but they're unreadable. "*What color is Drake's wolf?*" I ask.

"*Gray,*" he says, tilting his head. "*Why?*"

"*Just curious.*" Is he the gray wolf from my dreams? Or is it just a coincidence? I'll have to think about it more later.

Kane stands and starts back the way we came. "*We should get going, Elle.*"

Sighing I get up, not wanting to leave yet, but I want to come back so I won't push him. Maybe if I can show I will listen, Kane will bring me back.

When we get back to the tree line, we shift and get dressed. Once I'm covered I turn to see Kane putting his shirt on. Noticing something on his neck, I try to peer closer without him noticing. *It's a mark, Kane has a mate.* Buttoning up his shirt, the mark is covered. I look away, not wanting to get caught.

Kane looks at me, not giving any indication that I was caught staring. "Let's go," he says, walking in the direction of the house. I stay where I am. Only when he turns to look at me do I start to follow.

* * *

DRIVING down the road in his truck, Kane has the radio on a rock station, and he's drumming along to the beat on his steering wheel. He looks almost normal, like he's not driving around with a captive in his truck.

Reaching over, I turn down the radio.

"Hey! That's a good song."

"Why haven't you mentioned that you have a mate?" I ask, ignoring his protests about the radio.

He gapes at me. "How did ... why ..." Kane stumbles on his words, then he takes a deep breath. Letting it out he looks over at me. "What makes you think that I have a mate?"

I shrug. "I saw the mark when you were buttoning your shirt."

"Ahh, checkin' me out, were ya?" he laughs. "Do me a favor and don't let Drake catch you, I like my face how it is."

"I wasn't checking you out" I chide. "And you're deflecting."

"You really are annoying, you know that? Besides, it's none of your business."

"Maybe I wanted to send her a sympathy card, for putting up with your sorry ass."

The humor drains from Kane's face, sorrow replacing it. "That would be rather difficult, seeing as she's dead." He keeps his eyes on the road, refusing to look at me.

Wow, good going, Elle. That was a dick move, I chastise myself. "I'm sorry," I offer, not sure what else to say.

We sit in silence for a while, watching the scenery fly by. Now I feel horrible, I should have kept my mouth shut. I continue to berate myself– why do I always open my big mouth? When will I learn that it gets me in trouble?

"I had a son, too, and another pup on the way." Kane breaks the silence, pulling me out of my thoughts.

Sympathy for Kane washes through me. Obviously

losing his entire family has affected him. Who wouldn't it affect? Maybe Kane wasn't always a jerk— he shows kindness at times, maybe that's how he used to be all the time. Looking at him I try to picture him with a family, playing with his son, kissing his mate on the cheek, rubbing her round belly. I can see it easily. Perhaps losing them made him change to who he is now.

"How?" I ask. He looks at me with confusion. "How did they die?"

"How most of us do, a rogue attack. I had gone off with some others to stop a large group of them from getting into the living area." He grips the steering wheel, his knuckles turning white. "We missed some in the confusion and chaos. When we went back, we found the rogues who sneaked by us tearing houses apart looking for food and whatever else they wanted. We took care of them, and I ran home to make sure my mate and son were safe. I expected to find them locked in the bedroom scared, but alive." He takes a deep breath, his voice thick with emotion. My heart squeezes, hurting for him. "I found them pulled out into the back yard. They were dead."

Feeling a tear on my cheek I wipe it away. "I'm so sorry, Kane. I really am." I choke the words out. Without thinking I reach over and squeeze his arm. He stiffens under my touch and I withdraw my hand, clasping it in my lap.

"I left the pack, I never went back. I couldn't stay there, where all the memories I had of them haunted me. I wandered for a while, staying in various packs for a few weeks at a time and then moving on." Kane rolls down his window, and, clearing his throat he spits into the wind. "And now I'm here." He shrugs one shoulder. "I found my place in this pack, and it's here that I'll stay."

The truck slows, he shifts it into park and cuts the

engine. "Storytime's over," he says, opening his door. "It's time for work."

* * *

"WHAT AM I supposed to say to them?" I ask Kane as we walk down the road. The closer we get to the rundown houses the more nervous I get.

"Just introduce yourself and ask them how things could be better for them." Kane rubs his face. "Jesus Christ, this was kind of your idea."

"No, you threw me under the bus!" I accuse.

"Hey, it gets you out of the house, doesn't it?" Kane's attention drifts down the road. "What the fuck is he doing here?" I follow his stare and see Maxx talking to a few men I've seen come in and out of the main house. Kane turns to me. "Listen, I'm going to go talk to them and see why they're here." He looks at the house behind me. "Start at this house and go down from there," he says, pointing down the row of houses on the side of the street we're on.

My eyes widen. "You're going to leave me alone?" I don't know these people and they don't know me. They may slam the door in my face when they find out I'm Drake's mate. I'd do the same thing if I were them.

Smirking, Kane starts walking toward Maxx and the other goons. "You'll be fine, *Luna.*" He leaves me alone. *Okay, Elle, you can do this. Just knock on the door and introduce yourself.* Feeling marginally better after my little pep talk to myself, I turn around and face the house.

The roof is sagging and missing shingles, tarps cover parts of the roof. The porch has broken railings, some of the windows are boarded up, probably because the glass is broken and it's the only way to block the wind. It looks like it should be abandoned. The only sign that someone lives here is the garden, blooming flowers adding just a small bit of life and beauty to the yard. Some toys litter part of the yard, showing that kids live in this house.

I don't even make it halfway up the small walkway when the door opens. A small young girl, looking to be around seven years old, pokes her head out.

"Who are you?" she asks, her head tilting. She examines me, looking me over from head to toe and back up to my face.

Getting low so the girl doesn't strain her neck looking up at me, I introduce myself. "My name's Elle," deciding to leave off the "Luna" part. I don't want to scare her off. That wouldn't go well with the parents. "What's your name?" I ask her, making sure to smile and seem friendly.

The girl's eyes narrow, shaking her head, making her gold ringlets bounce around her face. "Mom says I'm not s'pose to tell strangers my name."

I laugh. "Well, I guess that's smart of your mom. And smart of you to listen to her." I wink at the little girl, she giggles, then turns and runs back into the house, leaving the door open. "Mom? MOOOOOM!" I hear her yell through the house and it makes me smile. "There's a lady outside!" She peeks her head out. "Don't worry, my mom's coming." Leaving the threshold of the house the girl skips down to me. "Why were you talking to Kane?"

"Well, he brought me here," I say, watching her face to see how she reacts.

She scrunches her nose. "You shouldn't talk to him, he's a bad guy." She points over to where Kane and Maxx are talking with the other men. "They're all bad."

"Kassie!" A woman in her thirties comes rushing out of the house, a baby on her hip and a toddler holding her hand. She looks down at her daughter. "You can't say those things," she scolds.

Kassie hangs her head, her curly hair covering her face. "I was just telling her that she shouldn't talk to them, Mom," she grumbles.

The mother's head snaps up, looking me over. "And who are you?" she asks, distrust written all over her face.

"I'm Elle," I say, unsure how much more I should say. *This was pointless, once they find out who I am they're going to run me out of here.* "I shouldn't have bothered you, I'm sorry." I turn to leave.

"Wait!" the woman calls out. I look at her. "I'm sorry, we don't trust new people here." She looks over at the group of men. "They tend to bring more trouble than what we already have." She lets go of the little boy's hand and holds hers out to me. "I'm Abigail. Abby,"

Smiling, I return her handshake. "And who's this?" I ask, nodding at the little boy with light curly hair like his sister's.

She pulls him out from behind her leg. "This is Charlie, and this," she shifts the baby on her hip, "this is Toby."

"You have a beautiful family," I say to her.

"Thanks. My mate is working, otherwise I'd introduce you. So what brings you here, Elle? Are you new to the pack?"

"You could say that," I say wryly. Raising my arms, I pull my hair back, tying it up in a bun. My shirt pulls up on my stomach. Abby's eyes glance down and then narrow. Noticing her stare I quickly tug my shirt back into place.

"Kassie, can you take Charlie and play in the yard?" she asks, not taking her eyes off mine.

Kassie huffs, "But, Mom! I want to talk, too!" she whines.

"Do as you're told! Or you'll have your father to answer to." Abby sighs. "Please, Kassie. I'm sure Elle will talk to you before she leaves."

"Okay," Kassie sighs. "C'mon, Charlie, let's go play." Taking her brother's hand, they make their way over to where their toys are.

Abby watches them for a moment before turning her gaze on to me. "Who are you?" She tucks a strand of her blonde hair behind her ear.

"I told you."

"No, you told me your name. That doesn't tell me who you are."

"If I told you, you'd tell me to get lost."

She adjusts Toby on her hip. "That depends," she says.

Sighing I give in, they're never going to trust me. "Drake brought me here to be his mate." She sucks in a breath. "It-it sucks, really sucks." The words catch in my throat. "I miss my home."

Abby takes my hand, holding it tight. "Listen to me, you need to run. You need to find a way to get out of here." She looks around to make sure no one else is around to hear what she has to say. Abby pulls me closer. "He's a bad man, though I'm sure you've figured that out." Her eyes flick to the group of men standing behind me. "Be wary of Kane, too," she warns. "He's not a good man, he jokes with you and makes you feel comfortable, then he'll find a reason to punish you. Please, believe me. Get out of here."

"There's no way—"

Abby cuts me off. "Then find a way. Find a way before it's too late and you lose yourself."

"Okay, I'll try. But what about you? Do you need help?" I look at her house and then the ones next to it.

She shakes her head. "No, dear, we get by. The outside

looks worse than the inside." Patting my hand, she gives me a small smile. "I hope you find your escape, Elle."

Abby calls Kassie and Charlie, ushering them inside. Kassie turns and looks at me from the porch. She smiles and waves before running in after her mother.

*　*　*

LEANING against Kane's truck I think about Abby's warning. I know I should be trying to leave, find a way out of here. But how? And what about Kane? He seems like he can be an asshole, but he's been somewhat decent to me, but the way she and Kassie talked about him makes me wonder.

Tucking that thought to the back of my head, I see a group of people sitting out on a porch a few houses down from Abby's.

Might as well try talking to them, I decide, squaring my shoulders as I walk down the street.

Kane sees me and winks, before turning back to his conversation. I spot Maxx next and he growls at me. Curling my lip, I snarl back. *Fuck you.* Maxx makes a move toward me. *Shit.* "Maxx, what do you think?" Kane calls Maxx's attention back to their conversation, saving me again.

See? He can't be as bad as Abby and Kassie said he is. He could've let Maxx come after me, but he didn't. Putting the thoughts I have of Kane away, I walk up the path to the porch where the small gathering is.

"Hello," I say, waving at everyone.

Some say "hi" back, most just stare at me, suspicion in their eyes. I take a deep breath, trying to calm my nerves.

"What's a beautiful young lady such as yourself doing

in this part of the pack?" an older woman says. Looking at her, you'd think she has to be pushing seventy. She has dark skin, with her silver hair pulled up in a tight bun. "A lady like you should be in one of those big houses with her mate, being spoiled and loved."

"Well, you got some of it right," I chuckle. "I'm Elle," I say to the lady and everyone else.

The old lady smiles. "My name is Athena." She looks me up and down. "So what part of what I said was true? I hope it's the love and spoiled part." She chuckles softly.

My smile falters. "I wish it was," I say to my feet.

"Well, child, you came over here for a reason." Athena points to a vacant chair. "Come on up here."

I oblige, walking up the steps and sitting in the chair next to Athena. I look at all the faces around the porch, some younger, probably in their twenties, others ranging up to their fifties and sixties.

"So, what part of what I said was true?"

Grimacing, I sigh. "Well, I live in a big house, but there is no love. I guess he's my mate, though." I let out a breath, might as well tell them the truth. "I'm Drake's mate, your Luna, I guess."

"Well, what the fuck are you doing here?" a young man asks. Someone shushes him. "Nah, I ain't shutting up." He walks over, standing over me, getting right in my face. "She's probably a fuckin' spy– she'll go back and tell the Alpha we're plottin' against him, then our rations will get cut down, and we'll have to work twice as hard." His nostrils flare, rage and hatred in his eyes.

I want to scream in his face. I'm sick of men trying to intimidate by getting in my face and shouting. Instead I take a deep breath, calming myself before answering.

"Actually, I was here yesterday. Kane brought me." I

nod my head in his direction, some turn to look at him. "I was upset when I saw your houses. You see, I've never seen a pack like this one, with the separation of classes and all. And seeing the state of your part, it made me sad. I wanted to help. Drake said I could, and that if I told him what was going on he'd 'fix it.'" Reaching up I rip out my bun, shaking my hair out. "But I know what he means by that. So I'll just tell him that you all refused to say anything to me."

They all stare at me, shocked, I think, at my honesty. "Look, I'm sorry, I shouldn't have come. It was stupid of me to think that I could change anything." Standing, I walk down the stairs. Drake isn't going to get any information from me that he could use to hurt these people even more. It's not happening.

"It may have been stupid, but it sure was a kind thought," an old gravelly voice says. Turning back to the porch I see a man, probably close to seventy, looking down at me. "We don't see much kindness or compassion from the ones up top. Sure is refreshing." He gives me a kind smile.

"Kind doesn't change that it was stupid. I don't want to cause you any more trouble." I look at the guy who got in my face.

"Stan has a reason to not like anyone from up top. Don't ya, Stan?" The man looks at Stan. "Well, come on now, tell her why you got so angry, son."

Stan glares at me but he motions for me to come back up on the porch. "You see," he says, looking around to make sure no one was listening who shouldn't have been. "They whipped me. I was late to my shift at the farm by ten minutes. My moms was sick, I was takin' care of her. Lost track of the time, ya know?" I nod, letting him know I'm following his every word. "I tried tellin' them that it wouldn't happen again, that my moms was sick, that I had never been late before. They didn't care."

Stan stops, breathing hard. Just talking about it is getting him worked up. "I got mad, you see, started sayin' some stuff I shouldn't have. Sayin' how most of us hated it here, and that things needed to change." Stan's pacing back and forth on the small porch – my eyes follow him, watching him get more and more agitated the more he talks. "They said I was rebelling against the alpha and that deserved punishment." He stops, breathing heavily. "I'll spare you from most of the details, but I left with a souvenir."

Stan lifts his shirt up, and what I see makes me gasp in horror. All over his back are scars. Scars on top of scars. *How?* And then I remember Kane has two whips. One has silver, and that would leave scars on us.

"I'm sorry."

Stan snorts. "Nothin' you did. That motherfucker over there did it." He points at Kane. *But why?* "Yeah, you should stay away from him, Luna. You piss him off right," he shakes his head, "you'll end up with scars, too."

"Hey! What the fuck are you talking about?" We all turn to see Maxx coming our way.

"Nothin', man, just gettin' to know our Luna," Stan says, pulling his shirt back down.

Maxx growls. "You're the one always starting shit, causing trouble." He points to the ground. "Get down here, I want to talk to you. What are you doing? Filling her head with lies? Trying to plot a way to get her away from the Alpha?"

"No, Maxx, there was no plotting." I grab his arm, trying to pull him back.

"Shut the fuck up!" He shoves me, pushing me down on the ground.

Kane helps me up. "Let's go, you don't need to see this."

"Don't want to see what? How you treat your people?" I snarl. "No, I think I'll stay."

Maxx takes a whip from his side and without thinking I rush over. "Maxx, no! Maxx! Stop!" I put myself between him and Stan.

"Move," he says.

"No."

He pushes me again and raises the whip. Before he can bring it down I slam into him, knocking it out of his hand. I climb on top of him, punching his face. He grabs me by the hair and throws me off of him. He turns me over onto my back with his foot and kicks me.

"Stop." Everything stills, Maxx stops his assault. Drake's here.

Drake looks down at me, then to Maxx. "What did I tell you about attacking her?" Drake asks Maxx.

"Alpha, she attacked me first, stopping me from delivering a punishment," Maxx says.

"He didn't need a punishment, we were only talking!" I look to Drake, pleading to him to listen to me.

Drake looks down at me. "It's not up to you to decide what warrants punishment."

"You fucking asshole! This isn't how you lead a pack that flourishes!" Pointing at the crowd gathering around to make my point, I go on. "These people, your people, look to you for guidance and leadership. And if all you give them is punishment and cruel treatment, they *will* try to defy you. And there's more of them than there are you." I meet his icy stare—I never knew ice could burn—

his eyes burning into my own. "And they will win, Drake."

Hearing whispers all around us, Drake breaks his stare and looks around at the pack members who have gathered.

He grabs my throat, pulling me close so my face is nearly touching his. "If I hear them whisper a word against me, I'll have a child whipped." His grin is malevolent, evil and sadistic. He truly is a monster. "Let's see how it works, shall we?" He shoves me away from him, Kane grabbing me to stop my fall.

My heart is going haywire, trying to jump out of my chest. *What's he talking about?*

"Bring me a child, any child," Drake orders one of his men.

No!

I hear a high-pitched scream. Kassie is being dragged from her house. Abby is crying, screaming, pleading with them to let her daughter go.

Anger flows through me. Pushing Kane off of me, I rush Drake, and, pulling him back, I punch him in the nose. I hear a crunch, I know I broke it. Grabbing a rock I bring it over my head, ready to smash his skull in. But someone stops me.

"You shouldn't have done that, Elle," Kane whispers in my ear.

"He was going to hurt her!" Not bothering to whisper, the words come out loud so everyone can hear. "He's evil, doing that to a child."

"No, he wasn't. He was provoking you, to see how you would react."

Drake spits blood. Wiping his face he glares at me, the malice glinting in his icy eyes. "You," he growls, "you *will* learn your place. I can see that I've been too easy on you."

He grabs my chin, forcing me to look at him. "You're going to learn today, sweetheart. Everyone is going to see what happens when they disrespect or defy me."

Letting go of my face he looks over at the men holding Kassie. "Let her go." They release their grip on her and she runs to her mother's arms, both of them sobbing.

"Get everyone to the post, I have a message to send." Drake looks at me. "And my Luna is going to be the messenger."

CHAPTER FOURTEEN

Elle

*D*rake is next to me in the back seat of his SUV while Maxx drives and Kane sits in the passenger seat. I don't know where we're going. Kane never mentioned a post to me.

Drake's rage has stopped rolling off of him. Now he's calm and collected. It's actually scarier than when he's mad.

No one says anything. We drive down the road in silence, just the rumble of the engine and the tires crunching over the pavement.

I look out the window and see people walking and getting out of vehicles. They're all walking in the direction the car is heading.

My wrists are bound in front of me. They're not taking any chances of me getting away from them. The metal digs into my skin, irritating it.

The car stops, Kane and Maxx step out, leaving me alone with Drake. I keep my eyes down, refusing to look at him. I can feel his stare boring into me. Normally I'd glare right back, but I don't want him to see the fear in my eyes.

"Realizing you've gone too far?" Drake chuckles. I don't respond, continuing to look at my hands bound in front of me. "Even if you did apologize, it's too late. Between you and me? I hope you do scream that you're sorry, I hope you scream to the whole pack that you'll never defy me again." Taking up a lock of my hair, he lets it fall through his fingers. "But I also hope you do defy me again, because I do enjoy making you scream. It's my new favorite hobby."

I jerk away, growling low, *'I hate you.'* Drake laughs, leaving the car. My door opens. Kane grabs my arm, yanking me out roughly. Another man grasps my other arm once I'm out of the car. There are people everywhere, forming a circle around Drake. They have a combination of worry, curiosity, and nervousness on their faces. Getting closer to Drake I realize it's not just he they're circled around.

It's a tall post, like a shortened telephone pole, standing in the middle of a circular cement platform. This must be the post Drake mentioned.

Kane and the other man, whose name I don't know, roughly pull me over to it. Once we're up to the post Kane unlocks one of the cuffs. Placing me in front of the post he grabs my arms, so it's like I'm hugging it. I can't move more than my head from side to side, scraping my face against the wood. I look at Kane, trying to find some answers but he doesn't look at me. "She's secure, Alpha," he says, his voice hard and gruff.

"Good," Drake replies. "Everyone," he calls out, his voice loud and deep with authority. "This afternoon you will be shown what can happen if my law, my word is defied." Drake walks around the post, around me. He points at me. "As some of you may know, about a few weeks ago I chose a mate, your luna. She bears my mark and yet every day she defies me. Today she has gone too far. The luna disrespected me, not only in front of my men, but also in front of some of you."

He pauses, looking around the crowd of people who are gathered around. "Today she will learn a lesson that will cut down to her bones. Maybe then she'll remember that I am the alpha and my word is law. This also goes as a message to all of you. If you defy me, this is what you'll get."

My shirt is ripped open down the back, exposing my bare skin to the air. My heart is racing, bile comes up to my throat, threatening to spill out my mouth. *I'm about to be whipped.* Drake moves behind me. I can't see anyone besides some of the faces in the crowd.

"Fifteen lashes, Kane. Make them deep," Drake drawls.

I don't hear Kane respond, I can't see what he's doing. Is he getting the whip he's threatened me with so many times before?

"Kane," Drake says again. I can hear the order in his voice. Kane still doesn't answer. "All right, then," Drake says, his voice low. "Maxx!"

"No," Kane says softly. *What? Is he going to stop this?*

Maxx laughs. "With pleasure, Alpha." His laugh is dark, humorless. It sends chills down my spine. I hear the whip crack on the concrete. Even though it doesn't strike me, the sound makes me flinch. "This is gonna hurt," Maxx jeers. I can't see his face but I can hear the smile in his voice.

"NO!" Kane's voice roars. He is going to stop this. A small bit of hope grows in my chest. Yes, he is. I saw his face earlier when he saw the bruises on me. He was disgusted, maybe even angered by it. Kane won't let this happen.

"What?" Drake snaps. "You dare to tell me 'no', Kane?" I hear footsteps, then Kane grunts— was he hit? "You dare to defy me? Perhaps you should be next."

"No," Kane says again. Feeling my body relax, I sag against the post. He's going to save me again. Just like he did in the hall with Maxx.

Maxx snorts, annoyed. "Cut the shit, Kane. Let me get on with this." He cracks the whip again, making me tense up. "You can be next if you want," Maxx taunts.

"No," Kane growls. I hear footsteps. *Fuck, I wish I could see what's happening.* "It's my job, Maxx. I'm the enforcer, not you." *What?* Any feeling of hope that I had evaporates. *He's just like them. No, worse. They never acted nice to me, but he did. He fucking played me and I fell for it.*

"Give me my whip, Maxx."

"You sure you got the balls for this? From what I've been seeing, you've grown soft for the bitch."

"Hand me my fucking whip, Maxx."

"Here," Maxx grunts. "If you don't break her skin, I'll do fifteen more. And then thirty on you," the threat clear in his voice.

"Fifteen lashes, Elle." Kane says, no emotion in his voice.

"Fuck you," I growl, the two words laced with all the venom and hate I have toward the three men standing behind me.

I won't scream or cry. I won't give them the satisfaction.

The whip cracks and for a moment I don't think it hit me, just air. Then my back is on fire, the air assaulting it, making it burn more. Tears fill my eyes.

"One," Kane says, loud and clear, for everyone to hear.

The whip cracks again, hitting me lower on my back. "AGHH!" I scream, unable to hold it back. The burn is unbearable. I have never felt pain like this before.

"Two."

The cracks come in different times, sometimes one right after another, sometimes he lets a minute go by before splicing my skin again. I'm screaming, tears running down my face.

"Please! Stop!" I sob into the wood. My knees try to give out, but there isn't enough space between me and the post to fall down. I'm stuck where I am.

Kane doesn't stop. He keeps going, his arm showing no mercy.

CRACK!

"Twelve!"

CRACK!

"Thirteen!"

CRACK!

"Fourteen!"

"This is the last one, Elle," Kane says softly.

Fuck you! I scream in my head.

CRACK!

"FIFTEEN!" I scream, my body collapsing as far as the post will let it. My back is raw, blood pooling over my sides onto the concrete below me. Every breath feels like it's going to rip me apart. I want to pass out.

"Fifteen," says Kane with a deep sigh. I hear something fall on the ground, someone comes over to me, then releases my restraints, letting me fall into them. "It's over, Elle. It's all over."

My eyes pop open, rage and hatred burn through me. "Don't touch me!" Finding strength in my rage I push him away, which makes me fall onto the hard ground on my open back.

"AGHHHH!" I roll onto my side, screaming in agony. *Make it stop, please.*

"Shh, let me help you up, Elle," Kane whispers, trying to soothe me. His voice is anything but soothing.

Ripping myself away from him, I glare daggers into him. "Don't touch me! Get away from me!" I sob. "Just leave me alone! I *hate you*. What would your mate think of you?" His eyes widen– it was a low blow, but he deserved it.

He stops advancing. He closes his eyes for a moment and walks away from me, leaving me on the cold ground.

Two men grab me under both my arms, being surprisingly gentle. It doesn't matter, every movement sends pain shooting through my body. I scream and cry out with every jostle.

The back hatch of Drake's SUV opens, the seat is down, Drake's already in the back seat that isn't folded down. The men lay me down on a blanket that was laid out. I hear the crunch of plastic underneath. Of course, can't ruin the interior with my blood.

Exhaustion takes over, I close my eyes hoping sleep comes quickly. Drake doesn't allow that. His hand fists my hair, dragging my head back so I'm forced to look at him. The movement sends the fire down my back again but I bite my lip, holding back my scream, but I can't stop the tears from flowing down my face.

"That was such a glorious sight, Eleanor." His eyes alight with lust, he grabs my hand and puts it on the erection bulging in his pants. "I've never been more turned on in my life," he muses. *Sick fuck.* "When we get home I'm going to fuck you so hard, you're going to pass out. Then I think I'll wake you up by shoving my cock in your ass. Yes.

We haven't done that yet, have we?" he asks. Looking down at me he traces my face with his finger. Not waiting for my reply, he goes on. "Yes, I think that's *exactly* what we will do tonight. I have to make sure you really understand that I own you."

I know he'll make good on those threats, but I don't care. I just want the pain in my back to stop. I don't even know which whip he used. The one with or without silver? Will today be etched into my back for the rest of my life? A souvenir, as Stan called it.

The car hits a bump, jostling my body. The pain is too much now. I let the darkness take over.

* * *

Kane

"Get away from me! Just leave me alone! I hate you!" Elle screams at me, crying, trying to get away from me. From the monster who caused her pain.

Ignoring her pleas, I keep reaching for her. I just have to explain myself. Explain that I *was* helping her. Her brown eyes pierce into me. "What would your mate think of you?" she says with vehemence. I stop reaching for her, the hole in my heart ripped open again, feeling raw like it did that day I found their bodies.

Closing my eyes, I back off. Standing up, I look down and see the pool of blood that poured off her back. My stomach knots. Turning my head in disgust I walk off the platform, away from Elle, away from Drake. I walk away from it all.

"Hey, Kane!" someone calls after me. I don't answer, I keep walking through the crowd that gathered and watched what happened to their Luna. No, they watched what *I did* to her. I whipped her until she bled, I whipped through the bruises that Drake left on her.

The crowd makes way for me, parents holding their pups out of my way, people scurrying out of my path. *They're afraid of me.* I never noticed it before. I was just doing my job, following orders. It wasn't until I saw Elle's face, heard her cries, her yelling at me to get away from her, that's when I saw how my packmates saw me.

I'm just like Drake in their eyes.

I can't take the stares anymore and I begin to walk faster. Pushing through the crowd, bumping into people. Once I'm free of the crowd I begin to run, I run into the safety of the tree line, where their stares can't see me.

Without stopping I shift, my clothes shredding to pieces. On four paws I sprint through the trees, jumping over rocks and fallen logs. My legs carry me away from the pack. It feels like I'm barely touching the forest floor, I'm running so fast.

I run for what feels like hours. The sun moves across the sky, sinking farther to the west. I stop running, panting, exhausted and thirsty. I look for a stream. Collapsing on the riverbed I shove my muzzle into the water, lapping up the cool mountain drink.

Why does her pain bother me? *Because you care about her.* I answer my own question. But do I? Do I care? *I never cared about the others Drake brought back.*

Oh yes, there were others. A lot of other potential mates who 'didn't make the cut' for his mark. They got the same treatment she did, but she has his mark. The others had the escape of death, but not Elle. She's stuck here with Drake.

So why is Elle different? Because she is different, not only to Drake, but to me as well. I never stuck my head out for any of the others. I didn't blink twice when I helped push their bodies into their graves. So why is Elle getting under my skin?

The look she gave me, that's what gutted me. She looked at me as though I was her biggest enemy. Not Drake, me. She saw what I did as a betrayal.

I have to fix this, I have to talk to her.

Turning around I race back to the town. I need to see how she's doing. I need to talk to her tonight. *I just hope she will listen to me.*

* * *

Elle

DRAKE MADE good on the promise he made to me in the car. Everything hurts, but my back is the worst.

I'm lying in a bed, not Drake's, because the blood would ruin his sheets. *Asshole.* If I wasn't in excruciating pain I probably would've slapped him for that.

As I lie on my stomach, Gerald applies a salve on my wounds. "Sorry, Luna," he says when I flinch away from his touch and growl. *Fuck, this hurts.* I stop growling. It's not Gerald's fault I'm in pain, plus he's helping me. *Which is more than I can say about someone else.*

I think that's what hurts most. Why did Kane do it? Why didn't he just let Maxx do it? *Because he's a bad man— Abby told you, Kassie told you. So did Athena and Stan.* They all said the same thing. Stay away from Kane.

He played me for a fool. I felt safe with him. Well, as safe as you can be in hell, I guess. But he never actually hit me, not like Max, and certainly not like Drake. Was it all a ruse to get me to trust him? Then he could pull the rug out from under my feet?

A knock on the door brings me back to reality. Gerald sets the bowl of whatever it is down and opens the door.

"Sir, I don't think now is the best time," Gerald says to whoever is there.

"I'm just checking on her, Gerald." I freeze, it's Kane. "Leave the bowl with me and I will finish."

"Kane, Luna," Gerald says and the door shuts, leaving me alone with Kane.

Kane walks around to the side of the bed. He resumes Gerald's task of putting the salve on my back. Hissing, I cringe away. "Don't fucking touch me!"

Ignoring my demand, Kane continues putting the globs of solution on the wounds. The wounds he put there. *Asshole. He's just like the rest of them.*

"Maxx is known for his strength and brutality when it comes to the whip. He cuts right down into the bone."

"So what you did was a sign of mercy? You think I should be thanking you?" I snap.

"It was merciful for me to take over. I didn't want to do it, Ells, but I couldn't let …" He cuts himself off, taking a deep breath. "I couldn't let Maxx hurt you. I know I hurt you, but trust me, I did you a favor."

"Fuck you, Kane." What he did wasn't a favor. He betrayed me. At least with Drake and Maxx I always know what I'm going to get. But I thought Kane was different because he treated me differently.

He was an ass, sure, but he never actually hit me or anything. And he always stuck up for me in some way. I thought maybe he was my friend, that he cared about me. But no, I see him for what he is, he's just like them, maybe even worse.

Drake and Maxx never offered me kindness and safety. Kane did, though, and then when the opportunity struck for him to give me the worst pain I had ever endured, he took it.

I hate it here. Tears stream down my face.

"I don't blame you," Kane says. I look at him, bewildered. I must have said it out loud.

All the pain of leaving home, of leaving my family behind comes crashing down on me. I feel my face get wet with tears, the sheet soaking them up.

Thinking of my dad, Sam, Meg, Jon, Connie, and even Noah opens the hole in my heart, leaving me gasping for air. My silent tears turn into gut-wracking sobs, making my back scream from the stress of the movements.

"I hate it here. I hate all of you," I choke out between sobs. "I hate being beaten and raped every night. I hate being away from my family. I want to go *home*. I wish I never stepped out of line that day."

"Wishing for a different outcome is fucking pointless and childish. I thought you would have known that by now." I look at Kane, his face hard. "If you want a different outcome, you have to make it happen. Not just hope everything changes."

"What?"

"You hate the beatings and being raped? You hate being a prisoner? Then change your status. Change how Drake sees you."

Raising my eyebrows I stare at him in confusion. "What the fuck are you rambling on about?"

Kane groans, tossing the bowl on the dresser next to him. "God, you're so fucking thick sometimes, you know that? I have told you before how to change things, but you don't listen."

"You've told me to submit, to give up fighting. I won't stop fighting, Kane," I vow. "I'll fight until the day I die."

He shakes his head. "I never once told you to give up."

"It's the same fucking thing."

"No, it's not, Elle. And I honestly don't think it's possible for you to stop fighting. You have to think differently here."

"I'm confused and you're rambling. Just spit it out."

"You have to show him you're different, Elle. He chose you because of your spirit, the fight you have in you. Use it against him. Find his weakness, become his weakness." Kane drops onto his knees and looks me in the eyes. "Make him fall in love with you."

CHAPTER FIFTEEN

Elle

Make Drake fall in love with me? Kane's advice, or lack thereof, keeps going through my mind. He left right after that, and I've been in this room healing for two days. Drake has, for the most part, left me alone, though he checks daily on my healing process to see 'when I can join him in his bed again.'

It's an impossible task. Drake can't love or feel anything like it. He's too sadistic, he enjoys giving pain too much to actually love anything. Infatuation and obsession could be possible, but doesn't he already show that when it comes to me?

The idea of willingly sleeping with him and submitting makes me sick, but if it's my own decision that means I'm in control.

What's the worst that can happen? More terrible things he's already done to me hundreds of times?

Fuck it, I'm going to try. I just have to figure out a way to make it believable. Can't lay it on too thick, that will be obvious. Happy with my plan, I crawl out of the bed, my back tight from the muscles stitching themselves back together.

Looking in the full-length mirror, I can see that I'm healing well. The welts are light pink and puffy, soft to the touch. Looking weeks old, not two days. They will be gone and smooth skin will return. Drake will be displeased. I saw the look in his eyes when he saw the damage done to my back. He enjoyed it, it turned him on. *Sick fuck.* Hmm, maybe I can use that to my advantage. I look at the clock. It's three in the afternoon. I have enough time to get myself ready for dinner.

I'm going to join him for dinner. Tonight I start the process of making Drake fall in love with me.

* * *

IN DRAKE's room I look in the closet for something to wear. Trying to convey sexy, keeping in mind the welts on my back. I need something flowy and comfortable, too.

I find a simple black dress with a low back. I throw it on the bed and taking off my towel I slip the dress on over my head. It's not too short, sitting mid-thigh, the neck scoops just below my collar bone. Not too revealing, but shows off the soft curve of my neck and Drake's mark. He'll really love that, my putting it on display that I'm his. *Ugh,* the thought makes me cringe. *You're going to be doing a lot more than showing the stupid mark, so get over it,* I chastise myself.

The back is perfect. It's low on my back, sitting right at

the hollow. It shows the welts perfectly, and also isn't sticking right to them so it's a plus for me. They're still tender.

I go into the bathroom and blow out my hair, adding volume and shine to it. Plaiting my hair into a braid that falls down over my shoulder, I move on to makeup. Not going for a sexy look. I don't want to be obvious, but I take the time to do more with my face than I have in the past few weeks. *Has it really only been just that? A few weeks?* It feels like I've been here for years. Putting on some coverup to hide the dark circles that seem to be a new permanent fixture to my face, I also add some mascara and eyeliner to make my eyes pop.

Satisfied with the woman in the mirror I take a deep breath and walk out the door. Finding my way into the kitchen, I run into Kane.

He takes me in, looking me up and down, settling on my face with his eyebrows raised.

"What are you looking at?" I snap. I still haven't forgiven him for whipping me the other day. I don't think I ever will.

A sly grin slowly spreads across his face. "You," he says. Kane shakes his head. "I can't believe you're actually going to try."

"You gave me the idea!" I huff. Crossing my arms, I stare him down. "Now," I sweeten my voice, making it soft, "Where is Drake?"

"Jesus," he laughs. "He's in his office." Kane walks out of the kitchen. "Come on, I'll take you to him." He's still laughing. *Jerk.*

"I can get there myself, thank you," I snap.

"Oh, I know you can, but I wouldn't miss this for the apocalypse," he chuckles.

Glowering at the back of his head I follow him down the hall to Drake's office. "I'm still mad at you," I say quietly. "Just because I heard what you said the other night doesn't mean you're forgiven."

"I know," Kane says softly.

When we reach Drake's office, Kane knocks on the door. "Enter." Drake's low voice penetrates the solid wood door.

"I've brought your luna to you," Kane says, opening the door, allowing Drake to see me. "At her request," he adds. I glower at him and he chuckles as he closes the door, leaving me alone with Drake.

Feeling Drake's eyes on me, I walk over to the shelves of books. Looking at the contents I let out a laugh, shaking my head.

"What's so funny, sweetheart?"

"There're no books here on how to be a sadistic asshole." I turn my head to look at him. He's staring at my back, like I knew he would.

Chuckling darkly, he moves over to me. "No, there are no books in this office about that." He touches my back, trailing a finger along a welt. "You're healing well, I see."

"You sound disappointed."

"Kind of. It was a glorious sight, seeing you being whipped, seeing you bound with nowhere to go. Hearing your cries for it to stop." He presses his lips to his mark on my neck. "Gets me hard thinking about it."

"You're sick and twisted, you know that?"

Drake grabs my arm, twisting it until I gasp in pain. "Why are you here?" he snaps.

I want to rip my arm out of his hand and slap him. But I'm not here to cause myself more trouble, I'm here to try and get under his skin.

Taking a deep breath I let it out, calming my anger from a raging blaze down to embers. "I was sick of sitting in that room," I say, looking at the floor.

He lets go of my arm and I walk over to the large window that overlooks the garden. "You've left me alone for the most part the past few days." Peeking up through my lashes, I watch his face. It's unreadable.

"I figured you'd appreciate the time off."

"I did. It gave me time to think."

His eyebrows shoot up. "Think about what?" he asks.

"About us, I guess." Sighing, I bring my eyes to his. "Look, I'm really hungry. Could we talk about this over dinner?"

Drake looks confused. It only lasts a second before he straightens up, his demeanor changing. He walks over to me until he's standing so close I have to tilt my head up to look at him. Suspicion in his eyes, he stares at my face, trying to read it. "Why?" he asks.

"Like I said, I've done some thinking," I say, adding some attitude behind my words. "If you don't want to have dinner with me, just say it." Without waiting for his response I head towards the door.

"Go tell Maxx and Kane to go home." Turning around I see him back at his desk, looking at the monitor. His gaze lands on mine. "We dine alone tonight." I acknowledge him with a nod, then once the door is shut behind me I lean against it, smiling to myself.

That was our first conversation that didn't end up with me having a new bruise. *Calm down, you have a long way to go before you can claim 'victory.'* I find Maxx and Kane in the entertainment room, watching TV. Leaning against the door frame, I smirk at them.

Maxx glares at me. "What the fuck are you smirking at?"

"Your face," I say, taking a seat on the couch Kane is occupying. "You know, you really should think about getting that unibrow trimmed and waxed. It looks like you have a large wooly bear living above your eyes."

Kane snickers beside me, keeping his face on the TV.

Maxx growls. "Calm down, that's an easy fix, Maxx. But the rest of your face ..." I shake my head. "Now that's going to cost a lot of money to fix."

Kane bursts out laughing. Maxx looks like he wants to kill me.

"Oh, and both of you need to leave," I say nonchalantly, looking at my fingernails. "That's an order from your alpha."

Kane's laughing comes to a stop and he looks at me with shock on his face. Neither one of them says anything. "Yeah," I sigh. "You're both going to have to figure out dinner on your own." I smile, knowing this is pissing Maxx off. Kane still looks dumbfounded.

Maxx stands, leaning over me. "I don't take orders from you," he snarls.

Remaining unfazed I look at my other hand. "I'm Drake's mate, that makes me your Luna, which makes this my house." My eyes flick to his. "Now get out." I see Kane leave out of the corner of my eye, hearing the front door open and shut. I look back at Maxx. "Maybe you should get your ears checked, too. Apparently you can't hear well. Leave, now."

"Fucking bitch!" Maxx snarls. Grabbing my braid he rips me off the couch, throwing me onto the floor. "I. Don't. Take. Orders. From. You."

"Maxx!" Drake walks into the room. "What did I tell you the other night about touching my mate?"

"Alpha, she insulted me and tried to kick me out of your house." Wow, a tattletale.

"Let her go," Drake says, the authority clear in his voice.

"But, but sir, she—"

"I told her to come in here and tell you to leave," Drake says coolly.

Maxx releases my braid from his grip. "Drake, I didn't realize it was a true order from you. I thought she was trying to slip out on you." *Now that's insulting, I'm not that dumb.*

"Whatever, I don't care. Just leave," Drake tells him. He rushes out of the room and I climb to my feet. Drake rounds on me. "Stop antagonizing my beta. Now, it's time for dinner."

He places his hand on the small of my back, leading me into the dining room. Once we sit down Gerald brings wine out for us to sip on until he brings the food out.

We sit in silence, sipping our wine. Gerald brings in our starter, French onion soup. It's delicious, as usual. I smile at Gerald– he's been the most kind to me the past two days. Hell, the whole time I've been here Gerald has been amazing. Something I'll always be grateful for.

It's not until our main course is served that I break the silence. "You know," I say as Drake looks at me, taking a bite of his steak. "I think I realized something, while I was recovering." I cut into my steak and take a bite, chewing slowly.

Drake eyes me. "And what was that?" he asks.

Shaking my head I grab my wine. "it's stupid, forget it." Taking a sip, I wait to see if he takes the bait.

"Tell me."

"Well, I'm your luna, right?"

"Hmm." Drake sets his silverware down, giving me his full attention.

"Don't you think that maybe you could treat me like one?" I look down at my plate. "I hate that you hit me." It's not a lie, I do hate it.

"You defy me at every turn. You deserve it."

"You took me from my home, my family, you didn't even give me a chance to adjust." I sigh, "I also know you enjoy it, inflicting pain on me. Why is that?"

Drake refills his glass and takes a sip. "It gives me control over you. I hit you, you scream in pain, making you cry. It's all from what I do to you. My effect on you." He smirks, "It's a powerful feeling."

I nod, even though what I really want to do is throw my wine in his face, grab the knife by my hand and stab him. Deciding it's not a good idea I take another sip of wine instead.

"You like feeling powerful?" I ask.

"Yes, who doesn't?" Drake looks at me from the corner Of his eye. "Being in control of someone's life, or in my case, hundreds, knowing you're the one who can make the call of who lives or dies, it's a feeling I can't explain."

"How many people have you killed?" I can feel my stomach twist in knots.

Drake muses for a moment. "You know, I honestly forgot how many." He seems bored. "I've taken out entire packs, sometimes killing everyone, even the pups." He doesn't seem disturbed by this at all, there's no remorse in his tone.

Sick, he's really sick. A thought passes through my mind,

maybe it will pique his interest. Maybe it will work, maybe it won't. Anything is worth a shot at this point.

"I've killed someone," I say quietly. Meeting his eyes I see something flash in them.

"Really?"

"It was a rogue," I nod. "He was stealing and destroying things in our pack." Pouring myself another glass I take a long drink, needing the liquid courage. "When we caught up to him, I asked him why he was there, he wouldn't answer. I snapped his neck."

Drake doesn't seem bored anymore. He's looking at me like I'm the most interesting thing he has ever seen. My stomach twists like it did that night— it didn't feel right, taking someone's life so easily. It still doesn't feel right.

"How did it make you feel? Did you feel your blood pumping faster through your veins?" It's working, he's loving this.

Closing my eyes I go back to that night, trying to remember exactly how I felt. Beneath the nausea and shock of what I had done, I realize then that Drake is right. I didn't enjoy it, but it definitely made me feel empowered. "Yes," I say. *Am I no different than Drake?* The thought is enough to shake me to my core.

Drake growls, and at that moment Gerald pops into the room. "You're excused for the night," Drake says, not even looking at him. "You can clean up in the morning." He's staring at me, the look of desire on his face.

"Alpha, Luna." Gerald leaves the room and Drake pulls me out of the chair.

He brings me down to the end of the table that wasn't used, void of plates and glasses. Drake seats me on the table, moving my legs apart so he can stand between them.

"Tell me more." Grabbing my braid he pulls my head back, exposing my neck to him.

Blanching, I shake my head. "I've only killed the one rogue."

"There has to be another incident that made you feel empowered." He trails his tongue down my neck. I shiver at the feeling– it doesn't feel good, my skin crawls under his touch.

"Rafe," I say. Drake pulls away, a dark look in his eyes. "A guy in my pack, he always challenged me. One day he lost it, attacked me. Tried to kill me."

"Obviously you're still here, so what happened to him?" Drake pulls my dress down off my shoulders, exposing my breasts to him.

Grabbing his face, I put my thumb next to his eye. "I gouged his fucking eye out." I press into his eye just enough to make my point.

Drake growls, grabbing my hand. He pins it to the table and presses me down. Pushing my dress up to my waist I hear his belt coming undone. Closing my eyes I wait for his assault.

* * *

When I wake up the next morning I'm surprised to see I'm not alone. *Fuck.* Stretching my limbs I don't feel the agony I have gotten used to feeling, I look down at my body. There're some bruises on my wrists and thighs, but that's it.

I think back to last night. Drake was . . . I don't want to say gentle, but he was definitely different. He didn't beat me.

Whoa, it's working already. I have to find a medium here. I have to still defy him to a point, not pushing too far. But I can't submit fully to him either. Well, that's just perplexing. Drake grunts, rolls over and sits up. He doesn't look at me, just gets up and closes the bathroom door. Hearing the shower turn on I relax.

Hmm, that was odd. Grabbing for my bathrobe I wrap it around me, finding comfort in the puffy fabric. Maybe in a few weeks or months, if I play my cards right, I can call my father.

I miss him so much. I miss Sam and Connie. I miss Meg, too. We were so close to becoming best friends, if we weren't already. Thinking of home makes me realize everything I don't have here.

I don't have any friends. Gerald is nice, he talks to me and allows me to taste test all the food I want, but I wouldn't say we're friends.

The closest person I have to a friend here is Kane, and that all changed when he demanded he be the one to whip me. I know he says he did it because Maxx is worse. Maxx would have made it hurt more. It's hard to believe, that was definitely the worst pain I have ever felt in my life. I don't know if I'll ever be able to forgive him for that. But I need a friend here, and Kane is the best option for one.

Sniffling, I wipe the tears from my eyes. "Why are you crying?" I hadn't realized Drake was out of the shower. He looks annoyed.

"I just miss my home." Sadness comes over me, I blink back tears as I look up at him.

He cups my cheek, wiping a tear that got away. "No one makes you cry besides me." Shoving my face away he walks into the closet. *Asshole.*

"Kane will spend the day with you," Drake drawls, coming from out of the closet. "I have more important things to do than babysit you."

What else is new? "Does it have to be Kane?"

"Would you rather it be Maxx? I'm sure he would gladly switch places with Kane."

"No thanks, I just healed from the last whipping. Maxx would find a reason for another one." I leave the bed, heading towards the bathroom.

Drake chuckles darkly. "I look forward to the next time you get whipped."

So much for my progress last night. Angry, I storm up to him, getting right in his face. "For someone who claims they like the power they get from inflicting pain, you sure use your men to do an awful lot of your dirty work," I hiss. "What is it, Drake? Are you a coward? Too weak to strike the whip yourself?"

His hand snaps up to my throat. "There you are," he says, squeezing my windpipe. I can breathe, but only just. "I was beginning to wonder where all your fire went." Drake presses his mouth to mine and my hands ball into fists, wanting to punch him. *No, I can't hit him,* I tell myself. *This* is the happy medium, this is the balance. Push him, but not too far. Piss him off, but not so he beats the shit out of me.

"I told you before, you'll never take that away from me," I choke out.

He chuckles. "Oh, I think a few more times at the post may change that." He releases me, I stumble back trying to regain my balance. A low growl rumbles in my chest. "Oh, and Eleanor?" Drake pauses, waiting for me to look at him. "Next time it will be me. And maybe next time I'll fuck you while you're still tied to the post, so everyone can see." He pulls open the door, slamming it shut behind him.

Well, fuck, that went well.

* * *

KANE and I are sitting on a rocky shore by a lake. He offered to get me out of the house and I accepted his offer. We haven't said much and the air around us is thick with tension.

He's an enigma, that's the only way I can describe him. One moment he's a total asshole, the next he's saving me from Maxx, then he demands to be the one to whip me, and now we're here, sitting on the rocky shore not saying anything.

I don't know where he stands in all of this. He's loyal to Drake, but he hates how Drake treats me. It's beyond confusing.

Kane picks up a rock. He rolls it in his hand before tossing it in the water, making ripples in the otherwise calm water.

"So," Kane says, pulling me out of my thoughts. "How's the whole 'get Drake to fall in love with you' plan going?"

"Like I would tell you," I scoff. Like I said, he's loyal to Drake. Who's to say he won't tell Drake my plan.

"I'm the one who gave you the idea, ya know." He throws another rock, this one larger so it actually splashes the water.

"I don't trust you," I say matter of factly. And I don't, not after the other day.

Kane sighs. Sitting next to me he looks at the ground. "Look, I already told you what that was all about. I told you *why* I did it. I didn't enjoy it, Ells. I'm not like him."

I contemplate his words, taking in his demeanor. "Is Maxx that much worse?"

"Yeah, he is. He had the whip with silver, too."

Instinctively I reach around and touch my back, now almost completely healed. By tomorrow or the next day it will be smooth, like nothing had ever happened. If Maxx had done it I'd still be bedridden, and I'd have large, angry scars to serve as a reminder.

"I understand why you think you helped, but you didn't. I thought that ... I thought we were ..." I can't get the words out. I trail off, not knowing how to tell him how I feel.

"Hey." Kane puts his arm around my shoulders, squeezing me. "For what it's worth, I'm sorry this has happened to you."

I whip my head around to look at him and he's smirking.

Shoving him away I stand up. "You're such a jerk!" I smile at him, remembering the last time he said those words to me on my first day here.

Kane laughs. I haven't quite forgiven him, but he's my only ally here. Even though I know he'll never openly oppose Drake, the little saves he does for me mean the world to me.

"We should head back." Kane has started walking toward his truck. I look at the sky. The sun has started its descent below the horizon. The smile falls from my face.

Now I have to go back and pretend I don't hate Drake with everything in me. I have to let him do horrible things to me and I can't fight back. If I could just get him to trust me, to let his guard down, I'll make my move. I'm going to get out of here.

CHAPTER SIXTEEN

Elle

It's been three weeks since I changed my strategy. I've been working diligently on trying to get Drake to fall in love with me. Though I think 'love' isn't the right term— I'm making myself irreplaceable to him. And I think it's working.

The more I comply and submit to him the gentler he becomes. And I'm not talking about making tender sweet love to each other. I just do as he tells me, and he still smacks me around. But the bruising is minimal. Now when I snap at him or do anything to piss him off he doesn't beat me bloody. No, he just shoves his dick in one of my holes, depending on his mood.

It disgusts me. I feel like a whore. I don't enjoy it, though lately I find if I rub myself I can get a little wet, providing lubrication. However that means Drake thinks

I'm reciprocating, and I'm attracted to him. *It's working in your favor, so shut up and deal with it.*

Sitting in front of the fireplace in the bedroom, I try to concentrate on a book, but I keep rereading the same sentence over and over again. As I toss the book aside the door opens.

"Good evening, sweetheart." Drake strides into the room, heading straight for the liquor cabinet. "Did you miss me?"

Like the world misses polio. "Mmm," I say.

"I couldn't stop thinking about how I want to fuck you tonight." He sits on the couch, in front of my floor nest.

"How romantic of you." I sneer. He chuckles, not saying anything else. I'm sure he already has a plan in his twisted head. "Do you have anything planned for Kane tomorrow that would keep him at the house?"

He eyes me suspiciously. "Why?"

"I just wanted to go for a run," I say shrugging. "It's hard to do that when my babysitter is stuck here doing work for you."

"He has more work to do than just entertaining you all day."

"Like what? Whipping people into submission?" I snap.

Drake's chuckle is low and dark. "Something like that. Why? Are you ready for more?"

"No, once was enough for me." I tilt my head at him. "I thought I was doing well behaving and all. Are you waiting for me to slip up?"

"Sweetheart, I'm always waiting for you to slip up."

I grab the book next to me, opening it, refusing to look at him. We sit in silence for a few minutes, me pretending to read while Drake stares at me.

"I'll set aside two hours for Kane to take you out."

"Thanks."

"When was your last yearly?"

My head whips up to him, shocked at his question. "Why? Are you afraid you might catch something? It's a little late to be worried about that."

"Are you on birth control?" he asks, ignoring my snarky comment.

"Yes. I got the shot a week or so before you took me. Why?"

He takes a long pull from his tumbler, watching me. "I'm going to schedule you an appointment with the pack doctor. You need a full examination to see if you're ready to bear my pups."

I take in a sharp breath and I feel the blood drain from my face. *What? No!* I can't be here that long, I can't bear his pups, give birth to them. That would tie me to him forever. I have to get out of here. Leave the damn continent if I have to. This cannot happen.

Drake nods and smirks at my appalled expression. He drains his gin, and motions towards the bed. "Strip and get on the bed. I'm going to enjoy your body while I can until it's ruined."

* * *

I'M WAITING for Kane in the garden. Gerald was out here earlier, chattering about tonight's dinner menu. I barely listened. I couldn't focus on anything he said. I've been in a fog all day. *I can't be here for another nine months.* The thought of carrying Drake's pups makes me want to vomit.

Raising little psychopaths, that's not something I want to do. Well, probably only one. The first-born male, that's what Drake would want to claim as his own. I'd probably raise the rest and worry about how they're treated by their own father.

But it's not happening. I just have to wait for the opportunity to present itself and I'm leaving this place.

"Hey, are you ready to go?" Kane asks, standing in front of me. How long has he been standing there? My thoughts have me so consumed I didn't even notice him out here until he was right in front of me.

"Yeah, let's go." I say, subdued.

As we walk to the tree line a thought comes to my mind. *Don't shift.* Hmm, if we get far enough away, maybe I can give Kane the slip and run. Maybe he'll let me go once I tell him Drake's plan.

Will Kane help me with this? He's loyal to Drake, not me. But there's always the possibility he may help me get away, he didn't like seeing my bruises before. I'll have to approach this carefully, depending on how he reacts to my news that in a year there may be a bouncing baby Drake joining us.

We get into the tree line, Kane stops and I keep walking. "Uh, Ells? Don't you wanna shift here?"

"Actually, I was thinking we could just walk," I say, turning around to look at him. He looks confused but not suspicious. "There's something I have to run by you but I don't want to talk about it at the house."

"Okay, let's go then."

Walking down the path I don't say anything right away. Kane doesn't pry, we just walk in silence. Once we're twenty minutes into our walk Kane stops me.

"Okay, as much as I'm enjoying this nature stroll, I was looking forward to running." He peers at me questioningly. "I thought you were, too. Isn't that why we're out here?"

"Drake wants to knock me up as soon as I'm deemed

healthy enough." Saying the words out loud makes it even more real. Dread fills me, tears sting my eyes. I turn away from him—I don't want him to see how much even the idea guts me.

Kane strides past me, not saying a word and I follow. We walk up the path, past our usual stopping point. He keeps glancing back to make sure I'm still following. He still hasn't replied to the bomb I just dropped on him. What's he doing? Where are we going?

After another mile or so he comes to a stop. "You're going to run, aren't you?" he asks. He faces me, his face unreadable. "That's why you didn't want to shift, so I couldn't warn Drake right away." He caught on to me, he knows what I am thinking. It's like he can read my mind.

My body stiffens. "You could just call him anyway," I mumble. "I'd be caught before I even made it off the territory."

Kane picks up a large rock. I gulp, *what's that for?* He walks towards me, his face expressionless. When he reaches me the corners of his lips curl up, making a small smile.

"Not if you make it so I can't call." He holds up the rock, pushing it to me so I have to take it in my hands. Kane looks at his watch. "You would have about a two-hour head start. You can make it if you go *now*." He turns his back to me and points to the back of his head.

"You want me to *hit you?*" I ask, baffled by his request.

"Yes, that way when they come looking for us when we're late going back, they'll find me unconscious." He gives me a pointed look. "Just don't bash my brains in, okay?"

"Why do I have to knock you out? Can't you just let me go now? And say I gave you the slip?"

"No, they wouldn't believe it. They'd figure out that I

helped you. And I don't feel like dying today, so, really, you'd be helping me out, too."

This is crazy! No, insane! I shake my head, and let my hand holding the rock fall down to my side.

Kane tilts his head, giving me a sly smile. "Tick tock, Elle. You're running out of time." His grin widens, his eyes narrow. "Unless you *want* to carry Drake's pups. And maybe you do. After all, it has to be confusing for you, trying to play with Drake's emotions. Maybe you're starting to believe the lie you spun."

"What? No!" How could he think that?

"You're the one willingly going to bed every night with him. Putting on makeup and dressing sexy."

"You're sick," I snap. "I'm only doing all that to find a way out!" I can't believe he's saying this. *He's* the one that gave me the idea. Not me, Kane, I'm just playing it out.

"And yet here you are. I've given you an opportunity and you're not taking it. So that makes me wonder, Elle, do you like it now? Do you like the way he fucks you? Does your pussy milk the come right out of—"

I smash the rock into his temple, cutting off his disgusting words, and Kane falls to the ground. Standing over him, still holding the rock, I wait to see if he's knocked out. Thirty seconds go by, then he groans. Leaning down my hair falls over my face, making a curtain covering both of us. "Guess I'm taking my chance after all." I bring the rock over my head and smash the back of his head this time.

Kane doesn't move, doesn't make a sound. I wait a few minutes, checking his pulse and heart rate. I know he's still alive.

Throwing the rock down, it tumbles and rolls, stopping

next to Kane's body. I notice blood trickling down his face from where I hit him.

I take one last look at Kane, then, taking off at a sprint, I fly through the forest, shifting mid-stride, my clothes ripping into pieces.

I run south– with no place in mind to go, I just run. Keeping my eyes and ears open to anyone in the area, I'm shocked to find no one. I don't slow down, I push myself to keep going. Even after two hours and leaving Drake's territory I don't stop. My lungs are on fire, my legs hurt, begging for a break. But my mind is stronger. I keep running.

* * *

DARKNESS HAS SETTLED over the forest. I found a large fallen-down tree to take refuge under. Exhausted from running for god knows how many miles, I curl up and surrender to sleep.

Something startles me awake. Pricking my ears up, I listen for whatever or whoever could be out there. Scanning my surroundings I don't see anything. I take in a large breath, trying to smell whatever it is that woke me up. Nothing. Just the normal smells of the forest. The sweet smell of pine sap, the sharp scent of evergreen firs. Wet leaves disintegrating into the dirt. But nothing out of the ordinary.

Forcing my body to relax, I lie back down, curling up to keep warm. After closing my eyes for just a few minutes, I'm back up on all fours, searching for whoever is threatening me.

"Eleanor, sweetheart."

My hackles rise— it's Drake. Growling into the night, I spin around, trying to see if he's anywhere close to me.

"*Come back, Eleanor. If you come back on your own, I promise I'll take it easy on you.*"

Liar, he won't take it easy. He'll probably take me close to death if I go back to him. I don't answer him, lunging over the log I continue running south. I'm already out of his territory. The mind link sounds far away, like a radio that is almost out of range.

"*Fine, do this the hard way,*" Drake growls in my head. "*I'll find you wherever you go. And I'll drag you back, chaining you up so you can't get away from me again.*"

Still refusing to answer, I fly through the forest. My muscles are screaming for me to stop. A few hours of restless sleep wasn't enough. *Keep running, Elle,* I command myself.

When I see daylight peeking its way over the horizon I slow to a walk. I have to be far enough away at this point. I have a pretty good head start. I notice a small clearing come up, and upon getting closer I realize there's a cabin. It doesn't smell like anyone's been here for a while, the air is too stagnant.

Shifting into my human form, I try the door handle. Locked. *Damn.* Walking around I check the windows. They're also locked. Frustrated, I look up at the sky. *C'mon! I need a little help here,* I say to absolutely no one.

Fuck it. I'll break the glass by the door handle and unlock the door. I only want something to wear while I'm human. A naked twenty-year old woman will definitely cause a scene.

I find a rock and bust through the glass. Reaching through I unlock the door and walk inside. It's a hunting cabin, nothing fancy. Two rooms, a kitchen and a bedroom.

Looking through the closet I find some pants and shirts. *Now I just need a bag to carry them in.* Aha! I see a backpack hanging on a hook. This will do. I shove the clothes inside.

I don't bother looking for food, I can hunt my own. "Thank you," I say to the small empty cabin as I close the door. Hopefully whoever owns it realizes I only took a few things.

I shift back into my wolf, grabbing the bag between my teeth and change direction. Heading east now, I have to find a bus or something to travel in so they can't follow my scent. With that thought in mind I search for a river. Walking in the water will help mask my scent, and typically if you follow water you'll find civilization.

* * *

I SPENT my day walking through the waters of a small river, cutting out onto the banks when the rapids got too rough for my liking. Apparently, water doesn't lead you directly to towns. Go figure.

Just a few more miles. If I don't find anything promising, I'll stop for the night and rest. I didn't have to walk much farther before coming up on a footbridge crossing the stream. Taking in the smells around me I can tell this bridge is frequented often.

I step into the bushes, shifting back into human form. Rummaging through the backpack I put on the clothes I stole from the cabin. They're too big, so I roll the pants at the waist and legs so they fit slightly better. I tie the shirt into a knot at the side so it's not so baggy. Grabbing the bag I climb up the bank and onto the trail. There's a sign, the big wooden kind that has an overhang on them that are in parks and national forests. Reading the map, I realize if I cross the bridge it will take me farther into the woods. If I go the other way, I'll only be five miles from the trail head's parking lot.

Adjusting the bag on my shoulder, I turn my back on the bridge. Where there's a parking lot there's a road, and roads lead to towns. I guess following water works after all.

It takes me a little over an hour to make it to the parking lot. I'm exhausted and hungry. I have no money, no cell phone. I'm screwed. Sighing to myself as I walk to the road, I see a sign that reads NEXT TOWN FRANKLIN 15 MILES. Well, shit, that's going to take me three hours, which wouldn't be so bad if I'd had a good night's sleep and some food in me.

I hope Kane's okay, I think as I walk down the road. When cars pass going in my direction, I hold out my thumb hoping someone will give me a ride. No one stops so I trudge on. I feel exposed on the road— what if Drake has his men out driving all over the place looking for me? The thought is unsettling, even though I'm pretty sure I did get a very good head start. Plus, I don't think Drake would waste resources randomly sending his men out to look for me in various locations.

A truck zooms by me. I don't bother holding my hand out. I've given up on that. I probably look like a crazy person who lives up on the mountain, no one is going to stop for me. The truck slows to a stop, the parking lights come on, and I see a hand wave out the window.

Running up to the truck I stop outside the passenger side door, and the window rolls down. "Well now, you look like you've had better days," a woman with gray hair, probably in her sixties, says to me through the window. "Where are you headed?" she asks, her eyes and smile genuinely kind.

"Uh, town," I say. I don't know where I'm going. I only know who I'm running from.

She pats the seat. "Well, get in. I'll give you a ride, darlin." Climbing in the truck I smell cigars, my guess being from her husband. She's not a wolf, that I'm sure of. Her scent is too domesticated. "Seatbelt," she says pointedly. I buckle myself in and she pulls out onto the road.

"My name's Pat," she introduces herself. "What's yours?"

"Elle," I say, cringing when I realize I told her my name and not an alias. *It's too late now*, I chide myself.

She glances me over. "I can't help but notice that you don't have any shoes."

"No, ma'am, I don't."

"That's kind of odd, don't you think?"

"Yeah, it is."

She eyes me, wary of my appearance. Looking in the side mirror I don't blame her. I'm a mess. My hair looks like it hasn't been brushed in days, twigs and leaves matting it down. I'm covered in dirt, wearing ill-fitting clothes and no shoes. I'm a goddamn train wreck. *No wonder no one stopped.*

"Where are you heading to, Elle?" I shake my head. I don't know where I'm going.

"Bus stop, I guess."

She laughs. "You have any money?" *Fuck, I forgot that part.* I sigh, feeling defeated. "No money, no shoes." Pat eyes me from the corner of her eye. "You look like you've been through hell and back, maybe twice. You're running from something."

Staring at my hands in my lap I don't answer. It wasn't a question, it was a statement. And she was spot on.

Pat turns the truck onto a dirt road. I look at her nervously. "I thought you were taking me into town?"

She shakes her head. "Honey, looking like you do now, with no money and I'm assuming no ID, you'll be picked up by the police in ten minutes. Now, I'm not trying to pry into your business, but you don't seem like the type to be running from the law. But you are running from something, aren't you?"

I let out the breath I've been holding. "Yeah, Pat. I am." The confession burns in my throat. I don't offer any more information, in fear of crying if I talk out loud.

Pat doesn't say anything for a while, letting me be alone in my thoughts. We pull into a driveway, and a beautiful log cabin-type house comes into view. She puts the truck in park and turns to look at me. "Did he hit you?"

I nod. "Yeah, a lot."

"Why don't you just go home?" she asks, "Don't you have family?"

The mention of home is my breaking point. The tears spill out onto my cheeks, falling into my lap. "I can't go there, he'll find me." It's the first place Drake would look for me.

Pat reaches over, rubbing my back. "There now, shhh, it's going to be okay."

Rubbing my sleeve across my face, I sniffle. "Thank you."

"Let me tell you what we're going to do." She looks at me expectantly. "We're going to go inside, and you can get washed up. My daughter, who is at college, has a bunch of clothes in the garage that she went through to donate." Pat looks me over again. "You seem to be a similar size so they should fit. Though anything is probably better than what you're wearing now." I laugh. Pat has the kindest eyes I have ever seen, full of warmth for a stranger she just met. "Then we'll see about getting you on that bus."

CHAPTER SEVENTEEN

Meg

"WHERE IS SHE?!" Drake roars in Sam's face. He and his men had rolled onto our territory with no warning, barreling down the road until they reached the packhouse.

Sam growls and squares his shoulders. "You shouldn't be here, Drake. I suggest you leave." The order is clear in Sam's tone. Drake backs up a step, still looking furious.

"Where is Eleanor?" he demands. "She attacked one of my men and took off." Drake looks at his men. "Find her, I know she's here."

Sam steps up to Drake. "Your men will do no such thing," he snarls.

"She's here, I know she is, and I'm going to find her," Drake spits. "She's mine, and I want her back. She has my mark on her, that means she belongs to me!"

"She's not here," I call out, walking toward them. Drake eyes me up and down, which sends creepy crawlies up my skin. "She's not here," I say again, looking him in the eyes. Sam grabs my arm, keeping me from stepping any closer to Drake. "Do you honestly think she's that stupid?" I snort. "This is the last place she would go, because she knows you would look for her here."

Drake glares at me. "You should teach your mate some manners when it comes to talking to other alphas."

That does it, I'm going to teach him some manners. "If you're so big and tough, how'd you lose her? Huh?" I snap. Sam wraps his arms around my waist so I can't get any closer to the asshole who took our friend. "You took her from us!" I yell at him.

"She came willingly," he hisses through clenched teeth. "I should destroy your tiny pathetic pack— she broke her word, who's to say now I can't break mine?"

"You didn't give her a fucking choice, you lunatic!" I scream. "You made her choose between her life or her pack's! That's not willing."

Sam holds my arms, pushing me back. "Meg, stop this right now!" Turning to Drake he sighs. "What will it take for you to leave?"

Drake smiles. "I just want to look around. Make sure she isn't hiding somewhere."

Sam closes his eyes. "Fine, but you'll have escorts."

What?

I'm beyond shocked Sam's allowing this. "What the fuck, Sam?"

He kisses me and I melt— fucking mate bond makes it impossible to stay angry at him. "Go to Roman, now!" Sam whispers in my ear. "Take Noah with you." He kisses my cheek before he walks over to Drake.

"Let's go, Noah," I say, grabbing his arm and walking toward his car.

Noah doesn't say anything. He's been really quiet since Elle's been gone. I wonder why that is. But now is not the time to think about that. "Head to Roman's place," I tell him once we're in the car.

After Elle was taken, Roman stepped down from alpha, asking Sam to take his place, just as Elle had asked him before she was ripped from his arms.

He hasn't been the same since. Who could blame him, though, his only daughter taken from him by a sadistic psychopath. After everything went down Sam made some calls around to other packs asking about Drake. Nothing he heard was good.

No one in the pack has been the same. Connie doesn't have as much sass to her. She's slowed down on the housework, too. I've picked up on it, seeing I live there now. I had to.

Sam has changed, too. He doesn't goof around anymore. He's not playful, all serious. It doesn't help that he's also alpha now. That's a lot of stress. Jon is still beta, working side by side with his son until he can step down when Sam finds a replacement. But that is easier said than done. It was supposed to be Elle and Sam leading the pack. Everyone thought Elle was going to be here forever, so now that she's gone it feels like the pack isn't complete.

"So," Noah breaks the silence. "We learned one good thing. He marked Elle."

I whip my head to him, puzzled. "And how the fuck is that a good thing?"

"Because it means she's alive and he intends to keep her alive."

"Okay, back up." I hold my hands out in front of me. "What the hell are you talking about?"

He sighs, rubbing his chin. "He's had other 'mates,' right?" Noah makes quotations around the word 'mate.' "But from what Sam's found out, they don't last long. You don't mark just any wolf you want in your bed for a little while. You mark the one you want around forever."

I scoff, "And how is that a good thing?" I can't imagine being bound to that beast for any length of time, let alone forever.

Noah looks at me. Parking the car in front of Roman's house, he smiles, "Because it gave her a chance to run."

"Did you love her or something, Noah?" I ask, unable to hold back the question burning on my tongue.

Noah's eyes pop out. "What? No! No, seriously, it's not like that." He responds to the 'really' look I give him. "Really, it's not. Elle looked out for me a lot. I'm not exactly the strongest wolf in the pack. She stuck up for me, let me hang around her and Sam. They didn't let Rafe mess with me."

No wonder he got all quiet when she left. Watching the person who used to stick up for you get kicked around and dragged off must be hard to deal with.

"But we know she's alive and fighting. And that's good enough for me," Noah says to me.

Nodding, I open my door. Roman has come out of the house, watching us with wary eyes. He's aged in the short time Elle's been gone. There's no light in his eyes anymore. They're full of sadness and loss.

"Roman!" As I run up the path, his eyes widen in concern.

He meets me at the bottom of the steps. "Meg? Noah? What's wrong?"

"Drake is here," I say, "looking for Elle."

"Elle?" He sits on the step, seemingly unable to hold himself up at the mention of her name. "Why's he looking for her?"

"She ran, Roman. She got away." I beam at him. "She found a way out and she took it!" He looks shocked.

"Wha- why- how?"

"Drake said she attacked one of his men," Noah claims, coming to stand beside me. "She's fighting, Roman. She hasn't given up."

Roman doesn't speak, lost in his thoughts. Different emotions flash across his face. Sadness, grief, anger, bemusement. Finally it settles on amused.

"That's my girl," Roman smiles.

CHAPTER EIGHTEEN

Elle

"'C'mon, you asshole! Let me in!" I yell at the big behemoth of a man staring down at me.

He just looks at me, unfazed by my little temper tantrum. "Sorry, miss, I have to wait for the alpha's permission."

"Ugh! How many times do I have to tell you that he knows me!" I glower at him. He shakes his head and points to a chair I can sit in while we wait.

I give up trying to get through his thick skull to just say "Elle is here to see you, alpha" and go and sit in the chair. The man nods, happy with my compliance. *Jerk.*

The past twenty-four hours have been interesting. Pat and her husband, Daniel, opened their home to me. They let me shower, gave me food, and even allowed me to crash in their daughter's room for a few hours. They gave me a few outfits from the donation pile, and as luck would have it, their daughter and I have the same shoe size, so I got a pair of old beat-up 'Chucks', too.

They gave me money for the bus, too. Pat and Daniel showed me the kindness I didn't believe existed outside of my pack. I've seen so much evil in the past month or so my view on the world has changed.

I got on the bus, getting off at various stops and towns, making my way to the only person I could think of who would offer me sanctuary.

So here I am, waiting for the alpha of this pack to come down to the end of the road that takes you into his territory.

"When's he going to be here?" I ask the man. Blake? Clark? I can't remember, nor do I give a shit.

He doesn't look up from his phone. "When he gets here" annoyance is clear in his tone.

Tires crunching down the gravel road pulls me from glaring at what's-his-name. The vehicle comes to a stop outside the small building. "Brock, what's going on that you need me down here?" A familiar gruff voice comes from outside. Brock goes outside to greet the person behind the voice.

Brock! That's his name. Oh well, who cares. "She says she knows you, alpha." *Oh, what a good soldier you are.* "She insists on seeing you."

A tall figure walks into the small room, making it feel crowded even though it's just the two of us in here. "Hey, Jared."

He glares down at me. "What the fuck are you doing here, Elle?"

Shrugging, I look up at him. He's pissed. "I was in the neighborhood. Thought I would stop by." Smiling meekly at him, I hope our past friendship helps me in this situation.

Jared jerks his head to the door. "Get in the truck, Elle." He sounds annoyed.

Taking my bag, I wave at Brock on my way out. "Thanks for keeping me company!" I say over my shoulder. Jumping in the truck I look at Jared. "So, how have you been?"

"Cut the shit, Elle!" he snaps. "Do you have any idea what position you being here puts me in?"

Well, shit, I didn't think about that. I didn't even think Drake had told anyone he had taken me as his mate. Guilt consumes me. I've put his pack in danger.

"I didn't think, I guess."

"Yeah, no shit you didn't!" He slams his fist on the steering wheel. "Fuck, Elle! I have a mate now! A pup on the way! A fucking pack full of people to keep safe!"

I can't look at him, the anger in his eyes is too much. Staring at the dashboard I reach for the door handle. "Look, I'm sorry. Just take me to the end of the road and forget I was ever here."

"Jesus Christ," Jared groans. "Stop, Elle, you're already here. It's almost time for dinner. You might as well stay."

"Thanks." I offer him a small smile and he laughs.

"Yeah, well, if I'm late for dinner again this week, Kayla will have my head."

"Well then, you better not be late."

We pull up to Jared's house. They don't have a main packhouse like my pack does. The alpha has their own house, and they live there until they die.

Seeing a curtain move in the window I wonder if that's Jared's mate, Kayla.

"Ah, fuck," Jared groans.

"What?"

"We're late," he says. "Well, maybe bringing home a stray will soften her up." Smirking, he leads the way into the house.

"Jared! Where the hell have you been?" a small dark-haired woman, her belly round with the expected pup, snaps. Jared puts his hands up in surrender.

"Babe, something came up and I had to—"

She points a wooden spoon at his chest. "Something always comes up! It's always something!" She pokes him in the chest to emphasize her words. "I've told you that once this baby arrives you won't be doing any late night—" She spots me. Shock on her face she looks back at Jared and me. "Uh, who's this?"

"Kayla, this is Elle. Elle, this is Kayla, my mate."

I hold out my hand. She takes it, still looking stunned that I'm in her house. "Nice to meet you."

"Uh, yeah. You, too." She turns on Jared, looking reproachful. "You didn't tell me we were expecting company."

"I told you, something came up." He points to me. "This is 'something'."

"Well, sit down," Kayla chastises, waving at the table. "There's plenty, Elle, please sit."

Kayla serves spaghetti and meatballs with garlic bread. I take a bite. The simple meal is amazing. I can tell the basil and tomatoes are fresh. The savory taste of the garlic butter toast rolls over my tongue. "Kayla," I say in between mouthfuls, "This is delicious. The sauce is homemade right?" I ask, pointing at my plate with my fork.

She chuckles, her face flushing at my compliment. "Thank you. If I had known you were coming, I would've made something else." She gives Jared a pointed look.

"Babe," Jared's voice is muffled, full of food. "I didn't know she was coming." Wiping his mouth, he looks at me. "Why are you here?"

I know he knows I'm mated to Drake. Otherwise he wouldn't have had the outburst he did in the truck. "I ran." I push my plate away, no longer hungry. The thought of Drake makes me lose my appetite. "I didn't know where else to go. I couldn't go home, Jared."

"It was fucking stupid of you to run, not just here, but in general," Jared snaps. Kayla jumps at the hostility in her mate's voice.

"Who did you run from?" Kayla asks me.

I look at Jared, trying to gauge how much I should tell her. His eyes narrow— he doesn't want her to know. "Don't worry about it, babe," he says dismissively. "I have to talk to Elle alone."

Her face contorts with fury. "Oh no you don't! You're not kicking me out of my own damn kitchen, Jared." She shifts her attention to me. "Who are you running from?"

Looking between them I weigh my options. I should listen to Jared since he's the alpha. However, Kayla seems like a force of nature you could compare to a tornado. Plus, she's pregnant, and I think I heard someone say you don't want a pregnant woman mad at you.

"I ran from my mate."

Kayla gasps. "But why?"

"He's not my mate by my choice. He gave me an ultimatum, either go with him willingly, or he'd slaughter my pack and he'd take me anyway." I swallow, trying to lubricate my mouth. "I chose to go willingly."

Kayla's hand covers her mouth, looking horrified. "And you knew about this, Jared?"

"Yes." He doesn't look at her, he sounds ashamed.

"And you allowed it?!" she cries out. "Why didn't you tell me? We could have done something!" Kayla's fists ball up on the table, sending Jared daggers with her glare. Jared looks like he has no idea how to calm her down. It's very amusing to watch.

"He couldn't have done anything," I say, trying to appease Kayla. "Drake isn't someone you want to cross. Trust me."

It then dawns on me how stupid it was for me to come here. Seeing Jared and Kayla, with her swollen belly, the thought of them getting hurt because I dragged them into the middle of my issues is like a punch to the gut.

Kayla and Jared are in a heated conversation about how they can help me. "Look, I'm sorry for coming here. I can leave tomorrow morning. But I would *really* appreciate a full night's sleep. I've been on the lam for three days and I've barely slept."

And I mean it. I'll leave at first light. It was reckless of me to come here. If I wouldn't put my pack in danger, how could I possibly put Jared's at risk?

I'll keep going. Stopping here and there, making money finding odd jobs to do for people. I'll find my way into Mexico and go south from there. Or maybe I'll do a big loop, go back up through Canada after going east and cut back west. Alaska wouldn't be too bad. Would it? It will be harder for Drake to find me if I zigzag through the continent. Eventually I'll be able to settle down somewhere. Maybe even find a pack that will take me in.

"How big of a pack does this Drake have?" Kayla's words cut through my thoughts, bringing me back to their kitchen table.

"Close in size to ours, baby," Jared says, grabbing the

plates and taking them to the sink. He starts washing them. "He's not an enemy we want."

"Are we allies with him?"

"No, but we're not enemies either. I made it clear that I don't like how he approaches things in his pack. But I also told him I don't want a fight." He shrugs. "Basically we agreed not to piss each other off. I'm breaking our agreement by having Elle here."

Kayla's gaze cuts to mine. Her face tells me she's deep in thought. "You said he's not your true mate?"

I nod, reaching for another slice of garlic bread to nibble on.

"How old are you?"

"Twenty."

"So you can still find your true mate?" she asks. Her eyes are full of excitement. What's she thinking about that's got her all happy?

"I mean, I guess, but it wouldn't help much." Seeing her confusion, I go on. "Even if I did find him, my true mate, Drake would just kill him and take me anyway." I glance at her and Jared. Kayla's face shows revulsion and Jared's has no emotion at all.

She taps her finger on her chin. "Maybe in *his* pack he could do that. But he couldn't do it in another pack. Not without starting a war." Her eyes have a devilish look in them.

"Kayla ..." Jared's voice is full of warning.

She whips around to face him. "Let her stay, Jared." Jared and I both start rambling excuses as to why that's a bad idea. Kayla gets up and wraps her arms around him. "If she finds her mate here he can't take her back."

Jared's eyes cut to mine, then back to Kayla's. His gaze

softens when it reaches her face. "Call me the fucking match maker," he growls and Kayla squeals with delight.

"You have three days to see if your mate is here," Jared says. "After that you have to go." It's an order. I'm not good at taking orders, but in this case, I'll do anything to not have to go back to Drake.

I nod. "Deal."

Kayla's beaming, rambling about loopholes. Jared bursts out laughing. Kayla and I share a confused look before looking at Jared. "What the fuck, dude?" I ask.

It takes him a minute to stop laughing enough to talk. "The last time I saw you, you were so adamant about not wanting a mate. Now you'll be going through my pack looking for him, like it's your last hope."

"That's because it is, Jared," I say solemnly. Jared stops laughing, Kayla looks at the floor, absentmindedly rubbing her bump. Grabbing my glass, I look at them. "It's the only chance I have."

* * *

"THANKS FOR THE COFFEE," I say to Kayla. We're both sitting at the kitchen table. "And the bed, too."

She waves her hand dismissively. "It's no problem at all." She sips her orange juice – something about only being able to have so much caffeine a day while pregnant. It sounds awful. I couldn't imagine not being able to have coffee throughout the day. But she doesn't seem to mind, smiling and humming to herself as she scurries around the kitchen.

Jared has already left, going to tend to pack matters. Seeing how different he is now with Kayla, not the same egotistical jerkwad he was the last time I saw him, makes me smile. Kayla spots it from across the room.

"What's so funny?" she asks, tilting her head.

"I was just thinking about how different Jared is from the last time I saw him." Laughing, I shake my head. "He's not the same arrogant 'I'm a man so I know better than you' Jared." The difference must be her. That's the only explanation for it.

"Ha," Kayla scoffs. "I put a squash to that when I first got here." Her gaze drills into me. "He saw me, threw me over his shoulder, and brought me back here." Her eyebrows scrunch in her scowl. "Fucking caveman."

"He did not," I gasp.

"Mmm, he sure did." She smacks her lips. "Tried doing the whole 'I'm the alpha, I'm the man of the house' spiel." Kayla dropped her voice low, doing a horrible imitation of Jared. I laugh– she's funny and spot on. "Of course, I did the only thing you can do in that situation, because they don't listen to words."

"What was that?"

"I cut him off. Every time he was a jerk and then tried making a move on me, I'd be like "Nope, not happening." She looks up to the ceiling. "*Then* he listened to me."

"Figures," I snort. "Take away sex and men don't know what to do with themselves."

Kayla nods, taking a sip of her orange juice. "So when do you want to go into town?"

Eyeing her belly I ask, "Are you sure you're up for it?"

"Psh, please. I'm not at the bedrest stage yet, and I don't plan on ever being there either." She sets her glass in the sink. "Now, let's go see if we can find you a mate."

* * *

My mate isn't here. I have been here for three days, walking all over the pack, visiting various places. And nothing. Kayla looks discouraged, upset that her idea didn't work. It was a good idea. A long shot, but a good idea.

It feels wrong, looking for my mate for the wrong reasons. Looking for him as a form of sanctuary and not for love.

Kayla groans, lounging on the couch, flipping through movies trying to find something to watch. "I'm sorry, Elle. I was hoping it would work."

"Nothing you or I can control. I'll leave here tonight. I don't want to overstay my welcome."

Hurt forms on Kayla's face. "I don't want you to go. I don't want you to be on the run for the rest of your life. You shouldn't have to live in fear of being caught and dragged back." She brushes a strand of hair out of her eyes. "it's just not fair."

She's right, it does suck. But if it's what I have to do, it's what I have to do. "Life isn't fair, Kayla." She rolls her eyes. "No, seriously. I made a choice to go with him. I made a choice to protect my pack. I went with him, he beat me and did horrible things to me, so I ran. I have to live with the consequences of my actions. So if that means I run forever, then I run forever."

"Still sucks," Kayla mumbles.

We go back to finding a movie, settling on *10 Things I Hate About You*. About halfway through Jared comes striding into the house, standing outside the living room.

Kayla perks up. "What's wrong?" she asks, sensing the urgency rolling off of him in waves. Jared's eyes cut to mine, staring into me with apology. *What's that about?*

He holds up his phone. "Drake is at the entrance."

My heart drops to my stomach. *He found me.* Kayla

jumps to her feet. "Stall him!" she urges. Rushing to Jared she puts her hand on his chest. "We can sneak her out one of the back roads."

Jared looks at his mate. I can see the inner fight he's having within himself. He'd do anything to make her happy, anything to keep her from being upset. "I'm sorry, I know it's not fair, but he's marked her. Elle belongs to him. Keeping her here will only put everyone in danger."

I hate being referred to as a possession– I don't belong to anyone but myself. Let alone that psychopath. But he's right. I have to give myself up, again. I can't be the reason for a war. I don't belong to this pack. Jared holds no obligation to me, despite our friendship. But sometimes that isn't enough.

"I'll go to him, there's no reason for him to step onto your lands," I say, standing up from my seat.

"No, there *has* to be something we can do!" Kayla cries. "You shouldn't have to go back to him."

"Babe," Jared consoles her, brushing his thumb across her face.

She smacks his hand away. "Don't you fucking 'babe' me! This is wrong!"

"You hardly know her, why do you care?"

"Because no one should be treated like a possession, no one should be beaten on a daily basis and forced to serve their abuser. It's inhumane."

Jared bristles. "We're not human, Kayla."

"You know what I mean. It's wrong." Kayla turns to me, grabbing my hand, and she starts pulling me to the room I stayed in. "C'mon, we'll sneak you out. You'll have to be fast, but you can do it."

My feet stay planted, refusing to budge. "Kayla, he'll

smell that I have been here. If he knows I've been here and I wasn't handed over when asked, he'll declare war."

Tears fill her eyes. "He's going to hurt you again."

"Probably." I'm not going to lie to her, or myself. I'll be lucky if Drake doesn't chain me up in a dungeon or something. I look at Jared. "Let's go."

My stomach knots the closer we get to the entrance road. My heart beats a million times a minute. I don't know what Drake will have in store for me, but I do know it's going to make me regret running.

Pulling up I can see Drake, Maxx, and Kane standing outside the SUV parked next to the little shack Brock made me wait in. Brock looks uncomfortable. When he sees Jared's truck he visibly relaxes. It could also be the convoy of trucks behind us. Jared isn't dumb, he brought some men with him.

Jared parks the truck. "I'm sorry, Elle," he says quietly, "I wish there was any other option."

I reach across the seat, pulling him into a hug. Drake snarls outside. *Fuck you.* "It's okay, Jared." He looks at me with disbelief in his eyes. "Really, I'll be okay."

"No, you won't," he says, calling my bluff.

Drake keeps snarling. "I better go. Before he rips me out of your truck."

Jared jumps out. Walking around the front of the truck he opens my door, helping me out.

We step in front of the truck and stand there. Drake makes no move to come get me. It's like there's an imaginary line no one can cross except me.

"Sweetheart." Drake lets the word out slowly, adding malice to the 'pet' name he's given me. "I've missed you."

I don't respond, looking from Drake, to Maxx, finally settling on Kane. *He's alive and here.* Drake notices my stare.

"Don't look to him for help anymore, Eleanor. After you left him unconscious in the woods, I whipped him back into shape." His smile is cold. "He got a lesson he'll never forget, didn't you, Kane?"

Kane meets my stare. His lips curl and he releases a vicious snarl. Gone is the friendly look in his eyes, he's Drake's man through and through. The 'lesson' he was taught must have reached through to him.

"Come here, Eleanor." Drake motions with his finger, beckoning me to him.

I can't move, I don't want to go back. I look to Jared, silently pleading with him to find a way for me to get out of this. *Please, don't make me go.* He doesn't meet my eyes. "I'm sorry, Elle, I really am." He grabs my arm and moves me toward the imaginary line. Back to my tormentor.

"Wait!" I cry. He stops, looking down at me. His face is devoid of emotion. "Call my father, tell him I'm still alive, and that I love him."

Jared's face softens and he nods. "I'll do something even better. I'll go see him myself and tell him in person."

"Thank you," I say softly. And I mean it, for everything he's done for me.

Squaring my shoulders, I walk across the line that apparently only I could walk over. I know I'm over it because Maxx and Kane step forward, grabbing me, shoving me to the ground on my knees before Drake. "Sweetheart," he murmurs, "how much I have missed you. Though I will say our time apart has given me a chance to plan your homecoming."

"A party? For me? You really shouldn't have gone out of your way like that." Sarcasm drips from my words.

Drake grabs my hair, yanking my head back. "That

pretty little mouth of yours still likes to talk, I hear. I know a remedy for that."

I laugh. "I hope you're not talking about your dick, Drake. That thing's so small I could recite the Constitution with it in my mouth, and you'd still be able to understand every word I say."

He slams his fist into my face. *Damn, not even a backhand first. Guess he's not playing nice anymore.* Not that he was ever nice. "Get her in the car," he snaps at Maxx and Kane. "I'm ready to get her home."

They haul me up to my feet, pushing me to the car. I wrench myself out of their grips. "Get the fuck off of me! I can walk, you know."

Maxx grabs my arm, pulling me into his face. "You will do as you're told, bitch!" His breath hits my face— being so close to his makes me breathe it in the foul odor.

"Don't fucking touch me!" I use my free arm and punch him in the face.

Maxx roars, "Hold her Kane. I'm going to teach her a lesson." Kane restrains my arms behind my back.

"Doing his dirty work now, are you?" I snap.

"Shut up," Kane growls in my ear. He's not saving me, not this time.

Maxx comes forward, his fist collides with my face. Blood gushes out of my nose. He doesn't stop there. He punches and kicks me until I sag in Kane's arms. He lets me fall to the ground, where Maxx continues his assault, kicking and stomping me into the dirt. He straddles me, punching my face again and again. I know my eyes will be swollen shut after this. My face will be unrecognizable for a few days.

When he finally stops Maxx gets low, his mouth next to my ear. "Kane didn't save you this time. He won't save you again. No one can." He sniffs my hair. "I hope Drake changes his mind about keeping you, because then I can have a turn with you. Show you what true pain is. But for now, I'll settle with this. You look at me the wrong way, I'll beat you just like this." He pulls away from me. "Put her in the car." I assume he's talking to Kane.

I'm picked up roughly and shoved into the car. I can barely make out Drake through my swollen eyes. "Hmm, looks like Maxx beat me to my welcome home present for you. Not to worry, I have more planned for you."

I don't miss the threat in his voice. I know whatever is waiting for me back at the manor isn't going to be fun, at least for me.

CHAPTER NINETEEN

Cedric

The past few weeks have been busy as we plan our strike against Drake to steal his mate. I'm still not sure what to do with her once I have her. Bryce is set firm on torturing her, and other things I said 'absolutely not' to. What he wants to do to her I couldn't even fathom doing to another person. I'm not a rapist, and no one in my pack will be if they want to stay alive. Bryce had settled with torturing her. I haven't turned the idea down, even though it's definitely not on my top favorite things to do. Sending Drake pictures of his mate beaten by anyone other than himself will really get to him. Or maybe it won't.

Cory and Reg are firmly against the torture. Saying just taking the woman will be enough to piss off Drake, that she's already been through so much hurting her some more wouldn't bother her.

I don't know what to do. I don't know how to handle this. I want my revenge but at what cost?

Cory walks into my office. "Man, you need some sleep or something." He stares at my face. "You look like shit."

I look down at my notes, ignoring his comments. "Did you get everything?"

"Yeah, got enough explosives to cause a landslide."

I nod. "Good."

"You know you can't be anywhere near Drake, right? He'll sense another alpha on his territory."

Rubbing my eyes, I groan. We have been over this a thousand times. "I know, Cory, I know. I'll stay at the rendezvous point, and once everyone is in place we'll detonate the explosives. That will hopefully pull Drake's attention away from his mate. Once they're on their way there, Bryce will grab her, taking out whoever stands in his way. After we have her, you'll bring her back here. We may have to consider taking longer routes to get back, though."

Cory nods. "Sounds good, except one thing."

"What's that?"

"Reg and I are with Bryce. Tom has the experience in this stuff, he can lead the others with the diversion part."

This is giving me a headache. "Why do you need to be with Bryce?"

"Because we don't trust him," Cory says simply.

That pisses me off. First Reg with Jasmine, now Cory with Bryce. Fuck this. "I trust him, so that should be good enough for you," I snarl.

"Well, it's not," Cory shoots back. My head jerks back, like he's just punched me. "Reg and I are with Bryce or we're not going at all."

"Whatever." He's put me in that fucking rock and a hard place, and he knows it. Cory knows we can't pull this off without either one of them. I have no choice but to give him his way.

Stifling a yawn, I rub my eyes. Those damn dreams keep waking me up at night.

"Man, seriously, what gives? Why are you so tired?"

"I don't know. I just feel restless, so I don't sleep well." I don't feel like talking about the dreams with Cory.

Cory eyes me with suspicion. He's not going to let this go.

"What's the matter? Doesn't Jasmine help you out with your stress?" He waggles his eyebrows at me like a complete idiot.

"No, yes, I mean, I don't fucking know anymore." Sighing, I stand and look out the window. Jasmine used to be the best distraction. But now with these damn dreams, that woman in them, though lately she hasn't been there. It's been me wandering the forest looking for her. Ever since the dreams started my feelings have changed toward Jasmine. Something inside of me doesn't feel like it's a good fit. And it's screaming at me loudly.

Cory stares at me, waiting for more explanation. Fuck it, what's the worst he's going to say? That I'm crazy?

"I've been having dreams for a few months now. They started off slow, maybe once a week. But now they're every night."

"What are you dreaming about? And what does that have to do with Jasmine?" Cory asks.

"I don't know if they have anything to do with Jasmine. But there's a woman in them. A she-wolf," I clarify. I look at Cory, who gives me a look that says 'go on.' "So I follow her around the woods, or lie with her by this spot where the trees clear the way for the sky to show through."

"Is she hot?" Cory snickers.

My lip curls up, a low growl rumbles on my chest. He holds his hands up in surrender. "Yeah, she is. Dark brown hair, brown eyes that seem to have embers in them. There's so much light in them." I look at Cory, who has his eyebrow cocked. "Smokin' hot body, too." I grin at him.

"Niiice. But I fail to see the problem here. A hot chick showing up in my dreams— if I weren't mated I wouldn't be losing sleep over it."

I sit in my chair, rubbing my face, again. "I didn't at first, lose sleep, that is. But one night another wolf showed up. A fucking big gray one. And he challenged me for her or something. I don't really know. I just know she shifted, turning into the biggest female I have ever seen. She was white and beautiful, I've never seen another wolf like her. I told her to run. And ever since then my dreams have been of me wandering the forest looking for her or waiting in that clearing for her to show up." I bow my head. "But she never does."

My heart aches, like I should be sad about not seeing her. *But why? Who is she?* I look up at Cory like he may have the answers to my questions. He stares at me, dumbfounded. "What do you make of it?" I ask, honestly hoping he has some insight to this.

"So it's the fact she's not there anymore that you are stressed out and not able to sleep?"

"Yeah, that's when I started waking up in the middle of the night."

"You said her wolf was white, and that she has brown hair and brown eyes." It's not a question, but I answer him with a nod.

Cory pinches the bridge of his nose. "Listen," he says, his eyes meeting mine. "If I say something, do you *promise* not to bite my head off?"

"Yeah."

"Here goes nothing," he mutters. "Have you ever thought that maybe fucking Jasmine is why you're stressed out?"

Oh, not him, too. First Reg, now him? "Who I fuck is none of your goddamned business, Cory," I snap.

He scoffs, "Man, I don't give a fuck who you have in your bed. But maybe you do."

"I enjoy her," I say, not quite sure what else there is to say.

Cory watches me— no, studies me is more accurate. "Man, don't you think maybe it's best if you take a break from Jasmine?"

I snarl at him. "What?!"

"Will you just *listen* for one moment!" he growls. "Fuck!"

Trying to calm my breathing, and my temper, I nod to him.

"As I was trying to say, before you rudely interrupted, was that maybe it would be best if you separate yourself from Jasmine." I glower at him. "At least until your birthday, man. I think your dreams are making up a woman as your mate and showing you you're on the wrong path. If you just take a break until the 'true mate bond' leaves you, maybe you won't be so stressed."

Leaning back I cross my arms. "Maybe."

Cory heads to the door to leave. "Just think about it, okay? You can't have your mind fighting against your heart and soul, or whatever it is that makes the bond work. It's gonna stress you out until you snap. And we have big plans coming up. So just think about it, okay?" He shuts the door behind him, leaving me alone with my thoughts.

In the back of my head I know Cory is right, but it's

been (mostly) Jasmine and me since I was eighteen. We've never officially been a couple, and there have been times where we've taken a break before.

But this time kind of felt different, it kind of felt like we were moving forward with our relationship.

But I don't love her, and she doesn't love me. Is the mate bond/call blocking it? Or am I trying to force something that doesn't fit? Like trying to put a round block in a square-shaped hole. It's never going to work.

Maybe Cory's right. Maybe I should take a break from Jasmine for the next few months.

The thought of a break makes me relax, like a weight is lifted off of me. Until I realize I have to tell her it's over, at least for now.

Fuck me.

* * *

JASMINE COMES into the kitchen where I'm currently staring at the dishes that need to be done.

"Hey, baby," she greets me.

"Hey," I grunt in response.

"You know, you're the alpha. You shouldn't be worried about silly things like the dishes."

"They've got to get done." Submerging my hand in the hot soapy water I grab a plate and start scrubbing it.

"So make someone else do it." Jasmine stands beside me, flipping her long red hair back. "You have more important things to take care of."

"What's that?" I wrack my brain trying to think of anything I might have missed today. But nothing pops out.

"Well," she purrs, placing her hand on my chest. Her

gaze is predatory, like she's hunting her prey. The prey being me. "I have some needs that need to be tended to."

"Well, this house is a mess. We've been so busy with other pack matters that the housework has fallen behind."

"So make someone else do it. You're the alpha, you can make people do this stupid mundane shit." Her eyes pierce into mine. "Aren't my needs more important than housework?"

Is that what she thinks being an alpha is? Ordering people around to do the shit I don't want to do? Is that what she thinks being luna is like? Sitting back enjoying a drink or going out shopping, while others pick up the housework?

I never remember my mother sitting around doing nothing. She was always busy, cleaning, cooking, tending to the garden, raising my sister and me. The only time I remember her taking a break was at night, when my father stepped out of his office, or coming back from some errand, they would sit and talk. And even then, they talked about business, like when he talked to her about any troubles during the day, it unloaded the stress off of him.

Jasmine doesn't do that. It's always about her, not about me, and certainly not about what she could do to help the pack. Pissed off, I throw the plate I'm holding back into the sink, sending soapy water sloshing onto the counter. "You're right, I do have something to take care of. You can do them." Turning my back on her, I head out the front door.

Three, two, one. I count back in my head, and right on cue Jasmine slams the door open, barreling at me.

"What the fuck was that, Cedric?" she shrills.

Here we go. I look up to the sky, praying for patience. I bring my gaze back to her. "You told me I had more important matters to attend to and to find someone else to do the dishes." I shrug. "You were there, not doing anything, You can do them."

Jasmine glares at me, shock and anger on her face. "You think I'm going to do them?"

"You eat here, you help clean up. Cory and Reg are busy. So, yeah, you can do them. And if you don't want to help out, you can stop eating and sleeping here." I sigh. "You're never here for me. It's always about you."

"I'm always there for you when you need it."

"No. You're not, Jas."

Her eyes flash. Going from angry to seductive, Jasmine walks over to me, rubbing my chest. "Why don't we take this conversation upstairs? You're stressed, let me help you out with that." She kisses along my jawline, my cock twitches.

Is this how she does it? Uses sex to get under my skin? Every time I try talking to her, we end up in bed, or on my desk, or the couch. She knows how to get my body to react, to want her. But it doesn't make up for everything else lacking in our relationship, or whatever it is. I thought it was different, but now I realize nothing has changed. It's just sex.

"No," I say, grabbing her hands and pushing her away. Stepping down the porch stairs I put some distance between us. "You can't just reap the benefits of being with me, of being my luna, and not do anything to help around the pack. It doesn't work like that. My mother did all sorts of stuff, she worked for her title and respect." I rub the back of my neck. God, this is uncomfortable. "Fucking me isn't enough."

Jasmine snorts. "Sorry to break it to you, Cedric, but I am *not* your mother. And look how well all her hard work around the pack went for her. She's dead."

I see red. She's right, she's nothing like my mother. I finally see her, Jasmine, I see her how Reg sees her. A spoiled brat looking for an easy way through life and using me to get it. She doesn't give a fuck about me or the pack. Just the Luna title and what she sees as an easy ride.

"Get out." My voice is steady, calm, but authoritative.

"What?" she asks, her eyes narrowed on my face.

"I said, get out. I need some space to think and without you constantly distracting me like a bitch in heat."

Quick as lightning, pain explodes across the side of my face, making my head turn from the impact. Turning back to face Jasmine, I see her hand falling back to her side. Her face is contorted with rage. "Fuck you," she snarls. Without another word she shoves past me, storming off the porch and down the walkway.

Well, fuck, that could have gone better. Hearing a chair scrape against the porch I see Reg walking toward me, doing a slow clap with her hands. *Has she been there the whole time?*

"What?" I growl at her, not in the mood for any more bullshit today.

"That was amazing. Can I get an encore?" she laughs.

"Fuck off, Regina," I snap. She scowls at my use of her full name, but I don't give a fuck. Turning away from her I head into the house, slamming the door behind me.

CHAPTER TWENTY

Elle

Drake made good on his promise— he gave me a "homecoming gift" I'll never forget. I'll carry it with me forever. My back twinges in pain, reminding me of what will happen if I try to run again. Drake whipped me, holding the whip himself this time. Twenty lashes, twenty large scars will be on my back for the rest of my life. He didn't go easy on me, using the whip with silver in it, so every time I see my back the scars will remind me what will happen if I disobey.

After Maxx beat me on the road before hauling me into the car I shut down. I don't fight back anymore. What's the point? It only causes me pain. Oh, the snarky sarcastic comments are there, but they stay in my head. I convey my anger and hatred toward them through my eyes.

The only good thing that has happened is I now have my own space. It's in the basement, cold and damp, but it's away from Drake. Gotta look at the positives in the situation. Though the chain around my ankle makes that difficult.

Drake visits every morning and night, beating me and then shoving his dick in me, getting off on my pain. I don't cry anymore, I refuse to give him the satisfaction of my tears. But sometimes I can't help screaming in pain.

The door opens. Wondering who's coming to deliver the next beating, I look at the door. The only people who come down here are Drake and Maxx, to deliver my daily round of torture. And Gerald, who brings me food and pain medicine to help me with my pain after the beatings.

My eyes widen in shock when I see it's Kane. I haven't seen him since the day I was picked up. Sadness tightens in my chest, I miss him, I realize. Looking in his eyes they're cold and dark. There's no more light in them. He's the other Kane, Drake's Kane. Not the companion I once had.

"What do you want?" I ask, my tone sour. "Are you here to beat the shit out of me, too? Feel like you're missing out on all the fun?"

He stares at me coldly. "Brought your dinner for you."

"Gerald does that," I say.

Kane shrugs, "He's busy. I thought you would like to eat tonight so I brought your food down for you. Throw it on the floor if you'd like, I don't give a fuck." He sets the tray down on the floor next to my mattress.

I can't read his emotions anymore, he's closed off from me. "Kane, why are you so mad at me?" I ask. "It was *your* idea, not mine."

"I'm not mad at you," he replies, his words flat with no

emotion. "I was taught a lesson about being weak, and it's not one I'll forget."

"So they got you pretty bad, huh?"

He chuckles. "Not as bad as you."

Scowling, I look him over. "Yeah, you look fine to me. I don't see bruises covering your body."

"Trust me, I have scars, too." Kane tosses something at me. Catching it in my hands I look at it. A bag, with two white pills in it. I look up at him, questioning him with my stare. "They're sedatives, they'll help you sleep so your back can heal faster."

"Why?" This guy gives me whiplash. His mood swings and personality changes make me dizzy.

Kane shrugs. "Just do me a favor and wait until after Drake visits you. He'll get suspicious if you're unconscious, and he knows I'm down here right now."

Shoving the pills under the mattress I look back at Kane. "Why?" I ask again.

"'Why' what?"

"Why is it that you act like you don't care? You act all cold towards me but then you do stuff like this. It's confusing, you know."

Kane watches me for a moment, then heads towards the door without answering. He stops with his hand on the handle. "Take any kind gesture you can get, Elle, because you won't be receiving much."

"So, what? You're going to beat me, too?" I don't think I could handle that, I think if Kane took part in Drake's and Maxx's activities with me it would truly break me. It's sad he's my only friend here— cold or not, he gave me the chance to run. That's more than anyone else has given me.

Kane finally makes eye contact with me. "No. No, I

won't do that." His voice is gruff, showing emotion now. "But don't blame me if they ask me to hold you down, because I will. But I'll never lay a hand on you, Elle, not like that." He shuts the door, ending our conversation.

"That guy needs some therapy," I mutter to myself.

He won't hurt me but he'll hold me down for them. He helps me escape but also helps Drake bring me back. He says no words of sympathy for my situation, but he brings me medicine to help. It's like he's Dr. Jekyll and Mr. Hyde.

Sighing, I push my thoughts about Kane aside and grab my food. The movement stretches the wounds on my back. *Fuck, that hurts.* I can't wait for these to heal. The scars may always be there, but at least they won't hurt.

A few hours later Maxx walks in. "Good evening, bitch," he sneers at me. I glance at him briefly, then look away. He's not worth my time.

My lack of greeting sets him off. "It's not polite to ignore someone when they talk to you." He pulls my hair, yanking me off the mattress. "Or did your father forget to teach you manners?"

The comment about my father stings, like I was slapped. But I don't say anything. My silence pisses him off more than my sarcastic remarks. He throws me on the ground, kicking me in the ribs. I grunt in pain. "Ahh, so you do have a voice. I was beginning to wonder." He smiles maliciously, delivering me another kick, this time to my gut. The dinner I ate threatens to come back up. *I hate you.*

Maxx keeps up with the kicks and I feel my ribs crack. His foot lands on my face, blood fills my mouth, the salty copper taste dripping down my throat. "No one here to save you this time, cunt."

"Maxx, that's enough," Drake orders. I didn't even notice him come in.

"Just teaching her some manners, sir," Maxx explains. *What a good soldier you are.*

Drake chuckles. "I'm sure she's had a good lesson today." He bends down and tilts my face up to his. "Haven't you, sweetheart?"

I don't say anything, but glare at him with all my hatred. "There, see?" he says, turning to Maxx. "Now leave us," the order is clear in his voice.

Drake lets me go and I scramble over to the mattress, not taking my eyes off of him. "You know, I miss your smart mouth," he muses. "The fights you used to give. It got me so hard, especially when I dominated you. You still have it in you, though." He glances at me. "Oh yes, sweetheart, I see the fire in your eyes still. I know there's still a fight in you. You may take whatever I give you physically, but mentally I know you're still screaming at me inside that pretty little head of yours."

I hate his rambling— just do what you came to do and get it over with. "You know, after your birthday, I'll be able to let you out of this room again." Drake pushes me down on the mattress, bunching my nightgown, the only thing he supplies me to wear, up to my waist. I hear his belt come undone, then he forces himself on to me, holding my wrists above my head. "Do you know why that is, Eleanor?" he whispers into my ear. I offer no reply, I stare at the ceiling above his head. "It's because you'll be bound to me completely. No chance of meeting your true mate. Once the timer's up on that, you'll be mine. Even your soul."

Still refusing to acknowledge him, I continue to stare at the ceiling. Drake carries on, uncaring that I don't respond to him. "You'll still hate me, that will never change. But you won't be able to leave, the bond won't let you. You'll be mine completely."

His words break through my armor, tears well up in my eyes. His words are more painful than anything else he has done to me. And that's because he's telling me the truth. I lie there, tears falling down my cheek onto the bed, as Drake continues his assault on me for hours.

CHAPTER TWENTY-ONE

Cedric

"All right, so Tom will lead his team on the east side of the territory, setting up the explosives every twenty feet or so." I draw my finger across the map to show everyone where to go. "Bryce, Cory, and Reg will be waiting here," pointing my finger to the opposite side of the map, a few miles away from Drake's house. "Once the explosives go off, most of Drake's men will go off to see what's going on. Wait a few minutes and storm the house. Grab Drake's mate and get the fuck out of there. Take out anyone in your path."

I look up, making sure everyone is following along. No one asks a question, so I continue. "I'll be here," I point at another location on the map, just south of the border of the territory. "I'll be in wolf form, watching everything that happens with Tom's team through Dean." Dean turned eighteen a few months ago and wants to help. I don't want him getting mixed up in anything that could happen, so he'll be in wolf form, watching and keeping me updated.

Looking at Reg so she knows I'm talking to her, I add, "You'll have the radio on, so I'll be able to hear you as well." She nods. Great. "I think that's it," I say, pleased with our plan. Either it works or it doesn't. It's a coin toss.

Reg clears her throat and all eyes go to her. "What about Abel? Is this our chance to get him out of there?"

I think about it for a minute. Abel has been there for a long time now. We could grab him if he's close. But then we lose our inside ears, and we will need them more than ever, no matter how tonight goes down. I shake my head. "No. Abel needs to stay." Reg looks at me, then nods. Okay, good. I didn't need that to be a fight.

"What do we do with the girl once we get her?" Bryce asks eagerly.

Cory and Reg stiffen. The whole reason they're going with him is because they don't trust him to not hurt the woman. Otherwise, they wouldn't have opposed the original plan.

I still don't know where I stand on how to deal with her once I have her. Part of me *wants* to cause her pain because it will drive Drake mad. While the other part doesn't know if I could do it—but that's what Bryce is for.

"Nothing," I say loud and clear. "Restrain her, cover her head, knock her out if you have to. But nothing else until you bring her to me." I stare Bryce down, making sure he understands there will be consequences if he disobeys my order.

Bryce doesn't show any expression. He nods. "Understood."

"Good." I let out my breath. "All right, go get ready for tonight."

A chorus of "Yes, sir," and "Yes, Alpha" fills the room.

Everyone leaves except for Bryce. He doesn't move from his seat on a low shelf.

Sitting in my chair, my eyes find his. "What's up?" I ask, leaning back, resting my feet on my desk.

He eyes me and doesn't say anything for a while. I exhale loudly. "Seriously, Bryce, what's up?" I'm getting impatient, and as much as I do trust him, his stare creeps me the fuck out. It's like there's nothing in there sometimes.

"What's your plan with Drake's bitch when we have her?" His term for the woman rubs me the wrong way. But I don't show it. It's not her fault he chose her. The poor girl is probably going through hell.

"I don't know, Bryce. Are you asking if I'm fully on board with torturing her?"

"C'mon, Ced. She's the mate of the bastard who killed your family. Not only that, he killed everyone in this pack who was over the age of twelve. He fucking deserves to pay, and you know it. And when we have her, that's how you can start collecting your debt."

"It doesn't sit well with me. Intentionally causing an innocent person pain, I don't like it."

"Who's to say she's innocent? She's guilty by association." He grins at me. "Besides, you don't have to be comfortable with it."

I look at him, confused by what he's saying. He leans on my desk, the grin still on his face. "That's what you have me for."

* * *

"EVERYTHING SET?" I ask Dean. I'm sitting on a large rock cut that juts out of the mountainside, giving me a good view of the land. Of course, I can't actually *see* anything because I'm so far away, but it makes me feel better being here and not sitting at my desk.

"Yeah, they just got done placing the explosives. We're going to cut back in a few minutes and set the first one off, then the rest are set to detonate at random intervals. Two minutes being the longest."

Damn, that will keep them occupied for a while. We decided on random times between each explosion because by the time one goes off and they reach the site, another one will go off, causing nothing but chaos. This will give Cory and them plenty of time to hopefully grab the girl with minimal resistance.

"Cedric, we're sitting on an old access road, about three miles down from Drake's house."

Cory's voice comes over the radio strapped into my backpack that holds my clothes.

Excellent, the road must've been clear enough to pass. We did a lot of research on the layout of the land. Reg went and found an old map that showed all the old logging roads. We picked one out that would get them closest to Drake's house. From the side of the road we were able to check out, it looked overgrown and forgotten, and probably not monitored heavily.

That's also how Tom's team got in as well, an old access road that looked like it hadn't been used in years. And with the darkness the new moon brings, it worked out in our favor.

"Headed back to the truck, sir," Dean tells me.

My heart is racing, adrenaline pumps through my veins. This is it, this is the moment I have been waiting for. Tonight is my first attack on Drake. Tonight the war begins.

Sitting in the darkness I wait. A few minutes later there's a flash of orange and red. *BOOM!* The noise of the first explosion echoes off the mountain. I grab my bag with my teeth, bolting down the mountain back to my truck.

* * *

Elle

DRAKE HAS me pinned to the floor on my stomach. He's taking his time tonight. *Why can't he just get this over with?* He's completely stripped me tonight, caressing my body like we're lovers. Every time he touches me I fight back the urge to throw up. He traces the pink, puffy marks on my back. "Beautiful," he says to either himself or me, I'm not sure which.

He moves off of me. Unbuttoning his pants, he presses against my entrance. There's a loud boom off in the distance, not enough to shake the house but it distracts Drake. He pulls away. "What the fuck is that?" I hear his zipper, he slaps my ass, hard. "Get up! Get dressed." His voice sounds urgent— apparently loud booms in the night aren't normal here.

Once I'm covered, he grabs my arm and yanks me through the door. Pulling me up the stairs and through the hallway, we run into Maxx and Kane.

"Alpha, there was an explosion on the eastern edge of the territory," Maxx says, his eyes wide. *An attack maybe?*

"WHAT?!" Drake roars. "Who would dare?"

They both shake their heads. "We're not sure, sir," Kane replies.

Drake looks down at me. "Here, take her." He shoves me into Kane, who catches me before I can fall. I hiss through my teeth because Kane happened to grab me where my freshly cracked rib is. "Keep her safe. No one gets her."

At that moment another explosion goes off, "Fuck! Let's go, Maxx," Drake orders and they rush out the door. I can hear the SUV start and speed away, presumably in the direction of the explosions.

"Come on!" Kane yells at me, pulling my arm, practically dragging me down the hall. My ribs hurt from him pulling on me and running. Kane looks back and must see the pain I'm in because he scoops me up in his arms and runs through the house.

"Where are we going?" I ask, wincing in pain as he jostles me around.

"Getting you the fuck out of here." When we reach the door he fumbles around me, grabbing the handle and wrenching the door open. We reach his truck and he sets me down. Another explosion goes off to the east. "Fuck, get in!" He runs to the driver's side and jumps in. Bracing through the pain I jump into the passenger side.

My heart is racing. Who could possibly dare to attack Drake? Kane throws the truck in gear and peels down the road, the engine revving as the speedometer races up the gauge. "Where are we going, Kane?" He doesn't answer me.

His silence makes me wonder if this was *his* plan. A plan to get us both out of this pack. I know he doesn't like it here.

That thought quickly changes when another vehicle comes down the road right at us.

"FUCK!" Kane roars, slamming on the brakes. The tires screech in protest against the road. I brace myself for impact, grabbing the oh-shit handle above my door. It never comes. Instead we come to a sudden stop, and the vehicle coming at us does as well. "Wait here," Kane says, opening the door.

"What? No! Kane, get back here!"

He doesn't listen to me and he exits the truck. As soon as he does, three people get out of the large vehicle in front of us.

One of them points a gun at Kane's head. *No!*

"What the fuck are you doing here?!" Kane growls, not seeming to be fazed whatsoever that a bullet could go through his head at any minute.

Another explosion sounds behind us. Someone opens my door and grabs me. Pinning my arms to my side, they haul me out of the truck. I didn't even see them come to my door. I was too distracted by the thought of Kane getting shot.

"Get the fuck off of me!" I scream, kicking at them.

"Fuck! A little help here, please?" my captor calls out.

"I got her." It's a woman's voice. She cuffs my hands. *Fucking bitch.*

"Let her go! You'll regret this, taking Drake's mate. It's fucking suicide," Kane shouts at them.

The man holding the gun smiles. "Fuck you." He lowers his gun. Firing it, the bullet hits Kane in the gut.

Kane falls, growling and swearing. His shirt darkens with blood.

"NO! No, Kane! Let me fucking go!" I scream. "Kane! Kane!" I try fighting their grips on me but they don't budge.

"Throw her in the fucking car!" the guy who shot Kane orders.

As the other two start dragging me, I see Kane trying to get up. The man shoots him again. This time Kane falls and doesn't get back up. "No!" I sob, "please! Don't kill him! Kane!"

The shooter gets in the driver's seat, leaving me stuck between the other man and the woman. He turns the vehicle, which I now recognize as a four-door Jeep, around and speeds down the road.

"What the fuck, man? Why did you shoot him?" the man next to me asks the driver.

"He might've sent Drake a warning we were here, I stopped him before he had the chance," the driver says coldly.

Using my restrained hands I start swinging on my new captives. "Fuck you! Let me go! Why did you shoot him?!"

The driver snorts. "You should be thanking us for killing that asshole."

I try jumping in the front, smashing him in the head with my elbow. The two in the back with me grab me, pulling me back.

"Jesus Christ! Could you two fucking handle the bitch, please?" the driver snaps. "Before she causes us to wreck. Fuck."

The man and woman grab me. "Listen, you need to calm down," the man next to me says. "That man up there, he'll do whatever he can to make you stop. And believe me, you don't want that. So please, calm down."

The man looks at me. His eyes seem honest. But I don't trust him, or any of them.

"Listen to Cory," the woman next to me says. I turn my head to look at her. "*We* don't want to hurt you," she gestures to the man, Cory, next to me. "But that asshole up front would love to have a reason to fuck you up." I look in her eyes trying to find any ill intent. I don't find any.

"Why did you take me?" I ask softly. Why would anyone

want to mess with Drake? He's ruthless and has enough warriors to destroy a pack.

"Because Drake fucked with us a long time ago. Now it's our turn to fuck with him," the woman says simply. She looks at me quizzically. "Was he your friend? The one Bryce shot?"

I shake my head. "I don't know. Sort of, I guess." I feel tears streaming down my face. I know I didn't want to see him die. The Jeep hits a bump, I wince and it doesn't go unnoticed.

"How bad are you hurt?" Cory asks me.

"I don't know anymore. Lost track of all the beatings," I say honestly.

Cory looks at me, sympathy in his eyes. *Who are these people?* He looks at the woman next to me. Having a silent conversation with their eyes, she nods to him.

"Cory's going to move up to the front so you can lie down if you'd like," the woman says. "The child locks are on both the doors and the windows, so don't try jumping out."

I wasn't planning on it. "Understood." Cory moves to sit up front with the Bryce guy. "What's your name?" I ask. "I know their names" – I nod my head to the front seat— "but not yours."

She chuckles. "I'm Reg."

"I'll assume you know my name since you all planned on kidnapping me."

Cory laughs. "Unless your name is 'Drake's Mate,' to which I'll offer my sincere condolences it it is, no, we don't know your name."

"It's Elle," I say scooting over in the seat, leaning back to try to get somewhat comfortable.

Bryce snorts. "You all might want to stop with the

fucking hand-holding best buddy bullshit until Cedric figures out what to do with her."

Wow, he's an asshole. "Who's Cedric?"

Reg looks at me, the lights from the dash making her blonde hair look like it's glowing. "He's our alpha."

Great, I get to deal with another alpha who gets a kick out of stealing people like they're objects. Fucking perfect.

* * *

I'VE SPENT the last few hours watching the scenery out my window, wrapped up in a hoodie Reg graciously lent me. My nightgown, even though it covered my back, left my arms and most of my chest exposed.

Reg had even undone my restraints so I could slip my arms through the holes. Bryce didn't like this and snarled until I was once again restrained. There's definitely tension among the three of them. *Maybe I can use that to my advantage.*

I wonder what their alpha is like. If he's anything like Drake or this Bryce guy I don't stand a chance. But Cory and Reg seem to be the complete opposite. They seem kind. Well, besides the kidnapping, restraints, and not blinking an eye when Bryce killed Kane.

You don't know that he's dead. He might be fine. Wounded badly, maybe, but hopefully not dead. Though who knows what Drake will do to him when he finds Kane and I'm not with him. Guilt consumes me. If he dies it's all because of me.

Taking back roads, twisting and turning through the night, there are no landmarks I can recognize or see in the darkness. I have no idea where we are or where we're going.

Reg is leaning on her knees, talking to Cory. He's

turned so he's facing her. I don't pay any mind to what they're saying. Until they both glance at me.

"What?" I ask them.

"Er, we're going to have to cover your face from this point on." Reg reaches beside her and grabs a hood. *Wonderful.* "Can't have you knowing how to get out." She shrugs. "Sorry, it's not personal."

Bryce growls. "Stop being fucking nice to her. We didn't rescue her. She's our goddamn prisoner. So fucking treat her like one."

Reg snarls back, "Fuck you, Bryce."

"I can't wait to get my hands on her." He glances back at me. "You'll wish you were back with Drake when I'm through with you." The look in his eyes is so sinister, I believe him.

Cory shoves him in the shoulder. "Keep your eyes on the fucking road. And you don't know that Ced is going to let you have your way with her."

"We'll see." Bryce's predatory eyes meet mine in the rearview mirror. I don't think I want to know what Bryce's way is.

* * *

Cedric

THE PHONE in my pocket vibrates. Pulling it out I look at the notification, swiping my thumb across the screen to read my new message. I smile when I read the text. Stowing the phone back in my pocket, I hear a car coming up behind me.

It's Tom's team. The truck stops and three people get

out of the truck, while a handful more climb out of the bed.

"Any problems?" I call out to the approaching figures.

Tom stops walking. Standing in front of me he grins. "No, sir. None at all. I was a little worried about this one," he points his thumb over his shoulder at Dean. Dean looks like he's just walked on the moon, his eyes wide with excitement. "But he listened to every order, and he didn't give a fuss about not being able to do much besides just stand there. He's a good pup."

Dean approaches us, probably from hearing his name. "I'm not a pup anymore." He stands tall before us, his eyes narrowed.

"I guess you're not," I chuckle.

"But it was so cool!" he exclaims, bouncing on the balls of his feet. "We got back to the truck and 'BOOM!' The first explosion goes off." If possible, his eyes grow wider. "Can I go on the next one?"

Tom and I laugh. "Yeah, Dean. You can. You proved yourself and your ability to follow orders in a stressful situation."

"Yes!" Dean whoops.

"Go get some sleep, you've had a long night."

His face falls and goes serious. "Sir, with all due respect, I would like to stay here. Wait for Drake's mate. I want to see what all the trouble is about."

I study him for a moment. He should be exhausted. They all should be. Looking around at the wolves making up Tom's group I see that none of them make a move to go home. None of them look tired.

It wouldn't be fair of me to ask them to risk their lives and not see what the whole mission was about. They want to see her, too.

My phone goes off again. I check the message, it's from Cory. "They're about twenty minutes out," I tell them.

The air fills with excitement and anticipation, and my heart begins to race. The feeling that I had on the mountain comes back multiplied by ten.

We stand there, outside under the night sky that's slowly lightening toward the east. Dawn is approaching. I stand and watch the road where they will appear. Any exhaustion I had from being up for almost twenty-four hours leaves me when headlights illuminate the tree line.

CHAPTER TWENTY-TWO

Elle

"We're almost there," Reg says to me. I'm surrounded by darkness thanks to this damn hood. Seriously? Wouldn't a simple blindfold suffice? Why do I have to have my whole head covered so I'm breathing in my own stale air? I don't respond, deciding it's best to go back to my silence.

The minutes feel like hours. I hate to say it but I'm nervous about coming face to face with the alpha who would dare to steal from Drake. No matter how bad Drake fucked with them it doesn't seem worth it to me. No, this guy *has* to be insane. Which probably doesn't work in my favor.

The Jeep stops, my heart rate accelerates. There's no way they can't hear it. There's no way they can't smell my fear. My breathing hitches. *Calm down, dammit.* I steady my breaths, slow deep breaths in and out. It helps, but my heart won't stop pounding. Better than hyperventilating, I guess. Adrenaline pushes through my veins.

I hear a chuckle from the front seat. I swing my head in that direction even though I can't see. "I can smell your fear." It's Bryce. My lip curls up, I let out a low snarl. "Oh, oh! She does have a fight in her." The doors open. "I'll get her," I hear Bryce's voice through the doors.

Moving away from the door so I don't fall out onto the ground, I lean against the seat. The door opens and I'm yanked out. I yell out in pain, the sudden movement causing my ribs to scream in protest.

"Shut the fuck up!" Bryce yells, pulling me up by the back of the sweatshirt. He pushes me forward. I stumble a few times until Bryce shoves me to my knees on the ground. "Here she is, Cedric," he boasts. *Asshole.* "Can you smell the fear rolling off of her?" I snarl from under the hood. Something hits the side of my head, knocking me back onto the ground. I'm hauled back up onto my knees. I point my head down so that if I could see I'd be looking at my knees.

"That's enough, Bryce," a deep voice calls out.

I keep my head down. Hearing footsteps approach, my body stiffens, preparing for the blow I know I'm about to receive. Only it never comes.

"Do you know why you are here? Why we took you?" the voice asks.

Something inside of me stirs at the sound of his voice. I shake my head, hoping the hood doesn't obscure the movement. He doesn't say anything else. No one says anything for a while. "What's your name?" he asks. Again, I don't respond.

"Her name is Elle," Reg says, her voice coming from in front of me. I assume she's standing behind him.

"Elle." He rolls my name over his tongue, like he's tasting a fine wine. "Well, I guess it's better than calling you 'Drake's Bitch.'"

I snarl from under my hood. "I belong to *no one*."

The alpha laughs. "If that was true, I wouldn't have had to steal you from him." He touches the scar on my neck. "And you wouldn't have his mark either, *Elle.*" He sneers my name, but his touch sends a flame across my skin. *What the fuck is that about?* I ask myself.

"Just kill me and get it over with," I snap. "It will piss off Drake and you'll be doing me a favor."

"And how would that benefit you?" His voice is by my ear and I shiver.

Taking a deep breath I force myself to relax. "Because I won't have to go back," I whisper to the ground.

His footsteps crunch around me. He's circling me, probably thinking of different ways to torture me. He stops in front of me again. Feeling his hand on my head I wrench away from his touch, and a low growl rumbles in my throat. "Don't fucking touch me!" I scream. "No one will touch me like he did ever again."

I hear him sigh. "I just want to take off the hood, that's it." His voice is low, almost soothing.

"I heard what Bryce said in the car. You're planning to torture me."

"Yes, that's true, to an extent. I'm honestly not sure what I am going to do with you. That will all depend on how you behave. But it is an option."

Feeling his hand on my head again I cast my eyes down, not ready to face my new captor. As the hood is pulled off my head, my hair tumbles around me. Not able to stop myself I look up. I stare into his green eyes. He stumbles back, eyes wide, staring at me.

Something inside me moves, a hole I didn't realize was there is suddenly filled. I continue to stare into Cedric's eyes, the eyes of my mate.

* * *

Cedric

MATE! Something inside of me screams in my head. What the fuck? How? Why? *Why her?*

Looking into her brown eyes I know it's true, I can't deny it. *She's the woman from my dreams.*

I can't speak, I think I'm in shock. How is it even possible that she, Drake's chosen mate, is my true mate? My head spins. The more I look at her the more I want to go to her. But she belongs to my enemy, she has his mark.

This is too confusing. I need to get away from her. It shouldn't be like this, it shouldn't be *her.*

Turning to Cory I bark at him, "Find her a room and put her in there."

Cory's eyes widen. That's when I realize everyone is here, watching me. "What?" he asks.

"Just fucking do it!"

He walks past me over to *her.* Reg is already there undoing the restraints on Elle's wrists. The three of them walk past me, Elle looking at the ground, not meeting my stare.

Everyone is staring at me. I can't take it anymore, I need to run. I need to process this whole situation. "Go home," I growl. Without looking at anyone I walk towards the tree line. I hear someone behind me. "What do you want, Bryce?" I ask, not turning around.

"What the fuck was that?" He sounds annoyed.

I shake my head. "I don't know."

"Man, I thought for sure you would've roughed her up a little bit in front of everyone." He pauses. "I think everyone did."

Breathing deeply I try to focus my thoughts. Part of me wants to run back and do exactly what Bryce had said. The other part, the much louder part, could never hurt her. *Why did it have to be her? It fucks everything up.*

"We'll regroup later today. Get some rest."

Bryce grunts, "Cedric, we need to show Drake how much we can affect him *through her.* Yesterday you seemed open to the idea of messing her up. Now you have Cory and Reg giving her the five-star treatment." He's pissed. Too fucking bad. "I should go back and find what room they put her in, rough her up a little, take some pictures maybe, then mail them to Drake."

"Stop!" I snarl.

He goes on like I never said anything. "I know you can't do the heavy- heavy shit, the shit that makes grown men puke, but that's what you have me for. I can do it. Let me go back there and show her what hurt really is." He's twisted, absolutely fucking insane. "Think about it, man. Think about how mad Drake will get if we send him pictures or videos showing his mate is being fucked by a different alpha, or any different man."

Rage burns in my chest, pumping through my veins with every heartbeat. Without thinking, I lunge at him, pinning him to a tree by his throat. *"You won't fucking touch her, Bryce,"* I growl in his face. Pulling him off the tree, I push him back into it. "If I see you anywhere near the room they put her in, you'll live to regret it. *She's mine.*"

Bryce holds up his hands. "Okay, fine. I won't." Something inside me tells me not to believe him, but he's never lied to me before. I let him down. "If you want her all to yourself you could have just fucking said so."

I don't say anything. I turn my back on him and shift. *Fuck, my clothes.* It's too late now. Bolting through the trees, I let my thoughts take over. The thought of Bryce, no, *anyone* hurting her sends daggers into my heart. I want to turn around and go back to her. Tell her she's safe and ease her fears of going back to Drake. How can I feel such a way for someone I have just met?

I'm not going to act on it. No. As long as we don't complete the blood bond we won't be bound together forever. The thought sends sadness through me in large waves. No, I can't be tied to her forever. Once my birthday goes by it won't be an issue. It's only a few months.

Maybe I should let her go. That won't work— she knows my name, and at least Bryce's, too. I'll assume she knows Cory's and Reg's, too. If I let her go Drake could find her, or maybe she'd run back to him and tell him where to find us. Either way, letting her go is a liability I can't take a chance on.

I turn around and sprint back towards my house. She's going to have to stay here. At least for a while. I just hope that the fucking bond doesn't mess with my plans.

She can't leave. Drake's mate is now my prisoner.

* * *

BACK AT THE PACKHOUSE, wearing a pair of basketball shorts that are left outside in case of situations such as these, I head into the kitchen. The house feels full, even though it's quiet. My eyes drift up to the ceiling, wondering which room Cory and Reg set her up in.

I'm too tired for this. Tired doesn't even come close to what I'm feeling, completely drained, exhausted.

Trudging up the stairs I make my way to the only place I want to be. My bed. *Only that's not where you want to be, at least not alone.* Shaking the thought from my head I open the door to my bedroom. A sound stops me. It's quiet, muffled, but there's no mistaking the sound of crying.

Of course they put her in the room next to mine. Standing in front of the door I find myself wanting to knock. What the fuck would I do? What would I say? Letting out a low growl I turn from the door, slamming my own door behind me.

I wonder if she heard me. I hope she did. I've seen her all of one time and for only a minute, and she's already got me all twisted. I'm fucked.

CHAPTER TWENTY-THREE

Elle

I heard him outside my door. I heard his growl, and then I heard the door slam.

Cory and Reg showed me up to the room I'd be staying in. They showed me where the bathroom was down the hall. I refused the food they had offered me. I wasn't hungry. They kindly left me alone, after telling me if there was anything I needed to just get them.

Their leaving me alone is what I wanted. I needed to be alone. The weight of everything that has happened to me finally came crashing down.

Leaving my home, my father. Leaving my friends and my happiness behind. Being forced to live with Drake and endure his cruel sadistic ways of pleasure. The rapes, the beatings— it all comes to the surface.

Tears fall from my eyes onto my cheeks. I wonder if

Kane's alive. The memory of seeing him get shot, the blood pooling onto his shirt is too much. I press my face into the pillow and scream. I scream and sob until my eyes can't produce anymore tears.

He was at the door when all I could produce were sounds. *Go away, leave me alone!* I wanted to scream at the door. But I also wanted him to come in and comfort me. But he never comes in, and the slamming door made his feelings obvious. Loud and clear. Part of me is sad that he didn't come in. The other half is relieved. I want nothing to do with him. Mate or not, he stole me. Stole me like I was a possession and not a person.

Eventually sleep overpowers me. I let it take me under, into a deep dreamless sleep.

* * *

THIRST WAKES ME UP, my lips and mouth dry from not having anything to drink in—I look at the clock—about fourteen hours.

Creeping to the door I open it and peer into the hallway. Seeing no one, I dash down the hall to the bathroom, locking the door behind me.

I'm so thirsty I drink straight from the tap like a water fountain. Once my thirst is quenched I look in the mirror.

I look like shit. And that's putting it mildly. The dark circles under my eyes look like they will never lighten. My hair is a disaster, there's dirt all over my face. I'm pretty sure it's hiding a new bruise, too.

I look at the shower. It's tempting to turn the water on and sit under the hot spray. But I don't have any clothes. *Shit.*

Putting my hand on the handle I figure I'll just go hide

in my room. I don't really want to wander around looking for Reg. I might bump into *him*.

The knock on the door makes me flinch.

"Elle? Elle, it's Reg. I, uh, I saw you go in there."

I don't respond. I stare at the door like the woman behind it is going to walk through it.

"If you don't give me some indication you're alive in there I'm going to kick the door in." Her voice is stern. I don't doubt for one second that she would, too.

Opening the door a crack I can see her peering in at me. She holds up a bag, like it's a peace offering. "Hey, you are okay. I was beginning to wonder."

Deciding not to be rude I say, "Yeah, I'm okay," looking at the floor, not meeting her gaze. "I wanted to take a shower but I realized I don't have any clothes."

Reg pushes the door open, I step back to let her in. She holds up the bag. "I brought you clothes. I don't think our jeans would be the same size, so I brought you some sweatpants. There's a shirt in there, too." She offers me a smile. She seems nice, but I'm still wary of her. She did kidnap me after all.

"Thank you," is all I can say, taking the bag from her.

"No problem." She's still smiling, seeming to not be affected by my coldness toward her. "I'll let you get cleaned up. There's a new hairbrush and toothbrush in that drawer. And towels here." She points in different spots around the bathroom.

Reg almost closes the door when it pops back open. "Oh, feel free to come downstairs and get something to eat. Cory and I will be down there."

Finally the door shuts. I bolt it shut behind her, glad to be alone again. Turning the faucet on I let the room fill with steam. Stepping into the hot water I can't help but realize Reg didn't mention *his* name. So he must not be in the house.

Dipping my head under the stream of water I let go of my thoughts, trying to wash all the dirt and grime off of me. Too bad that's all I can wash off.

After my long shower, I creep into the hall. I'm tempted to go back to my room, the room I know is safe. My stomach growls and cramps in hunger, making up my mind for me. I need food.

Peering down the stairs I look and listen for anyone downstairs. I hear someone talking, so there must be at least two people down there. *What if he's in there?* The thought makes me freeze on the steps. *Seriously? If you can survive Drake, you can survive this guy. But I don't want to see him.* I'm tempted to run back up the stairs but my stomach growls, once again making up my mind for me.

Taking a deep breath I continue down the stairs and turn into where the voices are coming from, hoping it's the kitchen.

It is. Cory and Reg are sitting at the end of a long, live edge table. A floorboard creaks under my foot, pausing their conversation, and they turn their eyes on me.

Reg offers me another one of her kind smiles. "Hey! You came down. Are you hungry?"

I nod, not quite sure how to respond to her. Their kindness is overwhelming.

She jumps up out of her chair. "Sit. What do you like?"

"Uh, whatever you guys had." I nod my head to the stove.

Reg looks over at the food in the pans. "You sure? It's just warmed up leftovers."

"I don't want to be any trouble," I say, shaking my head.

"Sit," she orders and I oblige. She makes me a plate and sets it on the table in front of me. It's steak and eggs with toast. Without any table manners, I start shoveling food into my mouth, forgetting I have an audience, Connie would smack me on the head if she ever saw me eat like this.

Swiping my last piece of toast across my plate, I pop it in my mouth. I really didn't know how hungry I was. I look across the table. Cory and Reg are both looking at me like I have two heads.

Cory bursts out laughing, making me jump. "Jesus, you can eat." He looks at me. "I've never seen a woman eat like that. And she eats a lot." He jerks his thumb at Reg.

She smacks him on the shoulder. "Cut that out!" she scolds. "Don't you know you never mention how a woman eats to her?"

"I didn't mean any offense by it." He looks at me. "Sorry if I made you uncomfortable."

I shrug. "It's fine. After having to live with Drake not much fazes me." *Except their kindness. It's unsettling.*

They stare at me. What did I say? "What?" I ask aloud.

Cory and Reg share a quick look with each other. "What did he do to you?" Cory asks. "Ow!" he exclaims as Reg smacks him again.

"Sorry," she apologizes on his behalf. "He," she gives him a pointed look, "doesn't know when to keep his mouth shut."

I don't say anything, looking down at the table. I don't want to talk about it. First off, I barely know these people. Second, if I talk about it, it makes it even more real. I'll break down like I did last night— well, this morning.

They must not have noticed my scarred back. They would know, then, the type of torturous shit I endured.

"It was bad. I wouldn't wish it on my worst enemy." There, that's all they're getting out of me.

Neither one of them says anything. Standing I decide to excuse myself. I'm not used to sitting around talking with anyone. Only if it involved insults and threats. That was my normal. I look around, not really sure what to do.

Reg has gone to the sink, cleaning up from the meal. Cory approaches me, his close proximity making me flinch. He notices and steps back. "Sorry. We won't hurt you, you know."

No, I don't know. Even Kane, my ally, hurt me. I don't trust anyone.

Cory sighs. "I was going to ask you if you wanted to watch a movie or something. You'll get sick of sitting in that room real quick if that's where you stay all the time." I narrow my eyes at him, telling him without words *I don't trust you.* "The living room is through there." He points through the doorway and across the hall. "And upstairs there's a study, the third door on the left. There are books in there."

He leaves the kitchen and walks out the front door. The water from the tap stops running. "You know," Reg says. I turn to her. She's drying her hands, watching me. "I know I can't begin to fathom what you have been through. I don't think I even want to know. But most of us here, with a few exceptions, are good people."

I turn away from her, heading back up the stairs without responding. *Good people don't kidnap others,* I think to myself. I almost open the door to the room I stayed in, but I don't want to go in there. I was given options. Instead I head down the hall. The third door to the left is open, so I walk inside.

There are books in here, that's for sure. Smelling the air

I can tell this room is used a lot. There's a large desk in the middle of the room, with paperwork spread across it.

Ignoring the desk I head straight for the books. Perusing the shelves, looking for something to read, I find myself smiling when I find classic Jack London books like *White Fang* and *The Call of the Wild*.

I've read them dozens of times. I want comfort, and these books will provide that for me. I take *The Call of the Wild* off the shelf and take a seat in the large overstuffed loveseat that's by one of the windows.

Immediately I get absorbed into the story and I read uninterrupted for a few hours. I'm at the part where Buck beats Spitz when someone enters the room.

"Well, well, well, what do we have here?" Bryce strides across the room until he's standing in front of me. I shrink back into the cushions– everything about him screams danger. He looms over me, getting right in my face. "You're looking a little too comfortable." He rips the book from my hands and it lands on the floor with a soft thud.

He grins down at me, his eyes menacing. "You shouldn't be this comfortable, you're a prisoner." Grabbing my face with one hand, he squeezes hard. "I should fix that." My stomach churns. *No, no, not again.*

Pushing away, I try to get by him. If I get to my room I can lock the door. I'll be safe there. But I'm not quick enough. Bryce yanks me by the hair and throws me to the ground. Gasping in pain I try to get up, but he's straddling my back. He pulls on my hair, bringing my head back towards him. "Oh, no you don't. I'm going to have my way with you. So calm down, relax, you may enjoy it."

"BRYCE!" It's *him*. "Let. Her. Go." The words come out slow, individual.

Bryce lets go of my hair, I let my face press against the

floor. "Cedric, she was in here, I figured it was off limits to her."

"Get off of her." His tone is low, close to a true order. Bryce stands up, I scramble to the wall, trying to make myself invisible. "What are you doing here?" he asks Bryce. I notice his eyes flick to me and back to Bryce.

Bryce laughs. "I came to see what was happening with her." He jerks his head at me.

"I told you not to worry about her. Now leave." Bryce grunts but does as he's told. "Oh, and Bryce?" Bryce looks at him. "You touch her again and I'll beat the fuck out of you." It's not a threat, it's a promise. Bryce glances at me one last time and leaves, shutting the door behind him.

He walks over to where the book is lying on the floor, picks it up and hands it out for me. I take it and my fingers briefly touch his. The connection feels like hot embers, burning into my skin. I pull away, taking the book from him. *That was odd.*

"Are you okay?"

I keep my eyes down, refusing to look at him. "Yeah."

His hand comes down and I flinch. Then I realize his hand is outstretched waiting for me to take it. *I'm not touching him.* Ignoring his gesture, I stand, still not looking at his face. "What's his problem?" I ask, glowering at the door.

He doesn't answer. I finally turn to look at him. He stands in front of me with a face full of mixed emotions. Curiosity? Anger? Confusion? It's hard to tell because they flit across his face so fast.

I study him. His hair is light brown and shaggy. A strong jawline, which you can make out even though he has a full beard. Not long, it's trimmed short, but full and thick. His t-shirt is tight around his muscles. Something to make any woman stop for a second glance, including me. *What is wrong with me?!*

A chuckle comes from him, making my eyes snap back up to his. "What?" I snap.

"You like what you see?"

Heat flushes my face. "I don't know what you're talking about." I can feel the fight in me coming back.

He flashes a devilish smile. "I saw you checking me out." *Arrogant asshole.*

"Actually, I'm trying to size you up. See what kind of an opponent you are." *Liar. And he can see right through it, too.*

Another chuckle escapes his mouth. "It's okay, I've been looking at you, too. And," he glances me up and down, "I like what I see."

I glare at him. *Cocky, he's cocky, that's for sure.*

He reaches for my face. I flinch, but he doesn't stop. He noticed it, though, and his jaw clenches in annoyance. He turns my face gently from under my chin. His eyes darken. "This is healing." He softly touches my temple. Fuck, I forgot about that bruise.

Being so close to him, him touching me is too much. Stepping back, away from his touch, I feel my body relax.

His demeanor changes, going from soft and playful to hard and stern. "What are you doing in here?"

"I was told there were books in here, so I came in to grab one." I look at the book in my hands and then the one on the couch. "Or two," I add, grabbing *White Fang* off the arm of the couch.

He softens again. "Those are some of my favorites."

"Yeah, they're good." I need to get away from him. Part of me wants to run from this room and lock myself into the room I'm sleeping in. The other part of me, the part reacting to the mate bond, wants me to stay. *I want him to touch me again.* No, I don't. It's just genetics, we'd make a good line of pups. That's all. It comes down to breeding. Not actual love or attraction.

I walk out of the room and scurry down the hall. Finding my room, I slam the door shut and lock it. Leaning against it, like that could stop him from getting in here.

But I don't find the safe feeling I was looking for here. No, it's back in that room with him.

I was absolutely terrified when Bryce was on top of me. I know what he wanted to do, I know what monsters do, and he's one of them. But as soon as I heard *his* voice, I felt safe. Like I knew he was going to stop Bryce.

I'm nervous around him, though. And that's because of how my body reacts to his touch. I wanted more. How could I want to feel more of his touch? After everything I've been through that should be *the last* thing I want. I still can't get over the fact that he stole me. Though he may be a nicer captor than Drake, he still stole me like I was a valuable possession. I'm still imprisoned, still not treated like a person. He hasn't offered to let me go, so what are his plans with me?

Sitting on the bed, I hold the books to my chest like a plate of armor over my heart.

CHAPTER TWENTY-FOUR

Cedric

Hearing her door slam makes me cringe. *What the fuck was that about?*

Taking a deep breath I head into the hallway, stopping by her door. I don't hear any crying this time.

I hear voices downstairs. "What the fuck are you doing here, Bryce?" Reg's voice travels up the stairs.

At the mention of Bryce's name I growl, storming down the stairs into the living room. He's lounging on the couch, drinking scotch by the looks of the amber liquid in his glass.

My eyes narrow on him. How dare he touch her! I rip the glass from his hand, throwing it at the wall, where it shatters into tiny pieces. "What the fuck were you doing?" I snarl in his face. Grabbing his shirt I shake him violently. "I told you to stay away from her."

Bryce doesn't look disturbed by my outburst. "I went up there to look for you. Saw her there, looking all cozy." He glares at me. "She's supposed to be a fucking prisoner, chained up and in pain. Not reading books like she's at a fucking bed and breakfast."

"What were you going to do to her?"

He shrugs. "Just rough her up a little."

He's lying.

"Get out." I let him go, stepping back so he has room to leave.

He stands and looks at me. "C'mon, Ced. Let me have a go with her. You're certainly not going to."

I snap. No one is touching her. I punch him in the jaw, sending him to the ground. "Get. The. Fuck. Out." The words come out in vicious snarls. "If you come into this house again and touch her, I'll fucking kill you myself." I'm shocked by my own words. Because I mean them. If he touches her again, I'll snap his fucking neck.

"Whatever," Bryce scoffs. He's at the door when he turns around. "You know, great leaders have been brought down by pussy. I'd hate to see that happen to you. You haven't even fucked her yet and you're already all twisted." He leaves the house. Looking out the window, I watch him walk down the pathway until he's out of sight.

Cory clears his throat. Closing my eyes, preparing for his and Reg's questions, I turn around and head straight for the liquor cabinet. I notice my glass supply is dwindling, I have to stop smashing them. They at least wait for me to sit down before rounding on me.

"What the hell was that all about?" Cory asks.

I look back and forth between the two of them. I sip slowly, stalling my reply. "When I went upstairs, he was antagonizing her." That's a flat out lie. "He was going to hurt her. I stopped him before anything could happen, but he had her on the floor and was on top of her."

I look at the floor. Seeing the terror in her eyes brought out something in me. I had to stop it. I couldn't let him harm her.

Reg scoffs. "She has a name, you know."

"I know," I bring the tumbler to my lips and drain the rest of the amber liquid. "Elle." I say her name as if I'm speaking a new language. "Why was she in my office?" I ask them. I know one of them told her to go up there.

"I told her she could find some books there," Cory says. "She shouldn't spend all day and night stuck in her room. She'll go nuts."

Reg doesn't say anything. She's watching me, like she's trying to figure out what's going on inside my mind. I hate when she does that. "What?" I snap at her, tired of her analyzing me.

"Why did you change your mind?"

"You want me to beat her? I thought you were firmly in the 'don't hurt the prisoner' camp.'"

"I am," she says. "But I have to wonder what happened to make you change your mind. What made you take off running like you saw a ghost or something?"

The way Reg is staring me down, I can guess she's already figured it out. *Why did it have to be her? Why is my mate Elle? What are the fucking odds of that?*

My hand grips the glass— I set it down before I can smash this one, too. "She's my mate." Sagging into the cushions, my eyes drift to the ceiling. To where *she* is. I wonder what she's doing up there. Reading? Sleeping? I picture her curled up on the bed. If I were up there she could be curled around me. I'd kiss her, then move us both so I would be between her legs. *I want her.*

"Bryce is going to be a problem." Cory's voice pulls me from my thoughts.

"What do you mean?" I shift in my seat so my dick isn't pressing against my zipper. *Could be pressed against something else.* I rub my eyes like it's going to erase the thoughts of her out of my head. The truth is, I couldn't stop thinking about her all day. She haunted my dreams, and now she's in my thoughts.

"He's adamant we do something with her."

My head snaps up. "No one touches her."

"Not even you?" He taunts. He's pushing me and he knows it. I want to punch the shit-eating grin off his face.

"Fuck off, Cory."

He holds his hands up, "Okay, okay. But seriously, you gotta do something with Bryce."

I know I do. But I don't know how to handle that at the moment. He's always been loyal, he's just doing what he thinks is best. If I tell him no, order him to leave her alone, he will. He may not like it, but he will listen to me. *But I already told him not to touch her and he didn't listen.*

"I'll talk to him," I sigh. "I'll tell him she's my mate. That may help him see why I don't want her harmed."

"So you're going to tell everyone?" Reg asks.

Glaring at them both because I want them to really listen to what I say, I reply, "No, this stays between us." It's better this way, it's not like I'm happy about this. And she's not exactly shouting the news from the rooftop. It's better that it stays a secret, for now.

It doesn't take me long to find Bryce. I decided it was best if I tell him tonight. That way he doesn't do something stupid. Again.

He's outside his house, sitting in front of a small fire. He nods to me in greeting. Sitting down in one of the folding camping chairs he has, I stare into the fire. "How's your face?"

Bryce chuckles. "Nothing that won't heal by tomorrow." He offers me a beer and I take it. We sit in front of the fire, drinking our beer and watching the flames flicker and dance. I watch an ember float up to the sky, following its travels until my eyes land on the moon, the smallest sliver of crescent in the sky.

"What happened tonight with Elle can't happen again, Bryce." I turn to look at him. There's no remorse in his face. "I told you the other night not to fucking touch her, but you did." I can feel the anger building up in me. He disobeyed me.

Bryce laughs. "Dude, what the fuck? She's a prisoner. We stole her. She's nothing more than a tool for us to use against Drake." He shakes his head. "I know she's good looking and all, but she's not *that* hot. What? Don't tell me you feel sorry for her?"

He's wrong. She is the most beautiful woman, she-wolf or human, I have ever seen. And I do feel bad. I have no idea what she has been through during her time with Drake, but I can bet it wasn't fun. The idea of someone hurting her makes my heart get caught in my throat. It feels like I'm choking. No, however long she is here, no one will harm her.

I growl, "She's my mate. So she's off limits, do you hear me, Bryce?" Meeting his stare, I finally see something on his face that isn't sarcasm. He looks shocked, even dumbfounded. "Do you understand, Bryce?" I stand over him. "Do you understand that if you harm her, I'll kill you?"

"Yeah, man," he scoffs. "I got it. I won't touch her."

Something tells me not to believe him. I'll have to make sure they don't cross paths. "You're no longer allowed at the packhouse. If you need me or I need you, call or text."

"Yes, alpha."

Turning away from Bryce I walk out of the light of the fire. When I arrive in front of my house I realize I'm too restless to go inside. *I need to run.*

I look around, making sure no one is outside or looking out their windows. Seeing no one, I strip right on my front lawn, feeling my bones and joint snap and reform until I'm on all fours. Bolting under the cover of the trees I let my senses take over. I let my mind go and let my wolf take over.

Elle

Looking out the window at the moon I notice movement on the front lawn.

It's him.

I watch him as he looks around him. He never looks up. He must've thought he wouldn't be seen because he strips down to nothing. The moon doesn't offer much light tonight, looking like a tiny sliver of white in the sky.

I don't know why I feel cheated out of something. I shouldn't even want to *see* him naked anyway. But I can't help but watch.

His body contorts, fur appears where skin once was. I stop myself from gasping or screaming.

Where he once stood, now a large black wolf stands in his place. *My wolf.* It's him, the one from my dreams.

Shocked, I can't move. I watch him as he takes off into the forest. I yearn to follow him. Even though I can't see him anymore I keep my eyes on the area he disappeared into.

I don't know how long I sit there waiting for him to come back. I don't even know *why* I am waiting. I shouldn't care. I should go climb into bed and hope for another dreamless sleep.

But I don't. I don't move until I see him come back, looking like a black shadow moving across the lawns. He stops where he left his clothes, once again looking around him but never up. Only after he shifts back to human and pulls his pants up does he look up. I realize I moved the curtain.

It's too late to move away. He already sees me. Our eyes meet. Though I can't really see his eyes, it's the feeling that spreads through me that makes me thinks he can.

Warm and safe. That's the feeling.

What a stupid feeling to have about my imprisoner. Disgusted with myself, I pull the curtains shut.

I shouldn't feel safe with him. I don't trust him. He wants what they all want, sex. Well, I hope he enjoys jerking off because he's not getting it from me.

But it could be good. The thought interrupts my inner rant.

Fuck that. Just because *HE*'s my mate doesn't mean shit to me. Nope. I don't think I could even go through with it, not after Drake, who ruined me in more ways than I can count.

HE probably doesn't even want me anyway. His enemy had me first. Ruined the goods. Marked me and raped me, only the devil knows how many times.

That's not what an alpha needs for a mate. *HE* doesn't have time to put his mate back together. No, it's best to just ignore everything until my birthday, or his, whichever comes first. Then we can go our separate ways. Never have to see each other again.

The thought of never seeing him again sends daggers to my heart.

Lying down on my bed I curl up with *White Fang*. I read and try to ignore the sounds of him pacing in the bedroom next to mine.

CHAPTER TWENTY-FIVE

Elle

I've been here for a week now. It hasn't been horrible. Actually, I'm pretty much left alone and allowed to go outside, eat what I want when I want. I can watch TV in the living room and not get asked what I'm doing all the time. I go into his study if I know he isn't in the house. I quickly grab a book and leave.

I try to make it so I don't see him more than once a day. When he's not right in front of me it's easy to hate him. To be mad that he hasn't let me go. But when we do come into contact, the air sizzles with electricity, currents flowing between us.

It's only when he tries to come closer or touch me the spell breaks and the fear takes over. He can't touch me. I won't let him.

When this happens I think he snaps back to reality, too,

because he turns out of the room and leaves. Usually slamming whichever door he goes out of behind him.

He's left for the day, gone to do whatever he does as the alpha in his pack. So I know it's safe for me to venture out of my room.

I head into the kitchen looking for something to eat before I figure out what I want to do today.

"Good morning, Elle," Cory greets me. I open the fridge to take out some eggs.

"Morning," I respond. Cory or Reg is usually here. One or the other, sometimes both of them. It didn't take me long to figure out that they're mates.

They argue and bicker all the time. But it's the way they look at each other, like even though they drive each other crazy, they can't live without the other. They remind me of Sam and me.

The thought of Sam makes me sad. I miss him. I miss all of them. I know I'll probably never see them again. I'll never see Sam and Meg become parents, I won't get to watch my father grow old, trying to keep up with his grandchildren. I'll probably never have pups now anyway, but that just shows how much my life has changed in the past few months.

"What do you have planned for today?" Cory asks, bringing me out of my thoughts and back into the kitchen.

Cracking an egg, I drop the whites and yolk into the pan, they hiss and sizzle in the hot skillet. "I don't know. I guess it depends on what I am allowed to do."

"What do you mean?"

"Can I go for a run?"

"Sure, I don't see why not." Cory doesn't look fazed by my question at all.

I'm bemused. "Aren't you afraid that I'm going to run? I am a prisoner after all."

"When have we treated you like one?" Cory looks annoyed. Like I offended him in some way.

"You aren't afraid that I'm going to run away?"

"Are you?"

I chuckle. Sitting down across from him I take a bite of my food. "No, I'm not. I guess I'm choosing to stay here. If I leave I may end up caught by Drake again." I trail off– the thought of going back there brings bile up to my throat. "No, I'm not going to take off from here."

He watches me for a while. Trying to calculate if I'm telling the truth or not.

"The path has markers. If you stay on it you shouldn't get lost."

I offer him a small smile. "Thanks."

He nods, taking his coffee cup with him. I hear the front door open and close, which leaves me alone in the kitchen.

I like Reg and Cory. Cory never makes any movements that scare me, he doesn't grab at me. I find it easy to be alone with him. He's goofy, too. I learned he's the beta, which shocked me because betas are usually serious wolves, who don't take any bullshit. And Cory is anything but serious ninety percent of the time.

Reg is like the mother to the pack. I've also seen her helping out with training drills.

Grabbing my plate I head to the sink. There's a pile of dishes. No one's asked me to do them, but I've been staying here and eating, might as well clean up and make myself useful.

Looking outside I can't help but notice there are no pups playing in the grass, causing chaos to their parents.

How odd. I know there're mated pairs here, so where are the pups?

Placing the last dish in the drying rack, I head outside to the porch. I find Cory sitting on one of the patio chairs, drinking his coffee.

"Why aren't there any pups here? I see plenty of mated couples here, yet the youngest ones I have seen are twelve or thirteen years old."

Cory stiffens, takes his time to answer. "Fear is good birth control, Elle."

What the hell does that mean? Yes, this is a small pack, but there are other small packs out there and they have a bunch of young ones. It makes no sense.

He must sense my confusion. "We don't want what happened to us to happen to any children we may have. We won't let the next generation become orphans, too."

"Wait, back up," I say, now even more confused. "Orphans? You're all orphans?"

He sighs, leaning on his legs, looking out into the yard, where Reg is. It looks like she's trying to train some wolves self-defense techniques. Cory looks back at me. "This is Cedric's story to tell, not mine. You want answers, talk to him."

Figures. Standing up I stretch. I'm itching to go for a run. I know Cory isn't going to budge, so I'm just going to get on with my day.

"Where's a good place to shift?" I ask him.

He points into the treeline. "There are bags and totes you can put your clothes into spread out along the trees."

"Thanks," I say, bounding down the stairs. Moving down the walkway, I notice a lot of people stop what they're doing and stare. They're probably wondering about the girl who doesn't leave their alpha's house. *Well, let them wonder,* I think to myself.

Paying them no mind I walk under the cover of the trees. I find one of the totes Cory told me about. Looking around I undress, put the clothes in the tote and shift.

I search for the path most pungent with the smell of other wolves and take off. Sprinting down the path, I let my legs stretch. *I should have asked about this days ago.*

Cedric

Arriving back at the packhouse I see Cory sitting on the porch. "Don't you have anything better to do than just sit there?" I ask.

"Someone's gotta be here to vet all your visitors." He grins that stupid grin— how does Reg put up with him? "Jasmine is here."

"What?" *Why?* I realize now that I haven't thought about her at all this past week. I've been so busy I haven't had time to think about her. *Too busy thinking about Elle in the room next to yours.*

Cory shrugs. "She wanted to see you, I told her you weren't here and to come back later. She shoved past me and went up the stairs."

She went upstairs? I hope she and Elle don't run into each other. Rubbing my head because now my day just got a whole lot more complicated, I ask, "Where's Elle?" My eyes flick to the second floor.

Cory doesn't miss it, his grin tells me he saw me look up. "She's not here," he says.

What? "Where is she?"

"She went for a run."

"Alone?" She could've taken off. "Why didn't you go with her?"

"I didn't realize she needed a babysitter." Cory lounges back in his chair, looking completely undisturbed that Elle took off on her own.

"She could have taken off," I growl.

Cory peers up at me. "Doubt it."

"What the fuck is that supposed to mean?" This is annoying. We may not be beating her but she's still not here of her own accord. I'd run if I had the chance. Who's to say she wouldn't?

He sighs loudly, like *I'm* the one who's being an idiot. "She's not going to run." I give him an incredulous look. "She's not that stupid, Ced. She knows this is the safest place for her to be. Where's she going to go? Home? No, Drake would find her there. She's not going to chance running out of here. Too much chance of him finding her."

I stare at him. I have no argument because he's right. This is the safest place for her to be. Cory's grin gets wider. "She went that way."

Without another word I turn and head down the porch, going in the direction Cory said she went. I find where she left her clothes and take mine off, setting them a few yards away from hers. Shifting into my wolf I start sniffing the air and ground.

I find her trail and take off following it. It doesn't take me long to find her, sniffing the area, trying to get her bearings probably.

Sitting back, I watch her. She hasn't noticed me yet. She must feel somewhat safe right now. When she catches sight of me her hackles rise and she snarls.

"Calm down, I'm not going to hurt you." I don't know if the

mind link will work, she may still be connected to Drake's pack.

Elle keeps snarling, not backing down. I guess she can't hear me. Lying down to show her I'm not a threat to her, I wait for her to relax.

She huffs, walking past me back down the trail. I follow her. Far enough so I'm not right on top of her, but I can still see her at all times. *Like in my dreams.*

I follow her back to our starting point. Shifting, I grab my pants and once they're buttoned I turn to look at her. I can't help it. She has her back turned to me, pulling the shirt over her head. I catch a glimpse of something on her back.

What was that? It looked like a scar. Without thinking I make my way over to her. "What's on your back?" I ask, wrapping my fingers around her arm so she stops.

She whirls around on me. "Don't fucking touch me!" she snarls, venom dripping with every word. "You have no right to touch me."

Letting go of her arm I hold my hands up, "I didn't mean to scare you. What's on your back? Are you hurt?"

"Like you fucking care." She's bristling, looking like an angry goddess ready to strike me down.

"Show me."

"Fuck you."

Sighing in aggravation, I look at her. "Why won't you at least tell me what it is?" Why won't she show me? I'm not used to being told 'no.' I don't like it.

"It's none of your goddamn business," she snaps, crossing her arms over her chest. I look down at the ground. It's then that I notice she doesn't have her pants on yet, her long legs exposed. They're well defined with muscle, but still feminine. My eyes travel up until I notice she's not wearing panties either. My cock twitches at the sight of her.

Ignoring the blood rushing to my groin, I meet her eyes. Defiant, angry, Elle stares me down.

"It is my business, you're my prisoner. Or did you forget that?"

Those were the wrong words to say. The fire ignites in her eyes, burning me with just a stare. "Fine!" she growls. "You want to see? I'll give you a show."

It takes me a second to realize that she's not just pulling her shirt up a little bit. She rips the whole thing off the top of her head and throws it at my face.

Elle stands there, completely naked in front of me. Her body is on full display for me to see. *Okay, now she looks like a goddess.* How can she be muscular but still so incredibly feminine? Her tits look like they would fill my hands perfectly. Her stomach is toned, but her hips flare out, giving her curves.

My eyes cut to hers. "Enjoying the show, asshole?" Her lips curl up into a snarl. It makes me remember why she stripped in the first place.

I walk up to her until I'm less than a foot away. Her breathing hitches in her throat at my close proximity. "Turn around," I say softly, looking right into her eyes. I don't care that they're looking at me with all the hate and anger she has in her. They are the most beautiful, intense eyes I have ever seen.

She glares at me for a moment longer and then turns around.

The sight of her back is shocking, I was expecting one or two scars when I saw the brief glimpse a few moments ago.

There're at least fifteen long, angry scars crisscrossing

her back. Seeing them infuriates me and a growl rumbles in my chest. *How dare he do this to her?* She tenses up, nervous from my reaction.

Tentatively I reach out and stroke one. She flinches from my touch. "I won't hurt you, Elle." I continue to trace the scars until I have touched every single one. There are twenty.

Marveling at the strength she must've had to endure such a trauma, I can't help but think of everything else she must've endured. "I want to rip his throat out."

She chuckles, it's low and humorless. "Get in line."

I cast my eyes down away from her. "Here." I hold out her shirt for her.

"Thanks."

For some reason I turn around to give her privacy to get dressed. Like I didn't just see her stand naked before me.

She steps beside me, just out of reach. *She doesn't like my touch.* The thought saddens me.

Elle doesn't look at me, just straight ahead. Maybe embarrassed that I saw the scars.

"Are you headed back to the packhouse?" I ask, hoping to ease some of this tension between us.

She shrugs. "Where else am I going to go? I'm your prisoner, remember?"

"Sorry about that." Stepping towards her I reach for her hand. "I shouldn't have said it."

She doesn't return the gesture, her hand limp in mine. But she doesn't yank it away either. "Why are you out here?" She ignores my apology.

"I came to look for you." I wanted to see her, I wanted to see her wolf. I know she's the woman in my dreams, but I needed to see if everything was true. But mostly I just wanted to see her. "You've been avoiding me. Seemed like a good opportunity."

She snorts. "Like you haven't been avoiding me, too." She removes her hand from mine, crossing her arms over her chest. "Let's not pretend this whole mate thing is what we wanted. At least for me it isn't."

What does she mean by that? And no, did I want the woman Drake claimed as his to be my mate? Fuck no, it complicates things more than I can wrap my head around. But I did want to find my mate, it just so happens to be her.

I don't have time to respond, she's already walking away from me. Leaving me behind. Rejecting me. This is good, though, right? When it's all said and done, we can go our separate ways. It's the best option.

Catching up to her I decide to walk back with her. Elle looks at me cautiously. "Just heading in the same direction as you," I say. It's a pathetic excuse. I could have waited or walked behind her. But she's a damn magnet.

Elle's right, we should keep our distance from each other. It would be easier, simpler. But the thought guts me. I hardly know her and yet I want to be near her. I want to know her. *It's just the mate bond, it wants us to complete it.*

When we get to the walkway of my house Jasmine comes out the front door. I had completely forgotten about her. She runs down the steps, throwing herself into my arms.

Elle

What the hell? Is she his girlfriend? Why didn't he say he had a girlfriend? And why do I care? I shouldn't care.

"Oh, Cedric! " she exclaims. "I was beginning to worry. I've been waiting for you for an hour." Wow, she's something. Waiting a whole hour for an alpha is nothing. You can be left waiting for hours sometimes.

Cedric looks uncomfortable, not returning her embrace. He steps out of it. *I'd enjoy it if it wasn't because some chick had her paws all over him. Whoa, that's possessive, Elle. What's wrong with you?* But I really don't like it, she needs to get the fuck off *of him now. And when did he become Cedric?*

"Jasmine, what are you doing here?" Cedric asks her. He doesn't seem happy to see her. Good.

Seriously? What is wrong with me? He touches my back, my scars, *after* he demands that I let him, *after* he calls me his prisoner. Now I'm over here bristling like I'm jealous.

Jasmine flips her long hair over her shoulder and bats her eyelashes at him.

"Well, it's been a few weeks since our fight, so I came to see if you wanted to reconcile." She draws a fingernail over his chest, which is still bare, he never put a shirt back on. *Oh, she wants to reconcile all right, in bed.* I feel a growl low in my throat. I quickly cough to cover it.

Cedric looks at me, a smug look in his eyes. Like he knows why I was growling. *Jerk, don't think much about it. It's just nature.* Jasmine's eyes finally leave Cedric and look at me.

"Oh! I didn't see you there." She gives me a phony smile. Wow, I don't like her. She's fake as hell. How could Cedric not see that? Obviously they had a relationship. "You must be what the fuss is all about."

"I didn't realize I created a fuss." I look at Cedric. He looks just as confused as me at her statement.

She laughs. It's not a real laugh, more like when girls try to laugh and look pretty at the same time. It's not genuine at all. "Well, I mean word around the pack is that Cedric kicked Bryce out of the packhouse. And that never happened before you." She flashes me her teeth in what could be taken as a smile, but to me she's showing that she's higher in rank than I am.

"That's none of your concern, Jasmine. You don't live here." Cedric's face is blank, showing no emotion. He places his hand on the small of my back. "Now I have some things to take care of, if you could please let us pass."

Jasmine's face contorts to rage when she sees his hand on me. She recovers and offers another faux smile, her eyes narrowing on Cedric. "Well, should you get done early," she looks at me briefly before her eyes flick back to Cedric, "you know where to find me." She walks away, her hips swaying. It's obnoxious.

"Well, she seems like a peach," I say, shaking my head. "Was she like your girlfriend or something?" I tilt my head up to him.

He smiles with a smug look on his face. "Are you jealous?" he asks, tilting his head, too.

"What? No!" I say way too loud and way too fast. His smile widens, he's enjoying this. "Ugh! I'm not jealous. I just think you must be an idiot for falling for *that* act." I jerk my thumb over my shoulder to where Jasmine was walking.

Cedric just continues to grin at me. "Ugh!" I turn and head into the house, slamming the door behind me, looking for sanctuary in the kitchen.

He must have followed me, I can feel his presence in the room. He comes up behind me, placing his hands on either side of mine on the counter, effectively trapping me.

My breathing hitches, my heart accelerates. I'm caught between fear and arousal. That's a feeling I never thought I would feel again.

Cedric leans in closer, pressing his chest against my back. "You are jealous." His voice is soft, but I can hear the smile he must be wearing.

"No, I'm not." My voice gives my lie away. It's too loud and high-pitched. *What is he doing to me?* I turn around to face him. He doesn't move his arms, still entrapping me against the counter.

Why hasn't he put his shirt on yet? I drink him in. Okay, more like ravaged him. Taking in every line, every muscle, I want to touch him. Without even realizing I was doing it, I reach out and touch his chest, running my fingers through the smattering of curly hair. His eyes darken, his chest rumbles in satisfaction from my touch.

Our eyes meet. He leans down and presses his lips to my neck. "You smell divine," he says, his lips brushing against my skin.

I relax into his touch. One hand snakes into my hair, bringing my face close to his. When our lips meet he devours them, and I reciprocate, just as eager as he to feel more.

Feeling his tongue on my lips, I open my mouth wider and let him in, allowing him to taste me. Cedric's hands move down my body. I freeze when he cups my breast. But he's so gentle, he doesn't rip my shirt off, or yank on them so hard it hurts. His thumb brushes my nipple, causing it to bud up under my shirt. I let out a moan, pressing myself closer to him.

Cedric kisses down my neck to my shoulder, and back up to my lips. His hand leaves my breast, traveling to the waistline of my sweatpants. His hand pushes past the elastic. I still don't care, I'm too busy reveling in his touch and our kissing.

He moves his hand to my core, his finger presses into my entrance.

The flame burning through me extinguishes, and the

ice takes over. I freeze. I'm back in Drake's room. *No, I can't do this.*

"Stop, stop, STOP!" I scream. He pulls away from me, looking completely taken off guard. I run to the other side of the kitchen, putting as much distance between us as possible.

Cedric looks at me. He doesn't look angry that I just stopped whatever it was we were doing. He looks confused and concerned.

"I—I can't do this," I tell him, looking at the floor. The ice is still in me. I wrap my arms around myself like it's going to help it melt.

"Can't do what?" His voice is gruff and thick with arousal. I almost walk back to him. He produces a heat that can warm me up again.

Instead I back up, heading towards the exit of the kitchen. "I can't, I'm sorry. You shouldn't want me—I shouldn't want you." Tears well up in my eyes. "He ruined me, Cedric. I may be your mate but you need someone strong by your side. He beat all the strength out of me." The tears choke me. "I'm not good enough for you."

Cedric looks like he's about to say something, but I turn my back on him and run up the stairs. When I get to my room I lock the door behind me, keeping him out.

CHAPTER TWENTY-SIX

Elle

*L*ying on the floor, beaten and bloodied. I look up and see Drake standing over me, holding a whip.

"You let another man, another alpha, touch you?" His voice is cold and icy like his blue eyes. "How could you let him touch what's mine?"

"I don't belong to you," I snarl.

Drake yanks me up by my wrists. Pulling on me until I'm against the wall. He chains me there, my arms above my head.

"Looks like I'm going to have to teach you another lesson, sweetheart," he drawls, his tongue licking my neck where his mark is. "But first, you need to learn what happens when you leave me. I thought you learned that the first time. Apparently I was too easy on you."

Hearing his footsteps recede I wait for whatever is coming.

The crack of the whip fills the room. My back is on fire again. I try to hold back my screams but the pain is too much. After the fourth lash to my back I can't hold it in anymore. I scream.

Cedric

A piercing scream shrills through the house, making me jump up out of a restless sleep. *Elle.* I bolt out of bed, pulling on my sweatpants when she screams again.

Wrenching the door open I see Reg and Cory in the hallway, concerned looks on their faces. I don't stop to talk to them. I have to get to her. Trying to open the door I find she has it locked. "Fuck!" She screams again, a scream of terror and agony. *She's hurt.*

Stepping back, I charge the door, ramming it with my shoulder. It gives way easily, granting me access to her room.

I turn on the light on the bedside table. She's cringing in pain from the unseen assailant attacking her. She's having a nightmare.

"Elle!" I pick her up under her arms, pulling her up into a sitting position. "Wake up, Elle, it's just a dream. Wake up!"

Her eyes open, wild and terrified. "Don't touch me!" She jerks and kicks at me, but I don't let go. "Don't hurt me, please."

"Elle, it's me!" I half yell, trying to get her out of her trance. "I won't hurt you, you're safe here."

She screams again, "My back! It hurts! It's on fire!" Pulling her into my chest I lift the back of her shirt up. There's nothing there, just the old healed scars I saw earlier today. She's reliving the brutal event all over again.

Elle sags into me, her body heaving with sobs. "Shh, it's okay. You're safe. It was only a nightmare." Her cries turn into whimpers as she relaxes into me even more.

I keep the growl from reaching my throat. I don't want to scare her. Seeing her so terrified of a dream brings out feelings I've never had before. I've always wanted to kill Drake for what he did to my family, my pack. But now I want him to suffer a long, slow, painful death.

"Holy shit."

Cory and Reg are standing in the broken doorway. They're staring at Elle and I realize I never pulled her shirt back down. The shocked looks on their faces mirror mine earlier today. We knew Drake was evil, but this brings it to a whole new level.

Pfft, like you're any better. You thought about torturing her, dickwad. The thought guts me.

I pull her shirt back down, and settle her on the bed again. Her fingers wrap around my wrist. "Don't go, please," she pleads. Staring up at me, her face still has fear etched on it.

The feeling that washes over me is surreal. *She wants me to stay?* "I'll be right back," I promise, tucking the blanket around her before turning to Cory and Reg. "We can fix the door in the morning," I say, dismissing them.

They share a look with each other. "Her screams woke some people up. There are some outside right now, worried, I think," Reg says. She peers beyond me at Elle. "Is she okay?"

"No," I answer honestly. "I don't think she is." Physically she seems okay, but I know there are more scars on her than the ones on her back. I just can't see them. "Take care of the ones outside. There's no threat they need to worry about." I shut the door the best I can since the latch is broken.

Sitting on the edge of the bed next to Elle, I look down at her. She's stopped crying, but her face is red and blotchy from the tears. Gently, I brush the hair out her face. She winces but then relaxes into my touch.

"Stay." Her eyes find mine. "Please don't go." She looks exhausted, the nightmare took a lot out of her.

Leaning over I turn off the light. She has the curtains open so moonlight spills into the room. She moves to the other side of the bed, scooting to make room for me. I slide into the bed, leaving my pants on. I'm going to sweat to death, but it's better than upsetting her again. And I'm pretty sure crawling into her bed naked isn't what she wants right now.

I expect her to stay on her side, maybe keep her hand on mine so she knows I'm still with her. I'm shocked when she curls into me, nuzzling the spot between my neck and shoulder. My cock likes this a lot and makes it known. *Not now*, I say to myself. Now is definitely not the time for that. I adjust myself so I don't brush up against her with my erection.

Elle's breathing slows, steadying in her sleep. I watch her. She's beautiful. It's hard to believe just a minute ago she was screaming, eyes filled with fear. Now she looks so peaceful snuggled up to me.

She's never had a nightmare here before. At least not one like that. What happened to cause it? Today in the kitchen, I followed the bond to her too far. I pushed her over the edge. My attraction and desire for her made it hard to think, I wanted her so bad. Especially seeing her get jealous about Jasmine. I don't care what she says, she was definitely jealous and it was a major turn on.

Elle was fine with everything we did, the kissing, the touching. Hell, she was just as into it as I was. But I was the asshole who took things too far. The moment my hand touched her wet pussy she froze, tensed up. I didn't notice at first, too busy marveling at how soaked she was for me. It wasn't until she screamed for me to stop and pushed me away I realized I had taken it too far.

"*He ruined me.*" Her words echo through my head. She was standing as far away from me as she could. She was afraid of me. The thought shatters me, I don't want her to be afraid of me. Looking down at her, snuggled into me, she's not afraid right now.

"*I'm not good enough for you.*" Oh, but you are, Elle. I know there's strength left in you, I'll help you find it. Even if you still want to leave me, I'll help you. You can lean on me until you're strong enough to walk alone.

I lie there watching her sleep, taking her all in, memorizing every line and curve to her face before I finally fall asleep.

Elle

Something presses against me, waking me from my deep sleep. A heavy arm is wrapped around me, pulling me close to someone's chest. Turning my head I see Cedric, fast asleep in my bed. *What the hell?* I try to scramble away from him out of the bed, but his arm tightens around me.

"Don't go," he mumbles, pulling me closer so my back is flush against his chest. Which also means his erection is pressed right against my backside. I roll over and face him. His eyes are still closed. At least now he's not pressed right against me.

Cedric takes a deep breath, opening his eyes, meeting mine immediately. "Good morning," he smiles. Rolling onto his back he lets me go.

"Uh, morning." I bite my lip. "So why are you in my room? In my bed?"

"You had a nightmare, I came in to comfort you." His

green eyes cut to mine, studying me. "You asked me to stay."

Noticing he's not wearing a shirt I begin to wonder what happened. "Did you ... um, did we, we didn't do anything, did we?"

His face hardens. "No, Elle, I wouldn't take advantage of you in a state like that." He sounds offended, angry even. "Nothing happened besides you falling asleep in my arms." He throws the blanket off, his shoulders tense. "But thanks for letting me know what you think of me." He's mad, really mad.

"I'm sorry," whispering so I'm barely audible. He stops at the door, which I notice is broken. "I told you yesterday; I'm ruined. Any good perception of men is gone for me. I'll always look for the bad before the good. And even then if I found any good, I may not trust it."

He doesn't look at me. "Last night you trusted me." And he walks out the door, out of sight.

Feeling like a pile of garbage for how this morning turned out, I bound out of bed and I knock on his door. He growls, "What?"

"I'm sorry. You're right that on some level I trust you, some part of me feels safe with you." I say this to the door, which has remained shut. "I shouldn't have assumed you did anything. It was wrong." I hear his footsteps come closer. He opens the door, looking annoyed and frustrated.

"When have I ever done anything to make you even think I would hurt you? Besides kidnap you."

"Well, yesterday you did call me your prisoner and made me strip."

He laughs— why is that so funny? "Oh, Elle, I just wanted to see your back. Yeah, I said you were my prisoner, but you and I both know I have never forced you to do anything. You could have walked away, and I would have let you go." He brushes his hand across my cheek. "*You* were the one who said 'I'll give you a show' and ripped your shirt off. Not that I'm complaining, I did enjoy most of it."

I blanch. He is right– it was my temper tantrum that had me standing before him buck naked. Cedric laughs at my expression, which I'm sure is mortified.

"Most of it?" I ask him. What about me didn't he like? And why do I care?

Cedric sighs. "Your scars, Elle. And I guess it's not the scars themselves, it's knowing the pain you went through to get them." His hand trails from my face down my arm to my hand where he laces his fingers through mine. I stare at our joined hands, marveling at how right they feel together.

"They are ugly."

"Nothing about you is ugly, Elle. Not a damn thing."

* * *

I LEFT him so he could shower, and I wanted one myself. Though I'm sure if I'd mentioned I wanted one as well he would have suggested something about saving water.

One thing I did notice, though, is I enjoy his touch.

What if I hadn't had my episode in the kitchen? We would have fucked right there on the counter, too absorbed in one another to care if someone walked in.

Shaking the thought from my head I turn off the water. But I did have the episode. Even though I'm not with Drake, he's still my captor. He still haunts me. *I hope it's not always like this.*

I dry off and get dressed, still rockin' sweatpants and t-shirts, looking like a bum. I need new clothes.

As if she has magic powers of mind reading, Reg pops

her head out of her room. "Hey! Elle! You got any big plans right now?"

"Umm, nope. My calendar is open." Like what else am I going to do? I've been lying around the house reading and watching TV the past week. Though I guess I'm allowed to go for runs now. Cedric didn't seem upset that I went out yesterday.

She smiles. "Good. 'Cause you know, as hot as you make that 'hot mess' look, you need some clothes." Her face drops. "Unfortunately, I can't actually take you out of the territory into town. Cedric put his foot down there, and honestly, he's right. Drake could be out there. The risk is too high."

And that's what I mean by Drake haunting me. Even though he's not there he is. "Online is fine. I know my size at least and what I like."

Reg grins. "Perfect!" She grabs my hand and pulls me downstairs. "My tablet is down here."

After what seemed like forever, I had a wardrobe on the way here. I'll have clothes, clothes that I get to pick out.

I never realized the power of clothes. When you're forced to wear something that isn't you it essentially strips you of your identity. Hopefully wearing my own clothes will help me feel even more comfortable.

I tell Reg I'm going for a run. She waves me off, saying something about finding Cory.

When I step outside I see Bryce and Cedric off to the side, talking about something. Cedric sees me, his attention from Bryce broken. Bryce follows his gaze and his grin widens, which creeps me out. Cedric says something to bring the focus back to their conversation. Thank god. I can't put my finger on it but there is *definitely* something wrong with Bryce. I know he wouldn't think twice about hurting me.

Once I'm in the tree line I strip off my clothes and shift. I need to run today, not mosey around. I take off at a sprint, watching the trees fly by as I race past them. This is the only time I feel truly free, running through the forest, not being chased, just for the fun of it.

Hearing paws thundering behind me I turn and see Cedric, his large black wolf charging at me. I stop to wait for him and he runs right past me. Spinning around I see he's stopped about twenty feet away, his head down, tail swishing high in the air. He barks and yips at me.

He wants to play. Taking off, I barrel at him. He dashes out of my way and takes off down the path. *Oh, he wants to race. Let's race, alpha.* I sprint after him. He's going to hate it when I beat him.

CHAPTER TWENTY-SEVEN

Elle

We have settled into a routine. I spend my day going through the house, helping clean up. I go for a run in the afternoon. Sometimes, if Cedric finds a way to excuse himself from whatever it is he's doing, he joins me. Then I find myself reading after dinner, sitting in his study with him while he works, making phone calls, going over the pack income, all the fun stuff that comes with being an alpha.

We sleep together every night, just cuddling, no funny business. During the day he steals kisses, each one more passionate than the last. I enjoy those moments. But he hasn't gone past that, not since the kitchen episode. And that was weeks ago.

Maybe I have to make the move to push farther. My body certainly wants more. Why can't my mind cooperate?

It's frustrating. Someday cuddling and stolen kisses won't be enough for him. He may go looking for a release elsewhere. The picture of Jasmine trailing her finger over his chest pops into my head. The thought makes me want to snarl.

"What are you thinking about over there?" I look up from the same page I've been staring at for the past five minutes. He looks amused.

"Nothing," I toss the book to my side. It lands gently on the cushion next to me. "The book wasn't catching my interest."

He tosses his phone onto his desk, motioning me to come over. I walk around until I'm standing between him and his desk. Cedric stands. Grabbing my thighs he pulls me up, placing me on his desk. Pushing himself between my knees, he kisses me. The kiss is hot, urgent. He devours my mouth. When he pulls away we're both panting.

"Does that capture your attention?"

"Mmm." I pull him back in for more and he chuckles.

"What were you thinking about?" He pulls away and I pout, upset he didn't kiss me again. He laughs– it's become one of my favorite sounds to hear. "Tell me, or I will go back to work."

My eyes narrow. "Is that a threat?"

Cedric grabs his phone. "I don't drop what I'm doing for just anyone. I figured whatever had you stewing over there must be important."

I sigh. Grabbing his phone from his hand I set it down. "I was thinking that I might be ready."

His eyebrow quirks. "Can you be more specific?"

Instead of telling him, I decide to show him. Pulling him into my embrace our lips connect. When I tug on his bottom lip with my teeth he growls in pleasure. Pressing myself against him as my hands move to the buttons on his jeans.

He freezes. "Elle," his tone low, a warning. I ignore him, my hands making quick work with the zipper. "What are you doing?" he asks, pulling away from me. He grabs my hands and stops them from completing their task.

"I figured you wanted more. More than just kissing and cuddling." I look away from him, too embarrassed to meet his gaze.

Cedric grabs my chin, forcing me to meet his amused eyes. "I do, Elle, I really do. But I have to ask you something."

"What?"

"Do you think you're ready? I'm fine with waiting."

I snort, "I guess my trying to pull your dick out of your pants wasn't clear enough." My voice is dripping with sarcasm.

"Not here."

My nose scrunches. "Huh?"

"I'm not fucking you on my desk for our first time, Elle." He pauses, looking up at the ceiling before looking at me again. "Maybe the second time, though," he grins.

Taking his hand in mine, I jump off the desk. "Let's go!"

"Wait, Elle."

"What?"

"I think we need to talk about this first."

Rolling my eyes, I huff. "Talk about what?"

"Are you sure you're ready?" he asks. "You can say 'stop' if it gets to be too much for you and I will."

He's giving me a choice, he's letting me know there's a way out if I want it.

"Okay." I pull on his hand, he yanks me back.

"Oh no, I want you back up on that desk."

"But you just said—"

"I know what I said." He picks me up and sets me back on the desk. "But I was really enjoying the prelude. And I want you to be hot and wet for me by the time we hit that bed." Giving me a devilish grin, he picks up where we left off.

The kiss deepens, becoming sensual and intense. His hands grip into my ass, pulling me closer to him. His hands move up my waist, keeping one hand on my back. The other moves up to my breast, teasing my nipple through my shirt. I moan into his mouth. Cedric takes this moment and frees himself from our kiss. Trailing his lips down my neck and back up to my ear, he nibbles my earlobe.

Every kiss, every touch sends sparks through my body. I want him. Now.

Someone knocks on the door. "Hey, Ced, are you busy?" It's Cory.

Cedric pulls away from me. I immediately feel cold from his absence. He's pissed that we were interrupted. "Is it important? Life or death?" he barks. I suppress a giggle, covering my mouth with my hand. He looks at me, amused by my reaction.

"Uh, no. I guess not," Cory says through the door. "I'll leave you to it."

Cedric shakes his head. "Now, back to my important business."

"Mmm," I say, running my fingers through his hair. He crushes his mouth to mine, building back up to where we were before we were interrupted.

I tug on his shirt, he gets the hint and rips it over his head. My hands move across his bare skin, feeling every line of every muscle. Fuck, he's hot. And I love that he has some chest hair that leads a nice happy trail down to his groin.

My shirt is bunched up over my breasts, leaving them exposed to him. He sucks my nipple into his mouth, I inhale sharply. His green eyes flick up to mine, intense with desire.

Cedric moves to give my other breast some attention when there's another knock on the door. "Jesus fucking Christ," he growls. "I swear to god if the pack isn't on fucking fire, I'm going to kill Cory."

"Let me handle it," I say. "Don't want you killing your best friend, you'll regret it later."

"Doubt it," he grumbles. "Wait." He pulls my shirt back down. "Best friend or not, if he sees you like that I will kill him."

I roll my eyes. "He's mated to Reg."

"I don't give a fuck, no one but me sees you naked."

Hmm, that's possessive. *Why do I like it?*

I open the door. It's Jasmine. "Oh, is Cedric in here?" She pushes on the door to open it wider but I tighten my grip, stopping her.

"He's busy."

She smirks. "Well, he'll make time for me," she declares, pushing the door again. I let it open. Her face drops at the sight of him. He's moved, now lounging on the sofa, his hair messed up, no shirt. He unbuttoned his pants, too. It's such a marvelous sight I almost forgot Jasmine standing there.

"As I said, he's busy." I shove her out the door. "And he will be for the indefinite future, so don't come back. If he wants you he'll come find you." I slam the door shut on her dumbstruck face.

"Stupid bitch," I mutter. I look at Cedric, looking amused by my interaction with his ex. "What?" I snap.

His face splits into a huge smile across his face. "You are jealous."

"Shut the fuck up, I'm not jealous," I argue, glaring at him. I don't know how, but his grin gets even wider.

"You're sexy when you're jealous." He walks over to me, wrapping his arms around my frame. He makes me feel tiny because he's massive. "You know, I got to thinking. As long as we're in here they're going to keep knocking on that door."

I look up at him. "So we should move this to your room? They won't bug you there?"

"No, that's my safe place. Life or death are the only reasons to bother me there." Without waiting for my response, he bends down, throwing me over his shoulder.

"Hey!" I squeal. "You fucking barbarian!"

He growls, giving my ass a hard smack. Striding across the hall he enters his bedroom, slamming the door shut.

"I think they got the hint."

"They better have." He flips me off his shoulder, effectively throwing me in the middle of the bed. The pillows fall around me and I laugh as I shove them away.

Cedric climbs on top of me. "Hmm, I think you have too much clothing on." Grabbing my shirt, he shimmies it over my head. Hitching his thumbs in the waistband of my yoga pants he eases those off my legs. He moans, "No panties?"

"Do you approve?" I ask, already knowing the answer.

He grins in approval. Kissing my navel he makes his way down my body. His beard scratches and tickles my thighs, sending sparks of pleasure all through me, making me moan.

I look down at him, our eyes meet. He's been watching me, watching my reaction. Pleased with his results he lowers his mouth on to my clit. My hips buck up. That's all he needed, that was his cue. Because now he's feasting on me, tongue lapping up my juices. My muscles tighten and I squirm on the bed, it's too much. My breaths come out in moans and pants.

Cedric must know I'm close to my release. He sucks my clit hard, I scream, my muscles spasm. I collapse in the bed, limp. "Holy fuck. I now know what spontaneous combustion is." Pleasure still flowing through me, I feel my legs tremble.

He chuckles. His pants fall to the floor with a soft thud. The bed dips under his weight and he settles himself between my thighs.

Cedric kisses me. "Keep your eyes on mine, Elle." I do as he asks. Feeling the tip of his cock at my entrance I freeze. *No!* I close my eyes, and all I see is Drake forcing himself on me. I have to get away. I can't do this!

"Elle! Look at me, it's me. You're safe." I open my eyes and look into his kind warm green eyes. Not the Icy blue ones that monster has. Taking a deep breath I calm myself.

"Keep going, I'm okay." I want this— no, I *need* this. That asshole isn't going to rule my life anymore.

Cedric looks at me, unsure if I'm telling him the truth. Grabbing his face in both hands I lift my head off the pillow and kiss him. "I want this, I want *you.*"

"Thank fuck," he groans as he pushes into me. Holy fuck, he's big. He stretches me until I feel like I'm going to split in two. "You okay?"

Biting my lip I nod. Cedric growls, pulling my lip out of my teeth into his. He rocks slowly, taking his time while I adjust to him, matching his rhythm. His cock slides through my slickness with ease.

Kissing me, he pulls away, kneeling while still inside of me. Grabbing my thighs he adjusts me. "Oh fuck," I murmur. It feels deep this way.

As he continues his slow strokes in me, I begin panting and thrusting to get to my climax that's right there, ready to burst. He pulls almost completely out, leaving only the crown of his cock in me. He moves his hips in short pumps, not filling me completely. I moan in frustration. *What's he playing at?* He chuckles. "So eager to finish this, are you?"

My eyes flick to his. "I'm close," I whimper. "Please," I beg. Being on the edge like this is driving me crazy. I need to come.

His growl is the only response I get before he drives into me. I scream, the movement making me push up on the bed. He leans over me, kissing my neck. "I wanted to go slow but, fuck, I'm having a really hard time not pounding this sweet little pussy of yours."

Oh god, he talks dirty. My walls tighten around him. I like it, I realize. "Do it. Please. Do whatever you want, I just want to come." I'm begging and I don't care, I just need him to *move*.

He starts thrusting again, but this time he doesn't keep the slow pace he had before. Cedric does exactly what he said he wanted to do. He pounds into me hard and fast, my legs lock around his back, holding him there. I dig my nails into his back, he growls, louder than the other times. Reaching his hand between us he finds my clit and presses on it.

I come. Hard. My arousal squeezes his cock as wetness flows out of me. I scream in pleasure again, and he doesn't slow his pace. I feel another orgasm building.

"Jesus Christ," he spits out between his teeth. My pussy tightens again, he pushes into me, pounding me hard into the bed. Not able to hold back any longer I let out another scream, riding through the waves of pleasure rippling through my body. "Fuck!" he roars as he comes, spilling his seed inside of me. I feel his muscles twitch above me.

Cedric pulls out of me but stays on top of me. We're both sweating and panting. He kisses me, soft sweet kisses, before resting his forehead on mine.

"Holy fuck, I never knew missionary could be so fun." He grins, kissing me again.

I giggle. Shifting underneath him I feel a wet spot on the sheets. I giggle again.

"What?" he asks, cocking his head to the side, amused at my bubbly mood.

"We need to change the sheets," I say sheepishly.

His eyes darken. "Well, that's how you know you had a good time and did it right." He kisses me before climbing off of me. I feel cold as soon as he's gone. I grab the sheet to cover my body. Scooting to the edge of the bed I wince, feeling sore. Cedric notices, concern written on his features. "Are you okay?"

"Yeah, just sore, a good sore," I say, smiling up at him.

"A good sore?"

"My limbs feel like Jello. And, um, don't let this go to your head but, um, you're kinda big, Cedric." My eyes glance at the part in question, my eyes widening when I see he's getting hard again.

Cedric gets a set of sheets from the closet and throws them on the bed. That's definitely going to my head, Elle." He laughs. "You want to shower?"

"Sure," I say, feeling a little crestfallen. I drop the sheet and head toward his en suite bathroom.

"Hey, what's wrong?" Grabbing my hand he pulls me into his chest, peering down at me, concern pulling the corners of his lips down. "Did I hurt you?"

"No," I say, shaking my head. "I just thought that maybe we could go again? But if you don't want to, that's fine, I'll take a shower." I start to walk away but he holds me tight so I can't escape.

"Elle, who said you were showering alone?" he asks before once again throwing me over his shoulder. This time he takes me into the bathroom.

CHAPTER TWENTY-EIGHT

Cedric

Sitting at my desk I look over the list of names of different alphas I have talked to, sighing in frustration at the lack of help I am getting for going head-to-head against Drake.

The only good thing is, I know he has no clue who took Elle from him. I know he's gone and searched packs for her but that's it. When word gets to me about it, I play dumb. I don't want anyone to know she's here. Drake doesn't even know we're here. He doesn't know he left a whole generation of werewolves behind after he slaughtered my pack.

I'm on the phone with Jared when Elle walks in. Wearing a shirt and jeans, she looks stunning, her long dark hair pulled over one shoulder. Her brown eyes find mine, determination set in them.

I realize Jared asked me a question and I was too busy watching Elle to hear it. "Sorry, Jared, what was that?"

Elle sits in the chair in front of my desk, raises an eyebrow. and smirks. *Yeah, babe, you are a distraction.* And she knows it, too.

Jared sounds annoyed when he repeats the question. "Yeah, that's fine. Thank you." I smile triumphantly as I hang up the phone.

"What was that about?" she asks, crossing her legs, leaning forward. It makes her tits push up in her shirt and I stare at them unashamedly. I love her body, the perfect balance of strong and soft. My cock twitches in my pants— he approves, too.

"Finally got an alpha to agree to at least talk about going against Drake."

"Alpha Jared?" she asks. This piques my interest. *She knows him?*

"Yeah. Apparently Drake did something that pissed him off a while ago. So he's been thinking about retaliation for a while now." I shrug. I don't care what his reasons are for changing his mind. It works in my favor. "You know Jared?"

She laughs. "Yeah, I know Jared."

My eyes narrow. "How do you know him?" I already know the answer. Everyone knows that Jared was a complete hound when it came to sex. Until he met his mate, that is.

"The same way you know Jasmine," she snaps, catching on to my jealousy. Elle sighs. "Look, his dad and my dad were alphas, they knew each other. So Jared and I would hang out."

"Hang out?" I spit through clenched teeth. *Fuck it, I don't need his help.* My thought is irrational because I *do* need his help.

She smirks and, walking over to me, she straddles my lap, settling herself on me. "You're sexy when you're jealous." She kisses me, I fist her hair, deepening the kiss. She rocks her hips, grinding on the bulge in my pants.

Breaking away from her mouth I look at her. "As much as I'd love to fuck you on my desk right now, I have a lot of work to do." *I hate being alpha sometimes.*

Elle gets up. "That's fine. I wanted to ask you about something anyway."

"What's that?"

"I need something to do, Cedric. I can't keep vegging around the house all day. I'm gonna get fat." She pokes her toned stomach to emphasize her point.

"I find that hard to believe," I chuckle.

"Ugh. Look, you want to go against Drake. So do I. I want to kill him. Let me help you." She sits back in the chair across from me. "We can help each other."

This is true, but I don't want her anywhere near him. Even though she has every right to kill him as much as I do. Maybe even more.

"I know how he thinks, Cedric. I lived with him. He's sadistic and evil, but he's smart and calculated. He's an opponent you don't want. You don't truly know what he's capable of."

Anger consumes me. "You don't think I know what he's capable of?" I snarl. She flinches back but straightens again. Her eyes flash in annoyance.

"Well, no one has told me a damn thing about your vendetta since I got here," she snaps. "I don't know what your issue is with Drake."

Closing my eyes I take a deep breath. She's right, I've kept her in the dark. I never once explained why I took her from him. "Drake killed my parents. He took out my entire pack." I hear her gasp but I don't look at her. "The only reason we survived is because my mom hid most of the kids twelve and under in a room that's in the basement. They never found us, so we were the only ones left."

I look at her. She looks sad, appalled, and angry. *But wait*, I tell her silently, *there's more.*

"There wasn't enough room for all the kids to go in that room. We wouldn't have fit. So my guess is they had all the teenagers take off into the woods. My sister included. Drake found them all and killed them. I think they raped some of the women and girls, too. Have you noticed the youngest person in this pack is nine? He was an infant when Drake came that night. Shoved into his older brother's arms, who was told to go hide until their mother came for them."

A tear streams down Elle's cheek, realizing that he's more than the monster who tortured her.

"'My mother told me to stay in the room and not come out until she came to get us. I don't know how long we were down there. But we ran out of milk for the babies, so we had to leave. Cory and I both went, being the oldest and all. What we walked out into will forever be seared into my brain. Our parents, aunts, uncles, cousins, they were all dead." My voice becomes thick with grief– telling her the story makes it feel real again.

"The hardest part of it all was finding the little ones who went with their parents and older siblings, trying to make a run for it." I glance at Elle. Her face is white, all the color drained from it. "He killed everyone, Elle. Even kids. I became an alpha at twelve years old because of him. So don't tell me I don't know how he thinks or operates. Because I do, and I know the world will be better off without him plaguing it."

She looks at me, eyes filled with tears and sympathy. "Cedric, I'm ... I'm so sorry." She chokes out the words and she tentatively steps toward me. I open my arms and she walks into my embrace.

"Let me help you," she sniffs. Her tears soak through my shirt— *she's crying for me*. "I can help you. I *want to*. He needs to die."

"Yeah, he does."

"Just promise me something." She pulls away, searching my eyes for answers I don't have.

"What's that?" Wiping the tears from her face ... *she's so beautiful*.

"Don't get yourself killed, then it would be all for nothing." She nuzzles into my chest. Kissing the top of her head, I hold her tighter. I don't say anything because it's a promise I might not be able to keep.

Elle

After Cedric told me his pack's story, grief for him and everyone in this pack consumes me.

I'm just a small notch in Drake's bedpost of horror. How could anyone massacre an entire pack? I know he threatened to do it when he first took me, but I didn't think he would kill everyone, including children. That justifies my decision to go with him. I'd rather it be me and only me who had to endure all of the pain. I would've had to anyway, but at least I don't have the deaths of my packmates on my shoulders.

Walking down the path leisurely, I think of home. What's my father doing now? Did he step down from alpha? Or did he stick with it to keep busy?

I miss Connie and her sass. I miss Sam, my strong and

quiet best friend. I wonder if he and Meg are expecting yet. It wouldn't surprise me if they were. They marked each other pretty quick into their relationship. Smiling at the thought of Sam being a father, I know he'll be a good one, great even, teaching his pups how to be patient and strong-willed. I'll never see it. I'll never see my father grow old and gray. Who's going to take care of him? It was supposed to be me. But I'm not there to do it now. The thought saddens me.

They will move on in their lives. I'll just be a distant memory. The only way I can go back is if Drake is dealt with. And that could be years from now, or never.

Maybe I can at least call him. Yeah, maybe Cedric will allow me to call my dad. I never asked Jared because Drake knew about him so it would be too dangerous.

But Cedric said Drake doesn't even know this pack is still here. I could call them, not tell them where I am but I can tell them I'm safe and happy. The word makes me stop short. *Am I happy?*

I think about how Cedric makes me feel safe and cared for. How I feel my strength coming back every day, like he's the medicine I need. Reg and Cory are both fun to be around, I enjoy their company. And the rest of the pack has been welcoming for the most part. With a few exceptions.

I begin walking back to the packhouse. I'm going to ask him if I can call my father. I don't see why he would say no.

Feeling emotionally lighter, I quicken my pace, eager to get back.

Cedric is on the front porch talking to Cory. He immediately turns to me, like my presence pulls him towards me.

"Hey, Elle," Cory says with a smile.

"Hi," I smile back. "I have a question for you," I say to Cedric.

"And what's that?" he says, taking my hand in his like it's a reflex for him.

Cory butts in. "If it's about that spot he has on his balls, I told him to get that checked *ages* ago," he chortles.

I roll my eyes. He can be a real idiot sometimes. Cedric punches his shoulders. "Fuck off, Cory."

Cory's still laughing. "I'm just pickin." Cedric glares at him before turning his attention back to me. His gaze softens.

"What's up?"

Taking a deep breath to steady my nerves, I tighten my hold on his hand. "I was wondering if I could call my father. I won't tell him where I am– actually, I still don't know where we are." I pause, taking another breath. "I won't mention your name. I just want to tell him I'm safe. I miss him so much."

He lets go of my hand, stepping back a foot. Cory eyes us both, watching our interaction.

Cedric sighs. "I'm sorry, Elle. I can't take that chance." At his denial I feel deflated, all the hope I had popped like a balloon. "Even if you take all the precautions you just listed it's still too dangerous. We don't know how closely Drake is watching your pack, waiting for an opportunity to find you."

My throat tightens, tears well up in my eyes. Looking down, I nod.

"I understand, I guess," I choke out, pushing past him, trying to get away so he doesn't see how much he just shattered me.

"Hey." He grabs my hand, stopping me from going into the house. "I'm sorry, Elle. But I can't take the chance." He lets go of me, I don't look up. Walking into the house I quietly shut the door behind me.

Running up the stairs, I shut myself in the first room I stayed in when I got here. I need to be away from him, and going to his room where his scent is all over the place won't help me get away. He reminded me right there that I am still nothing more than his prisoner.

Cedric

She ran away from me. I want to chase after her to explain, but I know she needs space right now. If she wanted comfort she wouldn't have gone into the house.

"Well, that was harsh," Cory's words break through my thoughts.

"What?"

"She wants to call her dad. What's the harm in that?"

"We don't know what measures Drake has gone through to find her." That's part of it. But I also don't want her to leave. If she calls them then she may want to go home, leaving me here without her.

Cory snorts. "That's fucking bullshit and you know it. Hello? This is the twenty-first century. We have burner phones for cryin' out loud. They're untraceable."

I don't respond because he's right. There are ways that she can call them and not be traced back here. "We don't know if Drake has someone in that pack. It's still a risk."

"You're something else, you know that?" he snaps. "If you had the chance to call your parents and someone told you no, how would you feel?" He glares at me. "I know I would give anything to be able to talk to my parents again. So would you."

Looking away from him, out to where I can see Reg and Tom doing some drills for training, I watch them. Not able to look Cory in the eyes anymore. "They're dead,

Cory, our families are dead. We will never talk to them again."

"Yeah, but *she can*. Her father isn't dead, Cedric. Give her the chance we never got. Let her talk to him."

I don't respond, taking a sip of my coffee instead. "Jared will be here in a few hours. I'll be in my study if you need me."

"Your mother would be ashamed of you," Cory says softly. The statement tears at my heart. I slam the door shut, so he knows he went too far. But he's absolutely right, my mother would be ashamed of me.

Heading up the stairs I look in my room. Elle isn't in there. I check my study but she's not there either. I hear something down the hall. Backtracking down the hall I follow the soft sounds. They're coming from the room she used to sleep in. *Why would she be in there?* It makes no sense, she's been staying in my room with me. Then it dawns on me. I step away from the door, back to my study. She wants to be as far away from me as possible.

I sit at my desk, ignoring everything I have to get done. Instead I rest my face in my hands, wondering how I can fix this.

CHAPTER TWENTY-NINE

Elle

J've been lying on the bed for hours and the tears have dried on my face. What's been happening the past few weeks with Cedric? Was I wrong in thinking it was more than just amazing sex?

When I asked about calling my father, I thought he would say yes. But he didn't. He threw that request in my face. *He doesn't care about me.* His actions proved I'm nothing more to him than a tool in his war against Drake. And a plaything at night. That's all I am to him.

Well, fuck him, I'm done. I won't help him, and I'm certainly not going to be in his bed anymore.

Hearing voices outside I peer out the window. It's Jared. I should go down and see him, show him that I am okay. But I don't want to see Cedric right now. If I do, I'd probably punch him. And that's not good etiquette when another alpha is present.

Cory and Reg join Cedric and Jared, they all walk into the house.

I listen as they walk up the stairs and down the hall. I hear the door to his office close. They must be having their meeting there.

He feels too close. I want to go into his office and sit by his side. But I'm not his luna. I'm nothing to him.

Leaving the sanctuary of the room, I creep down the stairs, easing the front door open. I sneak out, closing it quietly behind me.

I need to be outside, clear my head. A nice long walk on the trail will help with that. I glance up at the window. He's not there, he probably doesn't even realize I've left the house. Turning my back on the window, I walk across the lawns into the tree line.

Cedric

"So what changed your mind about helping me?" I ask Jared, looking between him and his Beta. Lee, I think his name is.

He sighs, leaning back in his chair. "I heard that someone had the balls to set explosives on Drake's land, causing a diversion so they could steal his mate." He pauses and his eyes narrow. "Was that you?"

I stare at him, refusing to answer. No way am I going to tell him it was me until I know what his motives are. Jared chuckles.

"Smart, not showing your hand." He sighs. "She was my friend, the woman he chose to be his. She got away from him once and came to me for help. I let her stay for a short amount of time, telling her she had to leave after a few days. I had my mate and unborn pup to consider." I listen, hanging on every word. "He found her and I had to hand her over. Actually, she volunteered. She knew the danger it would put my pack in if she tried to run and he found out I was hiding her."

Jared rubs his eyes, looking tired all of a sudden. "He fucking beat her right in front of me. Then had his two goons finish the job. She was unrecognizable by the time they were done." He takes a shaky breath. "And all I could do was sit there and watch, watch as they beat Elle bloody."

Wait, what? Realization hits me. Drake's mate, hiding her, he beat her. It was Elle. Elle is his friend. She did say she knew Jared, he has a large pack. It was a safe bet to go there. *She ran from him?* She never told me about that. The image of her scarred back flashes in my head.

"She's here," I say.

Jared's eyes widen. "Holy fuck, how did you pull that off? Is she okay? I'd like to talk to her."

He fires off the questions at me. Meanwhile I have questions of my own for him.

"You can talk to her after we're through here, I want to go over a few things first."

"She better be okay," he snarls at me. Cory and Reg reciprocate, snarling back.

"She's fine," I say to him. "Back off, guys," I tell Cory and Reg. They listen, both sitting back in their chairs.

Looking back at Jared, I add "she's fine." This appeases him and he settles back into his chair. "Like I said, you can see her later if you want. I'm sure she'd like to see you." I decide to get the inevitable out of the way. "She's my mate, my true mate."

"Holy shit." His eyes pop out of his head again. "So, he

can't take her back from you. I'm assuming you marked her and vice versa?"

"No, we haven't." The thoughts have come up a lot over the past few weeks. But she hasn't mentioned it. I don't even know if she wants to.

Jared, *tsks*. "Man, if I were you I'd get on that. That's a legit reason to get others to help you. Another alpha trying to steal your true mate? Been plenty of wars over that back in the day." I don't answer– he's right, but we have more things to talk about right now.

Jared looks around the room. "Hey, where's your other guy, the creepy one?"

"Bryce?" I ask, though he's the only 'creepy' guy I have around here. Jared nods.

"Yeah, Bryce. That dude freaks me out."

"I'm not sure where he is, actually." I glance at Cory and Reg but they both shrug. "He was supposed to be here." *That's odd.* Normally he's at these meetings. What's keeping him? My stomach knots, unsettled by Bryce's strange behavior.

I told him he could come to the packhouse for this meeting. *So why isn't he here?*

Jared shrugs. "Do we need him to be here?"

"No, I'll catch him up later." I look at the door, tempted to go check on Elle, but I decide against it, forcing myself to stay seated. *She's fine, safe in her room.* I tell myself this, trying to ease the nerves that are making my guts twist.

Elle

Walking aimlessly around the forest, while staying on the path, I want to scream in frustration. I want to go back to the house, storm into his office and strangle Cedric. But at the same time, I want to go in there and kiss him, let him hold me. *Fucking mate bond.* I can't even have a good pout session and be mad at him. Even though he deserves it.

He's never treated me like a prisoner before today. Actually, he treated me even less than. He refused to let me call my father. Even human prisoners are allowed phone calls. I need a lawyer.

A twig snaps and the sound makes me flinch. There's only one way a twig snaps like that. Someone stepped on it.

"Well, well, well, what do we have here?" I freeze at the voice. Bryce comes out from behind a tree. *Run!* my head screams at me.

"Bryce. Why aren't you at the meeting with Alpha Jared?" I ask, stepping back, trying to keep distance between us.

He steps around me, making me turn to keep him in my line of vision. "I could ask you the same thing. Seems he would want that pretty little ass of yours sitting on his cock while he talks the big talk with another alpha."

"You're a pig," I snap at him.

He laughs. "Men are pigs, Elle. All of them." He glances at me. "You of all people should know that." He continues walking, circling me.

My heart rate quickens. "Cedric said you can't come near me. You'd better get going. He usually meets me out here in the afternoons." I take another step back. "He'll be pissed if he finds you with me."

Bryce charges me. I turn to run but he catches me before I can get even five feet away. "Ah, ah, ah, I think he's a little busy right now. I don't think he's going to make it today. Why don't I join you?" He sniffs my hair. "We can spend some quality time together."

I throw my head back, smashing him in the nose, but he

doesn't let go of me. Bryce laughs. "Oh, you do still have some fight in you. I was hoping you'd fight back, it makes it more fun. You know," he trails a finger down my neck, of the mark that was forced upon me, "I'm surprised Cedric hasn't marked you, being mates and all. He always struck me as the guy who would complete the bond as soon as he found his mate." He spins me around, shoving me to the ground on my ass. "He must not want you, not forever anyway. He's definitely enjoying what's between your legs, though. We all hear you at night."

He kneels in front of me, getting right in my face, his breath blowing on my skin. "Once his vendetta is over he'll let you go. So tell me, Elle, how faithful are you to him, knowing he's going to use you and toss you once you're no longer convenient for him?"

"You're wrong," I counter, though is he? He's right, Cedric hasn't marked me. That alone makes the situation quite clear. Along with not allowing me to call my family.

Bryce chuckles, drawing his finger down my face. "You don't sound so convinced, sweetheart."

I cringe at the 'pet' name, the one Drake called me. I just look at him. "What are you playing at?"

"Well, I'm gonna do what I've wanted to do since we picked you up." He grabs my face, pressing his lips to mine. "I'm going to beat you so hard, you're going to wish you were dead, and then I'm gonna fuck you."

Bryce stands, bile fills my mouth. "Now I don't like things to be easy, so I'm going to make you a deal, Elle." He looks down at me, malice glinting in his eyes. "If you get to the tree line in front of the packhouse, I'll let you go. If not … well, you'll see when we get there. I'll be generous today, I'll give you to the count of twenty. That should be a good head start for you."

I stand up, not sure if he's serious. The packhouse is at least two miles from here.

"One," Bryce says, keeping his eyes on me.

"Two. Eighteen seconds left, Elle, you're wasting time."

I step back, turning on my heels. I race from his countdown.

Adrenaline pumping through me I sprint down the trail. *Fuck the trail.*

I jump over a dead log. If only I had time to shift, but that would slow me down. I run as fast as my legs can push me. I know I don't want Bryce to catch me. The sadistic look in his eyes told me he's not afraid of hurting me.

I hear him behind me, I push faster trying to stay ahead of him. Taking a quick right, I run on the path, trying to lead him in zigzags. I can't be too much farther away from my escape. If I can get close enough I can scream. Cedric will come. Even if he doesn't want me around forever, he still needs me. He will come.

Bryce is closing in on me. I can hear him gaining on me. I'm pushed forward, my body skidding across the ground. My skin burns where it breaks open, dirt getting into the small cuts, making them sting.

"You're fast, but not fast enough," he breathes in my ear. "I think we have some time— I'm going to have so much fun with you." He rolls me over, straddling me, holding my hands down.

"Why?" I ask. I don't know what else to say. I jerk underneath him. He moves both my hands to one of his and grabs my throat. He squeezes, making it so I struggle to breathe.

"Because it was all part of the plan, dear. Even Cedric's plan, he just let the mate bond get in the way. But I can carry it out for him."

Cedric

Leaning back in my chair, I'm satisfied with how my meeting with Jared has gone.

He clears his throat. "Can I talk to you alone?" His eyes cut to Cory and Reg, then to his beta before landing on me again.

"Go on," I say to Cory and Reg. They file out, Lee following close behind them.

The door shuts, leaving Jared and me alone. "Did you call that number I gave you a few months ago?" he asks with no prelude.

I wrack my brain trying to remember what he's talking about. "No, I didn't. Why?"

He grunts, leaves his chair and walks to the window. "They would be willing allies to your cause. Though they have their own reasons to want to take on Drake. They just don't have the power to."

"What the fuck are you talking about?"

"Alpha Roman, that's whose number I gave you." He looks at me from the corner of his eye, waiting for a reaction or something.

"Yeah, what's he got against Drake? Besides him being a sadistic asshole."

"Elle's his daughter, man. Trust me, they have every reason to want him dead. Drake took their future alpha from them."

Alpha's daughter, Elle was the future alpha? This makes no sense. "What?"

Jared shoots me an annoyed glare. "Elle, your mate, the woman you stole from Drake, is Alpha Roman's daughter. He had no sons, she was an only child. Training since she was twelve to become alpha. But Drake took her from them."

My mind swirls with the information he just pushed on to me. I shake my head, trying to make it all make sense.

"It's ironic because when she showed up on my territory she asked if she could find her mate. Looking for the only loophole to save her from Drake." He gives me a pointed look. "Obviously you weren't there."

"And why is that ironic?"

"Because she never wanted to find her mate, said it would fuck everything up for her to become alpha. That people would expect her mate to become alpha." He chuckles. "She wouldn't have it. And yet here you are, the man who steals her from Drake, being her *actual* mate? You can't make this shit up."

I stare at him, completely dumbfounded. *Is that why she doesn't want to stay?* Elle mentioned a while ago it would be best if we went our separate ways. Is that why? Because finding me would fuck up her plans of becoming alpha?

"She didn't want to spend her life breeding pups and stuck in the kitchen," Jared says. "She likes action, being in the middle of all the work and training."

"Is that what her mother does?"

"No, her mother died when she was two, I think. Elle never saw what a luna actually does, just the alpha."

I'm about to ask him another question when the door slams open. "Ced, Elle's not in her room," Reg says frantically. "I stopped to see if she wanted to get something to eat but she wasn't there. She's not in the house."

Standing from my chair I check my room. She's not there, nor in the bathroom. "Maybe she went for a run." I check my phone, looking at the time– it's about the time she'd be coming back. "Let's go downstairs and wait for her on the porch."

Jared follows me, eyeing me suspiciously. It's annoying, I wouldn't lie about her being here. I hold back my snarl.

We get out on the porch but I don't sit. Neither does Jared. "Where would she come out from if she went for a run?"

I point straight off the porch towards the tree line. "Over there." The more minutes that go by the more my guts twist. The same feeling I had earlier in my office when I wanted to check on her.

Cory comes running up to the porch with Dean. "Ced, Dean saw Elle go into the woods."

Dean nods. "When?" I ask him.

"'Bout two hours ago." He motions to Jared. "Not long after you guys went inside she came out of the house." I nod, forcing myself to relax. She just went for a run, she's mad at me, she had to run it off.

I make a mental note to talk to her more about calling her father. I shouldn't keep her from him. It's not right.

"That's not all, Ced," Dean continues. "I don't think she's alone."

"What do you mean?"

"Well, I saw Bryce heading this way, 'round the same time Elle was walking into the woods. He saw her and stopped. Waited a few minutes and followed her in."

What? No! "Fuck!" I yell, sprinting on to the lawn. That fucking asshole, he couldn't resist.

Jared comes up beside me, his beta following him. Cory's on my other side. I don't see Reg. I don't have time to think about why she stayed behind. I don't care. All I care about is finding Elle, hoping it's not too late.

CHAPTER THIRTY

Cedric

*F*ollowing both Elle's and Bryce's trails we run down the path. A scent stops me in my tracks. Blood. *No.* I take off down the trail, sprinting past everyone else.

The sight I come up on before me sends a rage through me I never knew I was capable of.

Elle lays on the ground, naked. Her skin is various shades of blue, purple and black. She's bleeding, too. I look up from where she lies. Bryce stands over her, holding his belt in his hands. He has some new bruises and cuts on his face. *She fought back.*

Bryce turns to look at me. "Cedric, you should have let me do this when she first got here." He smiles, turns away from me, raising the belt over his shoulder.

"*NO!*" I roar, charging him. I knock him to the ground,

pinning him there, bludgeoning his face with my fists. Blood gushes from his nose, new cuts form on his face. As I let him up, he spits blood.

"What the fuck are you doing?" I growl, seeing everything tinted red.

"What we originally planned to do with her." He spits, "Another few minutes and you would have come up on me balls deep in her."

I grab his shirt, shoving him against a tree. I smash his head into it hard. "You had no right to touch her! I told you not to! She's my mate! She's *mine*." I snarl the words, my spit hitting his face.

Cory and Lee both take Bryce's arms. "I did you a favor, Cedric. I did what you don't have the balls to do. You should be thanking me!"

"You're fucking delusional," I spit. Reg comes up behind me, holding up silver cuffs as explanation for why she wasn't right behind us. Seeing the silver makes me think of the belt. I pick it up. "Is this buckle silver?"

"No, I wish it was, though. I would have left my own mark on her if it was."

"Move," I say to Cory and Lee. They back up and I whip the belt across his face. His cheek splits open. Cory and Lee grab him again. I turn around to see Jared kneeling by Elle. A low growl rips through my throat. He looks up.

"She's alive, just unconscious." He holds up his hands, taking a step back. "The only good thing is the wounds will heal in a few days. She'll need sedatives, though." I nod. He walks past me to where the others are struggling with Bryce.

"Cuff him to the fucking tree. Keep two guards with him at all times. I'll deal with him later."

Kneeling down next to Elle, I take in all her injuries. It's bad– probably broken bones, and more bruised skin than untouched. I'm afraid to touch her, fearing I'll hurt her more than she already is.

"I sent Dean to get Tom and a few others, they should be here soon." Reg looks down at Elle. "She's unconscious, Cedric. Why don't you take her home?" I tear my eyes away from Elle, meeting Reg's sympathetic gaze. "Take her home, Cedric. We'll stay here and figure out who takes the first watch until you come back."

"Okay." Easing Elle into my arms as gently as I can, I pull her close to me. She whimpers. It's hard to tell from all the swelling, but I think she winces in pain, too. "It's okay, Elle. I've got you. I'll take care of you." I whisper to her, "I'm so sorry, Elle."

Jared walks beside me, matching my stride. We walk in silence, not saying anything. When we reach the house he goes in front of me, opening the door so I don't have to struggle.

"Where?" he asks.

"Up the stairs, last door on the right."

Jared races up the stairs. I take my time, careful not to jostle Elle too much. He has the door open ans I set her down on my bed, covering her with a blanket. I'm not letting her sleep in the other room, not while she's healing. If she wants to leave afterward she can.

I broke my promise to her. I told her she was safe here. I should have known Bryce wouldn't listen, that he'd look for any opportunity to harm her. I just didn't think he'd flat out disobey me.

Jared holds out a syringe to me. "Sedative."

"You keep these on hand?"

"No, I found it in your office." I look at him, annoyed he went through my office. "You were busy," he shrugs.

This isn't worth arguing about right now. I hold Elle's arm, deciding to go with her hand because it's the only spot I can see a vein. I pierce the skin with the needle and push the plunger down.

Her breathing transitions from short, labored pants of pain to slow, even breaths.

"You have to do something about your guy. From what I could tell you ordered him to stay away from her. He not only disobeyed your order, he took it to the next level, almost killing her." His gaze flicks to her before settling back on mine. "I know you haven't marked her, and I'm not about to put my two cents into that, but she is your mate. And killing an alpha's mate is a crime no one commits unless they plan on killing the alpha, too."

"I know."

He glances at Elle. "Let me know how she's doing in a few days." He slaps my back. "And for fuck's sake, call Roman."

I listen to his footsteps retreat down the hall. Once I hear the door shut, I crawl into the bed, carefully getting as close to Elle as I can without moving her.

"I'm so sorry."

When she's better we can talk about her calling her father. I should have let her in the first place.

You're such an asshole. The only reason I really didn't want her contacting her family wasn't because of Drake. That's only a small part of the reason. The real reason is that I don't want to lose her. I was happy in our little bubble. She seemed happy, too. I didn't want it to break. I'm a selfish prick.

Watching her sleep, I can't help but think how beautiful she is. Even with all the bruises and swelling, it's not only her physical features that make her beautiful. It's the spirit in her, the fight. I understand why Drake stole her and kept her for himself. Though he wanted to break her spirit, take her fight away, I can't imagine her without it. It's what makes her Elle.

She still has it, though. I saw Bryce before I got my hands on him. *She fought back.*

Night falls, blanketing the outside sky in stars. I've been lying here beside Elle for hours watching her sleep. The cuts on her face already show signs of stitching the skin back together. The bruises will take the longest, a day or two, depending on how deep they go into the tissue.

Someone stands in the doorway, blocking the hall light.

"Ced." It's Reg. She walks into my room, sitting on the edge of my bed. "It's time for you to go. I'll stay with her."

I get up, stiff from not moving for hours. I glance at Elle, still sleeping, looking peaceful despite her injuries. *I don't want to leave her.*

As if she can read my mind, Reg puts her hand on my arm. "She'll be okay, Ced. I won't leave her side." She gives me a small smile that doesn't reach her eyes.

Nodding to her, I walk out the door.

Walking under the moonlight, I stride across the lawns, into the cover of the trees. The moonlight doesn't filter through the leaves and my eyes adjust to the change of light.

Why did he have to cross this line? Why did I trust him to begin with? I've always known him to be twisted. But he's always been loyal to me, never once straying away.

That's why I have struggled so much with my decision. Execution or exile?

I have gone back and forth between the two options. I have killed before, rogues, but never someone I considered a friend. But he's not a friend, or a loyal member of my pack. Someone loyal wouldn't defy me and go after Elle. Especially after I told them she was my mate. Marked or not, she *is* my mate. And he tried to kill her.

There's orange flickering ahead. They must have started a fire. The flames make the shadows of the trees dance. Dean comes up to me.

"Any sign of remorse?" I ask him, already knowing the answer.

Dean's face is grim. "No, none at all. He hasn't spoken since you left earlier. How is she?"

"Sleeping."

"Guess that's the best thing for her, huh?"

"Yeah." I don't want to be here. I want to go back to Elle. I know she's safe, no one will get past Reg. The only threat to Elle right now is chained to a tree.

"Release him," I order. Cory and Tom undo the chains wrapped around Bryce and the tree, leaving his wrists bound behind him.

They push him forward, forcing him on his knees. Bryce stares up at me.

"I didn't betray you, I only did what we originally planned, before you knew she was your mate. *You* wanted this too, Cedric."

"You went after her after I told you to leave her alone. She's my mate. That should have been enough reason for you to leave her alone. But it wasn't. You have been loyal to me for a long time, Bryce. But I have to wonder why? Was it because I let you have your sick and twisted ways when it came to getting information? Or was it because you truly believed in our fight?"

"You know why. Stop with the stupid questions and get on with it."

Glaring down at him, I feel all the rage I felt earlier

seeing him stand over Elle, ready to strike her already broken and beaten body. Taking a deep breath, I calm myself. Though no one would blame me if I beat him within an inch of his life like he did to her, I can't do it. "You have been loyal to me for years, Bryce. Helping me out of binds I never could have gotten out of on my own. And for that, I'll show you mercy."

Bryce bursts out laughing. "You're a fucking weak fool. Tell me, Cedric, what's your verdict? Exile?" He spits. "You're weak, Cedric. You always have been. And that bitch is only going to make it worse. Without my help where would you be? You'd still be trying to plan out getting a man into Drake's fold. You're where you are because of *me*."

Looking around the fire I see the faces of those who showed up. I meet everyone's stare. None of them have doubt in their eyes.

I step forward, placing my hands on both sides of Bryce's face, looking him straight in the eyes. "I said I'd grant you mercy. I didn't say anything about sparing your life." Before he can say anything, I twist his head hard. Hearing the crack of his neck breaking I let him go, letting him fall to the ground.

"Get the truck," I say to Dean. He hustles off, following my order.

"Where are we burying him?" Cory stands beside me looking down at Bryce's body.

"Not anywhere on my fucking territory." I glance at him. "You ready for a long night?"

He nods. "Yeah."

* * *

Pulling the truck to a stop, Cory and I get out. Cory lets the tailgate down and grabs the shovels.

"No shovels. I'm not taking the time to bury this piece of shit."

He looks at me, shocked. "What are we doing with him?"

Walking to the edge of the gorge I lean to look down. We drove four hours to get here, a place I found on the map that is a town but doesn't have a large population. No people living here for miles. No law enforcement.

How many secrets does this gorge hold? Probably more than I would care to know. And it's about to hold one more.

"We'll dump him here."

"You're really not going to bury him? I mean, I didn't like the guy, but he was a member of the pack. We bury the rogues who are too far gone to join us."

"That's why he doesn't deserve a burial, Cory. I trusted him and he betrayed me."

He puts the shovels back in the bed, pulling Bryce's body out by the feet. I grab under the shoulders and we walk toward the edge of the gorge. It looks like a mouth, ready to eat anything that might have the misfortune of falling in.

Swinging his body back, we let go when it comes to the front of us. It disappears from view quickly, but the sounds of it hitting rocks, bouncing down the ledge, maybe even bones cracking, can be heard for a while.

We stare into the blackness that consumes the hole, even after all the sounds have stopped.

"Crazy, isn't it?" Cory's words pull my hypnotized stare from the gorge. My eyebrows furrow in confusion.

"What?"

He chuckles, leaving me to go shut the tailgate. Sighing, I get in the truck and he hops in on the other side.

"What's crazy, Cory?"

"The lengths we go to for the women we love." He stares out the windshield before turning to me.

I sigh. "I don't love her, Cory. I care about her, but that's as far as it goes."

"Whatever you say, man. But I know what I saw today." He looks back out the windshield. "You should stop fighting it. Both of you should."

I don't respond, keeping my eyes on the road, following the yellow and white lines illuminated by the headlights. Cory doesn't offer any more of his wisdom, he just checks his phone periodically. Texting Reg, I assume. I'm fine with this, it gives me time to think.

I don't love Elle. I care about her, that's it. I certainly don't want to see her hurt. I'm protective of her, but that's in my nature as an alpha, we feel protective over our packs. That doesn't mean I love her.

The memory of seeing Bryce standing over her, her body beaten and bloody, comes to the center of my thoughts. Gripping the steering wheel tighter, I let out a low growl. Cory gives me a confused look but doesn't say anything, turning his attention back to his phone after a few seconds.

I wanted to kill Bryce right there, I wanted to beat him like he did to her. But I couldn't leave her naked on the ground either. And the thought of someone else carrying her, taking care of her, didn't sit well with me. I had to do it. She's mine to take care of.

Leaving her earlier tonight to deal with Bryce was one of the hardest things I've had to do. I didn't want to leave her, I wanted to stay right there in that bed with her, watching over her.

My foot presses harder on the accelerator. I want to get back as fast as I can. She needs me. Or maybe I need her.

As I navigate the twists and turns of the road more memories of the past few weeks flicker through my head. When I first saw her face, realizing she was my mate. Seeing her in her wolf form, a beautiful strong white wolf. Seeing the scars on her back, the feeling of rage and also wanting to protect her from any other harm. The first night we slept together, Elle asking me to stay with her. Feeling so amazed that she trusted me and felt safe with me. How everything seemed right with her.

Elle's the missing piece of me. I've been fighting it because she's Drake's mate. No, she isn't. Elle is *my* mate. Drake stole her from her pack, and I stole her from him. He isn't getting her back, no one is going to hurt her again. *She's mine.*

* * *

Dawn is on the horizon when we pull up in front of the packhouse. Reg is standing on the porch waiting for us. When Cory approaches her, they embrace. It's passionate, like being away from each other for nine hours was unbearable.

I know the feeling. Stepping by them I rush up the stairs, I need to see her.

She's in the same spot as when I left. Though now I see she has one of my t-shirts on. Reg must've slipped it on her so she was covered better.

Brushing my hand gently across her forehead, pushing some stray hairs out of her face, I press my lips lightly to the top of her head. Elle takes a deep breath but then settles back into the slow steady breathing.

Now that I've seen that she's okay I head into the bathroom to take a shower. I need to wash tonight's sins off my body.

Once I'm clean and dried off, I throw on some shorts and a T-shirt. Crawling in bed, careful not to move Elle, I slide next to her. Taking her hand in mine, I watch her like I did hours ago.

Sunlight peeks through the window, casting light into my bedroom. Elle's bruises already look ten times better than they did when I left. They've faded from dark purple and black to blue, green, even yellow.

My eyes grow heavy with exhaustion, threatening to close. I know she's safe here with me. I realized hours ago that I don't just care for Elle, I love her.

But that thought brings sadness to me. I won't force her to stay with me, I won't force my mark on her. She already has one that she never wanted. She wasn't given the choice to say no to anything over the past few months. But I will give her that choice. I won't force her to do anything she doesn't want to.

Even if that means letting her go.

ACKNOWLEDGMENTS

I want to thank all of my beta readers— Rebecca, Brandy, Steph, Louise, Amanda, Dave and Kimi— without all of you and your support *STOLEN* wouldn't have happened. A thank you to my friend, Jon, who was right. And a huge thank you to my husband, for all his support and encouragement to follow my dream.

Made in the USA
Middletown, DE
23 March 2024

51489042R00213